UNDERWORLD

UNDERWORLD

A Dalziel–Pascoe Murder Mystery

Reginald Hill

CHARLES SCRIBNER'S SONS

NEW YORK

Charles Scribner's Sons
Macmillan Publishing Company
866 Third Avenue, New York, NY 10022

Library of Congress Cataloging-in-Publication Data
Hill, Reginald.
Underworld.
I. Title.
PR6058.I448U53   1988   823'.914   88-6479
ISBN 0-684-18931-3

The quotations on pages 5, 11, 87, 219, and 279 are from Dante's *Inferno*
translated by Dorothy L. Sayers and published by Penguin Books Ltd.

10 9 8 7 6 5 4 3 2 1

Printed in the United States of America

Hear truth: I stood on the steep brink whereunder
Runs down the dolorous chasm of the Pit,
Ringing with infinite groans like gathered thunder.

Deep, dense, and by no faintest glimmer lit
It lay, and though I strained my sight to find
Bottom, not one thing could I see in it.

Down must we go, to that dark world and blind.

UNDERWORLD

CHAPTER 1

'Another fine mess you've got me into,' said Detective-Superintendent Andrew Dalziel.

In his mind's eye, Peter Pascoe could see his superior's broad slab of a face twisted into a mock-exasperation intended to be reassuring. The picture had to be mental because he'd lost his torch in the roof fall which held him pinned helpless from the waist down, and Dalziel only used his light fitfully as he dug at the debris with his bare hands.

Mental or not, the picture was not to Pascoe's liking. In sick-bed terms, comfort from Andy Dalziel was like seeing the doctor edged aside by the priest. He tried to move again and felt pain run up his legs like fire up a fuse, exploding him to full consciousness.

'Jesus!' he gasped.

'Hurting? That's a good sign.'

'That's your expert fucking opinion, is it?' grated Pascoe. 'Where'd you pick up that priceless gem? Bart's was it? Or the interview room?'

'Watch it, lad,' warned Dalziel. 'I'll make allowances for delirium but I'll not stand insubordination. Any more of that and I'll . . .'

He hesitated.

'You'll what?' demanded Pascoe. 'Get me posted to traffic? Don't bother. I'll volunteer.'

'No,' said Dalziel. 'What I was going to say was, any more of that and I'll come down on you like a ton of bricks.'

There was a silence between the two men for a moment, and the moment was long enough to remind them that in this place there was no such thing as silence. Water dripped, earth dribbled, pebbles clinked, and from time to time there were creaks and groans as a hundred thousand tons of ancient rock tried to close this wound savagely ripped along its guts.

Then a new sound joined the others, almost but not quite the rattle of pain.

'Like a ton of bricks,' moaned Pascoe. 'Oh Christ, don't make me laugh.'

'Ton of bricks!' said Dalziel beginning to splutter. 'Ton of . . .'

He let out a bellow of laughter which ricocheted off the pile of rubble under which Pascoe lay and rolled down the old roadway behind them.

'Don't,' pleaded Pascoe. 'Please don't . . .'

But it was too late. The contagion of laughter was upon him and for a good half-minute the two policemen gave themselves over to hoots of merriment all the stronger because of the pain and fear they so inadequately masked.

Finally the merriment faded. Pascoe tried to keep it going a little time after it was completely dead. The alternative tenant of his imagination was a mouse voice squeaking that he was trapped in a dark confined space with no hope of rescue. It was, to misuse a phrase, a dream come true, his dream of the worst fate that could befall him. He closed his eyes, though in that place there was no need, and tried to win his way back to unconsciousness. He must have half succeeded, for he heard a distant voice gently calling his name and when his eyes opened, he was dazzled by a disc of white light which he tried desperately to confuse with the moon riding high above the lime tree in his garden on one of those rare nights when work and weather conspired to permit an *al fresco* supper and he and Ellie sat, wine-languid, in the summer-soft, flower-sweet, velvet-dark air.

It was a vain effort, a lie which never came close to being a delusion. The voice was Dalziel's, the light his torch.

'What?' he demanded.

'Nowt. Just thought there weren't much point ruining me fingernails digging if you'd snuffed it,' said Dalziel. 'How are the legs? Still hurting?'

'The pain seems to be getting further away,' whispered Pascoe. 'Or perhaps it's just the legs that are getting further away.'

'Jokes, is it? What are you after, lad? The fucking Police Medal?'

'No joke, sir. More like despair.'

'That's all right, then. One thing I can't stomach's a bloody hero.'

Dalziel belched as though in illustration and added reflectively, 'I could stomach one of Jack's meat pies from the Black Bull, though.'

'Food,' said Pascoe.

'You peckish too? That's hopeful.'

'Another good sign?' whispered Pascoe. 'No. I meant there wasn't any. Back at the White Rock. Did you see any?'

'Likely he'd not unpacked it. Well, he wouldn't have time, would he?'

'Perhaps not ... there was someone in there, you know ...'

'In where? The White Rock? In a cave, or what?'

'Back there ... the side gallery ... someone, something ... I can't remember ...'

'In there, you mean? Of course there was. Young bloody Farr was in there, which is why we're in here, up to our necks! Well, back to work.'

It wasn't the answer or at least only part of it, but his mind seemed to be refusing to register much since they had so foolishly left that marvellous world of air and trees and space and stars. He gave up the attempt at recall and lay still, listening to the fat man's rat-like scrabblings. Was it really worth it? he wondered. He didn't realize he'd spoken his thought, but Dalziel was replying.

'Likely not. They're probably out there already with their shovels and drills and blankets and hot soup and television lights and gormless interviewers practising their daft bloody questions. Nay, I'm just doing this to keep warm. Sensible thing would be to lie back and wait patiently, as the very old bishop said to the actress.'

'How will they know where we are?'

'You don't think them other buggers got stuck like us? Pair of moles, them two. Born with hands like shovels and teeth like picks, these miners. I can't wait to get my hands on that young bastard, Farr. This is all down to him, running off down here. Bloody Farr. He'll wish he were far enough when I next see him.'

Pascoe smiled sadly at the fat man's attempted cheeriness. He didn't believe that he and Colin Farr would ever meet again. His mind burrowed into the huge pile of earth and rock which held him trapped and his heart showed him Colin Farr trapped there too. Or worse. And if worse, how to explain it to Ellie in the unlikely event he ever got the chance? Any explanation must sound like justification. He would, of course, deny any imperatives other than duty and the law. Up there you had to keep things simple. There was no other way to survive.

But down here survival was too far beneath hope to make a motive, and the darkness was fetid with doubt and accusation. Time for the bottom line, as the Yanks put it. Place for a bottom line too. And the bottom line read like this.

Colin Farr. Trapped by the pit he hated. Driven into that trap by a man who hated him.

Colin Farr.

PART ONE

And see! not far from where the mountain-side
First rose, a Leopard, nimble and light and fleet,
Clothed in a fine furred pelt all dapple-dyed,

Came gambolling out, and skipped before my
  feet.

CHAPTER 1

'. . . the paddy broke down and we had to walk nearly the full length of the return to pit bottom and there was a hell of a crowd there already and tempers were getting frayed. They usually do if you're kept waiting to ride the pit, especially when other buggers push into the Cage ahead of you because they've got priority. It's not so bad when it's the wet-ride—that's men who've been working in water—though even then there's a lot of complaining and the lads yell things like, "Call that wet? I think tha's just pissed on tha boots!" But worst of all is when a bunch of deputies get to ride ahead of you which is what happened to us, and the sight of all those clean faces, grinning like they were getting into a lift in a knocking shop, really got our goat. As the last one got in, someone yelled, "That's right, lad, hurry on home to your missus. But you'll not get to ride there before the day-shift!" The deputy's face were white before, but now it got even whiter and he set off back out of the Cage like he was going to grab whoever it was that called out and start a rumpus, but some of the other officials got hold of him and the grille clanged shut and the Cage went up. Mebbe it shouldn't have been said, but first thing you learn down pit is not to bite when someone tries to rile you, and it certainly cheered up most of the poor sods still left waiting.

'I rode up with the next lot and that was the end of my shift and this is the end of my homework.'

'Thank you, Colin,' said Ellie Pascoe. 'That was really very good.'

'Ee, miss, tha don't say? Dost really think there's hope tha can learn an ignorant bugger like me to read and write proper?'

Colin Farr's accent had broadened beyond parody while his mouth gaped and his eyes bulged into a mask of grotesque gratitude. The others in the group roared with laughter and Ellie found herself flushing with shame at the

12

justified rebuke; but because she was by nature a counter-puncher, she replied, once again without thinking, 'Perhaps I'll settle for learning you to stop feeling insecure in unfamiliar situations.'

Farr's features tightened to their usual expression of amused watchfulness.

'That'll be grand,' he said. 'As soon as you've found the secret, be sure to let me know.'

He's right, thought Ellie miserably. I'm as insecure as any of them!

She hadn't anticipated this three weeks earlier when Adam Burnshaw, director of Mid-Yorks University's extra mural department, had rung to ask if she could help him out. One of his lecturers had contracted hepatitis in the Urals (Ellie had observed her husband teeter on the edge of a Dalzielesque joke), leaving a gap in a union-sponsored day-release course for miners. Ellie, politically sound, with years of experience as a social science lecturer till de-jobbed by childbirth and redundancy (both fairly voluntary), was the obvious stop-gap. No need to worry about her daughter, Rose. The University crèche was at her disposal.

Ellie had needed little time to think. Though far from housebound, she had started to feel that most of her reasons for going out were short on moral imperative. As for her reason for *not* going out, the great feminist novel she was supposed to be writing, that had wandered into more dead ends than a walker relying on farmers to maintain rights-of-way.

Preparation had been a bit of a rush, but Ellie had not stinted her time.

'This is something worthwhile,' she assured her husband. 'A real job of real education with real people. I feel privileged.'

Peter Pascoe had wondered over his fourth consecutive meal of tinned tuna and lettuce whether in view of her Messianic attitude to her prospective students, she might not be able to contrive something more interesting with leaves and fishes, but it was only a token complaint. Lately he too had started noticing signs of restlessness and he was

13

glad to see Ellie back in harness, particularly in this area. During the recent year-long miners' strike, when relations between police and pickets came close to open warfare, she had kept as low a profile as she could conscientiously manage. This had cost her much political credibility in her left-wing circles, and this job-offer from academic activist, Burnshaw, was like a ticket of readmittance to the main arena.

But there's no such thing as a free ticket. The dozen miners who turned up at her first class on Industrial Sociology seemed bent on confirming the judgment of Indignant (*name and address supplied*) in the letter columns of the *Evening Post*, that such courses were little more than subsidized absenteeism.

At the end of an afternoon of monosyllabic responses to her hard prepared but softly presented material, she had retired in disarray after issuing a schoolmarmly invitation to write an account of a day at work before the next encounter.

That night she served frozen pizza as a change from tuna.

'How'd it go, then?' asked Pascoe with a casualness she mistook for indifference.

'Fine,' she grunted with a laconicism he mistook for exclusion.

'Good. Many there?'

'Just twelve.'

'Good number for a messiah, but watch out for Judas.'

And here he was, Colin Farr, in his early twenties, his fair clear complexion as yet hardly touched by the tell-tale blue scars marking the other faces, his golden hair springy with Grecian curls, his every movement informed with natural grace. Put him in a tasselled cap and a striped blazer and he'd not win a second glance as he strolled through the Enclosure at Henley, except of admiration and envy.

Oh shit! she thought desperately. How classist can you get? It was wrong to call him Judas. He had merely invited her to betray herself.

At first indeed he had seemed a saviour when, just as she felt herself drowning in the silence which followed her request for a volunteer, he had risen like Adonis from a grassy bank and begun to read. It had been gratitude which had trapped her into that patronizing praise, and guilt which had stung her into that equally patronizing rebuke.

She took a deep breath, decided between inhalation and exhalation that the time was not yet ripe for an open analysis of the group dynamic, and said, 'Did you think it should have been said?'

'Eh?'

The change of direction was right. It had taken him by surprise.

'You said that perhaps it was wrong for someone to make that crack about the deputy's wife. Is that what you think?'

Slowly Colin Farr smiled. It was a slightly lopsided, devastatingly attractive smile and it seemed to say he now saw exactly what she was doing.

'What do I think?' he said. 'I think either a man can look after his wife or he can't and it doesn't matter what any other bugger says. Also I think that deputies deserve all the shit you can throw at them. Just ask these lads here what they reckon and you'll soon see if I'm right.'

She saw, and that night at dinner (steak and mushroom pie with braised red cabbage, incontrovertibly home-cooked) she attempted to convey both her delight and her surprise, delight that the ice had been broken and surprise at the depth of feeling revealed in the ensuing discussion.

'It's positively atavistic,' she said. 'These are young men talking as if they were back in the nineteen-twenties.'

'You always said the Strike had knocked industrial relations back a generation,' said Pascoe, shovelling another huge forkful of pie into his mouth.

'This is nothing to do with industrial relations,' retorted Ellie. 'It's tribal. Peter, if you're going to gobble your food and look at your watch at the same time, you'll end up putting your eye out. What's the rush anyway? Not another James Cagney film on telly?'

'No,' said Pascoe uneasily. 'It's just that I've got to go out.'

'You didn't say anything,' said Ellie indignantly.

15

'No? Well, I was going to tell you when I got home but somehow . . .'

'You mean,' said Ellie with detective sharpness, 'that when you got home and instead of the fast food you've been moaning about, you saw I'd rushed back from my class and slaved away cooking your favourite dinner, you lost your nerve!'

Pascoe smiled placatingly and said, 'Well, sort of. I *was* going to say something, but you were so keen to tell me about your interesting afternoon with the horny-handed sons of toil . . .'

'My God, I know who you really are! You're Indignant (*name and address supplied*), I recognize the style! So, tell me, what's so important that you prefer it to your favourite nosh, not to mention my intellectual company?'

'It's Mr Watmough,' said Pascoe.

'Watmough? You mean that creepy sod who's Deputy Chief Constable? I thought he was leaving?'

'He is. That's why I've got to go out. The brass will be laying on a farewell dinner, but tonight he's popping into the Club for a presentation from the plebs. I feel I ought to be there out of courtesy.'

'Courtesy? To a Social Democrat?' said Ellie scornfully.

The announcement of Watmough's resignation had been followed almost immediately by the leaked news that he was shortlisted as a possible SDP candidate for a winnable local seat. It was no secret that he had been bitterly disappointed when he failed to get the recently vacant Chief Constable's job. He'd been everyone's favourite, except for Detective-Superintendent Andrew Dalziel, who rated him, to quote, 'lower than a duck's arsehole and twice as wet'. How Dalziel could have influenced the result was not clear, but Pascoe had suspicions close to certainties that it had been the fat man's spade-like hand that had dashed the foaming cup from Watmough's foaming lips.

A period of dark brooding had followed. Watmough was already a small-time media personality with the assistance of Ike Ogilby, editor of the *Sunday Challenger*, flagship paper of the main Mid-Yorkshire news group. He had been hoping

to become a big-time personality via the Chief Con-
stableship, and thence launch himself into the political
empyrean. Now, faced with the choice of looking for other
Chiefs' jobs outside the area where his power base lay, or
attempting a low-level take-off, he'd opted for the latter.
  'Who's making the presentation?' asked Ellie.
  'Dalziel.'
  Ellie began to laugh.
  'You're quite right, Peter,' she said. 'You can't miss that.
It should be a night to remember. But first you'll eat up
your apple pie and custard. And you'll sit there and look
interested while I finish telling you about Colin Farr and
his mates. Are you sitting comfortably?'
  'Yes, miss,' said Pascoe.
  'Then I'll begin.'

CHAPTER 2

Colin Farr went to the bar and asked for another pint. It
was his fourth since he'd come into the Welfare not much
more than half an hour ago.
  'Thirsty work back at school, is it?' said the steward. His
name was Peter Pedley, but ever since he'd grown a bandido
moustache to age his childishly young features when he first
went down the pit, he'd been known as Pedro. His body
had long ago thickened to a solid barrel which was eighty
per cent muscle, and the childishness too had spread into a
mature joviality, though the moustache remained. He was
a man much respected both for his strength of body and his
resilience of spirit. In his mid-twenties he'd been advised
by the doctor that the bronchitis which had troubled him
since childhood was rapidly worsening underground. With
a wife and young family, he was unwilling to take the wage
cut and poor prospects of surface work, so he'd taken a job
as barman in a Barnsley pub, got to know the business
inside out, and eventually returned to the place of his birth
as the residential steward of the Burrthorpe Miners' Social

and Welfare Club. Two years later his resilience was tested to breaking-point when his youngest daughter, Tracey, aged seven, disappeared. The child had never been found. The consoling presence of and continued responsibility for three other children had kept Pedley and his wife from falling apart, but Mrs Pedley had aged a decade in the years since the disappearance and Pedro visited the whisky optic on his own behalf as frequently as on his customers'.

He rarely let it show, however, and he had a sharp eye for alcohol-based trouble in others.

Now Colin Farr supped two inches off the top of his pint and said, 'University, not school, Pedro. But you're right. It's thirsty work, all that talking.'

'Better than fighting,' said Pedley, amiably but with a hint of warning. He knew most of his customers better than they knew themselves. Four pints in half an hour was par for the course in some; with young Farr it spelt trouble.

The young man heard the warning and drank again, regarding Pedley over the rim without resentment. The steward still wheezed through the winter, but when Pedro Pedley sallied forth to sort out trouble, those close to it scattered and those safely distant settled down to enjoy the show. When Colin Farr lowered the glass, it was more than half empty.

'Where's Maggie,' he asked.

'She'll not be working tonight. She's badly. This is the day it happened.'

Their eyes met: Pedley's blank, Farr's searching.

'Is that right?' said Farr. 'Then naturally she'll be upset.'

And he went back to his seat moving with easy grace.

He was alone at one of the round formica tables. The Club's main public room was a cheerless place when almost empty. Full, you couldn't see the brown and beige tiled floor, or the cafeteria furniture, or the vinyl-upholstered waiting-room bench which ran round the flock-papered walls. Full, the plaster-board ceiling, steel cross-girder and glaring strip-lights were to some extent obscured by the strato-cirrus layer of tobacco smoke. And best of all, full, the whisper of a man's own disturbing thoughts was almost inaudible beneath the din of loud laughter, seamless chatter, and amplified music.

At the moment Colin Farr's thoughts were coming through too loud, too clear. He'd gone into the students' union bar at the University today. Its décor and furnishings had not been all that different from the Club's. The atmosphere had been just as thick, the voices just as loud, the music just as raucous. Yet he had left very quickly, feeling alien. The reaction had troubled him. It was uncharacteristic. He was not a shy person; he'd been around and hadn't been much bothered at entering some places where he'd been quite literally a foreigner. But the students' bar had made him feel so uneasy that he'd fled, and the memory of this uneasiness wouldn't leave him alone.

It had been self-irritation with his reaction that had made him so sharp with that Mrs Pascoe in the afternoon. Well, partly at least. And partly it had been her. Condescending cow!

He had finished his fourth pint without hardly noticing. He was thinking about getting out of his seat again, though whether to return to the bar or head out into the night he wasn't sure, when the door burst open and two men came in. One was Farr's age but looked older. They'd been in the same class at school, but, unlike Farr, Tommy Dickinson's career down the pit had been continuous since he was fifteen. Chunkily built, he had the beginnings of a substantial beer-gut, and when his broad amiable face split into a grin at the sight of Farr, his teeth were stained brown with tobacco juice.

'Look what's here!' he cried. 'Hey, Pedro! I thought only working men could get served in this club.'

'You'd best buy me a pint, then,' said Farr.

While Dickinson was getting the drinks, the other man sat down at Farr's table. He was Neil Wardle, in his thirties, a lean taciturn man. His face was as brown and weatherbeaten as any countryman's. In fact, like many of his workmates, as if in reaction against the underworld in which they earned their bread, he spent as much of his spare time as possible roaming the hills around Burrthorpe with his dog and a shotgun. He was charge-man of the team of rippers in which the other two worked.

'All right, Col?' he said.

'All right,' said Farr.

'Your mam all right?'

'Aye. Why shouldn't she be?'

'No reason. She didn't say owt about anyone coming round, asking questions?'

'No. What sort of questions?'

'Just questions,' said Wardle vaguely. Before Farr could press him, Dickinson returned, his broad hands locked round three pint glasses.

'It's no use, Col,' he declared in the booming voice which was his normal speech level. 'Tha'll have to play hookey from that school. They sent us that Scotch bugger again today. He can't even speak proper! Three times he asked me for a chew of baccy and I thought the sod were just coughing!'

Farr's absence meant that his place had to be filled for that shift by someone 'on the market', and men used to working in a regular team did not take readily to a new-comer.

'There's worse than Jock,' said Wardle.

Dickinson rolled his eyes in a parody of disbelief, but he did not pursue the subject. In matters like this, Wardle had the last word, and in any case, most of Dickinson's complaints were ritualistic rather than real.

'Teacher didn't ask you to stay behind to clean her board, then?' he asked slyly.

Farr wished he hadn't let on that one of his lecturers was a woman. His friend's innuendo was not masked by any great subtlety.

'Not today,' he said. 'I'm building up to it.'

'All right, is she?'

He thought about Ellie Pascoe. *A condescending cow* was how he'd categorized her to himself earlier. But that had been as ritualistic as Tommy's pretence that he couldn't understand Jock Brodie's accent. However, in-depth analysis was not what Dickinson was after.

'She's got nice tits,' he said. 'And she doesn't wear a bra.'

'Hey up! That's half the battle, then! Hey, did you hear the one about the lass who'd just got married and next time she met her old dad, he asked her, "What fettle, lass?" and she said, "Dad, can I ask you a question? That bit of skin at the end of my Jack's thing, what do you call that?" . . .'

Colin Farr's mind drifted away from the joke as his gaze drifted round the rapidly filling room. He knew all the men here by face, and most of them by name. Some there were who'd been young men when he'd been a boy. Some had been middle-aged then who were old now. And one or two had always been old and were now much much older. He knew them all, and their wives and their families, to the second and sometimes the third generation. He was looking at the past of a whole community here, traced in lined and scarred faces, in shallow breathing and deep coughs. Was that what was worrying him? He didn't think so. It was not the fact that he was looking at the past, he suddenly realized. It was rather that he could be looking at the future! It was here, in this room, in this loud talk, and laughter, and argument, in these wreaths of tobacco smoke and these rings of foam on straight glasses.

The bar in the students' union, there'd been foam rings there too, and tobacco wreaths, argument and laughter and loud talk. What there hadn't been was any sense that this was anyone's future. It had been here and now; fun and finite; a launching-pad not an endless looped tape. No sense there of raising a glass at eighteen and setting it down at eighty with nothing changed except your grey hair, gapped gums and wrinkled genitals!

In his ear Tommy's voice rose to its triumphant climax.

'"'Ee, lass," said her dad. "Ah diven't know what thy Jack calls 'em, but ah calls 'em the cheeks of me arse!"'

Colin Farr laughed, loud and false and desperate, and rose to his feet.

'Good one, Tommy,' he proclaimed. 'Good one. Let's have another pint!'

CHAPTER 3

The Police Club functions room was crowded, noisy and full of smoke. There was a sound like a spade flattening the last sod on a pauper's grave. It was Andy Dalziel's huge hand slapping the bar. Immediately the noise faded and even the miasma seemed to clear for a space of a couple of feet around the massive grizzled head.

The Detective-Superintendent, Head of Mid-Yorks CID, looked round the room till heavy breathers held their heavy breath, then he opened his speech with the time-honoured Yorkshire formula.

'Right, you buggers,' he said. 'You know what we're here for tonight.'

His audience sighed in happy anticipation. It occurred to Sammy Ruddlesdin of the *Evening Post* that his report (written in advance so that he wouldn't have anything to distract him from the boozing) was more than usually dishonest. In it he'd said that the crowded room bore eloquent witness to the high regard in which DCC Watmough was held by his fellows, while in truth, it bore eloquent witness to the low regard in which they knew that Dalziel held him. Most were here in the simple hope of being entertained by a valedictory vilification!

They were sadly disappointed. After a few ancient but warmly received anecdotes. Dalziel launched on a meandering and mainly complimentary account of Watmough's career. There were a few hopeful signs ('I knew him in them early days with Mid-Yorks. There were some as said he got a bit over-excited under pressure but I always said, you've got to flap a bit if you want to be a high flier!') but they never came to anything. Perhaps Dalziel was saving himself up for the Pickford case? This was Watmough's finest hour, occurring during a brief sojourn as Assistant Chief Constable in South Yorkshire when he had masterminded the hunt for a child killer. A salesman, Donald Pickford, had obliged by asphyxiating himself in his car and leaving a note of confession. Somehow Watmough, with media support, had turned this into a triumph of detection with himself modestly wearing the bays. He had returned rapidly on the crest of this wave to Mid-Yorks as Deputy Chief and had looked to have enough momentum left to carry him all the way to the Chief's office only three years later, till a malevolent fate had intervened.

This same malevolent fate was now approaching his peroration.

'We'll not soon forget what you've done for us in these past few years,' declaimed Dalziel. 'Like the man said, you touched nowt you didn't adorn. Now the time has come for you to move on to fresh fields and pastures new. And the time has come for me, Neville—and it's good to be able to call you Neville again after these past few years of having to call you *sir* . . .'

Pause for laughter, especially from Peter Pascoe who recalled Dalziel's more usual forms of reference, such as Shit-head, Lubby Lud, Her Majesty, Nutty Slack and Rover the Wonder Dog.

'. . . the time has come for me to present you with this token of our esteem.'

He picked up a box from the bar.

'Rumour has it you're thinking of going into politics, or at least into the SDP, so we thought this'd be a suitable gift.'

From the box he took a clock, turned the hands to twelve and set it on the bar. A moment later a peal of Westminster Chimes began to sound.

'We reckoned that with this, Nev, if you ever do get into Parliament, it won't matter whose bed you're ringing home from, you can always convince your missus you're at an all-night sitting in the House. Goodbye to you, and good . . . luck!'

And that was it. Not yet nine o'clock and the action over with not a bloodstain to be seen. The DCC, as relieved as his audience was disappointed, repaid Dalziel's moderation with a fulsomely sentimental tribute to his colleagues at all levels.

'Brings tears to your eyes, doesn't it?' said Pascoe.

Sergeant Wield, whose shattered visage looked as if it would absorb tears like dew off the Gobi Desert, said, '*De mortuis.*'

'Well, stuff me,' said Sammy Ruddlesdin behind him. 'Once through these hallowed portals and it's good-bye to all that 'ello, 'ello, 'ello, stuff and it's out with the Latin tags and literary quotes. Even Fat Andy was at it.'

It was clear Ruddlesdin had been enjoying the hospitality. Beside him was a short, stoutish man smartly dressed in a black worsted three-piece suit, a sartorial effect somewhat at odds with the handrolled cigarette drooping beneath a ragged and nicotine-stained moustache.

'I dare say you lads know my friend and colleague, Mr Monty Boyle of the *Sunday Challenger*, the famous Man Who Knows Too Much.'

'I think we've met in court,' said Pascoe. 'I didn't think our little occasion tonight would have had much in it for the *Challenger*.'

'The passing of a great public servant?' said Boyle with a W. C. Fieldsian orotundity. 'You surprise me. Dignity needs its chroniclers as much as disaster.'

He's winding me up, thought Pascoe. He opened his mouth to inquire what hitherto hidden connection with dignity the *Challenger* was planning to reveal when Ruddlesdin said, 'Careful, Peter. Our Monty Knows Too Much because he's got an extra ear.'

He drew back the *Challenger* man's jacket to reveal, hooked on to the third button of his waistcoat, a slim black cassette recorder, almost invisible against the cloth.

'Just a tool of the trade,' said Boyle indifferently. 'I don't hide it.'

'Voice sensitive too, and directional. If he's facing you in a crowded bar, it'll pick you up above all the chatter, isn't that right, Monty?'

There was not a great deal of love lost between these two, decided Pascoe.

'It's not switched on,' said Boyle. 'Mr Dalziel's valediction is, of course, printed on my heart. And I'd never attempt to record a policeman without his knowledge.'

He smiled politely at Pascoe.

Ruddlesdin said, 'Especially not in their club where visitors can't buy drinks,' and stared significantly into his empty glass.

Wield said, 'Give it here, Sammy. Mr Boyle?'

'No more for me,' said the crime reporter, glancing at his watch. 'I have some driving to do before I get to bed.'

'What's that mean? Farmer's wife or kerb crawling?' said Ruddlesdin.

Boyle smiled. 'In our business, Sammy, you're either pressing forward or you're sliding backward, have you forgotten that? Once you start just reporting news, you might as well bow out for one of these.'

He tapped the cassette on his chest before buttoning his jacket.

'Good night, Mr Pascoe. I hope we may meet again and be of mutual benefit soon.'

He made towards the door through which the DCC and his party were being ushered by Dalziel.

'Jumped-up nowt,' said Ruddlesdin. 'I knew him when he couldn't tell a wedding car from a hearse. Now he acts like the bloody *Challenger* were the *Sunday Times*.'

'Very trying,' sympathized Pascoe. 'On the other hand, tonight is very wedding and hearse stuff, isn't it? A column filler for the *Evening Post* perhaps, but lacking those elements of astounding revelation which set the steam rising from the *Challenger*.'

'When you buy a whippet you keep your eye skinned to see no one slips it a pork pie before a race,' said Ruddlesdin.

'Riddles now? You're not moving to *Comic Cuts*, are you, Sammy? What is it you're saying? That Ike Ogilby's put his minders on Watmough till he gets into Parliament?'

Ogilby was the *Challenger*'s ambitious editor, linked with Watmough ever since the Pickford case in a symbiotic relationship in which a good press was traded for insider information.

'No,' said Ruddlesdin confidentially. 'What I've heard,

and will deny ever having said till I'm saying, "told you so", is that yon clock's the nearest Watmough's likely to get to Westminster. This SDP selection he thinks he's got sewn up—well, there's a local councillor on the short list, a chap who's owed a few favours and knows where all the bodies are buried. Smart money's on him. And Ike Ogilby's got the smartest money in town.'

'Another rejection will drive the poor devil mad,' said Pascoe. 'But if it's not a personal leak in the Chamber that Ogilby's after, why keep up his interest in Watmough once he's resigned from the Force?'

Ruddlesdin tapped his long pointed nose and said, 'Memoirs, Pete, I'm talking memoirs.'

'Memoirs? But what's he got to remember?' asked Pascoe. 'He thinks a stake-out's a meal at Berni's.'

Ruddlesdin observed him with alcoholic shrewdness.

'That sounded more like Andy Dalziel than you,' he said. 'All I know is that Ogilby's not interested in buying pigs in pokes, if you'll excuse the metaphor. Mebbe my dear old jumped-up mate, Monty, is living up to his byline for once. The Man Who Knows Too Much. Wieldy, I thought you'd fallen among thieves! Bless you, my son.'

Wield had returned with a tray on which rested three pints. The reporter took his and drained two-thirds of it in a single swallow. Pascoe ignored the proffered tray, however. He was looking across the room to the exit through which Dalziel was just ushering the DCC and his party. Before he went out, Watmough paused and slowly looked around. What was he seeing? Something to stir fond memories of companionship, loyalty, a job well done?

Or something to stir relief at his going and resentment at its manner?

And how shall I feel when it's my turn? wondered Pascoe.

He too looked round the room. Saw the mouthing faces, ghastly in the smoke-fogged strip-lighting. Heard the raucous laughter, the bellowed conversations, the eardrum-striating music. He felt a deep revulsion against it all. But he knew he was not applying a fair test. He was not a very clubbable person. His loyalties were individual rather than institutional. He distrusted the exclusivity of *esprit de corps*. Not that there was anything sinister here. This scene was the commonplace of ten thousand clubs and pubs the length and breadth of the island. Here was the companionship of the ale-house, nothing more.

But suddenly he felt hemmed in, short of air, deprived of will, threatened. He looked at his watch. It was only five to nine.

'Time to go,' he said. 'I promised not to be late.'

'But your beer . . .' said Wield, taken aback.

'Sammy'll drink it. See you.'

In the small foyer he paused and took a deep breath. The door leading to the car park opened and Dalziel came in.

'Well, that's the cortège on its way,' he said rubbing his hands. 'Now let's get on with the wake.'

'Not me,' said Pascoe firmly, adding, to divert Dalziel's efforts at dissuasion, 'and don't be too sure he won't be back to haunt you.'

'Eh?'

He repeated Ruddlesdin's rumour. Rather to his surprise, instead of being abusively dismissive, Dalziel answered thoughtfully, 'Yes, I'd heard summat like that too. Makes you think . . . Ogilby . . . Boyle . . .'

Then he roared with laughter and added, 'But who'd want to buy memoirs from a man who can scarcely remember to zip up after he's had a run-off? It'd be the sale of the sodding century!'

Still laughing, he pushed his way back into the smoke- and noise-filled room while Pascoe with more relief than he could easily account for went out into the fresh night air.

CHAPTER 4

By half past nine, Colin Farr was moving between his seat and the bar with a steady deliberation more worrying to Pedro Pedley than any amount of stagger and sway.

'Young Col all right, is he?' he asked Neil Wardle as the taciturn miner got another round in.

'Aye,' said Wardle, apparently uninterested.

But when he got back to the table, he repeated the question as he set pints down before Farr and Dickinson.

'All right, Col?'

'Any reason I shouldn't be?'

'None as I can think of.'

'Right, then,' said Farr.

'What's that, Neil? A half? You sickening for something?' said Tommy Dickinson, his face flushed with the room's heat and his vain efforts to catch up with his friend's intake.

'No, but I'm off just now to a meeting,' said Wardle.

Wardle was on the branch committee of the Union. During the Great Strike there had been times when his lack of strident militancy and his quiet rationalism had brought accusations of 'softness'. But as the strike began to crumble and the men began to recognize that no amount of rhetoric or confrontation could bring the promised victory, Wardle's qualities won more and more respect. There'd only been one 'scab' at Burrthorpe Main, but many who had weakened and come close to snapping knew that they too would now be paying the price of isolation if it hadn't been for Wardle's calm advice and rock-like support. Since the strike he'd been a prime mover in the re-energizing of the shattered community. And it was Wardle who'd pushed Colin Farr into seeking a place on the union-sponsored day-release course at the University.

'Bloody meetings!' said Dickinson. 'I reckon committee's got a woman up there and they take a vote on who gets first bash!'

Wardle ignored him and said, 'There'll be a full branch meeting next Sunday, Col. You'll be coming to that?'

'Mebbe,' said Farr indifferently. 'They'll likely manage without me, but.'

'Likely we will. But will you manage without them?'

'Union didn't do my dad much good, did it?' said Farr savagely.

'It did the best it could and he never complained. Col,

28

you were grand during the Strike. It were a miracle you
didn't end up in jail, the tricks you got up to. Nothing
seemed too much bother for you then. But the fight's not
over, not by a long chalk. The Board's got a long hit list
and only them as are ready and organized will be able to
fight it.'

'Oh aye? Best day's work they ever did if they put a lid
on that fucking hole!' exclaimed Farr.

'You fought hard enough to keep it open in the Strike,'
said Wardle.

'I fought. But don't you tell me what I fought for, Neil.
Mebbe I just fought 'cos while you're fighting, you don't
have time to think!'

Wardle drank his beer, frowning. Dickinson, who hated
a sour atmosphere, lowered his voice to what he thought of
as a confidential whisper and said, 'See who's just come in?
Gavin Mycroft and his missus. They're sitting over there
with Arthur Downey and that cunt, Satterthwaite. Right
little deputies' dog-kennel.'

'I saw them,' said Farr indifferently.

'Here, Col, you still fancy Stella?'

'What do you mean?'

'Come on, Col, you were knocking her off rotten when
you were a lad, up in the woods by the White Rock. By God
I bet you made the chalk dust fly! And don't say it weren't
serious. You got engaged when you went off, and you didn't
need to, 'cos you were stuffing her already!'

He smiled at the perfection of his own logic.

'That's old news, Tommy,' said Farr.

'And you were well out of that,' said Wardle. 'Marrying
a deputy in middle of the Strike and going off to Spain on
honeymoon while there were kids going hungry back here!
That's no way for a miner's daughter to act.'

'What did you want her to do?' exclaimed Farr. 'Spend
her honeymoon camping on a picket line?'

'See! You still do fancy her!' crowed Dickinson.

'Why don't you shut your big gob, Tommy, and get some
drinks in?' said Farr.

Unoffended, the young miner rose and headed for the

bar. Wardle called after him, 'No more for me, Tommy. I've got to be off and look after you buggers' interests.'

He stood up.

'Think on, Col. If you're going to stay on round here, make it for the right reasons.'

'What'd them be?'

'To make it a place worth staying on in.'

Farr laughed. 'Clean-up job, you mean? Justice for the worker, that sort of stuff? Well, never fear Neil. That's why I've stayed on right enough.'

Wardle looked at the young man with concern, but said nothing more.

'Bugger off, Neil,' said Farr in irritation. 'It's like having me dad standing over me waiting till I worked out what I'd done wrong.'

'He were a clever man, old Billy,' said Wardle.

'If he were so bloody clever, how'd he end up with his neck broke at the bottom of a shaft?' asked Farr harshly.

'Mebbe when he had to transfer from the face, he brought some of the dark up with him. It happens.'

'What the hell does that mean, Neil?' said Farr very softly.

'Figure of speech. See you tomorrow. Don't be late. Jock never is.'

Left to himself, Colin Farr sat staring sightlessly at the table surface for a while. Suddenly he rose. Glass in hand, he walked steadily down the room till he reached the table Dickinson had called the deputies' dog-kennel.

The three men seated there looked up as Farr approached. Only the woman ignored him. She was in her mid-twenties, heavily made-up, with her small features diminished still further by a frame of exaggeratedly bouffant silver-blonde hair. But no amount of make-up or extravagance of coiffure could disguise the fact that she had a lovely face. Her husband, Gavin Mycroft, was a few years older, a slim dark man with rather sullen good looks. Next to him, in his forties, sat Arthur Downey, also very thin but tall enough to be gangling with it. He had a long sad face with a dog's big gentle brown eyes.

The third man was squat and muscular. Balding at the

front, he had let his dull gingery hair grow into a compensatory mane over his ears and down his neck.

This was Harold Satterthwaite. He regarded Farr's approach indifferently from heavily hooded eyes. Mycroft glowered aggressively, but Arthur Downey half rose and said, 'Hello, Col. All right? Can I get you a drink?'

'Got one,' said Farr. 'Just want a word with Stella.'

The woman didn't look up, but her husband rose angrily, saying, 'Listen, Farr, I'll not tell you again . . .'

Downey took his sleeve and pulled him down.

'Keep it calm, Gav. Col's not looking for bother, are you, Col?'

Farr looked amazed, then said with an incredibly sweet smile, 'Me? Nay, you know me better than that, surely? It's just that me mam wants Mrs Mycroft's receipt for potato cakes. It's all right if your missus gives me a receipt, isn't it, Mr Mycroft, sir?'

Mycroft was on his feet again, his face flushed with rage. Then Pedro Pedley was between the two men, collecting empty glasses from the table.

'Everything all right, gents?' he said pleasantly.

'Nowt we can't take care of ourselves, Peter,' said Satterthwaite, staring with cold dislike at Colin Farr. He was Pedley's brother-in-law and shared with his sister the distinction of using the steward's real name.

'Not in here, you can't,' said Pedley. 'Down the hole or in the street, you do what you like. In here you do what I like. Arthur, you've got some sense . . .'

He jerked his head towards the door. Downey gently took Farr's elbow.

'Come on, Col,' he said coaxingly. 'Let's go and sit and have a chat. It'd be like old times for me. Your dad and me had some good nights in here . . .'

'Not that many, Arthur,' sneered Satterthwaite. 'He didn't dare show his face in here much at the end. I'll give you that, Farr. You've got real nerve. I'd not have thought even you would have had the brass balls to come in here tonight of all nights.'

Farr swung towards him. His glass fell from his hand and

crashed to the floor, scattering beer and splinters. Downey flung his arms round the youth to restrain him. Pedley said, 'Belt up, Harold! Col, you get yourself out of here else you're banned. Now!'

Farr was trying to struggle free from Downey's restraint, then suddenly he relaxed.

'You know what, Harold?' he said. 'You're full of shit. It's time somebody took you apart but who wants to get covered in shit?'

Tommy Dickinson arrived from the bar, his face wreathed with concern.

'What's going off, Col?' he asked. 'I've got you a beer.'

'I think mebbe Col's had enough,' said Pedley.

'You're right there, Pedro,' said Farr. 'More than bloody enough!'

He pulled free from Downey, seized the glass from Dickinson's hand, drained it in a single draught and banged it down in front of Satterthwaite with a crash that almost shattered it.

'Take it easy, Col,' said Downey.

'You can fuck off too,' snarled Farr. 'Call yourself a friend? What did you ever do for my dad? What did any of you ever do?'

He pushed his way past Dickinson and headed for the exit door.

Dickinson slurped hastily at his pint and said, 'I'd best go after him.'

'He'll be better left,' advised Downey.

'What the fuck do you know?' said Dickinson rudely. But when Pedley said, 'Arthur's right, Tommy. Best leave him, for a bit anyway,' the chubby miner allowed himself to be led back to the bar where he was soon retailing a lurid version of the incident to eager ears.

Downey resumed his seat, looking anxiously towards the door.

'For Christ's sake, Arthur, why do you get so het up over a loonie like yon bugger?' demanded Satterthwaite.

'His dad were my best friend,' said Downey defensively.

'So you keep telling us when most'd keep quiet about

something like that. Or is it just that you think mebbe May Farr'll become your best friend too if you wet-nurse her daft bloody son.'

Downey's long face went pale but Stella Mycroft said slyly, 'Arthur just likes helping people, don't you, Arthur? Then mebbe they'll help him.'

'Oh, you can talk, then?' said Mycroft. 'I didn't hear you say much when that bastard were talking to you.'

'No need, was there?' said Stella. 'A lady doesn't need to open her mouth, or anything, when she's got three old-fashioned gentlemen around to defend her honour, does she?'

Satterthwaite snorted a laugh. Downey looked embarrassed. And Gavin Mycroft regarded his wife in baffled fury.

Outside the Welfare, Colin Farr had paused as the night air hit him, taking strength from his legs but doing little to cool the great rage in his head. He looked around as if he needed to get his bearings. The Club was the last building at the western end of the village. After this the road wound off up the valley to a horizon dimly limned against the misty stars. But there were other brighter lights up there, the lights of Burrthorpe Main.

Farr thrust a defiant finger into the air at them then turned towards the town and began to stagger forward.

Soon the old grey terrace of the High Street was shouldered aside by a modern shopping parade. Business, badly hit by the Great Strike, was picking up again, as evidenced by the brightly lit supermarket window plastered like a boxer's face with loss-leader Special Offers. Farr pressed his forehead against the glass, enjoying its smooth chill against his fevered skin.

A car drove slowly by, coming to a halt before the Welfare. A stout man got out. He stood on the Club steps rolling a thin cigarette, then instead of going in, he walked along the pavement towards Colin Farr.

'Got a light, friend?' he asked.

'Don't smoke. Bad for your health,' said Farr solemnly.

'You're an expert are you?' laughed the man. He was

studying Farr's face closely in the light from the supermarket window. 'It's Mr Farr, isn't it? From Clay Street?'

'Depends who's asking.'

'Boyle's the name. Monty Boyle. You may have heard of me. Here's my card.'

He undid his jacket and took a card out of his waistcoat pocket.

'I was thinking, Mr Farr,' he went on. 'We may be able to do each other a bit of good. I'm supposed to be seeing someone at your Club, but that can wait. Is there somewhere quiet we can go and have a talk, and a coffee too? You look like a man who could use a coffee.'

'Coffee,' said Farr, studying the card closely. 'And somewhere quiet. It's quiet here. And lots of coffee too.'

Boyle followed his gaze into the supermarket where a pyramid of instant coffee dominated the window display.

'Yes,' he said with a smile. 'But I don't think they're open.'

'No problem,' said Colin Farr.

And picking the man up as if he weighed fifteen pounds rather than fifteen stone, he hurled him through the plate glass window.

Fifty yards away the doors of a parked car opened and two uniformed policemen got out. The younger, a constable, ran towards the supermarket. Behind him at a more dignified pace walked a sergeant. The constable grabbed Colin Farr from behind as he stood laughing at the man sprawled amidst the wreck of the coffee pyramid. Farr drove his elbow back into the policeman's belly and turned to grapple with him.

'Now then, young Colin, behave yourself,' said the Sergeant reprovingly.

'That you, Sergeant Swift? Don't go away. I'll sort you out after I'm done with this bugger.'

So saying, Farr lifted the constable in the air and hurled him after Monty Boyle.

Sergeant Swift sighed and raised his night stick.

'Sorry, lad, I can't wait,' he said and brought it down with moderate force and perfect aim on the base of Farr's neck. Then he held out his arms to catch the young man's body as he fell into a darkness deeper and blacker than riding the pit.

CHAPTER 5

'And how was the people's poet today?'

'Sorry?'

'The young man in your class whose literary style you so admired.'

'He wasn't there,' said Ellie.

'Oh dear. A drop-out. I wondered why I found you so glum. Hello, Rosie, my love! How's life in the university crèche? Have they got you on to nuclear physics yet?'

Pascoe picked up his daughter and held her high in the air to her great delight.

'No, not a drop-out,' said Ellie. 'He couldn't be there because he's in jail.'

'Jail? Good Lord.'

Pascoe replaced Rose on the sofa and sat down beside her.

'Tell me all,' he said.

'He was in some kind of fracas with a policeman. I assume it was the kind of horseplay which, if indulged in with another miner, would have got his wrist slapped. With a cop, of course, it amounts to sacrilege.'

'You assume that, do you?' mused Pascoe. 'Is it an assumption based on evidence? Or, like that of the Virgin Mary, on faith and a dearth of eye-witnesses?'

Ellie's indignation was not to be diverted to the conspiracy of clerics, attractive target though it was.

'An educated guess,' she retorted. 'As for evidence, I rather thought you might have mentioned the case to me before this, or does it come under Official Secrets?'

'On the contrary. Assaults on police officers are, alas, so commonplace that they can go pretty well unnoticed, even in the Force. Like accidents to miners. As long as they don't put a man in hospital for more than a few hours, who cares? But you must have had his mates' version?'

'Not really,' admitted Ellie. 'He's the only one from his pit, so the others have only known him since he came on the course. One of them saw a paragraph about the case in his local paper.'

'So where is he from, this whatsisname?'

'Farr. Colin Farr. He works at Burrthorpe Main.'

'Burrthorpe. Now that rings a bell. Of course. Both mysteries solved.'

'I didn't know there was even one.'

'Mystery one. Why did it ring a bell? That was where one of the kids went missing that Watmough put in the Pickford frame. And our beloved ex-DCC never missed a chance of dragging the Pickford case into his many farewell speeches.'

'You mean this man Pickford murdered a Burrthorpe child?'

'Possibly. They never found her body. But Pickford's suicide gave Watmough the chance to load several unsolved child-molestation cases on to him, plus the Pedley girl's disappearance. Must have helped the serious-crime statistics a lot.'

'Jesus!' said Ellie. 'How comforting! And what was the other mystery? You said there were two.'

'Oh yes. Mystery two. Why don't I know about the assaulted copper? Because Burrthorpe's in the South Yorks area, that's why! Only just, mind you. Another quarter-mile and it would be on our patch, but as it is, the battered bobby is not one of Mid-Yorkshire's finest, therefore I know nothing.'

'How typically parochial!' mocked Ellie. 'How far is it? Twenty miles?'

'Nearer thirty, actually. That's quite a long way for your lad to come, isn't it? He must be very keen to get out of Burrthorpe Main once a week.'

'He's certainly found an ingenious way of staying out even longer, hasn't he?' said Ellie, a little over-savagely.

'Yes, dear. You don't know anywhere round here where a hungry policeman could get a meal, do you?'

Ellie rose and went to the door.

'It's salad,' she said as she passed through. 'I was a bit pushed.'

Pascoe leaned over and looked down at his daughter who returned his gaze from wide unblinking blue-grey eyes.

'OK, kid,' he said sternly. 'Don't play innocent with me. You're not leaving this sofa till you tell me where you've hidden the rusks.'

Next morning Pascoe, finding himself with a loose couple of minutes as he drank his mug of instant coffee, dialled the number of South Yorkshire Police Headquarters, identified himself and asked if Detective-Inspector Wishart was handy.

'Hello, cowboy!' came the most unconstabulary greeting a few moments later. 'How's life out on the range? Got running water yet?'

It was Wishart's little joke to affect belief that Mid-Yorks was a haven of rural tranquillity in which the only crimes to ruffle the placid surface of CID life were rustling and the odd bit of bestiality. Any note of irritation in Pascoe's response would only result in an unremitting pursuit of the facetious fancy, so he said amiably, 'Only downhill. In fact things are so quiet here I thought I'd give myself a vicarious thrill by talking to a *real* policeman about some *real* action.'

'Wise move. Anything in particular, or shall I ramble on generally while I'm beating up these prisoners?'

'You could fill me in on one Colin Farr, of Burrthorpe. He got done for thumping one of your finest last week.'

'Oh. Any special reason for asking, Peter?' said Wishart suspiciously.

'It's all right,' laughed Pascoe. 'I'm not doing a commando raid. It's personal and unofficial. My wife knows him, in a tutorial capacity, I hasten to add. She was concerned that he'd missed one of her classes, that's all.'

'Blaming it on the police in general and you in particular, eh?' said Wishart, who had the shrewdness of a Scots lawyer which is what his family would have preferred him to be. 'Burrthorpe, you say? Indian territory that. It was almost a no-go area during the Strike. You'll remember the great siege? They just about wrecked the local cop-shop. I believe they've rebuilt it like a fortress. There's a sergeant there I've known for years. I'll give him a buzz if you can hang on.'

'My pleasure,' said Pascoe.

In the ensuing silence Pascoe cradled the phone on his shoulder and burrowed in the bottom drawer of his desk in search of a packet of barley sugars he kept there. Man could not live on health food alone. When he surfaced, he found himself looking into the questioning gaze of Andrew Dalziel. Usually the fat man came into a room like an SAS assault team. Occasionally, and usually when it caused maximum embarrassment and inconvenience, he just materialized.

'Busy?' said Dalziel.

'Yes,' said Pascoe, carefully letting the barley sugar slip back into the drawer.

'Won't bother you, then. I just want a look at your old records. Mine are a mess.'

He peered towards Pascoe's filing cabinets, with the combative expectation of a new arrival at the Dark Tower. Pascoe, who knew why his superior's records were in a mess (if he couldn't find anything, he shook the offending file and shouted threats at the resultant shower of paper), rose in alarm. The phone was still silent.

'Was it something in particular, sir?' he said.

'I'm not just browsing if that's what you mean,' growled Dalziel. 'The Kassell drugs case will do for starters. I know you weren't concerned directly but I know too you're a nosey bugger, so what have you got?'

What's he doing digging up old bones? wondered Pascoe as he put the phone on the desk and went to the cupboard in which he stored his personal records.

'Thanks, lad. I'll keep an ear open for you, shall I?'

Sticking his head out of the cupboard, Pascoe saw that Dalziel was in his seat with the telephone at his ear, taking the paper off a barley sugar.

'That's OK,' he said with studied negligence. 'It's not really important.'

38

'It better had be, lad,' said Dalziel sternly 'Official phones these are. Some bugger rang Benidorm last week and no one's confessing. Wasn't you, was it? No. Not cultural enough for you, Benidorm. Can you find it?'

Pascoe resumed his search, spurred on by the need to get Dalziel out before the need arose to explain his query to South.

'Got it,' he said in dusty triumph a moment later. But it was too late.

'Hello,' said Dalziel in a neutral voice which, probably deliberately, might have passed for Pascoe's. 'Go ahead.'

He listened for a moment then exploded. 'Ripper! What do you mean he's a ripper? No, this isn't Peter. This is Dalziel. And who the fuck are you? You're not speaking from Benidorm, are you?'

He listened a while longer then passed the phone to Pascoe.

'Inspector Wishart from South,' he said. 'Says your man's a ripper down Burrthorpe Main. Gave me a nasty shock, that. This the Kassell stuff? I'll take good care of it, lad.'

'Yes, sir,' said Pascoe, who foresaw already the dog-eared, beer-stained state in which his lovely records were likely to return to him. 'Official inquiry, is it, sir?'

From the door Dalziel flashed him a smile as reassuring as a crack in new plaster.

'As official as yours, I expect, lad.'

He went out. Pascoe said, 'The coast's clear.'

'Jesus,' said Wishart. 'You might have warned me Geronimo had broken out again; let's do this quick, eh? Here's what the record says.'

That night he said to Ellie, 'I picked up some info on your protégé, if you'd like to hear.'

'Official version, you mean? Go on. I like a well-crafted tale.'

'Simply, he got drunk, took offence at something a stranger in the street said to him, got into a fracas and pushed the man through a shop window. That may have been an accident. Certainly, it turned out the man didn't want to bring charges. Which was odd. As evidently he turned out to be a journalist, one Monty Boyle, chief crime reporter on the *Challenger*. Makes you think . . .'

Ellie was not in the least interested in what it made him think.

'But the good old fuzz persuaded him to change his mind,' she said angrily.

'Not really. A couple of local cops witnessed the incident. When they approached, Farr attacked one of them, throwing him through the window too, and had to be restrained by the other. That was the assault he was charged with.'

'Now I've got it,' cried Ellie in mock delight. 'A bit of drunken horseplay, the kind of thing that passes for high spirits at Twickers or Annabel's, is escalated to a criminal assault by heavy-handed police intervention.'

'It's a point of view,' said Pascoe gravely. 'It's certainly true that if he hadn't assaulted the constable, the whole thing might have been smoothed over with a police caution.'

'But you can't turn a blind eye to saying boo to a bobby,' said Ellie.

'Not when he needs seven stitches in his hand,' said Pascoe. 'Incidentally, since you don't ask, the *Challenger* reporter was hardly damaged at all. It appears that Burrthorpe's not the kind of place you encourage cop-bashing. They had a full-scale riot there during the Strike and the police station was just about wrecked.'

'So a young man goes to jail and gets a permanent criminal record *pour encourager les autres*?'

'The record was there already,' said Pascoe. 'He had several counts against him during the Strike . . .'

'Who the hell didn't? And they can't have been all that serious, otherwise he wouldn't have kept his job under the famous victimization scheme!'

'True. But beyond and outside the Strike, he's obviously been a wild lad. Most serious was when he got done for assaulting a Customs officer at Liverpool. Before you ask, no, he wasn't coming back from holiday. He was a merchant seaman, didn't you know that? A good teacher should know all about her pupils. Anyway, it didn't amount to too much,

I gather. Farr felt he was being unduly delayed by official-dom and threw the man's hat into the ocean, then offered to send the man after it. He's very fond of throwing people around, it seems. But you can see why the magistrate wouldn't think a mere fine was enough in this last case.'

'Oh yes,' grunted Ellie. 'I suppose he was lucky to escape the strappado.'

'He only got a week. Five days with remission. He'll be back for your next class. What's the topic going to be? Law and Order?'

'Peter, that's not funny, merely crass,' snarled Ellie.

Pascoe considered.

'No, I don't think so,' he said quietly. 'It may not be *terribly* funny but I don't think it's at all crass, not between consenting adults in domestic bliss. As a professional communicator, you should be more careful. Intemperance of language is to thought what drunkenness is to courage: it makes a little go a long way.'

'Is that original? Or is it a quote from some other prissy, pusillanimous time-server?'

'Is that live? Or are you miming to the latest hit on the Radical Alliterative label?'

Ellie smiled, with only a little effort.

'I'll let you be original if you let me be live,' she said.

'Deal.'

He smiled back and went upstairs to see Rose, who was also smiling as she slept.

The difference was, her smile looked as if it went all the way through.

CHAPTER 6

'Carry your bag, miss?'

For a sliver of a second Ellie's hand started to proffer the battered old briefcase. She had felt unusually drained after today's class and had taken her time packing her papers while the cheerful chatter and clatter of the young miners faded down the corridor. When she finally followed them, Colin Farr had emerged from the door of the Gents as she passed. He was dressed in motorcycle leathers and carried a helmet.

'Real offer or just winding me up, Colin?' she said.

He fell into step beside her.

'Depends, miss.'

'On what?'

'Whether you think it's real or winding you up.'

'But which depends on which?' she wondered.

She also wondered, but this to herself, if Farr had emerged coincidentally by coincidence or if he'd been lurking in that doorway.

'Don't follow you, miss.'

'Yes, you do, Colin,' she said, smiling at him. 'That's one game you can stop playing. Another is calling me *miss* all the time. I told the others last week that if I was going to use their first names, they'd have to use mine. Even though you seemed a little abstracted today, you may have heard one or two of them call me Ellie.'

'Ell ee. Thought them were your initials, miss. Or mebbe a title.'

He grinned openly as he spoke.

They had reached the central landing. They were on the fourteenth floor of the Ivory Tower, a glass and concrete monument of the expansive and affluent 'sixties whose gnomonic shadow marked the passage of epochal as well as diurnal time on the scatter of redbrick buildings which had survived from the old civic university. Descent was by stair, conventional lift, or paternoster. The stairs were long and exhausting and the lift took an age to arrive, but Ellie usually preferred one or the other.

Farr, however, had made straight for the paternoster. The moving platforms were just large enough for two. He glanced at her, touched her elbow, and stepped forward. She stepped with him but as always the sense of the floor sinking away beneath her was so disconcerting that she gave a slight stagger and leaned against Farr whose arm went round her waist to support her.

42

'I'm all right,' she said, trying to disengage herself. But there was little spare room on the platform and he made no effort to move away.

'You'd not do to ride the pit,' he observed.

'Ride the pit?' she said brightly, aware of the closeness of his body and aware also that she was slipping beneath a protective carapace of school marminess. 'Let me see. That means go down the shaft in the Cage, doesn't it?'

'Aye. Down or up,' he said, smiling slightly.

He knows how uncomfortable he's making me feel, thought Ellie.

She said dismissively. 'At least the Cage is standing still when you get in.'

'You're right. And when it starts going down, you wish it'd stood still forever.'

His tone was so intense that she forgot her discomfiture and said curiously, 'You hate it that much, do you?'

Strangely this shift towards conversational intimacy seemed to affect him as the physical contact had affected her. He removed his arm and swayed away from her and said in a much lighter voice, 'Energetic buggers, these students,' nodding at the graffiti-scrawled interstitial floor beams. 'They must've had to go round three or four times to get them written.'

'That sounds like a considerable misdirection of effort,' said Ellie.

'Most things are when you look at them straight,' said Colin Farr. 'This is us.'

His hand grasped her elbow lightly, its touch chivalric rather than erotic, and they stepped out in a unity of movement worthy of Astaire and Rogers.

Outside in the cool air of the shadowy side of the Ivory Tower, they paused.

'I'm going over to the crèche,' said Ellie.

'The what?'

'The nursery. Where staff can leave their children while they're teaching. And students too.'

'Very democratic. I'm off to the car park. Where staff can leave their cars. But not students.'

'That'd be a male decision,' said Ellie. 'It's a wonder the attendant doesn't get you. He's a terror. It took three phone calls to persuade him I was entitled first time I came.'

'You should try a motorbike,' said Farr. 'You can be round the back of his hut before he notices.'

They stood in silence for a moment. Ellie glanced at her watch.

'See you next week, then.'

'Likely,' said Farr. 'If I can manage.'

'Colin, I was sorry to hear about your bit of trouble.'

She did not care to hear herself using the euphemism, but she was treading carefully. No one had mentioned the young man's week in jail today and she'd taken this as a signal that he didn't want it mentioned.

Now he gave her his crooked little near-smile and said, 'It were nowt. I've been in worse places.'

'The pit, you mean?'

'Oh aye. That's worse. But I meant worse jails.'

He grinned openly at her look of surprise.

'I've not just been a miner,' he said. 'I've been a sailor too. Did you not know that?'

'How could I?' prevaricated Ellie. 'I mean, you're so young!'

'Old enough. I went down pit at sixteen like all me mates. But I got a bit restless after a bit and when I was nineteen I jacked it in and went and joined the Merchant Navy. I were in for nearly four years. I came back to Burrthorpe just in time to go on strike for a year!'

'And will you go back? To sea, I mean.'

'Mebbe. I can't say.'

There was another silence.

Ellie said, 'I've really got to go and pick my daughter up. Till next week, then. Goodbye.'

'Aye. See you.'

She walked away. He watched as she passed from the shadow of the Tower into the sunlight before disappearing into one of the two-storey redbrick buildings on the scattered and disorganized campus.

44

He checked the car park was clear before loping towards the gleaming Suzuki 1100 which cost him more than he ever dared tell his mother in monthly payments. But it was money he didn't grudge. As he started her up, the attendant rushed from his hut shouting, 'I want a word with you!'

Farr waited till he was about thirty feet away, then opened up the throttle and sent the bike leaping forward towards the man.

'Jesus Christ!' he cried, jumping aside.

'See you next week!' yelled Farr over his shoulder.

He wove his way at a steady pace through the city traffic but once out on the open road he rapidly took the powerful machine up to the speed limit and held it there for a while. Then as the exhilaration of the streaming air, the blurring hedges and the throbbing metal between his legs got to him, he gave it full power and was soon cracking the ton on the straights.

It couldn't last long. Soon his eye registered the brief image of a police car sitting in a lay-by, waiting for just the likes of himself, and a couple of minutes later it was in his mirror, too distant to have got his number which in any case he always kept as muddy as he could get away with, but not receding. Ahead the road wound down a shallow hill to a small township which seemed to pride itself on having traffic lights every ten yards. Also there was a police station there, easily alerted by the car radio.

There were no turn-offs before he hit the town. He was travelling very fast downhill towards a sharp left-hand bend. Straight ahead was a tall hawthorn hedge with woodland behind it. There was a gap or at least a thinness in the hedge where it met a wall at the apex of the bend.

Instead of slowing for the turn, he twisted the throttle to full open. There might be something coming the other way; he might find the hedge more solid than it looked; even if he got through, the close clustering trees would be almost impossible to avoid.

He went straight across the road.

The hedge parted like a bead-curtain. He felt its branches scrabble vainly to get a hold on his leather jacket, then he

45

was among the trees, bucketing over exposed roots, leaning this way and that as he twisted through the copse, decelerating madly. His shoulder grazed bark, a low bough almost took his helmet off. Finally he mounted the steep mossy bank of a drainage ditch, let the bike slide from between his legs and lay on the ground, his ragged breath drawing in the odour of leaf-mould and damp earth while his pounding heart settled back into the monotonous rhythms of safety.

Distantly he heard the police car go by. He sat up and removed his helmet. He was hot in his leathers and he took them off too. Almost without thought, he continued undressing, peeling off shirt and trousers till he stood naked among the trees feeling the cool air playing on his feverish flesh. He was sexually aroused. He thought of Stella Mycroft. And he thought of Ellie Pascoe. His hand moved to his groin, but a sudden gust of wind heavy with a chilling rain got there first.

Like a pail of cold water over a rutting dog, he told himself sardonically. Thanks, God!

He pulled on his clothes and protective gear, pulled the bike upright and set out across country easing the bike along ploughed furrows but opening it up across pasture land. Sheep scattered; cows regarded him with gentle curiosity. A man on a tractor stood up and waved an angry fist, mouthing inaudible abuse. Colin Farr waved back.

Ultimately he hit a farm lane which took him out on to a minor road he did not know. Using the declining sun, he turned to the south-west and soon was back on a main road he recognized.

When he reached the outskirts of Burrthorpe, he stopped at a telephone box, went in and dialled.

The number rang a while, then the phone at the other end was lifted and the pips demanded his money before he could be heard, like ghosts gibbering for blood. He pressed in his coin.

A woman's voice said, 'Hello? Burrthorpe 227.'

He didn't speak.

'Hello?' Impatient now. 'Who's there?'

Still he kept silent.

And now the voice changed, the pitch lower, the tone anxious.

'Colin, is that you?'

But still he did not reply and the woman cried out angrily. 'Get stuffed!' and banged the phone down.

Colin Farr left the receiver dangling and went home.

CHAPTER 7

Ex-Deputy Chief Constable Neville Watmough awoke on the Friday morning after the SDP candidate selection meeting with that dull ache of the heart which warns the mind of a disappointment before the mind itself has recollected it.

He had been rejected. Again. The local councillor had won the nomination after a period of debate so short that in a jury it must have meant one show of hands in the corridor outside the court-room. The bastard was a *car salesman*, for God's sake, fit enough no doubt to sort out local problems of street-lighting and refuse-collection, but with little grasp of national or international affairs. As for his person—the suede boots, the two-tone shirt, the thin moustache which he kept on touching nervously while the anæmic tongue lubricated the narrow lips in preparation for yet another ingratiating smile—what kind of image was this for a Party with any real belief in its right to govern? Not that the selection committee itself had inspired any confidence. Schoolteachers, small businessmen, a solicitor's clerk, a token manual worker, and in the chair, that fat female JP who never missed any opportunity of scolding the police like a stern aunt from the Bench. At least in court you didn't have to look at her huge splayed legs.

Perhaps he had picked the wrong Party. Perhaps he should have listened to the frequent overtures from local Conservatives to become a bulwark of their Law and Order lobby.

But Watmough was not a stupid man any more than he

was immoral or opportunist, and over breakfast he settled down to sorting things out into their true relations in the chain of causality.

'It looks as if it could be nice enough to finish tidying up the garden today, dear,' said his wife brightly.

He smiled and grunted and sipped his coffee. It might have been pleasant to discuss things with her, but after three decades of conditioning to regard her husband's professional affairs as unapproachable, it would be as difficult for her to listen as for him to speak. Fleetingly he wondered if he had been altogether wise to treat, say, Mid-Yorkshire's traffic flow problems as confidential within the bounds of the Official Secrets Act. But he had made that decision and now must live with its loneliness.

At least, he told himself with some complacency, he did not blame his wife. She had accompanied him dutifully the previous night and said all the right things on cue. He guessed that he alone had detected her mighty relief when the chance that they might have had to move to London had been trampled on by those suede boots.

No; the cause of his disappointment had been bad timing. He had come too late into the race. Or rather, he had come too early. And the cause of that was his failure to get the Chief's job. Now *that* had been a real shock. No waking up the next morning then to the dull ache of disappointment, for he had been kept awake all night by its searing pain. It had shattered his hopes and scattered his plans, and worst of all, it had clouded his judgement. It had seemed a cleverly contemptuous act to chuck in his own resignation so quickly afterwards. He would have been wiser far, he now realized, to hang on and look around for a Chief's job in another part of the country. The local man, because he was known and taken for granted, was always at a disadvantage in such matters—except in the case of car salesmen, it seemed. No, he should have withdrawn, regrouped . . .

A clock chimed. *Ding dong ding dong. Ding dong ding dong. Dong ding ding dong. Ding dong ding dong.*

The sound filled him with sudden fury. He counted himself back to control with the hours . . . seven, eight, nine.

'I find those chimes a little irritating,' he said mildly.

'Do you, dear? I'm sure they can be turned off. Most things can.'

Was this irony? he asked himself in amazement. A glance across the table reassured him and he let his mind count another link back in the chain of causality.

The support of his colleagues, their simple loyalty, that too had been missing. That cunning old bastard Winter, the outgoing Chief, had never liked him. God knows what he'd said to the Committee. And as above, so below. That gross grotesque, Dalziel . . .

He shuddered at the memory.

At least he was now free of them, free to make his own decisions. Free to set the record straight.

There was his book, a serious review of the problems and future of modern policing, based on his own experience and observation, and leavened with accounts of some of the more famous cases he'd been involved with. It was a long way from being finished, of course, but he'd shown an outline and some draft sections to Ike Ogilby.

What was it Ike had said as he returned them?

'Very interesting, Nev. Should rouse a lot of interest in the so-called quality papers and the heavy chat shows. But a lot of it would be above our readers' heads. It's not as if you're claiming you get your ideas from God or anything really wild like that, is it?'

'I didn't show you the drafts with a view to *Challenger* publication, Ike,' he'd replied, genuinely surprised.

'Of course not. But I was thinking, Nev, in the remote circumstance things don't go right for you politically, this time. I mean—you could do worse than keep yourself in the public eye with a series of pieces in the *Challenger* . . .'

'But you said that your readers . . .'

'No, I wasn't meaning the main meat of your book, Nev. You wouldn't want to show your hand too early there, would you? I'm afraid the country's too full of unscrupulous senior cops who aren't above nicking a good idea. No, I was thinking of the more popular market. Memoirs of famous cases. Telling it like it was. We wouldn't need to take up all that much of your creative time either. I took the liberty of showing your draft to Monty Boyle, our chief crime man. He was most impressed. Monty could work with you. He'd do the leg work and stitch it all together. You'd have copy approval, of course, but this way it wouldn't interfere with your serious writing.'

'Interesting idea,' he'd replied. 'But hardly the thing for a parliamentary candidate.'

'Perish the thought,' said Ogilby. 'But have lunch with Monty anyway. Never any harm in having lunch, is there?'

So he'd had lunch, and found the journalist a civilized and entertaining companion. The man had asked if he'd mind if he ran his cassette recorder as they talked. 'It's best to keep a record, especially when it's informal. Things get missed. Or misunderstood. This keeps us both straight.'

'No, I don't mind,' said Watmough. 'Though it seems a waste of your batteries as I really don't envisage writing anything other than campaign speeches in the near future.'

'No, of course not. But as a crime reporter, I'm always keen to pick the brain of an expert.'

They had spent a fascinating hour talking about famous cases, then as they parted, the journalist had said, 'By the way, I know it's unlikely to happen, but if Ike ever does sign you up, don't settle for less than . . .' and he had named a quite surprising sum.

Since then, Ogilby hadn't referred to the matter. Would he bring it up again when news of last night's débâcle reached him? It wasn't that Watmough needed the money —there were any amount of run-of-the-mill security adviser jobs he could have if his excellent pension and good investments needed topping up—but he did need to make sure he maintained his public profile in preparation for the next selection short list.

If Ogilby didn't contact him it shouldn't be too difficult to contrive an accidental meeting. But he mustn't appear to be pressing . . .

In the hall, the telephone rang. He rose and went to answer it.

'Neville? It's Ike.'

He glanced at his watch and smiled. Ten past nine. These newsmen didn't let the grass grow under their feet when they really wanted something! Now what was that figure that Monty Boyle had said he should go for?

It was good to feel back in control again.

'Hello, Ike,' he said. 'And what can I do for you?'

CHAPTER 8

Peter Pascoe was getting used to going to work on Tuesdays in a bad temper. And an opinion pollster catching him en route would also have detected a marked swing to the right, at least as far as mining communities were concerned.

This morning at breakfast, Ellie had announced that she was planning to go down a mine. 'An experience shared is a gap bridged,' she declared. Pascoe, dismayed by the idea for a pudder of reasons, none of which he could identify reasonably, wondered whether this meant he was likely to find himself going to bed with a miner. Ellie informed him coldly that while reason was occasionally democratic, ridicule was always élitist. This, coming from a woman who fell off her chair at the ranting of radical comedians, had to be challenged. One thing led to another and the other led to the usual, which was Pascoe sitting at his desk in a bad temper on Tuesday morning.

After an hour of tedious paperwork, he had declined from a boil to a simmer when his door burst open with a violence worthy of the Holy Ghost fresh from Philippi jail. It was, however, no paraclete who entered.

'He's done it!' exclaimed Dalziel. 'I knew it'd happen. Reason said no, but me piles told me different.'

'Who's done what, sir?' asked Pascoe, rising to place himself defensively between the fat man and his records cupboard which Dalziel had taken to rifling at will during the past few days.

'It's Wonder Woman's memoirs. The *Challenger*'s going to publish them!'

'Good Lord. I heard he didn't get the nomination . . .'

'He'd as much chance of being nominated as an aniseed ball on a snooker table,' snarled Dalziel. 'We all knew that. But Ogilby was going around saying he'd read some of the memoirs in draft and it were like eating cold sago with a rusty spoon, so no one reckoned the *Challenger* could really be interested. But it was funny, the more folk said it were impossible, the more my piles ached.'

Pascoe was singularly uninterested in Dalziel's haruspical hæmorrhoids but he found himself marvelling as often before at the extent of his personal intelligence service. If it happened in Mid-Yorkshire, he knew it in hours; anywhere else in the county and he might have to wait till the next day.

'But if it's as bad as that, why should Ogilby be interested?'

'Christ knows! But he must reckon there's enough dirt in there to be worth digging for! They can make silk knickers out of a pig's knackers, them bastards! That Leeds vicar last week. Caught two youngsters nicking candlesticks and by the time Monty Boyle were finished, he had Headingley sounding like a mix of Salem and Sodom!'

'Monty Boyle!' exclaimed Pascoe. 'Of course!'

'You know something I don't?' said Dalziel incredulously.

Pascoe explained.

'It fits, doesn't it? The Pickford case was Watmough's finest hour. And it was during South's investigation of that Burrthorpe girl's disappearance that it all came to a head and Pickford topped himself, leaving a note confessing all. So if Boyle was sniffing around so that he could collaborate with Watmough on a tell-all series, he'd not want to draw rival attention to it by getting involved in a court case. Only, this was *before* the selection meeting, so Ogilby must have been pretty sure what the result would be.'

'I told you, everyone was. And if he hadn't been, he would likely have fixed it.'

'I'd better give Alex Wishart a buzz and warn him what's happening,' said Pascoe.

'Let Wishart take care of himself,' said Dalziel. 'You

concentrate on looking after those nearest and dearest. Like me.'

'But Watmough was mainly admin after he came back to us,' pointed out Pascoe. 'Not even the *Challenger* can make his time here interesting.'

'I wish I could be as sure, lad,' said Dalziel. 'But fore-warned is forearmed . . .'

'That's why you've been ruining my records!' exclaimed Pascoe.

'They were a bit mixed up,' said Dalziel reprovingly. 'You want to watch that. Well, mebbe you'll turn out to be right and it'll all be a storm in a piss-pot after all. But one thing I know for sure. If Lobby Lud says anything out of place about me, I'll hit him so hard with his clock, his head'll chime for a fortnight!'

He left like a mighty rushing wind.

Behind him Pascoe sat down and mused a little space. There were tiny clouds no bigger than a man's hand on several of his horizons. They might of course come to nothing or even break in blessings on his head. But when Dalziel got nervous, his colleagues did well to twitch.

And when Ellie started talking about going down mines, it was perhaps time to start looking beneath the surface himself.

First, though, he owed Alex Wishart a phone call.

The Scot listened in silence, then said, 'Well, I don't see how he can harm us by anything he says. He would hardly want to, would he? It was his triumph and you don't rain on your own parade. You're worried in case he takes a little side-swipe at Fat Andy, is that it? Mind you, from what I've heard, he's got it coming to him. Watmough's no genius, but he always struck me as a decent kind of man and an efficient enough cop.'

'Dalziel took against him. I think Watmough dropped him in the mire way back when they were both sprogs.'

'Doesn't just look like an elephant, eh? Well, I wasn't on the Pickford case myself, but perhaps I'll have a wee glance through the records just in case. Thanks for tipping me the wink, Peter. I'll be in touch.'

He kept his word quicker than Pascoe expected. Early the same afternoon the phone rang.

'Peter, I've been looking at the Pickford files. You've probably worked out yourself that your own involvement is only through the Tweddle child.'

Annie Tweddle, aged seven, had been found strangled and assaulted in a shallow grave in a wood about ten miles from the Mid-Yorks village in which she lived. There were no leads, and the case had been shelved for eighteen months when Mary Brook, eight, had been abducted from a park in Wakefield in South Yorkshire and later found buried on the Pennine moors. She too had been strangled after being sexually assaulted. A few months later, little Joan Miles of Barnsley had gone missing and the worst was feared. But now there was a common factor. Among the reams of statements taken in both cases there were references to a blue car, probably a Cortina, being seen in the vicinity. All similar cases over the past few years were reactivated. South, under Watmough, began to go through the computer print-outs of all registered owners of blue Cortinas in the area.

Then Tracey Pedley, the Burrthorpe child, had vanished too. Once more a blue car figured in the witness statements. And a week later a blue Cortina was found in a country lane near Doncaster with a length of washing-machine hose running from the exhaust into the rear window.

Inside was the body of Donald Pickford and a long incoherent letter in which he confessed by name to several killings and by implication to several more. Clinching evidence that this was not just some compulsive confessor driven by his madness to the ultimate authentication came in a set of detailed directions which led to the grave of Joan Miles in a marshy nature reserve only a mile away. Annie Tweddle was mentioned by name. Tracey Pedley wasn't. But once it was established that Pickford was likely to have been in the area at the time she vanished, she was put down with a few others as a probable victim.

'We did have to establish Pickford's alibi, or rather the lack of it, in the Pedley case, I think.'

'Yes, but that was hardly important,' said Wishart reprovingly. 'I was just trying to sort out where, if anywhere, you might be vulnerable to a bit of criticism.'

'I suppose Watmough could make a few snide remarks about us having got nowhere with the Tweddle investigation,' said Pascoe dubiously. 'But in fairness to the man, he never made any such cracks when he was here, and God knows, he was provoked enough!'

'So, no need to lose any beauty sleep, eh? Or ugly sleep in Andy's case. Before you ring off, Peter, there was one other thing. Insignificant, I'm sure, but it might interest you. I gave my old mate, Sergeant Swift, a ring. He was at Burrthorpe all through the Pedley case and through the Strike too, so what he doesn't know about the place isn't worth knowing. It was Swift who had the doubtful pleasure of arresting that lad, Farr, you were asking about. Now, when I told him about the *Challenger* printing Mr Watmough's memoirs, he told me that our friend Monty Boyle hadn't been put off by his encounter with that window. He'd been back a couple of times, buying drinks and asking questions, though he's given a wide berth to the Farr boy!'

'Asking questions about the Pedley girl, you mean? Well, that figures. Incidentally, was there any special reason why he should have approached Farr or was it pure accident?'

'He claimed it was just an accident at the time, but now Swift knows what he's up to, he reckons different.'

'But Farr can't know anything about the girl's disappearance or the Pickford case,' said Pascoe. 'You said he was away at sea till the Christmas before the Strike and the Pickford business blew up that September, didn't it?'

'Yes,' said Wishart. 'He was away, but his father wasn't. Billy Farr was the last person to see, or admit seeing, Tracey alive. In fact, he was in the frame for a bit. He was an old friend of the Pedleys, it seems, and had taken a real shine to the little girl. He often used to take her off for walks, him, her, and his dog. They'd gone brambling that day up in . . . let's see, here it is . . . Gratterley Wood, that runs along a ridge to the south of the village and there's a track runs up to it behind the Miners' Welfare Club where Tracey's father was—still is—steward. Mrs Pedley expected them back about five for the little girl's tea. But, according to Farr, Billy Farr that is, they were back within half an hour, about four o'clock. He said he wasn't feeling too well, and that's why instead of taking the girlie in as he usually did, he left her in the lane at the back of the club, just a few yards from the kitchen door. Trouble was, no one else saw her and there was no sighting of Billy Farr himself till he got home just before six, by which time the Pedleys were getting a bit agitated. Farr said he'd just been walking around by himself. Evidently he was like a man demented when he heard the girlie was missing, though demented with what wasn't clear to a lot of people.'

'Guilt, you mean?'

'There's nowhere like a mining village for gossip,' said Wishart. 'Naturally there was a big search for the girl. They found her bramble pail in the woods on a path running down to the road about a quarter-mile outside the village. There were a couple of sightings of a blue car parked off the road, but one of them was by Billy Farr's best friend, so that didn't carry all that much weight. Watmough certainly looked long and hard at Farr for a couple of days, then Pickford topped himself, and it was roses, roses, all the way for Mr Watmough and his modern investigative techniques which, we were assured, had pressurized Pickford into his suicide.'

'So it was merely Pickford's death that took the spotlight off Farr?'

'To be fair, I don't think so,' said Wishart. 'Watmough seems to have lost interest in him before Pickford killed himself. At least that's how I read the file.'

'And was there any doubt locally?'

'It seems so, though probably not a lot. Billy Farr was well thought of, a quiet fellow and a bit of a loner, especially since his accident which left him too lame to work underground, but much respected. Most people were happy to accept that Pickford was responsible. It had all the marks of one of his killings—except that they never found the body. But two child killers in the same neck of the woods

56

on the same day was unlikely, wouldn't you say? And Watmough wasn't averse to clearing up as many cases as he could in one triumphant swoop.'

'And the few who didn't accept this?'

'Swift tells me that before Pickford died they got the usual rash of anonymous calls and notes, pointing in every possible direction from the vicar to the NUM. Afterwards there was only one, a note, printed in block capitals. It said, YOU GOT THE WRONG MAN FOR TRACEY. DON'T WORRY. WE WON'T.'

'And how did Swift interpret this?'

'Sergeants don't interpret, they file, have you forgotten? But he recalled it on Boxing Day three months later when Billy Farr went missing and they found him at the foot of a sealed-off shaft in the old workings along the same ridge that Gratterley Wood stands on. Inquest brought in a verdict of accident. His wife said he'd gone out for a walk with his Jack Russell. There was no sign of the dog. Theory was that it had got into the old workings somehow and when Farr realized it was lost, he'd started looking down the old shaft, the cover was rotten, it broke, he slipped, and bingo! A day or two later there was another note arrived at the station. It said, CASE CLOSED.'

'It's a sick world,' said Pascoe. 'And this is why young Farr came back to Burrthorpe?'

'That's it. And he's been a bloody nuisance ever since.'

'To the police?'

'To every bugger as far as I can make out. Perhaps not the kind of company an ambitious young policeman's wife ought to be keeping.'

'Thanks for the "young", Alex,' said Pascoe. 'As for the rest, get knotted. But let's keep in touch over this one, shall we?'

'Take care, Peter,' said Alex Wishart.

Pascoe replaced the phone. The clouds on his horizons were still just the size of a man's hand. Only now the man seemed to have hands the size of Andy Dalziel's.

CHAPTER 9

Colin Farr awoke with a splitting head. The alarm clock by his narrow bed told him it was past eleven. He was on 'afters', the 1.0 p.m. to 8.0 p.m. shift. Last night he had started drinking as soon as he finished. There'd been some bother at the Club and he'd left. He couldn't remember much after that but there was the aftertaste of greasy chips in his mouth which suggested he hadn't come home to eat the supper his mother would have cooked for him.

Groaning, he rose, washed, dressed, and went downstairs to face the music.

His apologetic mood evaporated when he went into the kitchen and saw Arthur Downey there, sitting at the table drinking a mug of tea.

''Morning, Col,' the deputy said, smiling rather uncertainly.

'It's you,' said Farr. 'Run out of tea, your sister?'

'Colin, don't be rude. After last night, you should be ashamed to show your face in this kitchen. I had to throw his supper out, Arthur.'

His mother was standing by the stove from which came a smell of rich meat pastry. May Farr was in her forties, a tall, good-looking woman whose face and body could have done with putting on a bit more weight, and the rather becoming dark shadows around her eyes had not been put there with a brush.

'I'm sorry,' said Farr sitting down.

Downey seemed ready to accept that the apology included him.

'I just brought your mam some vegetables, Col,' he said. 'You don't have to go to sea to get scurvy, do you?'

'Don't you? Mam, I hope you're not making that pie for me. I couldn't face owt more than a cup of tea and mebbe a sandwich.'

'You missed your supper last night and I'll not have you going to work on an empty stomach.'

'They don't need their meals regular like us old ones, May,' said Downey. 'I bet you often got dragged out of your bunk in the middle of the night when you were at sea, Col, and had to work all day with next to nowt.'

'It weren't the bloody *Cutty Sark* I were on!' exclaimed Farr. 'All right, Mam, I'll have some, but not too much, mind.'

'Don't you miss it, the sea?' said Downey. 'I sometimes wish I'd given it a try when I were younger.'

'You're not old now, Arthur,' said May Farr, bringing a flush of pleasure to the lanky man's cheeks.

'No, you ought to sign on as a cabin boy,' said Farr. 'Or better still, stow away.'

Downey laughed and finished his tea.

'I'd best be off,' he said. 'See you down the hole, Col. Thanks for the tea, May.'

After the door closed behind him, May Farr said, 'Right, my lad, before we go any further, I'll not have you being rude to Arthur Downey or anyone else I care to invite into my house. Understood?'

'The bugger's always sniffing round here . . .' protested her son.

'You listen, Arthur were a good mate of your dad's and he's been good to me since . . . it happened. He'll always be welcome in this house as long as I'm here, understand? Besides, he grows best veg in Burrthorpe on that allotment of his.'

She offered this lightening of tone by way of truce which Colin Farr was happy to accept.

'Aye, it's not many lasses round here who get bouquets of broccoli,' he said slyly. 'You best be careful else you'll have folk talking.'

'What do you mean?' she said indignantly as she took the pie from the oven. 'Has someone been saying something?'

Her son smiled sweetly.

'There's not many round here would dare say owt like

that to me,' he said with an easy confidence she found more dismaying than comforting.

She heaped the pie on to a plate which she set before him. As he ate, he asked casually, 'Do you think you will get married again, mam?'

'How should I know? I've no one in mind, if that's what you mean. But this is wrong way round. It's me as should be asking you when you're going to get wed and settle down?'

'Me?' he laughed. 'Who would I marry when all the best ones are gone?'

'You're not still moping after Stella, are you?' she asked in alarm.

'Me run after a married woman? What a thing to say about your own son!' he mocked. 'All I meant was, you're the best, Mam, and they don't make 'em like you any more.'

She sat down and regarded him seriously, refusing to respond to his sentimentality.

'What does keep you here then, Col, if you've no plans for settling? I know you hate it, always did. And don't say it's for my sake. I'm all right now. I've got friends, real friends . . .'

'You mean Red Wendy and her mates in the Women's Support Group?' he laughed. 'With friends like yon, you need a man around the place to keep an eye on you.'

'You see, there you go again, Col, trying to put it down to me. Don't do that. Don't keep things hid deep inside you like he did. Yes, Wendy and the others are my friends. It may have ruined the Union, but there's me and a lot like me who can say thank God for the Strike. It showed me a road I'd not have found on my own. And you, Col; I thought when you started getting involved that mebbe you'd found a road too . . .'

'Me? Oh, I liked the action and the fighting well enough, but the only road I hope to find in Burrthorpe is the road out of it.'

'Then why don't you go?' she asked passionately. 'And don't pretend to be hurt, I know all your little acts, remember? You know what I'm saying. I wept the first time you went, after your dad hurt his leg. And I'll weep if you go again. But I were glad then too, glad that now neither of my men was going to be killed down that hole . . . Well, I were wrong about one of them, though God knows how . . .'

'There's more than God knows,' interrupted her son fiercely.

'Is that it, Col? Listen, son, he's dead, he's gone, does it matter how or why? There's nothing any of us can do will bring him back, so why waste your life boozing and fighting and causing trouble in the Club, and wandering round them old workings looking for God knows what . . .'

'Who's been gabbing? That old woman Downey, is it?' Farr interrupted once more. 'Jesus Christ, it's like living in a fish tank, this place! What do you have to do to get a bit of privacy?'

'Try living quiet, not raising hell wherever you go,' suggested his mother.

Colin Farr pushed his plate away and stood up.

'No one ever lived quieter than my dad and they didn't let him alone, did they?'

'Col, don't talk like that. What do you mean? What are you trying to do? Col, please, you've no idea how it upsets me to see you this way.'

There were tears on her cheeks. He put his arms round her shoulders and kissed them away. It was a gesture neither awkward nor theatrical. He had a natural grace in his movements which had made him stand out even as a child. He drew back and smiled at her, the smile which had so often won forgiveness instead of punishment, and complicity instead of accusation. Billy had sometimes said she was spoiling him but she knew how deep her husband's love went too.

'I'll go soon, Mam,' he promised. 'Once I'm sure you're OK and . . . once I'm sure. Now I'd best be off to work.'

She watched him walk away down Clay Street, marvelling as always that from Billy Farr's seed and her womb a creature of such grace and beauty could have sprung. At the corner he turned and smiled and waved his snap tin.

She waved back, then went inside and began to clear the dishes.

Colin Farr walked on, no longer smiling. The long brick terraces opening directly on to the pavement frowned back at him. They had been built a hundred years ago when Burrthorpe had suffered its first expansion from rustic hamlet to mining village. Perhaps they had looked more cheerful then. He doubted it. There had been other expansions since, most affluently in the late 'sixties and early 'seventies. The low hills to the east, the end furthest from the pit, were chequered with owner-occupied boxes. There were modern shops in the High Street (one with a new plate glass window) plus a bank and two building societies. The strike had hit hard, but the natives of Burrthorpe were used to taking and giving hard blows, and they would bring the good days back, if the pit survived.

Here was the irony which Farr felt every day of his life. It was like being fed by a tyrant you hated, yet if you slew him, you would starve.

He was in the High Street now, heading west towards the Welfare. The village was built in a blank valley running east to west. It was along the densely wooded southern ridge that the sweet infection of coal had first been detected. Here due to some geological fault the veins were broken and often near the surface, and possibly the uprooting of some ancient tree in a storm revealed the symptoms. There were records at the end of the eighteenth century of frequent disputes between the Burr estate which owned most of the land hereabouts and the locals who, delighted at having such a ready supply of fuel on their doorstep, ran drifts into the scrubby common land which abutted Lord Burr's woods, and didn't much care if they trespassed underground. At first his lordship's care was all for his trees, the game they harboured and the income they promised. But a new lord, the first one born in the nineteenth century, caught on that industrial progress simply meant a new system of serfdom to replace the old which had run its course. He initiated a series of fairly haphazard explorations of the south ridge, ravaging much fine woodland principally on the village side, out of sight of his country house. At last an engineer was employed who knew what he was doing. He looked at the mish-mash of workings on the south ridge, shuddered, turned to the north and after several months of exploration recommended that here was where the next generation of Burrs would earn the necessities of life such as London Seasons, Grand Tours, four shirts a day, and the most up-to-date treatment of their social diseases.

He proved right. Deep beneath the northern ridge rich new seams were found, running north and west. The pit-heads which rose here were completely invisible from His Lordship's house, and the remnants of Gratterley Wood still crowned the southern ridge to provide a nice bit of rough shooting for a couple of chaps on a morning stroll.

But that was long ago, aye, ages long ago, thought Colin Farr as he approached the Welfare Club. The mine belonged to the people now, the Burr estate had contracted, and you could walk freely through Gratterley Wood with more risk of having your head blown off by some poaching miner than an angry gamekeeper. Even the Burr mansion had declined to the clubhouse of the Burr golf club (miners welcome to join the Artisan Section), and all was well with the world.

Except that he was still walking up the long hill to clock on for his shift.

He needed a drink. He glanced at his watch. There was plenty of time for a leisurely pint in the Club, but he wished now that he'd come on his bike instead of walking so that he would have had the option of going to a pub outside the village.

Then, annoyed with himself for this weakness, he turned up the steps of the Welfare.

Pedro Pedley watched him enter the bar with a studiously neutral expression. Farr smiled with all his charm and said, 'Pedro, I'm sorry if I were a bit obstreperous last night.'

Before the steward could reply, another voice said, 'You're not obstreperous, Farr. You're just not fit to be around decent people. Peter, I thought this trouble-maker were banned.'

It was Harold Satterthwaite who spoke. He was sitting

close to the bar in company with a dark-suited, red-faced man, with a ragged moustache and an alderman's belly. Farr turned to face them as Pedley said, 'I decide who's banned in this bar, Harold. What is it, Col? A pint?'

'In a minute, Pedro. I just want a word with these decent people.'

He strolled towards the two men with a friendly grin on his face.

'Hello, Mr Satterthwaite, sir,' he said. 'And I know you too, don't I? You're that journalist I dumped through the shop window.'

'That's right, Mr Farr. Monty Boyle's the name,' said the stout man, returning the grin. 'Let me buy you a drink to show there are no hard feelings.'

'Thanks, Mr Boyle, but no, thanks. I think I was right about you first time we met. You come near me or my mam asking any of your nasty little questions and it'll be a brick wall I throw you through next time.'

'You hear that, Peter? Do you still say he shouldn't be banned, threatening members' guests like that?' demanded Satterthwaite.

Pedley who'd come from behind the bar put a restraining hand on the young man's arm. He shook it off and said, 'No sweat, Pedro, I'm not threatening this gent, just giving him some local colour, that's what newspapers like, isn't it? As for you, Mr Satterthwaite, sir, I'd not dream of threatening you because I just don't have the time to wait in the queue. But I'll tell you this for nothing. Sure as eggs, you'll be standing on your ownsome deep in-bye some shift, with nothing but the mice for company, or so you'll think, only someone will be creeping up behind you with a shovel to bash your thick skull in and toss you into the gob with all the rest of the shit!'

'You heard that?' exclaimed Satterthwaite looking round. 'All of you here heard that: By God, you'll not get away with threats like that, Farr!'

'Threats? Who's making threats?' said Farr all injured. 'I went out of my way to say I weren't threatening you, didn't I? No, it's all right, Pedro, I'm just going. Mustn't be late for shift, must I? Best sup up, Mr Satterthwaite, sir. Up to you important officials to set an example in timekeeping.'

Shaking himself loose from Pedley's renewed grip, he turned and walked out of the bar.

In the fresh air he took several deep breaths. Ahead stretched the road which led up to the top of the valley and the pit. There were men walking along it to clock on. He didn't feel ready for company and on impulse he turned off the road into the unmetalled driveway which ran up the side of the Welfare. This was the nearest way from the village up into Gratterley Wood. It was up this driveway, which became a lane and then a track, that Billy Farr and Tracey Pedley and Billy's dog, Jacko, had walked to go brambling that bright autumn afternoon.

And presumably too it was up here that Billy Farr had made his own last journey, that crisp Boxing Day morning three months later. The ridge was honeycombed with workings, their entrances sealed off by anxious man and heartless nature. There'd been many accidents over the years, the last during the Strike when shortage of fuel (and the irony was that the striking miners were the only people in the country short of fuel that winter) had led a team of youths to open an old drift. There'd been a roof fall which had almost killed one of them and for the rest of the Strike the ridge and woods had been more sternly policed than they had since the eighteenth century. Such was progress.

The subsequent sealing off process had been declared comprehensive and foolproof. But there still remained entrances to that dark world which childhood memory and adult ingenuity made accessible, and Colin Farr's ramblings, which so disturbed his mother, had not been all overground.

But today it was peace and oblivion he sought. Soon after the lane became a track, it unravelled into half a dozen green paths and he chose the one which led him into the heart of the wood. Here there was a large outcrop of creamy limestone, known simply as The White Rock. It had been a popular trysting-place long before the locals penetrated the earth any further than a ploughshare's depth, and the surrounding area provided any number of nooks and dells where a man and a maid could lie, safe from casual gaze.

Colin Farr settled beneath the White Rock and recalled those days when, a schoolboy still, he had first come here hand in hand with a girl. He'd felt little of the usual adolescent awkwardness in his relationship with girls. In fact, all of life had seemed easy in those days. You did what you wanted and if you wanted to do something else, you did that instead. No one made your choices for you. It was only later that he began to realize how much ignoring other people's choices limited your own.

He pushed the darkening thought away from him and tried to focus on brighter things. Mrs Pascoe, for instance. He couldn't make his mind up how he felt about her. It was different being with her, that was certain, she made him feel livelier somehow, sent bubbles streaming through his imagination. But at the same time she made him feel uncertain of himself, as if that adolescent awkwardness he'd never experienced had merely been lying in wait for him. He didn't like that. He found he was scowling again.

'Stupid cow,' he said out loud in an attempt to exorcize the image.

Suddenly he sat up. He had a feeling that he had been heard, as if someone stealthy enough to stalk him unobserved had been startled into movement by his unexpected outburst. And now he felt watched also, but his eyes gave him no support for the feeling.

He rose. It was time to go anyway. He set off along the crest of the ridge so that he remained in the world of trees and leaves and earth and sky for as long as possible, but all too soon he emerged at the head of the valley where the ground fell away to the road, then rose up again to the north ridge. Here they were, graffiti on the blue sky, the dark tower of the winding gear, the conveyor like a ramp into the bowels of a convict ship, the scatter of low sullen buildings all squatting amid mounds of their own waste. The pit-head, whose ugliness only hinted at the vileness of the organism beneath.

66

One of these buildings was the Deployment Centre where men coming on shift went to report for work. It was still impossible for Colin Farr to come in here and not see his father. This was where Billy had been put after his accident. This was the last place they had seen each other at the end of the young merchant seaman's final leave.

They'd said goodbye the previous night as Billy would have to be up at five to go on shift, but after breakfast Colin had been overcome by an urge to see his father again and had made his way up to the Deployment Centre. Spotting his father through one of the hatches, he called, 'Hey, mister, can you set a young lad on?'

His father had looked up anxiously and said, 'Is something wrong at home?'

'No. I just thought I'd see if this place had improved with age.'

'You needn't have bothered. It'll improve wi' nowt short of bombing.'

'Well, I'll say cheerio, then.'

'Right. Take care of yourself, son.'

'You too, Dad.'

They'd regarded each other for a moment, then turned away in unison. As he strode back down the hill he was full of anger with himself. He was far from clear what he'd hoped to do by going up to the pit, but he knew he hadn't done it.

Four months later as his ship wallowed in the Bay of Biscay against a Force Five which had stopped them from getting home for Christmas, the news had come over the ship's radio. His father was dead.

It was his last voyage. The pressures to stay in Burrthorpe were great. His mother was breaking under the strain. He was engaged to Stella Gibson. Neil Wardle had told him he'd got management agreement that Farr's old job would be available. Good will, it was called. Guilt, was what Farr called it. So he stayed. Within weeks his engagement was off. Within months his mother was improving and his pay was stopped for the duration of the Strike. But still he stayed, and still whenever he collected his 'checks', the metal discs with his number stamped on, he saw his father, framed in the hatch of the Centre and in his mind for ever.

'Come on, dreamer,' said Tommy Dickinson. 'Last as usual. Anyone'd think you didn't enjoy coming to this place!'

Together they went into the 'clean lockers' where they stripped and hung up their clothes. Then naked they walked through into the 'dirty lockers' where the miners kept their working clothes known as 'pit black'. It was no misnomer, thought Colin Farr as he took out the trousers, waist-coat and football shirt which he wore underground. Their original colour was beyond detection. Dampened by sweat and pit-water, smeared with oil and grease, impregnated with coal dust, to put them on was an act as symbolic in its way as the priest's assumption of the chasuble, the novice's of her veil. Only, what these stiff and stinking garments signalled was no embracing of a higher will, no movement to a higher plane, but the exchange of light for darkness, fresh air for foul, sky for earth. Their clammy touch was the embrace of the pit itself.

'You all right, Col? I'm not keen on working with buggers so hung-over they're only half conscious.'

Neil Wardle was sitting next to him, struggling into a pair of boots which had set like concrete since his last shift.

'I'm grand,' said Farr. 'You know me. Naturally quiet.'

'That's not what Satterthwaite says. He says you've been threatening him,' said Wardle. 'He'd like you out, Col. Permanent.'

They rose together and made for the lamp room.

Farr halted at the turnstile and turned to face the other.

'And what did you say?' he asked.

'I said bloody good riddance, what do you think?'

Colin Farr grinned.

'Thanks, Neil.'

'Aye but watch him, Col. He's after your blood.'

'Is that all? He can have that any time he likes.'

Farr went through the turnstile into the lamp room, so called because here the lamps were ranged in racks to be recharged during shifts. Each lamp had a numbered check on a hook above it. The safest way of passing a message to a miner was to hang it with this check. A man could ride the pit without many things, but never without his lamp.

There was a piece of paper hanging on his hook. He pulled it off, unfolded it, read it.

Crudely printed in block capitals, it read:

SG LOVES HS. TRUE. POOR YOU.

'Love-letter, is it?' asked Tommy Dickinson, coming up behind him.

Farr crumpled the paper in his fist, then tore it into little pieces and scattered them on the floor.

'Sort of,' he said. And went to ride the pit.

CHAPTER 10

It was Sunday morning. The ten churches were almost empty, the cells not much fuller. But when Dalziel addressed his one-man congregation, it was with a passionate sincerity which seemed capable of ameliorating both deficiencies.

'I swear to God I'll murder the bastard,' he said.

Pascoe lowered the *Challenger* and asked politely, 'Don't you want to hear this, sir?'

'Not as much as you do,' said Dalziel malevolently. 'Don't think I'm not noticing how well you control yourself every time I get insulted.'

'It's not easy,' admitted Pascoe.

He was reading from the trailer to ex-DCC Watmough's memoirs in which Ace Crime Reporter, Monty Boyle (The Man Who Knows Too Much) was promising a feast of sex, violence, blood, guts, and Amazing Revelations. Nowhere was Dalziel mentioned by name, but Pascoe couldn't feel his boss was being unduly sensitive.

He had just read: '. . . Nev Watmough told me that after his South Yorks triumph, returning to Mid-Yorks was like travelling back from the Twenty-first century to the Dark Ages. "The South was forward-looking, eager to keep pace with the technological revolution," he said nostalgically. "In Mid-Yorks they still preferred to fly by the seats of their broad and often very shiny pants. I've always believed that trouble starts at the top. And that's certainly where I found it in my efforts to drag my new command screaming and kicking into the Twentieth Century." . . .'

'Get on with it,' commanded Dalziel through gritted teeth.

'There's not much more,' edited Pascoe. 'Like we thought, he's starting with a bang on the Pickford case next Sunday. And in future editions we're promised such treats as *The Kassell Drug Ring—The Royal Connection? Who Killed Dandy Dick?* and *The Choker: Cock-up or Cover-up?*'

'Jesus! What did he have to do with any of them cases? What's he ever had to do with real police work? When he were a sprog constable, he couldn't write a report without stapling his tie in with it . . .'

'Don't be too hard on him,' said Pascoe provocatively. 'He's probably not writing much of his stuff either, not with Monty Boyle at his side. It'll all be ghosted . . .'

'Ghosted!' exclaimed Dalziel. 'I'll make a ghost of that moth-eaten string vest if ever I get my hands on him!'

He rehearsed the act in the air. His intention was apparently to strangle Watmough while at the same time gouging out his eyes. Pascoe felt that even with hands like Dalziel's, this was going to be a formidable task.

He said, 'Can he really get away with stuff like this? Isn't there a regulation? Something he signed?'

Dalziel considered, then shook his head. 'No, I'm sure Ike Ogilby's wide-boy lawyers will have covered that. But hang on! Mebbe he took some stuff out of the files that he shouldn't have, copies of records, statements, that sort of thing. I wonder if Trimble would cough up a warrant? It's time that little Cornish pixie started paying his debts.'

The Cornish pixie was Dan Trimble, Mid-Yorks new Chief Constable. The debt was for Dalziel's assistance in getting him the job, or rather in blocking Watmough's selection. The principal obstacle to repayment was that Trimble didn't have the faintest idea that he owed Dalziel anything, but as Pascoe knew from long experience, ignorance in such cases was no defence.

He said, 'I don't really think Mr Trimble's going to let you kick Watmough's door down, sir. Look, why make a fuss when there's other folk will make it for you? Digging up old cases always upsets a lot of people, relatives of victims, that kind of thing. He's obviously going to be dwelling on his Pickford triumph for a couple of weeks at least. There's nothing there to harm us. And by the time he gets himself back to Mid-Yorks, either someone will have slapped an injunction on him or Ike Ogilby will realize that our Nev's driving the punters back to their beds in droves on Sunday mornings, and spike the remaining episodes.'

Pascoe expressed himself thus cynically because he felt that at the moment the way to Dalziel's heart was through his bile. But beside his natural concern for the reputation of the police, he felt a genuine repugnance at this savaging of people's sensibilities for the sake of mere sensationalism. When he got home just before one, he found that he was not alone in his views.

He entered expecting congratulation that he'd slipped away from Dalziel and actually got back in time for Sunday lunch. But Ellie's expression as she met him in the hall was far from congratulatory.

'Have you seen it?' she demanded.

'What? The light? The spider? What?'

'This rag!'

The object she brandished looked anything but rag-like. He recognized it by instinct rather than eyesight as the *Challenger* compressed apparently by main force into papier-mâché. Producing his own copy, he flourished it and said, 'On guard.'

'Be serious!'

'About what? And why have you got that rag? I hope you wore a disguise to buy it.'

'It's Adi's.'

'Adi's?' he said, praying there was another Adi besides Adrienne Pritchard, radical solicitor and Women's Rights Group activist.

'She came round to talk to you, Peter. She reckons that

people could get hurt by these articles and she wanted a reasonable police view.'

No, she didn't. She wanted his destruction, for that would inevitably follow if Dalziel ever found out he'd been discussing police business with Ms Bitchard, as he called her. Suddenly simultaneous gouging and strangulation seemed well within the span of those vengeful hands.

He said, 'Ellie, you'll have to tell her, I disapprove of what Watmough's doing, but I'm not about to become Ms Pritchard's mole in the CID.'

'You tell her,' said Ellie.

'What?' He looked towards the lounge door with a condemned man's eight o'clock eyes.

'I asked her to stay for lunch. Wasn't it lucky you managed to get away on time for once?'

In the event lunch turned out to be quite enjoyable, particularly when he found himself opening a second bottle of Rioja. Adi Pritchard was no great beauty but she was a good conversationalist, and though he kept a careful eye on her he never got any sense of being pumped for indiscreet confidences. Even when the doorbell rang half way through and Ellie said, 'That'll be Thelma,' his suspicions were unroused. Thelma was Thelma Lacewing, dental hygienist, great beauty, and founder and driving force of the Women's Rights Action Group.

He greeted her with open arms, literally. Good conversation was OK but those limpid brown eyes spoke more fluently to the sensual ear.

He opened another bottle of wine, spoke wisely and well of the kind of man Neville Watmough was, told interesting and amusing anecdotes of his life in the CID, and was rather taken aback when Thelma started yawning uninhibitedly to show the strangely sexy depths of a delicate pink mouth crescented with the kind of pearly teeth a dental hygienist ought to have. She compensated by squeezing his hand apologetically as she said to Ellie, 'Must go. Have you got your great descent fixed yet?'

'Next week,' said Ellie. 'I'm going down Burrthorpe Main.'

'Burrthorpe? I know it. Good active women's group determined not to be sat upon after the Strike ended.'

'Always the problem with miners,' chimed in Adi. 'I defended a few of them and it was surprising how they followed a pattern. Shock troops of radicalism till it comes to their women, then they're stuck in the Dark Ages.'

'Perhaps,' said Pascoe brightly, 'if they sent all the women down the pit and made the men stay at home, they'd all soon arrive at a better understanding of sexual equality.'

This clanged like the last-orders bell and shortly afterwards the visitors left.

'Well, that seemed to go OK,' said Pascoe, flopping into an armchair.

'You thought so?'

She sounded irritated but Pascoe, who was feeling vinously randy, pressed on in the naïve belief that the way to melt a woman's heart was to be nice about her friends.

'I was surprised how reasonably Adi was approaching this business. She seemed genuinely concerned about the reputation of the Force as well as the feelings of the public. I was quite touched.'

'Yes, I noticed you were quite touched. And every time Thelma made a point, I noticed she was quite touched in return.'

'For heaven's sake! She's a mere child.'

'She's thirty if she's a day.'

'Yes, of course I realize that. But you've got to admit there is a childlike quality about her. Those eyes, that complexion, so fresh, so smooth. And not a trace of make-up . . .'

Something in Ellie's eyes warned Pascoe he was missing his way. He tried to get on the right path again by squeezing her hand and saying, 'What I mean, I suppose, is my attitude to Thelma is sort of avuncular.'

'Well, don't imagine you're going to work out your fantasies on me, Uncle,' said Ellie, coldly pulling away.

Irritated himself now, Pascoe retorted, 'At least I keep my fantasies above ground.'

'What's that mean?'

'What it says. You never told me you'd definitely fixed up this mine trip. And Burrthorpe. Why Burrthorpe? That's a long way to go to get your face dirty.'

'Because that's where the next visit is happening,' Ellie replied coldly.

'Is that so? Oh, I thought they'd have stopped work throughout the entire Yorkshire region and laid on a special gala to celebrate this great conversion.'

'Conversion?'

'Yes, isn't that what they do? Take the heathen bourgeoisie and bring them up blacker than black after total immersion in dust? Just think. One quick dip and you'll have expiated all your sins of birth and background and education and marriage—you'll have joined the working class at last! Welcome aboard.'

Ellie, who was rather sensitive that her origins were considerably less humble than Peter's, went to the door where she paused.

'Oh no,' she said. '*You* can't welcome me aboard. Not when you went over the side and swam away long ago, like all the other rats.'

She went out. Pascoe groaned and reached for a Rioja bottle. When he tipped it up, nothing came out. He peered inside with one eye and groaned again.

It was deep and dark and empty as despair.

CHAPTER 11

It was true what the Spaniards said about trouble. Once she fancied you, there was no shaking her off, so you might as well go looking for her as risk being surprised when she turned up at your wedding.

Colin Farr recalled this bit of wisdom, picked up in a Bilbao bar, during his shift on Tuesday afternoon. Monday had been great, the class had been really interesting with Ellie talking about the way the media distorted truth and often corrupted opinion rather than informing it. Afterwards she had been full of her visit to Burrthorpe Main on Wednesday. 'Pity I'll be on shift myself,' he said, 'else you could have come and had tea with my mam.' He could see she didn't know if he were joking and to tell the truth he didn't know himself.

That night as he went into the Welfare, he glimpsed Boyle, the stout *Challenger* reporter, standing at the bar with a couple of men Farr had no cause to like. He'd amazed himself by turning on his heel, getting back on his bike and heading off to do his fairly moderate drinking in a pub at the far side of the village.

He'd rounded this trouble-free day off by getting home early, drinking a cup of cocoa with his mother and laughing with her at some early pictures in the family album.

Tuesday morning he'd tinkered with his bike which was running a bit rough, then, leaving it half stripped down, he'd strolled to work, vaguely surprised at how little of the usual pre-shift tension racked his nerves.

But half way through the shift trouble found him out again. It wasn't surprising. A man can duck and weave through his free time, but work makes him a still target.

At first the trouble seemed merely operational.

They were advancing one of the gates or tunnels leading up to the coal-face. The roof here was notoriously weak and when they blasted the rip, instead of the looked-for twelve or fifteen feet, nearly thirty feet came down, leaving a great hole far beyond the reach of the metal support arches.

Colin Farr and Neil Wardle peered cautiously up.

'It's a bastard,' said Wardle.

'Aye,' said Farr.

They knew that someone was going to have to clamber up there among those pendulous boulders and jags of rock to construct a protective lattice of wooden beams above the advancing rings. Up there a ripper was alone, trying to support with his mind God knows how many tons of exposed ground, listening to its cracks and groans, feeling trickles of earth and spatters of stone, ready to leap desperately aside when a louder crack or some sixth sense warned him that a huge boulder was coming down to bounce like a rubber ball around the gate. It was a job no one could do and not be afraid.

Colin Farr felt the fear like everyone else. But fear of late had become a sort of barrier through which he could pass to a state in which no threat, not even of death, could touch him.

'I'll go,' he said. 'But tell 'em to switch that chain off.'

A little later the conveyor carrying the hewn coal along the face whined to a halt. It was a wise precaution. Being dislodged by, or jumping down to avoid, a falling boulder was dangerous enough without having the moving chain waiting to mangle you below.

Carefully Farr climbed up on to the ring and began his work. He'd only been at it a few minutes when there was an interruption.

'What the hell's going on here? Why's that bloody chain stopped?' demanded an angry voice.

It was Gavin Mycroft.

'Colin's up there, timbering the hole,' said Wardle as the deputy arrived.

'I don't give a toss what he's doing. We can't have the job held up like this. Get that fucking chain moving right away!'

'Now hold on,' said Wardle reasonably. 'You can't expect a man to . . .'

'I expect men to do what they're paid to do,' interrupted Mycroft. 'Every minute that lock's on is costing money. Aye, and it's costing all you lads money too, you know that.'

He raised his voice so all could hear. It was a telling argument for some. Bonus payments depended on the amount of coal moved per shift and as long as the chain stood still, there was a decreasing chance of reaching bonus levels.

'I thought you were supposed to be looking after safety,' said Wardle.

'What if I am? There's nowt unsafe about having the chain moving, is there? Not unless you're saying that the only safe pit's a pit where there's fuck-all happening!'

'There's a lot of truth in that,' retorted Wardle.

Colin Farr swung lightly down from the ring and said, 'I'll tell you what, Gav. If it's so fucking safe up there with the chain on, you get up and do it.'

The two men faced each other, each face brushed into visibility by the light of the other's lamp, Farr's dark with a patina of dust through which his eyes gleamed huge as a starving child's in their pale hollows, while Mycroft's much cleaner features worked in an uncontrollable fury whose roots went deep beyond the present situation.

'I gave an order,' said Mycroft. 'Get that lock off. Now!'

Neither man moved till the conveyor clattered back to life. Mycroft turned, eager to get away before anything could be said to spoil his triumph, but Farr's voice came after him.

'Hey, Gav,' he said gently. 'I'm not going back up there with the chain on.'

If Mycroft had kept on walking he might have got away with not much lost. At worst it would have given the men time to sort something out among themselves. But the deputy had paused at the sound of the voice and now there was no way for him to start walking again.

Slowly he turned.

'You're not?' he said. 'Right, then, Farr, if you can't do your work, you'd better fuck off out of the pit, then.'

Now there was no noise except for the moving chain.

Tommy Dickinson looked angrily at Wardle, who shook his head and sighed. They could do without this.

'Look,' he said. 'Gav, let's not be hasty about this . . .'

'What's hasty?' demanded the deputy. 'He won't work and I've told him his shift's finished. It'll all go down nice and official if that's what's bothering you, Mr Branch Secretary.'

'Gav,' said Wardle, 'let's not risk a dispute, not over something that's half personal . . .'

He realized it was a stupid thing to say as soon as he said it.

'Personal? What do you mean, personal?' demanded Mycroft on a rising note.

'Aye, what do you mean, personal, Neil?' asked Colin

Farr mildly. 'There's nowt personal between me and Gav, is there, Gav? He's just doing his job. So let's get it straight. You're telling me to go?'

'Aye. Go or not, your shift's stopped as from now.'

'In that case, Gav, pointless to stay, isn't it?'

In his hands Colin Farr held a ringer, the long crowbar used by rippers to pluck down loose rock. Now he raised it. Mycroft took an involuntary step back. Farr laughed and let the bar fall with an echoing clang to the ground between them.

'Remember, Gav, it were you that told me to go.'

He still spoke gently but to Neil Wardle the fury and the threat behind the words were unmistakable.

'Neil, what about the Union?' demanded Dickinson excitedly. 'We should all bloody go!'

'Fuck the Union,' Farr called back over his shoulder. 'Just be nice to Gav there, and he'll give you permission to go, no bother! See you, lads.'

Ducking low, he glided away down the gate.

'Gav,' said Wardle, 'you must be barmy. Right, lads. Let's get some work done, shall we?'

When Farr reached pit bottom, he saw the cage was almost ready to ascend. There was only one man in it. He didn't realize it was Harold Satterthwaite till he entered the Cage, but it wouldn't have made any difference.

'What's up with you?' demanded Satterthwaite as the ascent began. 'All that booze too much for you?'

'I've been sent off the job,' said Farr.

'Why?'

'For not being stupid as the bugger who sent me.'

'Who stopped your shift?'

'Mycroft.'

'Are you saying Gav Mycroft's stupid?'

Farr smiled at him slyly.

'He's down there for another two hours and I'll soon be fancy free in Burrthorpe,' he said. 'Who does that make stupid in your eyes, Mr Satterthwaite, sir?'

'You really think you can get away with anything, don't

you, Farr?' said Satterthwaite, provoked to anger. 'You think you know it all. Well, I can tell you, you know nowt!'

'Why don't you tell me then, Mr Satterthwaite, sir?' said Farr.

'No. I'll let you find out through experience. It'll be more fun that way.'

They were at the Bank. Satterthwaite didn't speak again but made towards the offices while Farr showered, dressed, and set off down the hill to the village.

The day was bright and sunny and Gratterley Wood hung over the road like a golden halo but Farr was not tempted to make a diversion. Straight down the road he went with the steady pace and unrelenting expression of a man who knew exactly where he was going. Entering the village, he passed through the grid of dark terraces which held his own home, keeping to the level High Street till the road began to rise again and dirty grey stone and pock-marked damson brick gave way to pastel-coloured walls with pebble-dash fascias beneath rib-tiled roofs, all bedecked with telephone wires and crowned with television aerials. Up the paved path through the neatly lawned front garden of one of these houses he strode, his finger outstretched to press the bell and lean on it till either the electricity failed or the wall fell in. But before he made contact, the door opened and he passed inside without a pause. Behind him the door slammed shut and a voice, equally violent, demanded, 'Col, for God's sake! What the hell are you doing here?'

He turned and looked at her. Stella Mycroft who had been Stella Gibson, known to him since childhood, and known to him in the biblical sense for the first time one velvet summer night in Gratterley Wood seven years ago.

'You look as if you were expecting me,' he said.

'What do you mean?' she said, her face tense with indignation.

'Flinging the door open, dragging me in,' he grinned. 'Real welcoming!'

'I didn't drag you in,' she retorted. 'I was lucky enough to spot you out of the window, I just hoped I could get you in before every nosey bugger in the street saw you. Some hope.'

'You could have pretended you were out.'

'You mean you wouldn't have rung the bell till it fell off the post, then kicked the door in? I know you, Colin Farr, and I saw the look on your face.'

'Oh aye. Then you'll know what I've come for.'

He went into the lounge. It was a bright and sunny room with lemon emulsioned walls and floral curtains to match the loose covers on the suite. An open fireplace had a fire laid in it, ready for lighting when the warmth of this autumn day gave way to the chill of night.

'You amaze me, you know that?' she said, following him. 'They only say things like that at the pictures. This is South Yorkshire, not South bloody California!'

He moved swiftly towards her and pulled her to him in a violent embrace that stopped her words before his mouth completed the job.

'You're bloody crazy,' she gasped when he finally drew his lips away. She tried to pull back, but he held her to him without any effort and kissed her again, running hands up and down her body from neck to buttocks.

With their lips parted again, her head moved this way and that as she darted glances round the room. Colin Farr smiled. She wasn't seeking an escape route. She was checking possible viewpoints.

He released her and began to strip off his clothes.

'What if someone comes?' she said.

'It'll likely be me,' he replied sardonically.

'No, you silly bugger, you know what I mean.'

'Pull the curtains, don't answer the door.'

'That'd be like advertising on telly round here,' she objected. But she was already beginning to unbutton her blouse.

Naked, they stood and looked at each other.

'Shall I light the fire?' she said slyly. 'It's a bit chilly like this.'

'We'll not need a fire,' he said, stepping towards her.

Their coupling was violent and swift, more like a battle

than an act of love. Spent, he collapsed across her, a dead weight, his face buried in her hair.

'You needed that,' she observed. 'You'd think you'd just got off that boat of yours.'

'I've been saving myself up.'

'I bet.' She pushed him off her and rose on one elbow to look down at him. 'All right, let's have it. What's going off?'

'What do you think?'

'I don't know. You come early off shift, straight up here, bang, you're in. What's going off?'

He said, 'How do you know I've come early off shift?'

'How do I know?' she echoed slowly. 'Well, I don't reckon you brought your snap tin just in case you fancied a jam buttie while you were in the stirrups! So come on, Col. What's it all about? I'm entitled to know who's being fucked here, me or Gav.'

He wrinkled his nose in distaste.

'You didn't use to talk like that, Stella,' he reproved.

'Didn't I? Mebbe I've grown up since last time we talked. Can you not see the difference?'

He let his gaze travel up and down her slim brown body, then took one of the pear-shaped breasts in his hand.

'Mebbe an extra half ounce there,' he said, hefting it. 'Otherwise no change.'

'Cheeky bugger,' she said, running her hand down the line of his flank. 'You've not changed either, except you're a bit rougher than you used to be. And you're still expert at wriggling away from questions you don't want to answer. Are you here because you've rowed with Gav?'

'Mebbe.'

'Is that all I'm going to get?' she asked angrily. 'What do you think you're playing at, Col? That business in the Welfare the night you got jailed. Receipt for potato cakes, Jesus! And them phone calls. It is you, isn't it? I can feel you on the end of the line.'

'Can you? I hope I feel hard.'

She said, 'Col, what *are* you playing at? All right, don't tell me. Mebbe it's best I don't know. But I'll tell *you* something. You're out of place round here. You don't fit. Why don't you go off again . . .'

'Back to sea? Every bugger wants that. I remember the fuss you made first time I went . . .'

'I thought we had a future then, Col.'

'I gave you a ring. And it was always good when I came back on leave.'

'Oh aye. Made a change from poking some foreign tart up against a wall in the docks, did it? No! Listen for a change, Col. I knew it were over, long before we finished officially. You knew too, only you never could make your mind up to actually do owt, not without being pushed. I reckon your mam and dad knew too. They went right off me at the end, and I used to get on so well with them, especially your dad. Was it something you wrote to them? Did you have the nerve to tell them before you could tell me?'

'I never said anything to them,' he protested. 'And it was you who chucked the ring back, remember?'

'Aye, because if I hadn't I'd likely be wearing it yet and getting nowhere!' she cried. 'For God's sake, Col, face up to it. You'd given up on me. You didn't come back to Burrthorpe because your girl was here, you came back because your dad jumped down that shaft . . .'

He rose to his feet in one sinuous movement.

'Jumped?' he said softly. 'Who says he jumped? Why should he jump?'

'All right. Fell! There, you see, that's what gets you going, isn't it? That's what it's all about.'

'You think so?' He stood astride her, looking down. 'When I came back, all right, I was all uptight about me dad and worried about me mam. You get obsessed. There's no room for owt else.'

'And now there is?' she said sceptically.

'I think so. I think I'll mebbe take all that advice and bugger off again soon. You're right, I don't fit round here.'

'I'm glad to hear it.' She rolled away from his straddling legs and stood up, ignoring his proffered hand. He regarded her with a frown of concentration, like a bullfighter before a difficult bull.

'Come with me,' he said abruptly, an order more than a request.

'What? Are you daft? Leave Gav, you mean?'

'Why not? You can't love him,' he said contemptuously. 'What's he got to offer you? This?'

He looked around the bright room.

'This?' she said angrily. 'Aye, this. And what's wrong with it, Col? I'm twenty-four and what I've got already is more than my dad's ever given my mam, and she's nigh on fifty-four. Gavin's a good man, and he'll get on. He's got a good job . . .'

'A gaffer's job,' sneered Farr.

'Why do you say it like it's something dirty?' she demanded. 'Mebbe I'll take that kind of crap from some silly half-pissed bugger who thinks the Union's Godalmighty, but I'll not take it from you. What's the Union ever been to you, Colin Farr, except an excuse to crack a few heads open in the Strike? What's *anything* to you?'

'You are. You're everything.'

'Listen to the way that you say that!' she exclaimed. 'Like a line in a play that you've got to say so you can see what happens next.'

He considered this, then nodded as if in acknowledgement of its truth.

'What *does* happen next?' he inquired with polite interest. 'You and Gav live on here happy ever after, is that it?'

'Mebbe not. But it'll not be you I leave with, Col.'

'Oh? There've been other irons in your fire, then? I've heard a few distant clangs.'

She began to gather her clothes together.

'Always clever with words, Col, I can recall you at school. You should've taken the chance then and gone some place where being clever with words made you more than just a big-mouth.'

'Stella, what *am* I going to do?' he burst out.

His voice was so vibrant with emotion that she almost weakened. Then behind the candid, appealing gaze she thought she saw a glint of what could as easily be amusement as despair.

'You're going to get dressed and get out of my house,' she said composedly. 'It'll not be long till knock-off and I want you long gone when Gav gets back. Me, I'm going to have a nice hot bath. It's gone a bit chilly. Mebbe we should have lit the fire after all.'

She went out, knowing a good exit line when she spoke one. Upstairs she began to run her bath, all the time listening. Suddenly the phone rang. She rushed into the bedroom, but as she picked up the extension she heard Farr's voice saying, 'Hello?'

There was no reply. After a moment the connection was cut. Farr's voice said, 'You listening upstairs, Stella? Seems I'm not the only one you get funny calls from.' Then he laughed.

She slammed the phone down. A little while later she heard the front door bang. She rushed to the window and peered from behind the curtains. He was already out of the garden and walking down the road, moving with cat-like ease and balance.

He didn't look back.

With a sigh that was nearly all relief she went into the bathroom and lowered herself into the warm and scented water. She felt quite drained of strength, both physically and mentally. She didn't want to think about what had just happened or what might happen next, and she readily gave in to the feeling of drowsiness that drifted over her with the tendrils of steam.

Some time later she woke to find the steam had all condensed and the water was nearly cold. She got out of the bath and towelled herself vigorously, enjoying the rough material against her water-tender skin. She was able to think now of her encounter with Colin, reducing it with each stroke of the towel to a fragment of pure sensuality. There was no getting away from it, compared with the other men she'd known, he pushed her into an extra dimension of pleasure. But it was not a dimension that played any significant part in her blueprints of possible futures.

She went into the bedroom where she was surprised to see how late it was. Fortunately the oven's automatic timer was taking care of Gavin's supper. She dressed quickly, but even so she was still making up her face when she heard the front door open and her husband's voice call, 'Hello, love. It's me.' She analysed tone and inflection, found nothing to concern her, and called back, 'I'm up here. Down in a tick.'

But as she began to descend, she heard his voice again and needed no analytical expertise to know there was trouble.

'Jesus!' he exclaimed from the living-room. *'Stella!'*

She went in. Her husband was standing before the hearth. In the grate the fire had been lit and was now just a bed of glowing embers. But it wasn't this that had caused his outcry.

Before he left, Colin Farr must have put both his hands into the soot-furred chimney, then pressed them against the wall above the fire-place and drawn them slowly down. It looked as if two monstrous black arms were being raised in supplication or in threat.

'Stella, what the hell has been going on here?' demanded Gavin Mycroft.

PART TWO

      ... I fell to quaking
At a fresh sight—a Lion in the way.

I saw him coming, swift and savage, making
For me, head high, with ravenous hunger raving
So that for dread the very air seemed shaking.

CHAPTER 1

Nothing in her conversations with her class or her reading of their essays had prepared Ellie for the sheer terror of her first descent in the Cage.

She was the only woman in the group of visitors which included two local councillors—one Labour, one SDP—two Frenchmen who had something to do with the EEC, and an elderly research student from Doncaster who bombarded the harassed-looking pit-manager with disturbing mnemonics like MINOS, MIDAS AND FIDO, and most sinister of all, IMPACT.

It was IMPACT that stayed in her mind as they entered the Cage and she heard a melodramatic hiss of compressed air as the drawbridge they'd just crossed was withdrawn. Somewhere a bell jangled. And suddenly they were moving.

The acceleration was rapid. In seconds Ellie felt the rush of air through the sides of the Cage brushing her face and winnowing the few strands of hair not tucked up beneath her borrowed helmet. No one spoke, not even the politicians. Ellie waited for the Cage to attain a steady speed but to her horror its acceleration did not seem to be stopping. Suddenly there was a great clap of noise like a huge paper bag exploding or the collision of air-waves as express trains pass in a tunnel.

Someone shrieked. Ellie suspected it was her but she didn't care. Her mind told her it was only the counter-balancing up-cage on its ascent, but down here reason was not enough. Religion took over, or rather its poor relative, superstition. Her hands joined in a tangle of pleading fingers and her mind gabbled the childish prayer which had remained a pre-dormitive necessity well into her pyrrhonic adolescence.

Godblessmummyanddaddyandgrandadandgrandmaand unclegeorgeandauntiemadgeandcousindickandtimmyand roverandsamuelwhiskersandmepleasegodthankyouvery muchamen.

In the light of the beams from their helmet-lamps the speeding walls of the shaft streamed past.

Suddenly everything reversed direction. The walls rushed by the other way, the Cage was now ascending! She knew it was an optical illusion, but again knowledge was ineffective against terror.

And now came a sudden jerk on the cable sending them all staggering. The walls reversed again. Once more they were falling. The cable's snapped! Ellie told herself. She could hear one of her companions retching drily. Another jerk, then another. It's the brakes, she assured herself. We're slowing down. It's only the goddam fucking brakes!

At last the Cage was perceptibly slowing. The shaft became visible as more than a speeding blur. There was light outside, a strident glare of orange and white neon strips. The cage hit its restraints, bounced, and sank back into blessed stillness. A moment later the gate was opened and they filed out into the pit-bottom, drinking deep breaths of the warm air that blew in their faces, their relief so great that it was some while before they became aware of the humid stench of it. Mr Kavanagh the pit-manager took his farewell at this point.

'I'll leave you with one of our most experienced deputies,' he said. 'Mr Satterthwaite here will show you round and answer your questions. Stick close and do as he says, and you'll be all right.'

This Satterthwaite in whose tender care they had been placed looked to Ellie as if he might be distantly related to Andy Dalziel. Broad, solid, mean-eyed, square-jawed, he should at least come in useful if the roof fell in.

'If you'll follow me, gents,' he growled with all the en- thusiasm of a jailer inviting his charges into the exercise yard.

'And lady,' gallantly corrected the SDP councillor.

'Oh aye,' said Satterthwaite. 'This way.'

'So, I'm an alien, in a man's world,' thought Ellie. She recollected what Adi Pritchard had said about miners: social radicals, sexual fascists. Well, she wasn't going to sit down under that!

Her determination to assert herself was not easily satisfied. The two councillors were engaged in a private competition as to who could show the most intelligent interest and any gaps they left were immediately filled by the student's technically pedantic questions about automation, both proposed and effective. The Frenchmen, perhaps in reaction against their unconcealed terror during the descent, were now suffering from a bad attack of *galanterie*, which involved much *après-vous*-ing and the placing of guiding hands on shoulders, elbows and occasionally an area at the base of the spine which if not an erogenous zone was certainly border country.

Satterthwaite, whether through inclination or ignorance, replied to most questions with that great Yorkshire stand-by: *Oh aye*, which can be made affirmative, interrogatory, sceptical or satirical by an almost Chinese subtlety of intonation.

Ellie's use of the patois picked up from her students clearly didn't impress him much either. In the end she abandoned questions and concentrated on observation. One thing she failed to observe was Colin Farr. Of course most of the miners they saw at work were difficult enough to distinguish at close quarters under their patina of sweat and dust, and became totally anonymous at any distance. But when they saw a team of rippers at work Ellie knew at a glance even from several yards away that Colin was not among them. How did she know? she asked herself. The answer was at once unsettling and exciting. Stripped to the waist as these men were, his easy grace and fluidity of movement could only be even more distinctive. She turned away from the thought, found it followed her, so turned it inside out by using his grace and beauty as a foil against which to see this most hideous of man-created working environments.

An hour later, with every muscle in her body aching, she re-entered the Cage, her mind as heavy as her flesh so that she hardly felt any of the descending terror as she rode the pit this time.

She felt as if she could never be clean again. Even a good

half-hour in the deputies' showers only seemed to touch the surface, though a careful examination in the mirror revealed a state of pink cleanliness which suggested the trouble was mainly within. When she blew her nose and saw the state of her handkerchief, she realized that *within* covered the physical as well as the psychological, which in a way was a relief.

She said her goodbyes and thanks, then went to the car park. As she approached her Mini, a figure moved between the cars a couple of rows away. Even that slight movement told her who it was.

'Hello, Colin,' she said as he approached with uncharacteristic uncertainty. 'I looked out for you down below. I thought you said you were on afters.'

'Should've been,' he said. 'I got sent off yesterday. There was a bit of bother. Nowt to worry over. It'll be sorted by tomorrow and I'll be back down, worse luck. Any road, I thought as I were doing nothing, like, how'd you fancy that cup of tea at me mam's?'

Ellie restrained herself from looking at her watch. She knew precisely what time it was, knew also that if she drove like the clappers, she might just be back within the outermost time-limit promised to her friend, Daphne Aldermann, in whose care she had left Rose.

On the other hand, Rose clearly adored Daphne and her spaciously elegant house with a fervour which, though politically reprehensible, was socially very convenient. An extra hour of baby-sitting would probably not bother Daphne, or at worst only keep her back from some totally non-productive activity. Besides, Daphne, who at the very best might pass for a Social Democrat in the dusk with the light behind her, had collapsed in helpless giggles when Ellie had told her where she was going.

'I'm sorry,' she hiccoughed. 'It's just that . . . going down a pit . . . it's so *you*!'

Ellie had managed a smile too. She was not after all one of the humourless Left. But Daphne owed her one!

'I'd love a cup of tea,' she said. 'Hop in.'

*

The visit didn't start too well because May Farr was unable to conceal that it came as a complete surprise to her.

'I've not got much in, I'm afraid,' she said. 'And the place is in a mess. Colin should have warned me. I might have been out or anything. They don't believe we've got lives of our own to lead, do they?'

She smiled at Ellie, reassuring her that the irritation was aimed at her son and inviting her to join in her general analysis of the sex. She was a good-looking woman, in her forties, Ellie judged, perhaps already into the change which might account for her pallor and shadowed eyes. Her smile was Colin's, open and charming, and she had the same easy grace of movement which a man might interpret as sensual.

Ellie tried to recall how long May Farr had been a widow. Were there any new men in her life, she wondered, or had she settled for the role of grieving widow-woman with doting son?

Thinking of roles, she suddenly realized she was playing one for all it was worth. It was the role of the dedicated teacher telling a proud mum how well her precious child was doing at school.

What the hell do I mean, *playing* the teacher? Ellie asked herself in alarm. I *am* the bloody teacher! That's the only reason I'm, here, so let's have less of this role-playing bit!

But at this moment she caught Colin's eye and he gave her a conspiratorial wink which at the same time complimented her on her success and implied another level of relationship which his mother might not understand.

They drank tea and ate some cake, a plentiful supply of which existed after all. Ellie and May Farr made polite and not too obtrusively stilted conversation and the young man relapsed into a watchful silence which he finally broke by announcing he still had some work to do on his motorbike.

'You're not bringing bits into my kitchen,' said his mother emphatically. 'There was more oil there than in the Persian Gulf yesterday.'

'No, Mam,' said Colin Farr long-sufferingly, and went out.

Ellie viewed his departure with some surprise. Why was

she being left alone with this woman? Why had Farr brought her here in the first place?

She caught May Farr's eye and they exchanged polite smiles and she realized that much the same thoughts must be going through the older woman's mind.

She glanced at the clock on the mantelpiece. In every sense it was time she was gone.

'I really must be on my way,' she said, wondering as often before why one was conditioned to sound apologetic about something which could only be a mighty relief to the hearer. 'A friend's looking after my daughter and I reckon that she'll have been driven to breaking-point by now.'

'You've got a girl? How old is she?'

Ellie told her and saw May Farr deduct Rose's stated age from her own estimated one.

'Just the one, is it? So far, I mean.'

'That's right. And you? The same?'

'Aye. Just Colin. So far.'

'Oh, I'm sorry, I didn't mean . . .' but Ellie's confusion faded as she saw the woman was laughing at, and with her.

'What's your husband do, Mrs Pascoe?' May Farr now asked with that uncomplicated because perfectly natural curiosity which was typical of Yorkshire.

Ellie hesitated. She had consciously avoided any reference to Peter's profession when taking her class, fearful that their discussions on questions of law and order might be inhibited or even distorted. But she had never had to speak the lie direct.

Now she heard herself saying vaguely, 'Oh, a boring office job, files and form-filling, the usual thing,' and feeling surprisingly treacherous.

'Is that your husband?' she asked as a (she hoped) not too obvious diversion, indicating a framed photograph standing next to the clock. It was a snapshot, slightly out of focus, of a thin man with wind-tousled hair against the background of an unruly sea. He was looking straight into the camera with shadowed, introspective eyes and just enough of a twist to the lips to suggest he had been instructed to smile.

'Billy never cared to have his picture took,' said May

Farr. 'I've not got above four photos of him taken since we were wed.'

'No, he doesn't look as if he was enjoying the experience,' said Ellie.

'He never found it easy to enjoy himself, Billy,' continued the widow, half to herself. 'He always seemed, I don't know, suspicious of happiness. Even before his accident.'

Ellie said, 'Accident?'

She'd heard of only one accident, the fatal one. Clearly May Farr wasn't referring to that.

'When he did his leg in. Didn't Colin mention it?'

'No. The mine, was it?'

'What else?' said the woman bitterly. 'His leg were crushed. They did wonders on it at the hospital by all accounts but it still left him hardly able to bend his knee. But you don't want to hear this, Mrs Pascoe. You've got to get back to your kiddie.'

'A few more minutes won't hurt,' said Ellie. 'She's in good hands.'

May Farr hesitated. Why does she want to talk to me about her husband at all? wondered Ellie. Someone outside her own tight little community, perhaps? Shit! There I go again, patronizing. She's probably got friends here at least as understanding, loving and trustworthy as mine.

Then it came to her. It wasn't Billy Farr the woman wanted to talk about, it was Colin. The teacher role hadn't completely reassured her. She saw an older, married woman, perhaps moving out of her class for a bit of rough, and felt that some kind of warning-off was needed.

And was it? Ellie was distracted from this outrageous line of thought by May Farr's resumption.

'They gave Billy a job on top,' she said. 'He didn't say much, he never did. It were always hard to know what were going on inside Billy. Colin's the same. You can never be certain. Never.'

There it was, the first warning.

'He felt it, I could see that, ending up on top at his time. Not just the money, but his old workmates. Oh, he felt it. Then Colin jacked it in, the pit I mean. Said he wanted to

94

go to sea. I don't know where he got the idea from. I never wanted him to go down pit in first place and there were no need. He wasn't stupid at school, could have done anything. But like I said, there's never any knowing with our Colin and there's even less telling. Once he decides something, it's wasted breath trying to get him to change.'

Second warning. Ellie said, 'But you must've been glad he was out of the pit. Both of them in fact.'

'Glad? Aye, part of me was, at first anyway. But you don't get owt for nowt in this world, especially not happiness, Mrs Pascoe. Price I paid for having them out of pit was Colin not coming home except once in a blue moon, and Billy sitting quiet as a cat staring into the fire or wandering off by himself with Jacko, that were his little terrier. I never knew what he were thinking, Colin neither. They both had dark hidden places inside of them, Mrs Pascoe. Not bad, I'm not saying bad, but dark. Mebbe if you work down the pit a bit of it gets inside you after a while.'

Third warning. Why not cut the cackle and say that Col was mad, bad, and dangerous to know?

The door opened and the young man in question appeared looking none of these things. Indeed with tousled hair and an oil stain on his cheek, he looked about sixteen.

'Mam, here's Wendy,' he announced.

A painfully thin young woman entered wearing baggy jeans and a loose knit sweater which emphasized her skinniness. Her eyes were almost feverishly bright and she was smoking a cigarette which the yellowness of her fingers suggested was neither the first nor the last of the day.

'Didn't know you were entertaining, May,' she said, looking at Ellie with open curiosity.

'This is Mrs Pascoe, she runs the course at the college that our Colin goes to. This is Wendy Walker. She runs our Women's Group.'

'The Strike Support Group? The Women Against Pit Closures?' said Ellie.

'Aye, that's what we are now. It's us the University should be spending its time on, not these lads.'

'Yes. How many are in your group?' asked Ellie, irritated

95

with herself. For some reason she'd never even considered the possibility that May Farr might be a member of the Support Group. She'd fallen into the old chauvinist trap of defining her solely in terms of her relationship with men: the grieving widow, the protective mother.

'Twenty at best, more like ten what you might call hard-core,' said Wendy.

'You may have met a friend of mine who's done some work with the Groups. Thelma Lacewing.'

'Thel?' Wendy's mouth widened into a nicotinous grin. 'You a mate of Thel's? She were all right. She's got a grand throwing arm!'

Colin reappeared accompanied by a tall, gangling man with a not unattractively long face, like a sad sheepdog's. He was clasping a carrier bag out of which smiled the full-moon face of a cauliflower.

'Here's Arthur,' he said. 'You ready for off?'

It was clearly Ellie's dismissal. She rose swiftly before May Farr could protest at her son's rudeness and said, 'I must dash. Look, I've really enjoyed meeting you. Thanks for the tea. I hope we can meet again sometime. You too er . . .'

'Wendy. Give my best to Thel. Next time she comes, get her to bring you. It's always good to make contact with the outside world!'

The thin woman's tone was both friendly and mocking.

Outside Ellie said, 'You didn't introduce me to your friend.'

'Friend? Oh, him. He's no friend of mine. Arthur Downey. Bloody deputy. He were my dad's best friend once. He's been sniffing around Mam ever since Dad died. He looks just like a bloody great lanky hound, doesn't he? Luckily she's got more sense. Good job someone in our family has.'

They were at the car. To her surprise he opened the door and got in the passenger seat.

'I'm sorry, Col, but I've really got to rush.'

'That's all right. Drop me along the road somewhere. I could do with a good walk. Get the taste of that sodding hole out of my lungs.'

She started up the car and set off.

'Do you really hate the pit that much?' she asked.

He laughed harshly and said, 'Bloody right I do. There's precious few as loves it, that's for sure. But I always hated it, hated it and feared it from a kid.'

'Then why did you go down?' she asked.

'Not much else to do round here,' he said.

'Come on,' said Ellie. 'Your mam said you were pretty bright at school.'

'You have been having a right cosy chat, haven't you? Did she get out the photo album and let you see me in my nappies?'

'She loves you and worries about you very much,' said Ellie quietly. 'But she didn't need to tell me you were bright. So what happened? This isn't the bad old days when there really were no choices.'

'You think not?' He shrugged. 'All right. I were bright enough at school to get something better than the pit, everyone reckoned. Not that there was much better round here. Clerking mainly with a lot less money and the chance of being made redundant any day. Oh aye, the big un-employment rush was starting when I did my O-levels. They said, Stay on at school, another two years and then mebbe college. I told 'em to get stuffed. I was sixteen and fed up with being a kid. They said, Be sensible, listen to our clever advice or you'll end up down pit. I don't know which were worse, the bloody pit being a threat or an expectation! I got mad and said, If I go down pit it'll be because that's what I decide to do, not what you buggers tell me I've got to do! And I went off that day and got myself set on.'

'What did your parents say?'

'Mam was furious. She'd not hit me for three or four years but she made my ears ring that day, I tell you. Dad were always a quiet man. He just said, "You've made up your mind to go down. See you make up your own mind to come up." I soon found out what he meant. I hated it and everyone told me I'd not stick it, so I had to stick it, didn't I? And I did stick it for nigh on three years till my dad had his accident. Did Mam tell you about that? He ended up with a locked knee and one leg shorter than the other. He didn't get much compensation either. This deputy, Satterthwaite, said the lads had been larking around during their break when it happened. They often do muck about a bit, you've got to do something else you'd go mad. But not Dad. He'd just sit there quiet. Downey were there too. He could've said something, but he reckoned he was looking the other way. Bastard! He'd just got made up and I suppose he wanted to show Satterthwaite he knew which side his bread were buttered now. So there wasn't as much compensation as there should have been. Union took it up but they got nowhere as usual. Not that the money bothered Dad too much. It was ending up on pit-top that got to him. He'd been a collier all his life. He had more pit-sense than all the deputies put together. They all used to turn to him for advice. Except Satterthwaite. That's why the bastard re-sented Dad so much. For him to end up with a surface job at his age really finished Dad. You could see it in his eyes. All that he knew was useless to him now. It wasn't just his leg that got shattered, it was his whole picture of himself. That's when I came up too, when I saw that.'

He fell silent. Ellie was driving very slowly, not wanting to take the youth too far, not wanting to stop him talking.

'I went and joined the Merchant Navy, don't ask me why,' he resumed. 'I'd never given it any thought before and the nearest I'd ever been to the sea had been a week at Brid one summer. Mebbe it was because I thought it'd be as far away from mining as I could get.'

'And was it?'

'Sometimes. Sometimes it seemed worse. At least at the end of a shift down pit you're your own man. But yeah, it mainly was a bloody sight better, and it was good having your money saved for you as there was bugger-all to spend it on. Come the end of a trip, you could have a right good time.'

Ellie tried to imagine what a right good time looked like to Colin Farr. Booze and birds? It seemed more likely than books and Beethoven. Was she being culturalist?

She said, 'But you came back?'

'Aye.'

'Because your father died?'

'Aye.'

'And you stayed because of your mother.'

'Aye,' he repeated, but this time he didn't sound so sure.

'Did she ask you to stay?'

'No! She wanted me to go off again,' he exclaimed. 'She said she'd be fine and the last thing she wanted was to see me back down the pit. But I said no, I'd stay.'

'That was very thoughtful,' said Ellie.

'No it wasn't! It had nowt to do with Mam, or at least not directly,' burst out Farr. 'There were stories. About the way Dad died. I overheard a lad saying it were suicide. I half killed the bugger before they got me off. After that most of 'em were a bloody sight more careful. But I knew they'd still be on with their stupid bloody gossip behind my back. And I reckoned the further off I was, the braver they'd get. So I stayed.'

'To protect your mother?' said Ellie.

'I suppose so. Incidentally. But mainly to show them buggers that I didn't care. But *they* better had, if they didn't want to end up in the gob with a broken jaw.'

'In the gob?'

'The hole left where they've taken the coal out of the seam. Don't you read those bloody essays you make us write?'

'Yes, of course. Sorry. Colin, what's been going on today?'

'Nowt,' he said harshly. 'What do you mean?'

'Oh, come on!' said Ellie. 'Why'd you take me to meet your mother and then leave us together?'

'Mebbe I wanted to give her a chance to discuss your prospects and ask if your intentions were honourable!' he sneered.

Containing her anger with difficulty, she brought the car to a halt by the roadside but didn't switch off the engine.

'It's been an interesting day, Colin,' she said very formally. 'Thank your mam again, will you? And I'll see you next week.'

He sat looking gloomily out of the window without speaking. She stole a glance at her watch. Daphne would be in that state of icy politeness which in the privately educated daughters of C. of E. archdeacons passes for rage.

'Colin . . .' she began.

His reaction was astounding. He turned towards her, placed his right hand on her left shoulder and thrust his left hand with considerable force up her skirt between her legs.

For a moment simple astonishment excluded outrage. She looked at him, eyes and mouth rounded in a dramatic mask of surprise. His face was very close but he made no effort to kiss her. His hand was pressed hard against the narrow gusset of her panties, but the fingers were still.

Then outrage came and she hit him, an open-handed slap across the face with as much force as the swing-limiting confines of the Mini permitted.

Immediately he withdrew his hand, released her shoulder, and turned his head to stare out through the windscreen once more.

It took another moment for Ellie to regain her powers of speech.

'And what the hell was all that about?' she demanded.

'Nothing. I thought you might fancy a quick jump,' he said indifferently.

'Oh no you didn't!' she retorted. 'Don't give me that! Even when you were pissed out of your mind in some dockland knocking shop, your approach'd be subtle compared to that!'

'You think so?' he said. 'All right, you're the clever one. *You* tell *me* what I was after!'

'I don't know! You were watching me, weren't you? You just wanted to see what I'd do. You wanted, I don't know, to shock me, defile me even, is that it?'

'Defile?' he savoured the word. 'Sort of sacrilege, you mean? Like gobbing on a crucifix, something like that?'

He was mocking her and she did not feel in any state to trade verbal blows.

'Get out,' she said. 'Just bloody well get out!'

He climbed out of the car and closed the door gently behind him.

She set off instantly, accelerating rapidly. She never once glanced in her rear view mirror for fear of seeing him. But after she had driven half a mile she had to pull into the side of the road once more.

With awkward tyro movements, she lit a cigarette. She was shaking, she was amazed to discover. She tried to tell herself it was rage, but she knew it was not. It was the aftermath of that moment of sheer nerve-fracturing terror when she had been absolutely certain he was going to rape her.

'Oh, you bastard,' she said. 'You cocky little bastard!'

It was five minutes before the shaking stopped enough for her to drive back to town.

CHAPTER 2

The following Sunday Pascoe drove to a newsagents where he wasn't known and bought a *Challenger*. Sitting in his car, he turned with scarcely a pause past the page with the topless blonde and settled down to the first episode proper of Watmough's memoirs.

'Bloody hell,' he said after he finished, and immediately began the unpleasant task of reading the article again.

It outstripped his expectation in several ways. The language was even more lurid than he'd guessed, details were given of Pickford's assaults on his victims which had never appeared before, and there were quotes from recent interviews with relatives, plus the revelation (with address) that Pickford's widow had remarried and gone to live in Essex. These were obviously the work of Monty Boyle, but it all came out under the imprimatur of Neville Watmough.

As far as Mid-Yorks went, there was the expected sideswipe at their inefficiency in dealing with what turned out to be the first Pickford killing, that of Annie Tweddle. But this was nothing compared with what was hinted at in the trailer for the following week.

What of the body that got away? Little Tracey Pedley was never found. Did Pickford abduct her and subject her to the same terrible fate as the others? At the time the evidence seemed to point that way. But upon examination how flimsy that evidence seems. Before Pickford's suicide it amounted to little more than the alleged sighting of the by now notorious 'blue car' off the road near the place where her pail was found. And after Pickford's death the best the police could do was establish that he had no alibi for the time of Tracey's disappearance.

But what if the police got it wrong for once? What if Pickford did have an alibi?

There were always those in Burrthorpe who were never satisfied with the official explanation and their doubts may have been rekindled three months later when the last witness to admit seeing Tracey alive himself died in strange circumstances. Coincidence? Like the coincidence that it was his best friend who gave the most positive sighting of the blue car?

'A tragic accident,' said the coroner. But there were those who whispered of remorse, or even retribution.

But suppose they too are wrong as the police may prove to have been wrong? Suppose the killer of Tracey Pedley is still alive and perhaps even having his evening pint drawn by the father he so cruelly bereaved . . .

What do I think?

Find out next week. Only in the *Challenger*!

Bastard! thought Pascoe.

As he drove home he wondered if he should draw Ellie's attention to the fact that it was her protégé's father who was being blackguarded here. Not that she'd said much about young Farr or her class since their row the previous Sunday. She wasn't usually a sulker and he'd expected a detailed account of her trip to Burrthorpe Main, but there'd been only the most basic of responses to his truce-offering inquiry.

He found her reading a colour supplement.

'I got a *Challenger*,' he said. 'Thought I should keep up to date.'

'Why bother? Crap's crap no matter when,' she said, not looking up.

'I thought you might be interested to see if Adi had been able to do anything about Watmough's article.'

'Has she?'

'If she has, I wouldn't have cared to see the original version. This one's grisly enough for my money. There's a bit about Burrthorpe in it.'

She turned a page of her supplement indifferently.

'It sounds like he's got something nasty up his sleeve. For us, I mean.'

'Us?'

'Us, the fuzz,' he joked. She didn't smile, but said, 'What's it to do with you?'

'There was only ever circumstantial evidence linking Pickford to the Pedley girl's disappearance. He worked for a press tool manufacturer near Huddersfield. That afternoon he had an appointment over here at Tanyard-Lees, the fork-lift truck works on the Avro Estate. Its forty-five miles as the crow flies. He left his office at three-thirty. Burrthorpe's well south of his route but if he had diverted there he could have made it easily by four. Tracey was last seen alive by a local man just after four.'

He paused, saw no response, went on. 'If Pickford kept his four-thirty appointment on the Avro Estate, he just couldn't have picked up Tracey. That's where we came in. As it was on our patch, we did the checking at Tanyard-Lees, and we confirmed that Pickford didn't make it.'

'And now Watmough's saying you made a mistake? It's possible, isn't it? Anyone can.'

'Sure. But I can't see it.'

For the first time she looked up.

'What? So it's infallibility now? Who was the Pope on this occasion? You or Fatso?'

'Neither. It was Wieldy. And he's the nearest thing to infallible we've got, especially on something as simple as this.'

'Perhaps it was too simple,' said Ellie. 'You're not saying Watmough's been holding back on something all this time?'

'No, of course not. He's a lot of things but dishonest isn't one of them.'

'So, if some new information came up, he'd bring it out, even if it marred his triumph slightly?'

'Yes, said Pascoe. 'I suppose so. But what new information could there be about something as straightforward as this? No, I reckon it's just a bit of *Challenger* titillation.'

'Then you've nothing to worry about, have you?' said Ellie, returning to her article which appeared to be on interesting things to do in the kitchen with squid.

Was this yet another threat to his well-being? wondered Pascoe.

He folded up the *Challenger*, left it neatly on the coffee table and went to phone a friendly warning through to Wield.

At nine o'clock on Monday morning, Sergeant Wield turned off the main road through the Avro Industrial Estate into the service road running alongside the Stalag security fence which wrapped itself round the premises of Tanyard-Lees.

Most of his colleagues must have seen yesterday's *Challenger*. The prospect of seeing the worm turn yet again to nip Andy Dalziel on the ankle was almost irresistible. Wield had resisted because he knew what rags like the *Challenger* would do to someone like himself if they got the chance. Once they had got close and Dalziel had been the most substantial bulwark fending them off. So he owed something to Andy Dalziel.

He also owed something to Peter Pascoe. Of all his colleagues who must have worked out what the article was getting at, only Pascoe had picked up the phone to make sure he didn't come in the next day unprepared.

Well, he was going to be better than prepared. He was going to be justified. He'd gone over it all last night a thousand times. He'd come here as instructed, checked every way possible whether Pickford had kept his appointment, and returned with confirmation of the answer everyone logically expected. No, he hadn't.

The only doubt that snagged in his mind lay in that

phrase 'that everyone logically expected'. He knew how easy it was to see what you expected to see. It was a principle he'd lived behind most of his life.

But he still couldn't believe he'd fouled up.

What he could believe was that the *Challenger* had 'persuaded' someone to 'recall' that perhaps Pickford had shown up that September day after all.

He halted his car at the entrance barrier, got out and went into the gatehouse.

The gateman looked up from his newspaper and said, 'Yes, sir?' He was a man of about sixty, grey-haired, ruddy-complexioned, with the kind of face that knows things about central heating and carburettors.

'I'd like to see Mr Wattis, please. Is he in yet?'

'Who?'

Wield consulted his notes. He'd called in early at the station that morning to check out the file.

'Mr Lewis Wattis. He's assistant controller, Purchasing. Or was.'

'*Was* it is, sir,' said the gateman. 'Mr Wattis retired two years ago, mebbe more.'

'Oh. Do you have an address?'

'Forwarding, you mean? Who knows?' The gateman looked slowly upwards then let his gaze slip slowly down.

'Dead?' said Wield.

'Same year he retired,' said the gateman. 'It's often the way, though I'd not have expected it of Mr Wattis. He wanted to be retired, you see. He wasn't going to be pining away for this place!'

Wield stood at the counter, his face showing none of the bafflement he was feeling. It was Wattis that Pickford's four-thirty appointment had been with. It was Wattis who had assured him that Pickford had not turned up. Naturally Wield had double-checked at the gatehouse. No one could enter the works without passing through here and signing the book. Donald Pickford's name did not appear.

'Was it business, sir, or private? If it was business, I can give Purchasing a ring and see if anyone can help you,' offered the gateman.

If not Wattis, who then had the *Challenger* dug up to say that Pickford *did* keep his appointment? His eyes, inward-looking, refocused outward and the gateman's friendly knowing face swam into definition.

Wield said, 'How long have you been here, Mr . . . ?'

'Moffat. Twenty years, more,' said the man.

'So you'd be working here when the Pickford killings took place?'

The man's face registered consternation.

'Here, look, so that's it. Sorry, mate. I can't say anything about that. You'd better buzz off. I've got work to do.'

'Who says you can't say anything? Your friends at the *Challenger*?' said Wield aggressively.

'Yes, that's right,' said Moffat. 'Mr Boyle warned me some of you lot would likely be along and he said to tell you I'd sold what I know to the *Challenger* and if you want to find out about it, you can buy a copy next Sunday!'

Wield said incredulously. 'Boyle told you to say that to the police?'

'Police? You're police?' replied the man with equal incredulity.

Wield produced his warrant and Moffat said, 'Yes. I see. Sorry, but you didn't look like . . . No, Mr Boyle said if the police came round, then naturally I should tell them all I know.'

'And also why you didn't tell all you knew a couple of years ago,' said Wield grimly.

'That's easy, mate. I was never asked!'

Wield, who'd been sure that either someone had lied in the past or was lying now, listened to Moffat's story with a growing sense of his own culpability.

Moffat had been on holiday when the Pickford suicide made headlines.

'I read about it on the beach at Rimini,' he said. 'When I read he were a salesman for that tool company, I remember thinking, I wonder if he were that fellow who came to see Mr Wattis?'

'But he didn't come to see Mr Wattis,' said Wield. 'Mr

Wattis was sure he hadn't kept his appointment. And his name wasn't in the book.'

'No,' said Moffat. 'The thing was, he was late. Just ten minutes, but that was enough for old Wattis. He was a bit of a joke really. Just treading water till his time was up. And off to the golf course like a flash if he got half a chance. Pickford must have been the last thing he had on his plate that day. He'd give him five minutes, then off. He went out just as Pickford came in. That's how I recall the time. I glanced at the clock when Pickford said he had a four-thirty appointment. It was just gone four-forty. I told him it were too late. I said I'd ring through and see if they could fix up another day, but I tipped him the wink that it'd likely be a waste of time. You see, with Mr Wattis being so demob happy, no one treated him serious any more. You could be pretty certain any salesman they steered towards him wasn't someone they intended doing business with! Pickford didn't seem to be bothered, just said thanks and went off. So his name didn't get in the book and the only person he saw at Tanyard-Lees was me, and no one ever asked me!'

'He came back off holiday three weeks later,' Wield told Pascoe on his return to the station. 'His stand-in, that's the fellow I saw when I looked at the gate book, went off to his usual duties and never mentioned my visit. Why should he? I just looked in the book, and there was never any mention of Pickford's appointment at the Plant in the papers, Wattis retired a month later, went down to Cornwall and died, and Moffat never thought any more about his possible encounter with Pickford till Monty Boyle came round with a handful of fivers.'

'You're sure he's telling the truth?' said Pascoe.

'Certain. More important, perhaps, Boyle's obviously certain too, certain enough to go public with it. Even ten minutes late wouldn't give him enough time to divert to Burrthorpe and kill that little girl. Christ, what a cock-up!'

'Come on, Wieldy, you can't blame yourself. You were asked to check what looked a ninety per cent certainty according to the way South, that is, Mr Watmough presented it to us. You checked it the best way you could. No one can blame you.'

'Tell that to the *Challenger* on Sunday,' said Wield. 'Tell it to Mr Dalziel *now*.'

'I'll come with you,' said Pascoe.

'To hold my hand? No need. He'll likely just send me to bed with no supper.'

'I'll come anyway. And talking of supper, I've been meaning to ask you round for a bite one night.'

In fact the notion had just popped into his head, but even as he said it, he recognized he was merely confirming a stage in their friendship.

'Great,' said Wield. 'When?'

'Make it tomorrow, if that's OK. Eightish?'

'Eightish it is. If I survive.'

The condition seemed less of a joke when Dalziel flung open his door as they approached and glowered at them like a jealous Italian catching his wife and brother *in flagrante delicto*.

'Well?' he snarled. 'Is it true?'

Wield nodded unhappily.

'I'd not have thought it possible of you,' cried Dalziel, more than ever like a man betrayed. 'How'd it happen? Mental breakdown, was it?'

Stoically Wield gave his explanation. It was clear, concise, and void of excuse or special pleading.

'So,' said Dalziel. 'Clever cunt, this Monty Boyle. I think we'd better have a word with him. See to it, Peter. Poor old Nev!'

Pascoe looked at the fat man in surprise. Sympathy for Watmough? And from a man whose usual position on the Christian forgiveness ethic was that no enemy ever fell so low that a kick in the teeth couldn't drive him lower.

'I mean,' said Dalziel, 'this makes us look Charlies, right? But it takes a bit of the bloom off Lobby Lud's success, doesn't it? And with a bit of luck Boyle may have dug something else up that drops old Nev right in it without splattering us in the process! No wonder Ike Ogilby wanted to sign him up.'

'I don't see why Boyle couldn't just have done an article about this himself,' said Pascoe.

'Don't be dim, lad. Which would you rather read—confessions of a randy vicar or accusations from a ranting bishop? *J'accuse* wins Pulitzers but *mea culpa* bangs up circulation figures.'

Even Wield's face registered astonishment and Dalziel's lips slid back from his great brown teeth like the curtain rising on a Wieland Wagner set at Bayreuth as he grinned in delight.

'Now let's sit down and see if we can do some real police work, shall we?'

CHAPTER 3

In depression as in toothache, rational analysis is no palliative. Ellie knew that a gloom had settled upon her since her visit to Burrthorpe but knew no way to disperse it. A recent ritual clearing out of the family medicine chest, aimed principally at Peter who had the mild hypochondriac's reluctance to dump old pills, had washed away her own little store of uppers and downers, putting that particular temptation out of reach. Drink made things worse, and long walks in the very fresh air didn't make them any better. She could see that Peter was puzzled by her dullness, and in particular by the absence of the full action replay which her descent into the pit would normally have produced. It wasn't that images of the visit did not fill her mind. Closing her eyes in sleep brought a darkness which was rapidly filled by the bobbing lights of helmet lamps. Tunnels curved away with gates branching off in all directions, and as she moved along on the ever accelerating paddy, she had the retrospective fancy that she was in the bloodstream of some monstrous creature, being sucked along a main artery by the audible pumping of its huge heart. And at that heart stood a solitary figure, Colin Farr, his naked body caked with glittering coal dust like a fell of dark pricked with a myriad stars. Then she was in the car with his hand between her legs and in the back seat his mother talked sadly of her pit-maimed husband lying dead in the darkness at the foot of the old shaft.

She was able to toy with these dreams in a variety of ways, but no amount of no matter how eclectic a self-analysis could lighten her depression. She told herself that the terrifying otherness of that underground world which in itself would probably just have provided good copy for a radical dinner-party had somehow, indeed almost literally, been rammed home into her subconscious by the brutal indifference of Col Farr's assault. Had he simply made a pass at her, that would have been different. In the Ivory Tower's paternoster she had experienced his physical proximity like an electrical current. But this had been something else. It might just as well have been his 'ringer' which he had thrust beneath her skirt. There had been something intensely impersonal as well as whatever was intensely personal in that gesture. It meant separation, dismissal, perhaps even contempt. She made up her mind to ring Adam and call off the rest of her classes.

But on Monday afternoon she was there as they came drifting in, and with them, neither ostentatiously last nor challengingly first, Colin Farr. She caught his eye without meaning to, and he rubbed the back of his hand across his nose and gave a little grin, sheepish almost, like a small boy acknowledging his fault but sure of his forgiveness. Instantly the dullness lifted from her mind like a morning mist and she had to take deliberate control to keep the returning lightness from catching at her voice.

That class was one of the best she had taken. There had been a big CND rally in London the previous Saturday which Ellie had been severely reprimanded by Thelma Lacewing for not attending. She had, however, partly retrieved her position by pointing out that as part of her group's study of media distortion, she had asked them to read the account of the rally in whatever Sunday paper they normally took, and to come along on Monday ready to discuss it.

110

'Forget personal belief or knowledge,' she said. 'Let's just discuss the rally and the issues in the light of what you've gleaned from the paper you normally read.'

It took a while to divert the class from their fascinated curiosity into her reaction to visiting a pit, but once discussion of the papers got under way, the miners were soon competing to make their points.

At the end of the session which had overrun by nearly half an hour, Colin Farr took his time in packing his insubstantial gear together and soon only he and Ellie remained in the room.

'That was good,' he complimented her. 'I enjoyed that.'

She felt an absurd amount of pleasure.

'Thanks,' she said. 'How's your mam?'

'Why?' he asked, immediately alert. 'Did you think she looked poorly?'

'No,' she said. 'It's just the kind of polite inquiry us middle class academics make. Sometimes it's meaningless. Sometimes it stems from a real interest.'

'And what's it stem from this time?' he asked.

'Real interest. I liked her. I hope she liked me. Did she?'

He smiled, no sheepish child's grin this time, but sardonic and watchful.

'You oughtn't to ask questions unless you want to hear the truth,' he said.

'That's the only reason I ever ask questions,' she retorted with spirit.

'In that case,' he said, 'Mam said you seemed quite a nice kind of woman.'

'Oh.' Ellie considered. 'Is that good or bad?'

'Well, she might've said you seemed quite a nice kind of lady,' said Farr.

'And would that have been better or worse?'

'What do you think?'

He rose from his chair and strolled slowly towards her. She felt all her muscles tense. He halted only a foot away.

She said, controlling her voice with difficulty, 'If you're planning the mixture as before, Colin, I should point out that I'm wearing an extraordinarily sturdy pair of jeans today.'

To her surprise he flushed beautifully.

'Look,' he said. 'I wanted to say I was sorry about that. Sometimes I do things ... I was upset, I don't know why ...'

'Upset by me?'

'I don't know what!' He spoke sharply. 'Only sometimes when things get a bit mixed up in your mind, it seems to make sense to get 'em all straightened out, nice and simple, even if it means forcing one or two of them a bit. Don't you ever feel that?'

'You certainly acted as if you were about to force me. I was terrified.'

'Were you?' He sounded genuinely taken aback. 'I'm sorry, I didn't realize. Oh shit. It just seemed to make things simpler if I thought of you as a middle-class bird who fancied a bit of rough.'

'Well, thank you, kind sir!'

'No, I'm sorry, that's not what I really think. I knew it wasn't true, even when I tried it on. That's why I did it like I did, I reckon, because I knew it was just a gesture. I'm really sorry, though. Do you believe me?'

'You'd have got a real shock wouldn't you if I'd flung myself on top of you and started tearing your clothes off!' said Ellie pensively.

He began to smile, the true Colin Farr smile, slow, charming, incredibly attractive.

'I'd have tried to act like a gentleman,' he said.

He was still very close and Ellie suddenly felt a thrill of danger and knew this time it came from within as much as without. It was time not to be alone with this youth, but she wasn't yet ready to part company with him altogether.

'Have you time for a cup of tea or something in the refectory?' she asked. 'I'm parched after all that talking.'

'What about your lassie?' he asked. 'Don't you have to pick her up?'

Oh God, here we go again, she thought. Poor old Rosie!

'She's in the crèche,' she said. 'I'm late already, but they

112

don't usually mind. I'll just ring up to make sure they can hang on to her another half-hour. You could do a bit of tidying up after your mates if you like.'

She gestured at the newspapers strewn around the tables. This feeble attempt to retreat to a teacher–pupil relationship did not go unremarked.

'Yes, miss,' he said.

She went out and along the corridor to Adam's office. He wasn't in, but he had given her a key so she could use the room to store any material she didn't want to lug around with her. It took her a few minutes to get through to the crèche, conjuring up pictures of some dreadful crisis with Rosie, mutinous from neglect, at its centre. But no, all was well, a matter-of-fact voice assured her, and yes, another half-hour would make no difference.

But when she returned to the classroom she saw that a few minutes had made a very great difference.

Colin Farr was standing with one of the discarded newspapers in his hand. His face was pale and drawn and suddenly the resemblance to his mother was quite marked.

'Colin, is something wrong?' she asked.

'Mebbe. I don't know.'

He threw the paper on to the floor and made for the door. She followed him.

'For heaven's sake, what's the matter?'

'I'm sorry,' he said over his shoulder. 'That cup of tea'll have to wait.'

They reached the landing and without pause he stepped on to the paternoster. Unthinking, Ellie followed him, falling heavily against his taut young body as the moving platform dropped away. He put his arms around her to steady her, but he did not take them away. The descent seemed dream-like. Her eyes were closed and when he stepped out, almost carrying her with him, and she opened her eyes once more, she would hardly have been surprised to see the neon glow and whitewashed walls of pit bottom all around them.

He said, 'I've got to get home. See you next week.'

Then he kissed her briefly and turned and loped away towards the car park.

She watched him go till rationality came seeping back.

What in the name of God am I doing? she asked herself, and glanced around, sure that an ambush of curious eyes must have gathered to view this silly old slag who was behaving so daftly.

There was no one to pay the slightest interest. Recalling she'd left her bag in the seminar room, she summoned a lift. The paternoster's cramped cells seemed to be flying upwards at an impossibly dangerous speed. The lift was a long time coming and an even longer time ascending and by the time she reached the room, she was perfectly composed. She picked up her handbag, checked her face and hair in the pocket mirror and prepared to leave.

Her foot kicked the paper Colin Farr had dropped to the floor. She picked it up. It was the *Challenger* and it was open at the page containing Episode Two of Watmough's alleged memoirs. Her eye caught the word *Burrthorpe*. Peter had been talking about this yesterday, she recalled. She had affected indifference. No, not *affected*. Yesterday she had been indifferent. But not now.

She read the piece swiftly, then more slowly re-read the final paragraph. She recalled her conversation with Mrs Farr. There seemed no doubt; the dead witness, the man about whom this terrible insinuation was being made, must be Colin's father.

When she'd finished, she stared at the photograph of Neville Watmough which stared seriously back from alongside the headlines.

'You bastard!' she said. 'You shitty bastard.'

CHAPTER 4

'Mr Downey. Your sister said I'd find you here. Can I have a word?'

Arthur Downey was kneeling on a small mat, facing east, his face devout with concentration.

'What? Oh, it's you. Hang on.'

He rose slowly and shook off the soil from his hands.

'Digging up some rhubarb roots for forcing,' he explained. 'You interested in gardening, Mr Boyle?'

Monty Boyle looked around the immaculately kept allotment and shook his head.

'No time,' he said. He manoeuvred himself till he was straight in front of the other and opened his jacket.

'I'm surprised to see you here, Mr Boyle,' said Downey. 'After what was said in the *Challenger* yesterday.'

'By Watmough, you mean? I can't be held responsible for what an ex-policeman says.'

'It's you who's been asking the questions round here. You should take note—there's a lot who'd say anything for a free drink, and take it back for another.'

'Is that so? Well, I promise you, I personally never write anything I can't prove.'

It was true, but only in the way that most of Boyle's pieces were true; i.e. there was just enough truth there to support a whole precarious edifice of speculation. Next Sunday's episode was all set up but he needed a new startling revelation for the week afterwards.

'So you think you can prove I'm a liar? Round here, you can get yourself thumped for saying things like that!'

Downey's long face creased beneath an ill-fitting expression of belligerence.

'What makes you say that, Mr Downey?' asked Boyle, all injured innocence.

'That article yesterday, it seemed to say that yon fellow Pickford couldn't have been round Burrthorpe that afternoon. And I'm the one who saw his car. And it said I were a good friend of Billy's, implying I might have been covering up for him.'

'Like I said, I don't write the articles, so I don't know what Mr Watmough's getting at. But it's a question worth asking, Mr Downey. Would you have lied for your friend?'

The agony this question caused was written so clear on Downey's face that even a journalist's heart could not be untouched.

'Look, no one's saying you're a liar, Mr Downey. You

didn't say you saw Pickford's car, you said you glimpsed a blue car parked off the road that runs along the bottom of the ridge, right?'

'Yes.'

'And it was quite close to the track down through the woods where the child's bramble bucket was found.'

'Yes.'

'And this was the truth?'

A pause as if to check for traps.

'Yes,' he said.

'And I believe you. So, next question, Mr Downey. Is there anyone round here who drives, or used to drive, a blue car about the size of a Cortina?'

'I can't rightly say,' said the deputy after another agony of concentration. 'Probably plenty. But I can only think of one off-hand.'

'Who's that?' asked Boyle.

'You know him, I've seen you talking to him. Harold Satterthwaite.'

'Oh yes. He's been very helpful, Mr Satterthwaite.'

'Has he? He's all right, Harold, a bit rough but all right. Except for one thing. He never cared for Billy, and he likes young Colin even less.'

'I gathered. What do you make of Colin Farr, Mr Downey?'

'I don't know. He's not happy here, that's a fact. Mebbe it'd be better if he took himself off again. Trouble seems to follow him. Like some people are always having bad luck. Have you noticed that? How bad luck seems to pick on the same folk all the time? But Colin's Billy's son and I'll not hear a word against him.'

'No?' Boyle smiled. 'Funny thing is, despite all his trouble, and with one or two notable exceptions, most people seem to be of your mind. The world seems to love Colin Farr. Even I find it hard to dislike the lad and all he's done for me is throw me through a window!'

'I'm finished here,' said Downey. 'You're not going by the Club, are you?'

'I can do. Will they be open?'

'Soon enough. Hang on.'

He went into the small wooden shed and came out with a cauliflower and an aerosol can. The cauliflower he handed to Boyle, saying, 'Try that. Lovely flavour. You'll be amazed,' as he sprayed the aerosol round the edge of his vegetable patch.

'Keeps the animals off,' he said. 'There's a wilderness out there but they still seem to prefer a bit of cultivation.'

Boyle looked around. 'Wilderness' was extreme, but certainly many of the neighbouring allotments were looking very neglected.

'You should have seen it during the Strike,' said Downey nostalgically. 'Every inch packed with veg that year. We mounted pickets at night to make sure nothing went missing.'

'I thought it was all brotherly love and community spirit during the Strike,' said Boyle cynically.

'Oh yes. We're sent into this world to help each other, I sincerely believe that, Mr Boyle. But there's always some who don't want to be helped, and others who just want to help themselves. I'll just lock up.'

Boyle went to his car and tossed the cauliflower on to the back seat. He also took the opportunity to run back and replace the full tape on his cassette recorder before Downey joined him. He switched it off temporarily. No point in recording the noise of his motor. In fact, probably little point in recording much more of Downey. But there might be others at the Club. Satterthwaite for instance, who owned a blue car and was always so keen to bad-mouth Billy Farr. It could be worth talking to Satterthwaite again. And Pedro Pedley, a very hard man to get anything quotable out of. How would he react to the idea floated in the *Challenger* that his daughter's killer might still be on the loose? Unless, of course, it *had* been Billy Farr. But that would be a pity. A live killer was worth a much bigger spread than a dead one. That could be the way to prise open May and Colin Farr's mouths. Hint at evidence emerging that . . . that what? The trouble was, no evidence *was* emerging, just rumour, innuendo, theory. None of which he objected to, but he had to have that pinch of truth which would act as leavening to all the rest.

'Ready?'

Downey had come up quietly behind him.

'Right. Hop in.'

As he started the engine, his car phone rang. It was a luxury Ogilby had conceded only after a string of vandalized public phones had delayed a terrific rape story which Boyle had stumbled upon a few months earlier.

It was the editor himself.

'Monty, where are you?'

'Burrthorpe.'

'I thought so. Look, we've really stirred things up,' said Ogilby gleefully. 'Some victim's rights lawyer threatening us with an injunction. A woman too, Pritchard, I think she was a big mouth during some of the Strike trials, so see if you can get a few quotes down there, the more sexist the better. I'm giving her a headline next Sunday, though I don't expect it'll be the one she wants. Also, the police are inquiring after you at ever decreasing intervals so we've certainly caught their interest too.'

'Oh yes. Will you just keep telling them you can't make contact at the moment?'

'Naturally. Hot on a good dirty trail, are you?'

Boyle glanced at Downey who was busy trying to clean the earth from out of his fingernails.

'Oh, yes, I shouldn't be at all surprised,' he said.

CHAPTER 5

It was five minutes to opening and Pedro Pedley was wrestling a beer keg into position in his cellar when he heard someone coming down the stone stair. The steps were light as a dancer's, but naturally, not furtively.

'Hello, Col,' he said without looking up. 'Got a thirst on, have you? I'll be with you in a couple of minutes.'

Farr said, 'You saw the *Challenger* yesterday?'

'Aye,' said Pedley. He finished coupling the pipe to the keg, then sat on it and looked up at Colin Farr, who had stopped half way down the stairs.

'I were in here yesterday dinner-time. Why'd you not say anything? Why'd no one say anything?'

Pedley tugged at his moustache and said, 'What did you want people to say, Col? For all anyone knew, you'd read it yourself and were ready to stuff the first bugger daft enough to mention it.'

'That's what they thought? But what about you, Pedro? You were entitled to mention it. In fact I reckon you were bound to mention it!'

'Mebbe. But in me own time, not over the bar with all them dirty lugs flapping.'

'Time's now, Pedro. So what do you think? Do you reckon there's even the millionth chance there's any truth in what that lousy bastard's implying?'

Pedley sighed and said, 'What do I get if I say owt but *no*, Col? Will you try to bust my head open with one of them kegs?'

'He were a good friend to you, Pedro,' exclaimed Farr. 'And he loved that lass of yours like she were his own.'

'Did he? I always thought so. But he didn't see her safe home that day, Col, like he'd always done before. He never explained that to me, not proper. No don't interrupt. Hear me out. You've got to understand; what me and Maggie have been through changes your view of folk. It's not so much you stop trusting 'em as you stop trusting your own judgement of 'em. I went to the inquest they held on that bastard Pickford. If he were the one as took our Tracey, I wanted to know all about him, I wanted a true picture so I could at least dream about tearing him apart! Know what I heard? I heard his wife tell what a lovely man he were, how he loved dogs and children, how he went on sponsored charity runs, how she'd never believe in a million years that he'd done what he said in his letter. His mother were the same only worse. It got me thinking, I tell you.'

'What did it get you thinking, Pedro?' asked Farr softly.

'Only this,' said the steward with equal softness. 'If you want the ninety-nine per cent of me that says, there's no more way good old Billy Farr could've harmed our Tracey than pigs can fly, you've got it. But if you want the other fraction, well now! *That* doesn't trust my own judgement any more, *that* reckons that after Pickford there's no bugger in the world who's not capable of anything and everything! That's it, Col. That's what you asked for. So what's it to be? The fist or the keg? Only be warned. I'll not just sit here and take it.'

Colin Farr's body, taut before, was now trembling like a cable under breaking strain.

He flung back his head and cried, 'He were my dad!'

And Pedley slowly rose and whispered, 'And she were my daughter.'

'Will you come in for a drink?' asked Arthur Downey through the window of the car which Boyle had brought to a halt just short of the Welfare.

The journalist hesitated. He wanted to see Pedley but not while he had customers to serve. Before he could make up his mind, the door of the Club burst open and Colin Farr came rushing down the steps. His motorbike was lying half on, half off the pavement as if he'd been in too much of a hurry to put it on its rest. He dragged it upright, mounted it in a fluid movement which even the turmoil evident in his face could not render less than graceful and sent it screaming round the side of the building into the potholed lane that ran up to the ridge.

There is a tide in the affairs of journalists, thought Monty Boyle, or something like that.

'Not tonight,' he said. 'Excuse me.'

And he sent his car in pursuit of the speeding bike.

It was a vain effort. Fifty yards and the potholes were beginning to claim him. He stopped the car, switched off the engine, reached into the glove compartment and came out with a torch and a pair of field glasses. Far ahead through the trees he glimpsed the bike's permanently lit head-lamp flickering still at great speed. But there was a limit to the places that its rider could be going. The hunt was far from dead.

Already dying for a cigarette, Monty Boyle set out along the track. Up here the answer lay. Up here Billy Farr had come with Tracey Pedley. And back up here little Tracey had come alone, after being left alone.

If she had been left alone.

'No,' screamed Colin Farr into the windy air.

It was a dank October evening with low clouds, bringing an early dusk. Autumn it had been when Billy Farr and Tracey went brambling, but by all accounts a balmy Indian Summer day with Gratterley Wood still in rich leaf and the air still warm enough for bees to buzz in and lovers to lie in. And hard winter it had been when Billy Farr had come up here for the last time to this same spot his son reached now. It was an area of scrubby common once scarred by spoil and diggings, but now with its wounds mostly healed over with coarse grass and undergrowth. Here and there, like druid's circles erected by some prehistoric botcher, stood rings of palings, laced with rusty barbed wire and adorned with ivy and bindweed and fringed with nettle and burdock. More than the stone which marked his grave, these were monuments to Billy Farr's death. Here the council workmen had come to seal off all known entrances to the old workings like pharaohs' tombs, no doubt presenting some distant generation of archæologists with an interesting problem.

Meanwhile the tomb-robbers were not to be denied.

Colin Farr let his bike freewheel down a diagonal of the ridge till the undergrowth and saplings at the fringe of the wood brought him to a halt. Laying the bike on its side, he took a torch from the pannier and went forward on foot. Suddenly he stopped and spun round. There was nothing to see except a graceful scatter of silver birch, their trunks scarcely thick enough to hide a man. He pressed on, finally halting by a bank of dusty gorse bushes. Once more he looked round. Once more his eyes failed to back his instinct.

Watched or not, he knew there was no turning back. He

was in the grip of a compulsion as strong and undeniable as sex. It might take him into the dark places he feared, but sometimes they seemed light enough beside the darkness he found inside of him.

He pulled at the gorse bushes, ignoring the pricking of his hands. They parted to reveal a narrow deep fissure. Out of this those early rustic miners had hewed their first black harvest home.

Colin Farr switched on his torch and, stooping almost to his knees, wriggled inside.

An hour later as darkness fell on Gratterley Wood, a dog fox sniffing the air to see what kind of night it was likely to be was disturbed by a thin wailing cry. Above, he'd have put it down to an owl. But this hadn't come from above, it had seemed to emerge from the ground itself. The fox listened carefully but there was no repetition. So, deciding the noise was irrelevant to his purposes that night, he turned and went on his way.

It was late when Colin Farr got home.

'Col, is that you? Where've you been?' called his mother from the kitchen. 'Your supper's ruined. Col!'

She'd come to the kitchen door and seen her son. He was dirt-stained and scratched, but it was the look on his face not his physical condition which disturbed her.

'What's happened?' she demanded. 'Have you been fighting? It's not Harold Satterthwaite, is it?'

'No! It's nowt to do with him,' exclaimed Farr. 'I've been down the old workings, Mam. Down where Dad died.'

'Oh God,' said May Farr, collapsing against the doorpost as the strength ebbed from her legs. 'What have you done that for, Colin? What took you down there? Was it that bloody paper? I hid it so you'd not see it, but there's no way to keep anything quiet in this place!'

'No, Mam, it weren't the paper. I've been down the workings a dozen times before.'

'But why?' -

'I had to know if Dad . . . I had to *know*, and where else was there to look?'

He stared at her with a defiance which was more heart-rending than a direct appeal for help.

'If he killed himself, you mean? Is that it? Why'd you need to look, Col? You could've just asked me. You should've been able just to ask yourself! Instead you go risking life and limb . . . It were an accident, Colin. Likely Jacko got lost and he were looking for him and some idiot had taken the cover off . . . it were an *accident*, nothing to do with . . . anything.'

'Nothing to do with Tracey, you mean? Just coincidence? Up there where he'd last been with her, Jacko goes missing and Dad goes looking for him? It's a nice story, Mam, but if it's true, then how do you explain this?'

He held out a circle of imprinted metal.

She took it and looked at it, bewildered but fearful.

Then slowly he unzipped his leather jacket, and she screamed inaudibly and slid all the way to the floor as out of it spilled a confusion of delicate ivory bones.

CHAPTER 6

Pascoe was amazed to find himself under violent attack the moment he got home on Monday evening. It took him some little time to work out the angle of assault and the nature of the armament, and when he did he had to double-check.

'Hang on,' he said. 'You're blaming me for what Neville Watmough's writing in the *Challenger*? Is that it?'

'No. Yes. In a manner of speaking, you are responsible, aren't you?'

'Speak to me in that manner, that I may hear and be instructed,' said Pascoe gravely.

Ellie was not to be mocked into truce.

'It's you, it's Dalziel, it's the whole bloody way the police function, isn't it? You don't think of people as people, they're statistics, so many crooks and potential crooks. So many victims and potential victims. You don't care about feelings, not till someone starts knocking you in the media and then you come all over hurt. Look, you cry, we're giving you protection, aren't we? And it's our lives, not yours, that are at risk out there on the front line, so you should just sit quiet at home and thank your lucky stars that you've got the best police force in the world to go along with the best TV, the best Royal Family, and the best Health Service, look at all the frogs and wogs who come here for freebies . . .'

'Hang on!' said Pascoe. 'Aren't we getting just a little incoherent? What about some of that fine old academic discipline we used to get before the war? If you want to bitch about the *Challenger*, bitch away and I'll bitch with you . . .'

'Bitch? Bitch? What's with this sexist language? You give yourself away every time you open your mouth. Peter, you're in quicksand and you can't see it. You're sinking. Every day you're becoming a bit more of a Dalziel clone. No, all right, I take that back, he is absolutely unique! But you could be a Watmough clone, respectable, polite, self-important, thinking that a life spent shovelling manure qualifies you to pontificate on agricultural policy and technique.'

'I thought you said it was quicksand I was sinking in,' said Pascoe. 'Whoops, before you tell me that I always flee to frivolity in the face of defeat, let me quickly slip in that I've asked Wield for supper tomorrow night. Perhaps you can serve him the food we're quite clearly not going to get tonight.'

'Wield? Why? I knew you were friends—well, friendly— but you've never asked him for a meal before.'

'I've asked him now. OK? I thought you liked him.'

'Yes, I suppose I do. How's he been? I haven't seen much of him since he came out.'

'He seems OK. As for coming out, I can't say I've noticed very much change.'

'As you never noticed anything in the first place, that doesn't surprise me,' said Ellie acidly.

This reference to the fact that he had been amazed at the revelation of Wield's homosexuality while both Ellie and Dalziel found it completely unsurprising was a low blow. She knew how much he blamed himself for his insensitivity.

Well, in this age of equality, both sides can fight dirty.

He said, 'To get back to Watmough and the *Challenger*, would I be right in saying what all this is really about isn't human rights but the Marvellous Boy of Burrthorpe? Has he been weeping dusty tears on your shoulder all afternoon?'

It was a savage blow. Ellie momentarily reeled but, like the fighter she was, rallied magnificently. All night long the noise of battle rolled, with pause only for hasty mouthfuls of a scratch supper and a couple of hours' necessary sleep. Breakfast was a cross-table bombardment and hostilities would certainly have been resumed in the evening by the fireside's glow if it hadn't been that Wield was coming to supper.

He arrived dead on time, clutching a bunch of red roses and a bottle of white wine. He was casually dressed in a pair of elegant light blue slacks, a pale lemon open-necked sports shirt and a diamond patterned lambswool sweater.

He said, 'I've left my leathers in the garage. I hope that's OK.'

Pascoe and Ellie avoided exchanging glances.

'Leathers?' said Pascoe faintly.

'Yes. I came on the bike,' said Wield.

'Of course,' said Pascoe. 'The famous motorbike. Darling, you must have heard me mention the famous motorbike.'

He did glance at Ellie this time and saw he was overdoing it.

'Come in,' said Ellie firmly. 'It's great to see you again. Can I . . . ?'

She looked at his burdens.

'Oh yes,' said Wield. 'I brought you these. I hope they're what you like.'

Carefully he handed Ellie the bottle of wine and Pascoe the bunch of roses. They both looked at him for some signal that the distribution had been an error, but that gnarled and knotted face gave no more away than the bark of an old elm tree.

Then he smiled and said, 'You can swap if you think I'm being sexist.'

Ellie began to laugh a fraction before Pascoe.

'I really am glad you've come,' she said. 'Let's have a drink while Peter's putting his flowers in water!'

It was a delightful relaxed evening. Wield let down three or four of his outer defence barriers, and though Pascoe got a sense of plenty of layers in reserve, the shrewd and humorous man revealed was a pleasant guest to have at anyone's table. Ellie demurred at calling him Wieldy but the sergeant refused to reveal his Christian names on the grounds that they might discriminate him.

'Wieldy's fine,' he said. 'As long as you make no cracks about "unwieldy". I had enough of that in training.'

After supper they were sitting talking with a Glen Miller record on low in the background when the phone rang. Pascoe answered it and a man's voice, young and Yorkshire and not very distinct, asked if he could talk to Mrs Pascoe. Relieved that at least it wasn't a summons to duty, he went back to the lounge and summoned Ellie. After she had gone into the hall, he offered to refill Wield's glass.

'Best not,' said the sergeant. 'I'm always getting stopped. Our car lads think anyone on a bike's a Hell's Angel who's probably breaking the Highway Code by eating a live chicken as he rides. One of these days I'll get some smart kid who'll show how impartial he is by breathalyzing me.'

'You think we should get special treatment?' wondered Pascoe, who had not found Wield's temperance infectious.

'Not special. Neither specially good nor specially bad. The same. Equal.'

'That should be easy enough to arrange,' said Pascoe.

'You reckon? Try being a motorcyclist. Try not being a cop,' said Wield. Then he added in a voice a little lower but quite audible, 'Try being gay.'

'Thanks but no thanks!' Pascoe heard himself say, then, 'Oh shit, Wieldy, I'm sorry, it's the booze.'

'No, it's not,' said Wield equably. 'It's a conditioned response. The station canteen, the Club bar, that's the kind of thing you've got to say to show your credentials. I've done it myself in the early days.'

'And now?' asked Pascoe.

126

'And now? I've been in a kind of limbo these past few weeks. I'd said to myself: No more, I'm coming out, from now on in I'll be myself. But what's that? I mean, for me to start going up to people who know me and saying, "Have you heard? I'm gay!" that's so far from what I *am* that it'd almost be as dishonest as the way I was before. I've never been promiscuous, or mebbe I conditioned myself there too, and with these scare stories about AIDS around, I'm certainly not about to start. I did go into the Jolly Waggoner on Childersgate one night, you know, the one they call the Gay Galloper. I bought a drink and someone said, "My God, darling, the fuzz are really scraping the barrel for their *agents provocateurs*, aren't they?" I drank up and left. I mean, what else was there to do? I couldn't see any future, or much point, in standing on a chair and trying to persuade them all I really was gay. More to the point, I found myself thinking it was none of their bloody business. In fact it's no one's except mine. I am what I've made myself and that's the way I'll stay till I make myself something else. So no crap. I'll never lie again about being gay, but I'll not take a full page spread in the *Post* to advertise it either. Does that make sense to you, Peter?'

This was certainly the longest and most personal speech Pascoe had ever heard Wield make.

He said, 'What do I know? But yes, it makes sense to me, for what that's worth.'

'A lot,' said Wield seriously. 'Right. That's that. And don't worry. If you don't go on about your sex life, I'll not go on about mine! Is there owt new about Mr Watmough?'

Pascoe accepted the change of direction with a relief he felt slightly ashamed of.

'I gather there's a lot of pressure from high up to get him to shut up, but I doubt if he's really in control now and it takes lawyers with a good case to shut someone like Ogilby up. I've tried two or three times to get hold of Monty Boyle, but he's never available and he never rings back. I think I'll have to go out looking for him. But there's no way next Sunday's piece won't be printed, I'm afraid.'

Ellie came back into the room. Pascoe knew at once that

there was something bothering her. She said, 'I'm sorry, but I've got to go out.'

Pascoe said, 'What's up? Not your father, is it?'

Ellie's father in Lincolnshire had for some time been drifting into the happy but hazardous land of senile dementia. He was quite capable of going for a walk on a country path which had been replaced by a four-lane highway twenty years ago.

'Oh no,' said Ellie. 'Nothing like that. It's just one of my students. He sounds a bit agitated about something so I think I ought to put in a bit of the old pastoral care.'

Wield began to rise, saying, 'I really ought to be going . . .' but Ellie put her hands on his shoulders and pressed him firmly down again.

'No, don't make me feel guiltier than I do,' she said. 'You stay, finish the bottle. Or Peter will make you some more coffee.'

'Do you have to go?' asked Pascoe petulantly, because petulance hid his real feelings.

Ellie smiled without much humour.

'That's usually my line when Dalziel rings, isn't it? And don't tell me that's different. I'll be as quick as I can.'

She left too swiftly for him to reply. He thought of going after her and continuing their discussion in the hallway but he knew that would only upgrade it to a row. A moment later they heard the sound of Ellie's car.

'I hope she missed your leathers,' said Pascoe, trying for brightness.

'I thought Mrs Pascoe—Ellie—had given up her job at the College,' said Wield speculatively.

'This is a university course, extra-mural,' said Pascoe. 'Miners.'

'Miners?' said Wield. His face as usual gave nothing away. Pascoe wished he could feel as sure of his own control. He'd never heard the voice on the phone before, but he'd recognized it instantly with a certainty which his conscious mind had dismissed as absurd. Colin Farr, the Marvellous Boy. Colin Farr.

CHAPTER 7

'Why am I driving so fast?' Ellie Pascoe asked herself 'I'm like some kid rushing out on her first date, terrified she'll be late and he'll have gone on without her!'

The comparison was not as amusing as it should have been. There was a light drizzle in the air, enough to smear but not to clear the screen. Wield was going to need his leathers. She pressed the cleaner button but no water squirted out. She remembered now that she'd noticed the bottle was empty last time she'd tried to use it. She slowed down, straining her eyes to see through the dirt-striated glass. Ahead a signpost pointing down a minor road said *Lardley 6 miles*. She turned down it. There was no cat's-eyes and any number of ambiguous forks but finally she saw ahead of her the obscure light of a telephone box standing at a five-lane crossroads.

Anyone else would have been sheltering inside but Colin Farr was sitting on the grass verge with his back against the door and his eyes closed. Between his legs was a bottle. As she got out of the car she saw with horror that his golden curls were caked with blood, his face was bruised and his jerkin and jeans were torn.

'Colin, what's happened?' she asked anxiously. 'Are you hurt badly?'

He opened his eyes, laughed and said, 'Why? Will you kiss it better?'

'For God's sake, get up and get into the car,' she said angrily. 'If you want to get pneumonia as well, that's your business, but I don't.'

She climbed back into the car and a moment later he opened the passenger door and slumped in beside her.

'Right,' she said firmly, determined not to risk having sympathy mocked again. 'What's going on? You weren't all that coherent. Have you been in an accident?'

'Very sharp of you, Mrs Pascoe,' he said. His voice was slurred.

'Was anyone else involved?'

He started counting on his fingers.

'Well, there was me and the bike and the tree,' he said. 'That makes three.'

He burped and she smelled the sweet heavy smell of rum. The sailor's drink.

'You've been drinking,' she said.

'Christ, you sound just like my mam, or a bloody wife!' he said. 'Yes, I've had a couple of jars. So what?'

'So you shouldn't have been driving,' she said weakly.

'I wasn't,' he said with his slow smile. 'I had my eyes closed and me hands on me head. If they built straight roads round here, I'd likely still be going.'

'Why did you ring me, Colin?' she demanded.

'Why'd you come?' His voice was stronger.

'I thought you were in trouble.'

'And that bothered you? Must be bloody good money they pay you at yon university to come running like this! Was that your husband that answered the phone?'

'Yes.'

'Didn't he mind you rushing off like that?'

'He didn't say what he thought.'

'Silly twat,' said Farr.

Ellie said, 'All right, Colin. I'm pleased you're not badly hurt and I see now I misunderstood you. So, out you get. Have you got plenty of change? You may have to ring quite a few taxi firms before you find one that will come out here.'

'Eh? What's up?' demanded Farr.

'You were right. They don't pay me anything like enough to oblige me to put up with drunken jokers,' said Ellie. 'So out.'

He didn't move. Then he said in a low voice, 'I'm sorry. I don't know how to talk to you . . . no, that's daft . . . it sounds like I'm a peasant and you're a princess and that's not what I mean! It's just that I feel I've got to meet you head on somehow, like it were a kind of challenge . . . I mean, like when I rang up, I expected you'd just tell me to

130

sod off. It were like riding along with my eyes closed. You know what's going to happen so when it does, it just sort of confirms things, means you were right to expect the worst. But you said you'd come, right off, no fuss, so I don't know what to expect, and I'm a bit pissed and my head hurts and I've got to fight back else you might have an advantage . . . Listen, why'd you come?'

'Not to put you down, that's for sure,' said Ellie. 'Why'd you ring me? Are you in some sort of trouble?'

'Trouble?' he said in such a low voice she could hardly hear him. 'Am I in trouble or is he in trouble . . . or out of trouble . . . like Dad . . . a way out of trouble . . . to take . . . to give . . .'

'Colin,' she said urgently, 'has something happened? At home? At the pit?'

He slumped back and closed his eyes. Ellie for a heartstopping moment thought he'd slipped into unconsciousness, or worse. Then his lips started to move again. She put her ear so close she was almost touching and she could feel his breath light as a summer breeze that hardly stirs the grass.

'. . . blood on your coal . . . they say . . . blood and flesh and bones and brains . . . dark place for a dark deed . . . man can't toil all his life in darkness without drinking some of it in . . . not possible! Not possible!'

His voice suddenly rose to a scream and she jerked her head back. His eyes were open again and watching her.

She said, 'Colin, what are you talking about?'

He frowned in concentration, then pulled the bottle from inside his leather jerkin and took a long draught. Ellie said, 'Oh Colin, must you?'

He seemed to consider the question seriously then replied, 'Yes, I must.'

But he replaced the bottle in his jerkin.

He said, 'You know what Mam said when Dad had his accident? She said, "At least it means he'll end up dying in God's good air and not down that stinking hole." She's always been a one for finding good in bad, my Mam. She told me she felt glad when I went to sea. She cried because I were going but she felt glad too. She thought it meant that

131

I'd be like Dad, able to die in God's good air, or at least God's good water, eh?'

He laughed. It sounded contrived.

He went on, 'I got to thinking of it today. I shouldn't have gone on shift. Last night I thought I'd never go underground again, but after what Mam told me . . . well, I had to think, and dark seemed right place to think . . . he killed himself though, stands to reason, mebbe not because . . . I don't know . . . but he had left her, hadn't he? He'd have loved a little lass of his own . . . after me Mam couldn't . . . that's why he were so fond of . . . bloody Satterthwaite! that bastard deserves everything . . . but I shouldn't have . . . it was so black down there, I had to get out, I had to get out, I told Jim I were sick . . . all the way along the return I could feel the dark flooding after me like water, and all the way up in the Cage. Seeing that sky again . . . oh God!'

He stopped, leaned his head back and took in a deep breath as though reliving the experience. Ellie found she'd put her hand over his and he turned his over to grasp hers loosely. It felt easy, companionable, safe.

She said, 'You still haven't told me what you're doing out here.'

'I didn't want to go home and worry Mam, so I got on me bike and went for a ride. And I stopped for a drink. And it seemed a good idea. So I stopped for some more. And when I got properly bevvied up, I crashed the bike, came staggering on here and rang you. All right?'

His voice was loud and harsh.

Ellie said, 'Why me? Why not a garage? Or a taxi? Or a friend?'

'I thought I did,' he said. 'Ring a friend.'

'Crap,' said Ellie firmly.

'You mean you're not my friend?'

'I mean I'm not the kind of friend you ring up when you've crashed your bike!'

'Now that's a real middle-class luxury,' he mocked, suddenly wholly himself again. 'Having categories of friendship.'

'I like it when you give yourself away,' said Ellie calmly. 'You've got to be really clever to play dumb all the time.'

'And mebbe you've got to be a bit thick not to know when it's best to play dumb,' he retorted. 'All right, here it is. After I'd been drinking a bit I got to thinking I'd really like to sit down and talk things over with someone, not with one of my mates or anyone who had owt to do with Burrthorpe, but someone who'd mebbe see things a bit clearer from the outside. You were the only one I could think of.'

'Thanks,' said Ellie.

Farr laughed. 'Truth were your idea,' he said. 'Any road, I don't know if I'd have done owt about it, but when I came off the bike and got to this box, I meant to ring a garage, like you said. But then I thought; Why not her? See what she says, what she does. There, that's how it was. Satisfied now? Or shall I lie back here while you ask a few more questions?'

'Colin, I'm not a psychologist,' said Ellie carefully. 'Nor am I a schoolteacher. Either we talk on level terms or we don't talk at all.'

'Level terms?' he sneered. 'What do you know about anything? How could you understand owt? Middle-class cow!'

She was beginning to feel uneasy at these swings of mood. Was it the drink that caused them? Or his head wound? Or something deeper, darker?

'You're right,' she said. 'I can't understand for a start why you've stayed on at the pit as long as you have if you hate it so much.'

'How the hell should I know?' he demanded. 'Look, I went back after Dad died, like I said. That were to show 'em, to shut 'em up. Then the Strike started. You remember the Strike? Or did you mebbe not notice in the academic world? It lasted a year, just on. It was pointless leaving then. It would have looked as if I were giving in, letting my mates down. Besides, at least you didn't have to go down that bloody hole. There were some good times. It brought us all together. Sometimes I'd think I must be mad, freezing on a picket or having my arse kicked by a bloody police horse, all to save a place and a job I hated! Then I'd go down the Welfare, see how everyone was pooling their resources and pulling together, and I'd start to feel that mebbe there was something here worth all the shit, that mebbe it had taken the Strike to awaken it and it'd not go back to sleep in a hurry even when the Strike were over.'

'And were you right? Have things changed permanently?'

'For some people, mebbe. Some of the women say so. Good luck to 'em if they can keep it up.'

'But for you . . .?'

He shook his head, winced, shook it again as if defying the pain.

'So, if things didn't change for you,' said Ellie, 'why *are* you still there?'

'Just because it went back to what it was before!' he exclaimed angrily. 'Because people were still saying things, because . . . oh, a hundred becauses, not one of 'em you're like to understand . . . then there was that bloody copper writing in the paper. That's the last straw, I reckon. Since I saw that and realized it was all going to be raked over again, I've been going around, I don't know, looking for someone to kill it feels like, even if it's only myself!'

He pulled the bottle from inside his leather jerkin once more and took a long pull.

'Colin!' she said.

'Want some? Sorry it's empty.'

He laughed and threw the bottle out of the window. The air was full of the sweet smell of rum.

'Time we got you home,' said Ellie grimly, starting the engine.

'What's the hurry?' he asked with a sudden change of mood. 'Dark night, country road, let's get in the back and get to know each other.'

'Christ, Colin, I thought we got that out of the way last time.'

'No! That were just a game. This time I really fancy you.'

He swayed towards her and embraced her. She didn't struggle till she smelt the rich rum stench of his breath. He

134

tightened his grip and tried to force her round to face him.

'What'll you do when you're finished with me?' she demanded. 'Drop me down a shaft?'

He released her instantly.

She said, 'I'm sorry.'

He said, 'You can go to hell!' and started fumbling with the door, banging his head in frustration against the glass as he failed to find the handle. His head wound seemed to have opened up again. There was a smear of brown down the window. Suddenly desperate to be back among lights and people, Ellie put the car in gear and set off along the road. For a few moments it seemed as if he might still try to get out, then he slumped back in his seat, closed his eyes and let out a long groan of pain or despair. Then he was still.

What the hell am I doing here? Ellie asked herself. How did I get into this?

The road was narrow and winding. She should have wiped the smeared screen before starting but she certainly wasn't going to stop now and see to it. With relief she saw an illuminated sign ahead which told her she was approaching the main road. From here it shouldn't take long to get to Burrthorpe and dump her dangerous cargo. After that, all she had to worry about was getting home and explaining to Peter what she had been doing.

The main road was broader and straighter and she managed to pick up a bit of speed, so much so that when a poorly lit section of road works loomed up, she didn't see them till the last moment and had to swing the wheel savagely. There was a bang as her nearside wing caught one of the plastic warning cones and sent it spinning towards the verge.

'Oh shit,' said Ellie as she straightened the car up. And 'Oh shit!' she repeated with redoubled force as her hitherto disregarded rear-view mirror blossomed with a blue flashing light.

She did the right things, getting out of the car and walking a few steps back to meet them. For once in her life she hoped that she might be recognized as Inspector Pascoe's wife but these two were strangers to her. They courteously asked to see her licence and insurance, neither of which she had.

'I came out of the house in a bit of a rush,' she explained.

'Oh aye? Have you been drinking at all, missus?'

'No!' she denied indignantly.

'Well, we'll have to ask you to take a breathalyser test,' said the constable. 'You've committed a moving traffic offence.'

'What the hell was that?' she demanded, ready to take a stand against random testing.

The policeman merely glanced back towards the road works.

'Oh, that,' said Ellie. 'They ought to light the things properly.'

'Not very well lit, is it?' agreed the constable. 'Just blow in here, till you inflate the bag.'

She took the breathalyser and blew with all her strength. The policeman examined the results. Then to her amazement he said, 'I'm sorry, madam, but this is positive. You'll have to come with us for further tests.'

'You're joking!' exclaimed Ellie indignantly. 'There's something wrong with your machine.'

'Mebbe,' agreed the constable with the patience of one who has heard it all before, 'But we'll find that out back at the station, won't we?'

Ellie opened her mouth to let out her gale-force indignation when suddenly she remembered. Of course she had been drinking. How many bottles of wine had Peter and Wield and herself got through over supper? It seemed such an age ago that it required a piece of conscious computation to work out that barely an hour had elapsed since she'd dashed from the house with not a thought for what she had drunk that night.

Was it worth explaining this to the policeman? Or was this perhaps the moment to forget her principles and drop Peter's name into the conversation?

The decision was postponed by an unexpected interruption. It was a laugh, long, merry, drunken. It came from Colin Farr who had opened the passenger door the better to eavesdrop on Ellie's exchange with the constabulary.

'Drunk in charge of a drunk!' he hiccoughed. 'That's grand. Lecturing me, and you're full of pop yourself!'

The policemen exchanged glances and one of them wandered across to Farr.

''Evening, sir,' he said politely. 'I'm afraid your friend isn't going to be able to drive you any further and I don't think you had better take over the car, had you? Best come along with us too, eh?'

'Get fucked,' said Farr, all merriment ceasing as if cut off by an electric switch.

'That's a nasty cut, sir,' said the policeman. 'Have you been in a fight or something?'

'Just a little accident, Officer,' said Ellie hastily. 'Colin, you wait here. Either I'll be back or I'll fix for a taxi to pick you up.'

'No need,' said Farr, trying to stand up. 'I'm fine. I can foot it back to Burrthorpe from here. But I'm not . . .'

'What's your name, son?' interrupted the policeman.

'Not the same as yours, so I'm not your fucking son, am I?' snarled Farr.

'Now don't you get stroppy with me, lad!'

'Look, his name's Colin Farr,' said Ellie, wanting to defuse this situation. 'He's nothing to do with this, is he? I mean, he's just a passenger, so can't we just go to your station and get this silly business sorted out?'

'Farr? Colin Farr from Burrthorpe?' To Ellie's horror the nearest policeman suddenly seized Colin's arm in a tight lock. 'Right, sunshine. You'd better come along with us after all. Oh no, none of that!'

Colin had swung his free arm at the man's face and next moment he was bent double, shrieking in pain, as the policeman savagely thrust the locked arm up between his shoulder-blades. The other cop was leaning into the car, talking into the radio.

'What's going on?' demanded Ellie. 'I'm dreaming this! What the hell do you think you're doing?'

Farr was forced past her and thrust into the rear seat. Ellie was contemplating an assault on the arresting constable's back when she felt her arm gently taken by the other man who had finished on his radio.

'Don't make things worse,' he said wearily.

'What's happening? Why are you arresting my friend?'

'Friend, is he? You should mebbe pick your friends more carefully.'

'And you should mebbe pick your victims more carefully!'

And Ellie heard herself doing what long ago she had vowed she would never do, parading her relationship to Peter, and her mainly pretended intimate acquaintance with every senior officer from Dalziel up to the Chief Constable, in an effort to extract privileged treatment. Dubious at first, the man ended up convinced, but not overly impressed. It was like using the ultimate weapon and seeing it explode like a soap-bubble.

'Look, I'm sorry, Mrs Pascoe, and I'll see your husband gets informed, but you'll still have to come in with us.'

'Can't you get it into your skull, I'm not worried about my husband being informed,' said Ellie, sadly disillusioned. 'It's *me* that I want informed. What's going on?'

The man hesitated then said, 'All I can tell you, Mrs Pascoe, is that half an hour ago we got a call from South Yorkshire asking us to keep an eye out for your friend, Colin Farr. Said he'd most likely be riding a motorbike.'

'But why? What's he supposed to have done?'

'He works at Burrthorpe Main, doesn't he? Well, at the end of the last shift they found a man dead down the pit, a deputy name of Satterthwaite. And the South Yorks force would like your friend Mr Farr to help with their inquiries!'

CHAPTER 8

'I don't believe any of this,' said Pascoe.

On his arrival at Burrthorpe police station, he had been neatly intercepted by Detective Chief Inspector Alex Wishart of South Yorks CID whose presence in this outpost of his constabulary empire was not reassuring. Something serious was going on. Quickly Wishart gave him a brief outline of events as they involved Ellie.

'What it comes down to is that my wife has been picked up drunk in charge of a murder suspect?'

'That's how I might put it if I were writing for the *Challenger*,' said Wishart. He was a small, neat man with a residual Scots accent which had survived his transplant to South Yorkshire some thirty years earlier. Pascoe enjoyed his dry humour, and liked and respected him.

'Where are they?' he asked.

'Farr's up at the hospital. He's got a lot of injuries and I want it firmly established that they're nothing to do with us. Your good lady's here but not being very cooperative. Listen, Peter, I'd really like to smudge this breathalyser business out of sight. It's an unhelpful complication and the reading was just on the borderline anyway.'

'So what's the problem?'

'The Press,' said Wishart. 'The locals are here already and no doubt the big boys will be sending out scouts. Someone will talk. It might even be your good lady, the way she's going on about citizens' rights and police brutality. Once the hacks find out she's married to a cop they'll have a field day.'

'What are you saying, Alex?' asked Pascoe.

'Urge upon her the merits of silence, even if it's only relative. And explain that we've got to go ahead with the blood test. It'll almost certainly be under the limit by now, so that will be one less thing for the Press to sink their fangs into. Oh, and it would be nice to have her statement all signed and sealed by the time I get back.'

'From where?'

For answer Wishart jerked his thumb downwards.

'You're going down the pit? Jesus!' said Pascoe with a shudder.

'I don't much care for the idea myself. It'll only be a token to get the forensic boys under way. Looks bad if the investigating officer doesn't show his face at the scene of the crime.'

'It's definitely a crime, then?'

'You ought to see the body,' said Wishart grimly.

'It's been brought up already?' said Pascoe in surprise.

'Peter, you don't leave bodies down a coal mine. When they found him, they thought it must have been an accident so naturally they brought him out. Soon as a doctor saw his injuries though, we were sent for.'

'These injuries . . . ?'

'Looks like several violent blows to the skull with a length of metal, but we'll need to wait for the PM for details. No doubt about assault, though.'

'Where does Farr fit in?'

'He knocked off early saying he felt sick. His team leader, a man called Wardle, told him he'd better let Satterthwaite, the official in charge of their section, know. Evidently there's been bad feelings between Farr and Satterthwaite, with threats of violence. Farr went off. When he left the pit yard, he didn't go home but just vanished.'

'And on the strength of that you put out a call for him?'

'No, though his reputation plus this previous trouble with Satterthwaite might have been enough. But there was another deputy, a man called Mycroft, who saw Farr on his way out. He said Farr asked if he'd seen Satterthwaite and he directed him to where he thought he might be. Also I thought it might be a good idea to have his pit-black checked by forensic. There'd almost certainly be traces after an attack like that. But when he looked for Farr's gear in the dirty lockers, it wasn't there. So then I put out a call. But I'm treading very carefully, Peter. It's tribal round here, you've got to be careful not to upset any local ju-ju. So wish me luck. I'll not be long if I can help it. Make yourself known to Sergeant Swift. I've told him you're coming. Whatever anyone else says, he runs this joint!'

Wishart left and Pascoe went in search of Swift, a grizzled middle-aged man who didn't greet him with any enthusiasm.

'You'll find your wife upstairs, sir. Second floor, first on left.'

The rebuilt Burrthorpe police station was, perhaps literally, big enough to withstand a siege, and, perhaps wisely, they'd put Ellie as far away from the public areas as they could without locking her up.

'Peter, what's going on?' she demanded angrily as soon as he came through the door. 'I've been stuck in here for nearly an hour.'

'You make it sound like a dungeon,' said Pascoe. 'The door's not locked.'

'Not physically perhaps. The Scots dwarf who put me in here said he was a friend of yours and implied that if I didn't stay put, it might mean a public beheading for you!'

'He was exaggerating,' said Pascoe. 'It would probably be private. But thanks for worrying. I hear you were breathalysed.'

'Yes, I bloody was! I bet you weren't, and you probably drank twice as much as me.'

'You're not implying privilege, are you?'

She shook her head and said, 'Not really. Yours is not a name to conjure with, as I found out the hard way.'

'Ah. Trying some conjuring, were we? Well, you'll be pleased to see just how impartial and incorruptible we are,' said Pascoe. 'Which means you'll have to take a blood test.'

'What?'

'That's the procedure. You wouldn't want us to vary the procedure, would you?'

'Peter, don't muck about. They've got Colin somewhere in this kremlin and they're trying to pin a murder on him. Who the hell's bothered about breathalyser tests?'

'Ellie,' said Pascoe, very quiet and controlled. 'Farr isn't here. He's been taken to hospital for a check-up. He will be well taken care of. Your job now is to take care of yourself. It would be well, for instance, to establish that you were not indulging in some kind of mobile drunken orgy when apprehended.'

'Apprehended? You make it sound like there was a car chase like in one of those awful cop films you love watching.'

'That is just how it may sound unless we are careful,' said Pascoe wearily. 'Look, the doctor should be here soon to take the sample. Don't be too impatient. Every minute gets you nearer legality. Then you'll have to make a statement.'

'Statement?'

'Yes. You're a possible witness in a murder case, remember?'

'Witness of what, for God's sake?'

'I don't know,' said Pascoe. 'I wasn't there. I'll fix up for someone to come and help with the statement. No, I don't mean write it, just the lay-out and to witness your signature.'

'Can't *you* do that?'

'Not a good idea. I've no standing here, thank God. Also I'll give Wieldy a ring and make sure our daughter isn't holding him hostage.'

'Oh God. I'd forgotten Rosie,' she said in alarm. 'You left her with Wield?'

'What did you want me to do? Bring her here?'

'No. Of course not. I'm sorry. I'm sure he'll be fine.'

There was a knock at the door and a tired-looking man with a doctor's bag came in.

'Mrs Pascoe?'

'That's her,' said Pascoe, 'I think.'

He went out and wandered around till he found an empty office with a telephone. He sat down and rang his home number. There was a heart-chilling delay before the call was answered.

'Hello?' said a gruff voice eventually.

'Wieldy?'

'Who else? Sorry if I took a long time. I was outside.'

'Don't tell me. Looking for a kitten up a tree?'

A few days ago a neighbour's kitten had got stuck up a tree in the Pascoe's garden. Rosie had heard it crying and had been delighted when Pascoe rescued it and brought it into the house. Her delight, however, had turned to anger and grief when the neighbours had gratefully claimed it. Clearly determined that the next one was going to be hers, she now heard kittens crying in every gust of wind.

'You should have warned me,' said Wield.

'If I'd warned you about everything, I'd not have left yet. Cats apart, is everything all right?'

'Grand, thanks. And you?'

'It's getting sorted. I'll tell you about it when we get back, which I hope won't be too long. Meanwhile make yourself at home, and if you get knackered waiting, don't hesitate to bed down in the spare room.'

'Will do.'

'And thanks, Wieldy. Cheers.'

'Hello. Who're you?'

A spotty-faced young man was standing in the doorway, uncertain whether to be aggressive or not. Pascoe made up his mind for him by flashing his warrant card and learning in return that this was Detective-Constable Collaboy.

'Just the man,' said Pascoe. 'My wife's along the corridor writing a statement. She's a witness in the Satterthwaite case. When she's finished, she'll need someone to go through it with her and then witness her signature. Could you see to that?'

The young man agreed without enthusiasm. Perhaps Ellie's reputation had already spread. And if it hadn't, it was soon going to, Pascoe thought with a sinking heart as he led Collaboy into the room where he'd left Ellie, and found it empty. As they'd walked along the corridor, his ear had caught and dismissed as none of his business a distant hubbub of upraised voices. But somehow deep in his small intestine he had known it was his business all along.

He ran lightly down the stairs. The noise grew louder as he approached the station desk area and when he pushed open the door, he saw that his small intestine was blessed with the same power of divination as Dalziel's piles.

Pressing round the desk, behind which stood Sergeant Swift, was a crowd of people who were thinking seriously of becoming a mob. Prominent, almost pre-eminent, among them was Ellie. Pascoe stood and watched her for a moment. She always flung herself wholeheartedly into debate. Her hands reinforced her arguments as clearly as sign language to a deaf man. He watched them as they stabbed emphatic fingers at Swift, cut through his denials with scything sweeps, clutched at her bosom in righteous indignation, fluttered to her flaming cheeks in shock, cupped her ears in disbelief. She was beautiful and he loved her and he would not have her change one iota, except that maybe at this moment it would be nice if she were sitting at home, dandling Rosie on her knee, while his slippers warmed before the fire.

Thrusting such recidivist thoughts from his mind, he advanced to join the merry throng. Central to it was a woman in her early forties, thin, pale, a pretty face, but her eyes deep shadowed by worry or illness or both. This, he quickly inferred, was Colin Farr's mother. Supporting her, metaphorically, though his hand did rest comfortingly on her shoulder, was a long skinny man, angular of limb and body, with a narrow anxious face. Behind them crowded a chorus of Burrthorpians of both sexes. It seemed that Mrs Farr was claiming a mother's right, potent in lore if not in law, to see her son. Ellie had clearly joined in the debate, and the locals, though by no means tyros in the art of simple abuse, had quickly acknowledged a virtuoso and settled back to enjoy the performance. Pascoe listened for a while and though he too could not but admire the force and the rationality of his wife's arguments, he felt that an impartial judge would finally have to award the sergeant the laurels for his patient repetition.

'Ellie,' Pascoe interposed finally. 'He's not here. I told you before. Listen to what the sergeant says. *He's not here.* He's gone to the hospital.'

It was clear that Ellie, having till now concentrated all her rhetoric on police mendacity, was quite prepared to switch in mid-trope to police brutality. Pascoe cut her short by addressing himself politely to the woman. 'Mrs Farr? I think you'll find your son has been taken to the County Hospital. There's nothing to worry about. It's quite normal in these matters.'

'Who're you?' demanded the thin man with an ill-fitting attempt at aggressiveness.

'Detective-Inspector Pascoe, and you sir are . . . ?'

'Downey. Arthur Downey. I'm a friend of May's, Mrs Farr's.'

'Pascoe?' said the woman. 'Any relation to her?'

Ellie said quickly, 'This is my husband. He's from Mid-Yorks, nothing to do with this case.'

144

'Cock-a-doodle-doo,' said Pascoe, *sotto voce.*

'Does our Colin know about him?' asked Mrs Farr.

Ellie glanced quickly at Pascoe.

'No,' she said. 'It never came up.'

'Cock-a-doodle-doo,' murmured Pascoe.

'It came up when you came round for tea,' said Mrs Farr scornfully. 'I remember asking you what your man did.'

'Cock-a-doodle-doo,' crowed Pascoe for the third time but his heart was no longer in the joke. Ellie had made no mention of going home to tea. Dear God, it sounded like an old-fashioned courtship.

Ellie's demotion from rabble-rouser to police nark was immediate and absolute. She made no effort to resist as Pascoe drew her aside, only saying, 'Thanks a million.'

'For the truth? Think nothing of it. Which should be easy. As you clearly do. Now let's concentrate on getting away from here. You've given a sample?'

'Yes. And I've got my own in case one of these bastards decides to slip some gin in it.'

'A wise precaution. That just leaves your statement. This is Detective-Constable Collaboy who has kindly volunteered to assist you in this business. Oh, by the way, since you ask, Rosie's well. Wieldy on the other hand has been introduced to the joys of phantom kitten rescuing.'

It was perhaps a low blow but it worked.

'Oh shit,' said Ellie and went off meekly with a bemused Collaboy.

Pascoe went in search of the small canteen in the basement. Here he sat and drank a cup of coffee that was so awful in every particular that he bought another just to confirm it was no flash in the pan. Then he went up to the desk where all was now peaceful.

'Quieter now, Sergeant,' he said.

'In here mebbe,' said Swift. 'But they'll be out there waiting.'

'You're not really expecting trouble, are you?' said Pascoe.

The man shrugged.

'You weren't here during the Strike, sir. Ever see that

145

film, *Zulu*? Well, that's what it were like in here that night we had the bother. Except that in the film the redcoats stood their ground. We had more sense. We ran! Since that night, I've been ready for anything. A mob's like a dog. Once it's bitten, it can always do it again.'

'Good Lord,' said Pascoe, impressed. He went to the door and peeped out, feeling more like Wayne in *Rio Bravo* than Caine in *Zulu*.

'No one out there at the moment,' he said.

'No one to be *seen*,' said the sergeant.

Pascoe closed the door.

'I'll just see how my wife's statement's coming along,' he said.

He went towards the stairs. Behind his back, the sergeant smiled faintly, then became serious as the door opened and Chief Inspector Wishart came in, looking surprisingly happy for a man who'd just been down a mine to investigate a murder he didn't want.

'Inspector Pascoe!' he called to Pascoe's disappearing back.

Pascoe turned and viewed the Scot's approach with surprise.

'When you say you're not going to be long, you mean, it don't you?'

'I told you, just a quick look. But I really wanted to get back before you left, Peter,' said Wishart putting his arm round Pascoe's shoulders and ushering him up the stairs. 'A funny thing's happened. We were on this wee train, the paddy they call it, and I must have been looking a bit uneasy because the pit manager who was with me said, 'Don't let it worry you. Just think that up there only a few hundred yards at most is Little Hayton.' Well, that rang a bell. There's a nice pub there, does lovely meals. I went there once last time I was in this neck of the woods. But then it struck me. Little Hayton's over the line. It's not South at all, it's in Mid-Yorks. So when we got to the spot they found Satterthwaite, I said, 'What's up there now?' And he worked it out on this map he's got of the workings.'

'Where's all this getting us?' asked Pascoe uneasily.

146

'A long way from here,' said Wishart gleefully. 'Peter, a crime belongs to the Force whose patch it's found on, right? Well, this chap Satterthwaite: even allowing for a large margin of error and the fact that he was found under a couple of thousand feet of earth, it is incontrovertibly Mid-Yorkshire earth he was found under. Peter, I honestly believe this may turn out to be your body after all!'

CHAPTER 9

Dan Trimble, Chief Constable of Mid-Yorkshire, was a small man with a sharp face and prominent ears. He was still very new in the job. His predecessor, Tommy Winter, had tended to let things slide in his final phase, preferring to deal with trouble by devolution and absence. Trimble, by contrast, preferred to meet problems face to face, and one of them was facing him now.

'I reckon it's like mineral rights,' declared Dalziel.

'I'm sorry?'

'The bloody coal doesn't belong to the farmer whose field's up above, does it? It belongs to them as mines it, which in this case is the Coal Board as represented by Burrthorpe Main, which is South's baby.'

'A body is not coal,' said Trimble.

'Tin.'

'I'm sorry?'

'You'd be more used to tin, sir, coming from Cornwall,' said Dalziel with the benevolent beam of a man willing to make allowances.

In fact Dalziel quite approved of Trimble whom he'd backed very profitably in the selection stakes. But neither professional approval nor personal profit could be allowed to obscure basic issues such as who ran what in Mid-Yorks. He knew he couldn't win this present argument but he also believed there was nowt like a few teeth marks in the ankle to make a postman tread carefully next time he came bearing bad news.

147

'We've got to learn to bow gracefully to the inevitable, Andy,' Trimble said.

Aye, but you've not so far to bow as me, thought Dalziel with the amiable scorn of the large for the small. That he didn't say it out loud was a measure of his relative respect for the man.

'And this is what's been decided,' continued Trimble. 'The investigation of Harold Satterthwaite's death will be a joint operation. It makes sense even if there hadn't been this absurd complication of whose body it really is. It makes sense because South's Head of CID is currently on special assignment in Ulster and Chief Inspector Wishart is a little junior for what looks like a potentially troublesome case; it makes sense because we've already become involved to some extent; and in the opinion of some of the policy makers, it makes sense to provide a buffer between a highly sensitive community and a local force they haven't yet re-learned to trust.'

'So we're a buffer now?'

'Well, you certainly have the build for it, Andy,' smiled the Chief Constable, running his gaze up the CID man's mountainous frame. Supposedly, one of the privileges of rank was not having to worry about what you said, but when Trimble peaked at Dalziel's face, he saw his remark registered there like a price in a till.

'I'm not altogether convinced of all these arguments myself, Andy,' he went on hastily. 'But I am convinced of the overall usefulness of a joint approach. I hardly need tell you that this involves two basic principles. One is to solve the crime. The other is to make sure we get our share of the credit. OK?'

'Aye,' grunted Dalziel without enthusiasm. 'One more thing, sir: I understand there's a promotion meeting later today. My lad, Pascoe: what's holding up his promotion to CI? There's buggers I'd not trust to come in out of the rain leapfrogging ahead of him.'

'Rain is the favoured environment of frogs,' said Trimble mildly.

'You what?'

'Nothing. Andy, you must know that promotion is not in my gift. Mine is merely one voice among many, and as a comparatively new off-comer, it's not even a particularly strong voice. But if there's any special case you wish me to advance at the meeting . . .'

'Aye, there is. Mebbe you can pass this on to the many,' said Dalziel.

A quarter of an hour later, on his way to his office, he met Wield.

''Morning,' he grunted. 'You look bloody rough.'

'I had a disturbed night, sir.'

'Oh aye. Anything I ought not to know about?'

From a lesser man there might have been a hint of sexual innuendo. From Dalziel the signal flashed like the lamp on a police car.

'I was looking after Mr Pascoe's kiddie.'

'You'll know all about this Burrthorpe business, then. Well, it's our business too, as from now. Come on. Let's get the ground cleared, then mebbe we can make a start.'

Dalziel's approach to ground-clearing made more use of the bulldozer than the hoe. He rang Burrthorpe, asked for Wishart, requested a progress report, listened yawningly for thirty seconds, then said, 'In other words, nowt? What's the matter with this lad, Farr? It'd save me a drive down there if you could charge him in the next couple of hours.'

'There's nothing concrete to tie him in,' said Wishart. 'We haven't found the weapon. And no one in Burrthorpe's saying anything, at least not to us.'

'What about his clothes?'

'He changed and showered before he left the pit, so we went to collect his pit-black, that's the gear he wears to work in. Only it wasn't there.'

'Sod me. There you are! What do you buggers in South want? Doves and a voice from a cloud? Find it and you've likely got the sod!'

'We're looking. The gateman remembers him going out on his bike, but reckons he wasn't carrying anything like a bundle of clothes and a pair of boots, so we're concentrating on the yard itself. I think our best bet could be an admission when Farr's fit enough to talk. The hospital'll be checking him over shortly.'

'Oh aye! In that case, I'd best come down myself. When? Oh, any time, lad. Any time at all.'

He put down the phone, grinned at Wield and said, 'That'll be something for 'em to look forward to. Now, Wieldy, what went off last night?'

'I think you ought to ask Mr Pascoe that, sir,' said Wield.

'All right. If the bugger's got in yet.' He picked up the internal phone, pressed a couple of buttons, and said, 'Peter! You've never got out of bed? See if you can manage to stagger up here. Wieldy thinks there's one or two things I should ask you about last night.'

He banged the receiver down and glared at the sergeant as if daring an objection. But Wield's mouth stayed shut and his face remained as unreadable as the weathered inscription on a tombstone.

Pascoe entered without knocking.

Dalziel said, 'You look worse than he does and he's got a head start. I get landed with someone else's case on someone else's patch, and I'm supposed to be helped by the living dead! Questions, Peter. Your missus, what's Farr to her?'

'A student.'

'And her to him?'

'A lecturer.'

'Oh aye? Me, I was never at college, so you tell me, Peter. Did you ring up a lot of your lecturers when you got pissed and fell off your bike?'

'No. But this is different. A different kind of course, a different relationship. These are mature students, the course is developmental rather than academic.'

'Not much mature about this lad, Farr, from the sound of him,' growled Dalziel. 'How'd you feel when Ellie shot off to pick him up?'

Pascoe rubbed his thin features with his hand, like a man who has just walked through a cobweb.

'Why are you asking these questions?' he asked.

'Just so I'll know whether I can use you on this case or not,' said Dalziel. 'Can I?'

Pascoe said softly, 'The reason I was late this morning was I took Ellie's own blood sample to the hospital to be tested. I'm happy to say it came out well below the limit. That, as far as I'm aware, disposes of the only possible objection to me assisting on the case.'

'That's all right, then,' said Dalziel genially. 'Why'd you and the sergeant not say that to start with and save us all this idle chatter? Right, Peter, I want you to get hold of Boyle and Watmough. I recall asking you to have a word with Boyle earlier in the week, but I suppose you've done bugger-all, as usual.'

'He's never in. But why do you want me to see Mr Watmough?'

'Because he claims in the *Challenger* that there are people in Burrthorpe who know exactly what happened to Tracey Pedley *and* to her killer. One of them's quoted as saying, "We never trusted the law much here in Burrthorpe, not even before the Strike. What's a child killer get these days? A few years inside with good grub and colour telly, then he promises to behave and they turn him loose till next time! No, it's best if you take care of your own, the good and the bad. We learned that a long time since." I want to know who, if anyone, said anything remotely like that. I want to know who's been hinting all this time that Colin Farr's father did that poor lassie in, and I want to know in particular if the name of Harold Satterthwaite comes up in connection with this or any other rumour. Oh, and you might ask Mr Watmough politely if he could let us have sight of any personal notes he may have made relating to the disappearance.'

Pascoe knew he should never be surprised by Dalziel, but he constantly was. Of course, he might already have had a long chat with Wishart and been thoroughly briefed on Farr's background. But it was more likely, he told himself bitterly, that the fat bastard had tapes of all his phones conversations with Wishart.

But even that didn't explain the full extent of Dalziel's apparent knowledge.

He said, 'I don't recall reading anything like that in Mr Watmough's article last Sunday, sir. He hinted he was going to prove it probably couldn't have been Pickford who abducted Tracey Pedley. And he mentioned a rumour in Burrthorpe that the killer was local and had himself committed suicide. But all this stuff about local vigilantes, where does that come from?'

'Next Sunday's piece, lad,' said Dalziel softly.

'*Next* Sunday . . . ?'

'You didn't think I was going to sit on my arse while that long streak of owl-shit smeared my name and do nowt, did you?' said Dalziel, his face set in a mask of malevolence that made Wield look like a matinee idol. 'Forewarned is forearmed. But I didn't reckon on the Good Lord dropping him quite so plumb into my lap.'

'You think the Good Lord killed Harold Satterthwaite then, sir?'

Dalziel regarded Pascoe for a moment, then decided to accept this as a joke rather than a reproach and let out a snort of laughter.

'Mysterious ways, right enough!' he said. 'Mysterious bloody ways. Me and God both!'

Pascoe didn't push any further. In fact, there was nowhere to push. Whatever Dalziel's personal motives, interviewing Watmough was a necessary step.

He said, 'One thing, it may be a bit hard not to let on that I've got advance knowledge of next Sunday's article.'

'No, it won't,' said Dalziel. 'Because you haven't! You don't think Ogilby's lawyers are going to let him print a word of this once they hear what went off last night? No, before he's through, he'll be down to reminiscing about his exciting days in traffic. Where they're always looking for lively ex-CID men. So let's start acting like real detectives, eh?'

Pascoe smiled wanly and left. Behind him Dalziel and Wield exchanged glances which to the casual eye might have looked like a freeze-frame from *Frankenstein Meets Godzilla* but in which they registered their mutual concern.

'He'll be all right,' said Dalziel. 'Wieldy, I want Farr's movements after he left the pit. Best to back-track him from that phone box. Check where they found his bike, then get your legs across that phallic symbol of yours and track him back to Burrthorpe.'

'Yes, sir. But won't Mr Wishart . . .'

'Mr Wishart reckons Farr's going to tell him all. Me, I reckon he's over-optimistic. Farr talks body-language to cops, I gather. He throws them through plate-glass windows. I want to sort this one out proper, for all our sakes. Especially for . . . Just get to it, Wieldy!'

And back in his own office Pascoe was trying to ring Ellie as he had done from the hospital lab, as soon as he got the news about her blood sample. Now as then the phone rang and rang.

He went to see ex-DCC Watmough.

CHAPTER 10

Colin Farr woke from a dream-haunted sleep in which he ran in terror down the tailgate pursued by a runaway tram loaded with a tangle of naked limbs. Half awake, for a moment the image of those twisted arms and legs became erotic instead of necrotic and he deliberately pushed himself away from terror towards a fantasy in which he shared his bed with Stella Mycroft and Ellie Pascoe.

Ellie. Last night came back, not suddenly because in fact it had never been far from his consciousness either waking or sleeping, but with the sad insistence of dawn to a still weary traveller.

He was in trouble. Cautiously he moved to check whether he was also in pain. There was certainly the echo of pain in various parts of his body, but the only pang positive enough to be worth wincing over was at the back of his head. He raised his hand to rub it.

'Awake, are you? You must be the only bugger in this place that's not been awake for hours save them as snuffed it during night.'

The speaker was a police constable slouched in an armchair by the hospital bed. He yawned widely, showing well-filled teeth.

'Me, I'd just nodded off when they started beating bedpans in my ear. Hungry? You've missed breakfast but as it's near on nine o'clock, they'll likely have got lunch on the go.'

'Cup of tea'd be nice,' said Farr. 'What are you doing here?'

'Guarding you,' said the constable, rising and heading for the door.

'What from?'

The man laughed. He was middle-aged, well-built, but with muscles running to flab. He had the red face of a jolly monk.

'What from! That's good. What from!' He opened the door and called, 'Sister, he's awake. Tell doctor, will you? And is there any chance of a cup of tea? Better still, two cups. Thanks, love.'

He returned to the bedside.

'We'll see about breakfast after the quack's checked you over,' he said.

'I'm not hungry,' said Farr.

A nurse came in, shook a thermometer and put it in Farr's mouth. While it was still there, a white-coated Asian doctor appeared and examined the chart at the foot of the bed. The nurse removed the thermometer and showed it to the doctor who gave her the chart to make an entry, then approached Farr and shone a pencil light into his eyes.

'Any pain?' he asked.

'Bit of a headache.'

'You shouldn't drink so much. Follow my finger with your eyes. Good.'

He pulled back the sheet and probed and prodded at shoulders, chest and legs.

'India rubber and iron by the feel of you,' he said.

154

'Does that mean he can be shifted?' said the constable hopefully.

'Shifted? Why?'

'We're keen to question him.'

'I'm keen to keep him alive. You'll have to ask your questions here under strict medical supervision. Liquid diet, Nurse. And that doesn't mean more beer, Mr Farr. I'll see you later.'

'Bloody foreigner,' said the constable. 'Still thinks we use rubber truncheons. Nurse, can I have the phone?'

The nurse wheeled in a mobile phone and the policeman rang Burrthorpe and reported the situation.

'Anyone been asking after me?' said Farr to the nurse.

'Your mam came up in the night and saw you sleeping. I think she's been on the phone this morning, but I don't know about anyone else.'

The constable finished his conversation and replaced the receiver.

'Can I use that?' asked Farr.

'No way, sunshine. Who do you want to ring, BUPA?'

'What about visitors? Can I have visitors?'

Now the policeman laughed.

'You'll have visitors all right,' he said. 'But don't expect many grapes.'

The first visitor was Detective Chief Inspector Alex Wishart. Though grapeless, he at least started conventionally, inquiring after Farr's health. But when the young man replied equally conventionally that he was all right, Wishart moved smoothly into his proper role, saying, 'Fit enough to answer a few questions, then?'

In the corner Detective-Constable Collaboy was taking notes. The uniformed constable whom Wishart addressed as Vessey had been dispatched to enjoy a cup of tea. It would be easy lying here in a warm comfortable bed listening to this soft-spoken courteous Scot to forget what was going on.

'So you felt unwell and you told Neil Wardle you were going to leave. And he said . . . ?'

'He told me to be sure to let Satterthwaite know.'

155

'Why Satterthwaite?'

'He were the deputy in charge of that section.'

'Fair enough. And was that all that Wardle said to you?'

'I can't recall owt else.'

'Didn't he say something like, "And be careful, Col. No bother, no matter what he says"?'

Farr put his hand to his head and said slowly, 'He said, "If the bugger says anything, tell him you don't want any bother and will he take it up with the Union."'

'You see. You remember very precisely when you try.'

'More than you do from the sound of it,' said Farr.

'Why did Mr Wardle think it necessary to make this warning?' asked Wishart.

'Deputies don't like men going off in the middle of shift,' said Farr.

'Is that all?'

'No, but it's an important part of it and I'd like to be sure your girl's got it down.'

Collaboy looked up angrily and Wishart said, 'It's all right, Constable. Miners' humour. The trick is not to bite, isn't that so, Mr Farr?'

'The trick is knowing when it's meant,' said Farr.

'I see. To resume: accepting that there might be an irritated reaction from a deputy as part of a general principle, what particular reaction or interaction between you and Satterthwaite was Wardle warning you against?'

'Am I supposed to understand all that?' mocked Farr. 'And me just a poor working lad.'

'Me too,' smiled Wishart. 'Shall we both play stupid or would you rather develop the role alone?'

Farr nodded, not in response but at some judgement of his own.

'Harold Satterthwaite didn't like me and I didn't like him,' he said. 'There was likely to be trouble most times we met. Just verbal, though it had come close to blows odd times. That's what Neil were getting at.'

'Any particular reasons for this friction?'

'Mebbe, but I think they were almost as much effect as

cause. When you got down to it, we just naturally hated each other's guts.'

'That's very frank of you, Mr Farr.'

'No point in lying about what every big mouth in Burrthorpe knows. But it doesn't matter anyway as I never saw the sod on my way outbye.'

'Did you look for him?'

'Not very hard. I just wanted to get out.'

'Did you ask anyone if they'd seen him?'

Farr smiled. He looked not much older than seventeen when he smiled, thought Wishart. As beautiful and as dangerous as a fallen angel. My God, am I on the turn? he mocked himself. But his professional mind was thinking of Ellie Pascoe and the effort her husband had put in to keeping up an appearance of simple domestic upset rather than personal crisis. It wasn't yet clear to Wishart how much Pascoe was still fooling himself.

'I think you know I did,' Farr answered. 'I ran into another deputy and told him I were going off shift and asked him to tell Satterthwaite.'

'This was Mr Mycroft?'

'That's right. And before you ask, I don't get on very well with him either.'

'You seem to have a problem with authority, Mr Farr.'

'No problem,' said the young man with easy assurance.

'Mr Mycroft says he advised that you ought to see Mr Satterthwaite personally.'

Farr shrugged and winced.

'I can't have been listening,' he said. 'I was in a hurry to get out. I just got on the paddy and didn't stop till I was back on the bank.'

'Your ringer,' said Wishart. 'That's what they call it, isn't it? Your working tool. Did you take that with you when you left Wardle and your other workmates?'

'I dare say so. Or mebbe not. Someone else would need it, wouldn't they?'

'I assume so. Wardle and the other man, Dickinson I think it is, seemed uncertain, though on the whole they favoured seeing you leave empty-handed.'

157

'It's funny how people find it hard to remember, you must find that all the time,' said Farr.

'Too true. You showered on the way out, I suppose.'

'Bloody right! And it were a bloody sight hotter than it normally is at proper knock-off time.'

'And you'd normally leave your pit-black in the dirty lockers?'

'I'd hardly take it with me, would I?' said Farr but his scornful assertiveness faded even as he spoke. 'Hold on. You mean it's not there? And you think I hid it in case there were traces of blood or anything on it?'

Now it was Wishart's turn to smile.

'That's very sharp for a poor working lad,' he said. 'Why didn't you go home?'

'What?'

'You were ill. Why not go home and seek rest, relief, medical advice?'

'The fresh air made me feel better. I didn't want to worry my mam by getting back early. I thought I'd just go for a ride around till it were my normal time for getting back.'

'But you were already well past that when you rang Mrs Pascoe.'

'Look, she's got nowt to do with any of this.'

'I don't suppose she has. Why did you ring her in particular?'

'I don't know. I suppose I just wanted to talk to someone who had nowt to do with Burrthorpe or the pit.'

'And she came to mind first?'

'First and last,' said Farr savagely. 'All the other buggers I know on the outside are likely tossing around in the Bay of Biscay. And I'd not have rung 'em anyway.'

'Why?'

Farr answered hesitantly, as if dealing with a question of his own.

'I made some good marras but not for talking to, you understand. Oh, if I got into a fight or into bother with the pigs or if I were strapped for cash, they'd stick by me, no question. But sorting things out in your mind, that takes something . . . different.'

'Like Mrs Pascoe?'

'Aye. She might be a bit stuck up and a bit of a do-gooder, but she'd know what I was on about and be able to listen and not end up by saying another pint would put me right, or I ought to get active in the Union, or wasn't it time I found a nice girl and settled down and had a family?'

'So you rang her. Her husband answered, I believe.'

'Aye.'

'But you didn't ring off?'

'Eh?' Farr looked puzzled, then he laughed scornfully and said, 'I'm not her fancy man, if that's what you're thinking. Why the hell should I ring off?'

'Husbands can misunderstand things,' said Wishart, watching him closely. 'For all you knew, Mr Pascoe could have been a short-tempered heavyweight boxer.'

'Could have been. I doubt it, but. Women like her usually end up married to teachers, them kind of twats.'

'So you never talked about Mr Pascoe?'

'No. Why should we? Hey, he's not a heavyweight boxer, is he?'

Wishart smiled and shook his head. It had bothered him that Farr, possibly on the run after committing murder, should ring up the house of a police inspector and be unconcerned when a man answered the phone. But Ellie had obviously decided that her close links with the filth wouldn't create a climate of confidence in her class.

'What did you want to talk to Mrs Pascoe about?' he inquired.

'What?'

'You rang her because you wanted to talk to someone with a different outlook from your marras. That was what you said, wasn't it? All right. Talk about what?'

'That's my business,' retorted Farr.

'It could be mine,' said Wishart.

'How's that?'

'If you wanted to talk to her because you were confused about what to do after bashing Harold Satterthwaite over the head and dumping his body in the gob, that'd be my business, wouldn't you say?'

159

'Aye.'

'So?'

'So ask Ellie . . . Mrs Pascoe, if that's what I wanted to talk about, and when she says no, you'll see I'm right and it's none of your sodding business, won't you?'

Wishart regarded him shrewdly and said, 'I dare say the truth is what with the booze and that bang on your head, you can't really be sure yourself what you did talk about.'

It was a subtle bait. Amnesia must look a very tempting escape route from these persistent questions, but once taken it was damnably hard to follow.

Farr shook his head, winced and said obstinately, 'No, I don't forget things, not even them I'd like to forget.'

He sank down against his bank of pillows and his eyes closed. If his smile bore him back to boyhood, this weariness was more regressive still, turning him into a lost child. Wishart felt a sudden pang of conscience. The doctor had set a strict time limit on questioning of his patient and Wishart had assured him that at the first sign of fatigue, he would desist. But his professional instinct was to press on now while the defences were weak.

But before he could speak, there was a sound of voices outside and the door burst open. Wishart looked round guiltily, sure it was the doctor, come to accuse him of the third degree. Instead he saw two strangers, one male, middle-aged, balding, dressed in a creased blue suit and clutching a battered briefcase in nicotine-stained fingers. The other was female, in her thirties, with spiky red hair, dressed in an apple green jump suit, and carrying a glossy leather document case under her arm.

Wishart, suspecting Press, rose instantly and prepared to be outraged.

'Who the hell are you?' he demanded.

They both spoke at once and as neither seemed prepared to concede the primacy it was only the coincidence that they were both saying more or less the same thing that allowed Wishart to grasp at their thread.

'You're *both* his solicitor?' he said incredulously.

'Wakefield,' said the man. 'Neil Wardle asked me to come on behalf of the Union.'

'Pritchard,' said the woman. 'A friend of Mr Farr's was concerned that he might be unrepresented.'

Wishart felt like Solomon called to judgement. Perhaps he should offer the patient to be dissected. After all, they were in the right place for it. But before he could pronounce, a third figure appeared, like Jove in a masque, rising to mend mortal destinies. It was Dalziel, flushed and breathing hard after climbing the stairs to avoid the concentrated contagion of a hospital lift.

''Morning, Chief Inspector Wishart,' he said. 'What's this? A public meeting?'

During Wishart's explanation, it seemed to him that Dalziel's flush pulsated like a nuclear core as he looked at Pritchard. But there was nothing but sweet reason in his tone as he said, 'No problem, is there? The client chooses the lawyer, not the lawyer the client, Mr Farr, which of these legal eagles would you like to crap on you?'

Colin Farr, who had kept his eyes resolutely closed during all that had passed hitherto, recognized in Dalziel's voice that summons which cannot be denied.

He sat up, regarded those present with unwelcoming eyes, and said, 'None of 'em. You can all fuck off. And that includes you, Porky!'

CHAPTER 11

In the hospital car park Adrienne Pritchard climbed into an ancient green Mini.

'What happened?' demanded Ellie. 'You've been gone hardly any time.'

Laconically the solicitor told her tale. When she got to the bit when Colin Farr called Dalziel *Porky*, they both laughed.

'I'm sorry you've wasted your time,' said Ellie. 'I shouldn't have dragged you out here.'

'You did rather give the impression your boy was being held in a dungeon with no access to legal aid, whereas . . . well, never mind. He looked fine, by the way.'

'Did he?'

'Yes, I could see you were dying to ask but afraid of giving yourself away. A little pale with interesting shadows under the eyes. Very Romantic poetish. I could see the attraction.'

'Adi, there is nothing going on!'

'I'll see you in court,' said the other disbelievingly, opening the car door and struggling out over the coils of unreconstructed seat-belt. 'Ellie, why don't you get a decent car? Two minutes in this heap and your husband would be on his way to the car showroom—by taxi!'

'Are you going back to town?' asked Ellie.

'You've guessed. There's nothing for me here. If young Lord Byron up there does decide he needs a lawyer, he'll be all right with that shark the Union sent along. Are you heading back too? I'll drive along behind you if you like, to pick up the pieces.'

'No, thanks, I've got a couple of things I want to do here.'

'By yourself? Well, as long as you don't frighten the horses. See you.'

Ellie watched Adrienne get into her shiny red sports car and roar away.

'At least mine's British,' she muttered turning the ignition key to produce a pneumonic wheeze. Before she could try again, a fist like a fender rapped against the passenger window which was almost immediately filled by a face like a flitch.

'I thought it were you,' said Dalziel with delighted surprise, opening the door and climbing in. 'Just visiting, I hope? A rich relative, is it?'

'Don't muck around, Andy,' said Ellie irritably. 'You know it was me that got Adi Pritchard to visit Colin Farr. So Peter was right when he said you lot might get landed with this case.'

'Yes. I've got him working on it himself. But don't worry. He's a long way away from here.'

He tapped his nose in a gesture both salacious and con-

162

spiratorial. Ellie was not certain which element most offended her, but what she *was* sure of was that in-fighting with Dalziel was like trying to tickle a grizzly to death. The only valid approach was with a flame-thrower from fifty yards.

She said, 'I hope you get the man who killed Mr Satterthwaite very soon. Now, if you'll excuse me.'

He didn't move but said, 'Reckon we've got him already. Your friend, Farr. Bird in the hand, like they say.'

'What evidence do you have?' she asked angrily.

He smiled and said softly, 'I didn't say we'd got any evidence yet. Just that we've got *him*. Evidence'll turn up. Weapon. Bloodstained clothes. Something he did or said on his way out of the mine. Or later when he got himself kaylied and came off his bike. Said nothing significant to you, did he?'

'You've read my statement,' evaded Ellie.

'Aye, I've read it,' said Dalziel. 'Funny, that, I thought. Here they were, sitting in a car—it'd be this car, would it? very cosy—and neither of 'em said owt to the other. Some people might take that the wrong way, of course.'

'You dirty-minded old sod,' said Ellie, her resolve not to be provoked bending as easily as it usually did.

He looked at her in amazed indignation, and said, 'Nay, Ellie. You've got me wrong. I never meant owt like that. All I was trying to say was, if you don't fill in the detail of what you and him did say, some folk might think you were trying to cover up for him. Now I know how easy it is to think things aren't worth putting down in a statement, all the ordinary trivial chat. "Nice weather we're having, have you seen the price of eggs in the market? That's a lovely dress you're wearing, my sister in London had one just like that four or five years ago." The sort of thing you and your mates pass the time of day with over your morning coffee.'

I'll kill him! thought Ellie wildly.

Steadying her voice she said, 'No, we didn't talk about the price of eggs or the dress he was wearing.'

'No? Then what did you talk about?' asked Dalziel. 'No, don't answer me now. Have a good think about it and then you can broaden out your statement when you call in at the local station later on.'

'At the station?'

'Aye. That was why you drove all the way down here, wasn't it? To modify your statement and mebbe check up on the result of your blood test.'

Her expression showed him that she had forgotten all about the test and also that Pascoe hadn't been in touch with her since he called at the lab that morning. Probably because she had already left to winkle out Pritchard. Possibly because he felt in the mood to let her sweat a little longer. Well, it was none of his business to interfere between man and wife. Yet.

He said, 'Aye. Could be serious that, Ellie. Lose your licence, big fine. They're really cracking down. So I'll see you later likely. Cheers now.'

He opened the door and unwedged himself from the low seat. As he got out, Ellie saw with anticipatory delight that the coil of seat-belt had wrapped itself round his ankles.

Dalziel stood upright, stretched, raised a huge arm in farewell, and walked away. Around his legs the belt tightened, tautened, and snapped, as without a stumble or a hesitation he strode towards the hospital.

Disappointedly, Ellie turned the key again. The engine came to life with the reluctance of one who has gone happily to his long rest after a race well run. Adi was right, it was time she had a decent car, it was time she asserted herself in a hundred ways.

It was also time, she told herself with a return to humour as she nosed out of the car park, that the Women's Movement recognized that five minutes with Andy Dalziel was worth a month's budget of professional propaganda.

Fifteen minutes later without any conscious debate or decision she found herself parking round the corner from the terraced house in which May Farr lived with her son.

She felt herself observed as she approached the front door and not just by the police car parked further along Clay Street. Burrthorpe must be abuzz with what was going on. They might close ranks against outsiders but within the

164

tribe there would be no shortage of slanderous speculation, prurient analysis and malicious gossip.

The door opened before she could knock.

'Come in,' said May Farr, 'before the whole street clocks you.'

She led the way into the little front room. Ellie had a sense of someone else in the house, probably in the kitchen.

'Right,' said the woman after checking that the net curtains were draped for maximum obfuscation. 'What do you want?'

She stood facing Ellie, her arms folded under her breast in the classic working-class pose of female aggression.

Ellie said, 'I was up at the hospital and I thought I'd come and see you.'

'Did you see Colin?'

'No, but I gather he's all right, physically I mean.'

'You didn't see him? I'd've thought they'd've let *you* in.'

'Because my husband's a policeman?'

'You said it.'

'Mrs Farr, you'd be surprised how few privileges being married to a copper brings you. Don't get me wrong. I'm not complaining. Nor am I apologizing for Peter. It's his job. It's what he is. And if he did something else, it'd be a loss to the police and the public alike. A loss to people like you and Colin, Mrs Farr.'

'And what are people like me and Colin like?' asked the woman with undiminished aggression.

'In trouble,' said Ellie gently.

May Farr digested this.

'Sit down,' she said finally. 'We'll have a cup of tea. There's some massed.'

Ellie would have preferred coffee or better still a stiff scotch, but she knew that the offer of tea was like salt in a Bedouin's tent. Also it gave May an excuse to go into the kitchen and update whoever it was she had in there.

The tea appeared in the same delicate china cups that had been used on her previous visit. Conversation waited till the ceremony of milk, sugar and tasting was complete.

'Right, Mrs Pascoe,' said May Farr. 'I admire the way

you've stuck up for your man, but if you're not ashamed of him, why'd you lie about him when I asked you last time?'

'Because it didn't seem to matter then. I mean the truth would have mattered perhaps. It might have set you and Colin against me.'

'You think we all hate the police, do you?'

'A lot of you have had some cause, I think.'

'Is that what your man thinks too? No, forget I asked that. It's your business, married business. What I do want to know is why you're so keen to stick your neb into our business, Colin's and mine?'

'I didn't so much stick it in as have it rubbed in,' retorted Ellie, with whom a little humble pie went a long way. 'He rang me last night, asked me to help him. I didn't volunteer.'

'You didn't refuse either. You're not after Colin, are you, missus? He's not your what-do-they-call-it? bit of rough, is he?'

'I wouldn't call your son a bit of rough, Mrs Farr,' said Ellie steadily. 'I like him but I'm not after him. As for him, he could be after me but I'm not sure he likes me.'

'It was you he rang.'

'I don't know how surprising that was because I don't know who else he might have rung,' said Ellie. She was aware of the ambivalence and evasion at the heart of nearly all her answers, but her main concern was to keep things simple and straightforward as far as her own part in this drama went. Back home she might be Cressida, but here in the Greek camp she was just a walk-on part.

May Farr frowned, then nodded and said, 'You're right. Not many.'

She relaxed noticeably, perhaps because the odds on Ellie being a predatory middle-class nymphomaniac had lengthened.

'What's going to happen to him, Mrs Pascoe?' she asked suddenly. 'What have they got on him, can you tell me that? I rang the police station and they told me nowt, then I rang the hospital and they didn't tell me much more. So what's happening, Mrs Pascoe?'

166

Ellie was saved from reiterating her ignorance by a knock at the front door.

'Now who's that?' said Mrs Farr irritably without making any move to find out. But someone was moving. Ellie heard the door being opened, the sound of voices, then the sitting-room door was pushed ajar and a head appeared wearing what she had thought of last night as the expression of an anxious horse. She reached for the name. Downey.

'Sorry to interrupt, May, but it's Stella, Stella Mycroft, Stella Gibson as was.'

'I know who Stella Gibson married, Arthur,' said May Farr in a rather exasperated tone. 'What's she want?'

'I just wanted to find out how Colin was,' said Stella, pushing past Downey into the room and looking at Ellie with undisguised curiosity.

What she saw, Ellie did not care to speculate. Seeing ourselves as others see us might be a desideratum of general social philosophy but it didn't apply when the other in question was in her early twenties, with an exquisite sensuous figure, silver blonde hair and a face whose small features had a delicate beauty which not even a heavy hand with the make-up could disguise.

'Does Gavin know you're here?' asked Mrs Farr sharply.

The girl shrugged. Even that was a sensuous movement.

'I don't have to get permission to ask after an old friend,' she said. 'Any road, he'll be as keen to know what's going off as everyone else.'

'Oh, I don't doubt they're all taking a lively interest,' said the older woman bitterly. 'Well, they'll have to be disappointed, I know as little as they do and a damn sight less than they can make up!'

'Is he still in hospital?'

'Yes, but they say he's OK, thank God. Stella, they say your Gavin saw Colin on his way out of the pit. What's he say happened?'

'Nothing much,' said Stella. 'What's Arthur think? He was down there too?'

'Oh, Arthur,' said May as if Downey weren't there. 'He'd not say owt he thought might upset me. But I always got straight talk from you when you were going with our Colin. At least I thought I did.'

So that was it, thought Ellie. An old flame. Perhaps not wholly extinguished either. She examined her feelings, recognized jealousy, and realized with perhaps more concern how little surprised or dismayed she was by the recognition.

'Folk are saying that Col hated Harold's guts,' said Stella, watching Ellie though she addressed her words to May. 'They're saying that he's always had a wild streak and that it'd not surprise them if it turned out he'd put paid to the bastard like he threatened often enough. That's what they're saying.'

'I asked for it straight,' said May Farr with a humourless smile. 'Do these folk say why Colin should have hated Harold Satterthwaite?'

Stella Mycroft hesitated, then said, 'Them things some folk hinted about Colin's dad and the Pedley kid, Harold Satterthwaite were the worst of all, he really believed them.'

'Nay, Stella, no need to bring all that up,' protested Downey indignantly. 'Not now. Aren't things bad enough?'

'It's all right, Arthur,' said May Farr. 'No other reason you can think of, Stella?'

'What other reason would Col need?' said the younger woman. 'You should know best how he felt about his dad?'

It was like watching a No play, thought Ellie. You could sense the drama without really understanding it. Certainly there was little love lost between these women. Did the elder resent the younger for having thrown her son over? Or the younger blame the elder for making him unmarriable?

'Aye, I should,' said May Farr. 'I'll get you a cup of tea.'

'No, I mustn't stay,' began Stella, but the other woman was already out of the room. Arthur Downey looked reproachfully at Stella and said, 'Can't you watch what you're saying?' before he too left.

'Silly sod,' said Stella. 'Hangs around here like a toothless guard dog!'

'Are they . . . ?' said Ellie.

'He'd like to, I reckon, but he's not exactly action-man,

our Arthur. No, I reckon May would have to start anything if anything were going to start. One thing's certain: Arthur's not spent a night in this house since Billy died else the local CIA would have had it all on tape!'

'So Mr Downey lives by himself?'

'He lodges with his sister and her husband in the next street. He and Billy were big mates, at least Arthur used to tag along behind Billy like a dog. Then Arthur got made up to deputy. Well, that didn't help. They're funny about deputies, this lot, I should know. And not long after, Billy Farr had his accident and had to take a job on the bank. Arthur and him got back to being a bit closer after that maybe, but not much. Billy didn't seem to want to know, really. There was a lot of people reckoned he turned right unsociable after his accident but I always thought he were a lovely man. I was engaged to Col, and while he was away at sea, I used to come round here a lot and we'd look at Col's cards and work out where he was, and Billy used to make a great fuss of me. Me and little Tracey. I always reckoned he'd have liked a daughter of his own.'

'Tracey was the child who disappeared?'

'That's right. You'd know all about that. After that Billy really was unsociable. I don't think I got a kind word out of him from that day on. Nor her either. You'd have thought ... any road, I thought it'd be different when Col came back, and it was, or mebbe it was the same. We dragged on a bit, but it ended with me giving him his ring back. We were standing on the bridge over the mineral railway. A train went under and I remember he just dropped the ring over into a wagon full of coal. He were always half mad.'

That's my boy, thought Ellie. Ever the symbolist. But never my boy, nor this woman's either, though clearly she still felt some claim.

Another part of her mind had been trying to work out why Stella Mycroft was being so frank with a total stranger. Native Yorkshire tactics were usually to ferret out other people's business and keep quiet about your own. But two things dawned on her.

One was that Stella didn't need to be nosey because by

now the local CIA would have programmed everything they could find out about Mrs E. Pascoe into the central computer. The other was that this gratuitous stream of reminiscence was not aimed at bringing her into the life of Burrthorpe but excluding her from it. Look, Stella Mycroft was saying; see how much closer we can be to each other even in our hates and quarrels than you can ever hope to be even in your affections. See how my life has been entwined with Colin's long before you ever set your strange and stranger's eye upon him. Understand that all these odd things that go on in this village have everything to do even with the least important of us who live here and nothing at all to do with an incomer like yourself!

It was a formidable attack, no less destructive because it came from the flank, and probably from the hip. Stella hadn't come round to this house where she was clearly unwelcome to see her "rival" off. She'd come to find out about Colin.

Typically, Ellie counter-attacked.

'You got bored with waiting for Col to make up his mind, did you?'

'No,' said Stella, unperturbed. 'I'm a good waiter. But I'm not an Arthur Downey. I won't dance around and look ridiculous. I should have known when Col left in the first place how little I figured in his decisions. But I gave him the benefit and waited. Oh, I didn't languish but inside I was waiting. But when he finally came back and I realized that had nowt to do with me either, I said, Sod it! and six months later I married Gavin. Rebound? Mebbe. But you do rebound off a stone wall, don't you, Mrs Pascoe?'

'I see you know my name, Stella,' said Ellie in her best garden-party voice. She felt she was losing on points and needed a space to review tactics.

'Everyone round her knows your name and your husband's name and number too by now,' said Stella viciously, as if suddenly tired of this game. 'And most on 'em can't understand why you don't just bugger off out of it and leave us to look after our own affairs!'

'I'll go when I know whether or not Colin killed that

man,' said Ellie spiritedly. 'You've told me what "folk" are saying. What do *you* say?'

The answer she got was totally unexpected.

'Of course, he bloody killed him!' exploded Stella. 'You may not have known Colin long, but long enough surely to know that one day sooner or later he was bound to kill someone. It's there inside him, have you never felt it? Mebbe it's in his blood, I don't know. But he was bound to kill someone some day, and now it's happened and his only hope is that your man and the other pigs will be too thick to pin it on him. They got so used to fitting up lads who'd done nowt during the Strike, that mebbe they've forgotten how to deal with someone who's so obviously guilty!'

'How can you be so sure?' demanded Ellie. 'I thought you were supposed to be his friend.'

'That's right,' said Stella Mycroft, regarding her with an expression of mocking triumph. 'I'm his friend. And you run to your friends before you run to your teachers. It was me he rang up first last night, *me*! That's how I know he's guilty. Because he bloody well told me so!'

From the doorway there came a crash. Ellie turned. May Farr stood there, her face grey as morning, at her feet the shards of a china cup lying in a pool of amber tea.

CHAPTER 12

Neville Watmough looked drawn and strained, but it was when he greeted Pascoe like an old friend that the detective knew the man was in trouble.

'Peter, come in, how are you?' The use of his first name was a giveaway in itself. The ex-DCC had never felt able to go beyond the formal courtesy of 'Mr Pascoe' in office.

'Let's go into the study, shall we? What about a drink?'

Pascoe couldn't hold back a glance at the mantelshelf where the presentation clock showed it was only twenty to eleven.

'Too early?' laughed Watmough. 'Time has less significance when you're retired. Coffee, then?'

'No, thank you, sir,' said Pascoe, distrusting all this cosiness.

'Well, sit down anyway. How's everything back at the works? I must drop in sometime soon and have a chat before everyone forgets who I am.'

'I don't think there's much chance of that,' said Pascoe, only conscious of the sarcastic vibrations as he finished the sentence.

'I should explain,' he went on quickly, 'that I'm here on duty.'

'Not a social call, then?' said Watmough, not sounding very surprised.

'No, sir. The point is this. You probably heard on the news about this killing at Burrthorpe Main Colliery last night?'

'Yes. And that you had a man helping with inquiries.'

'That covers a multitude of possibilities as you know, sir. The thing is, there's a chance that there might be a tie-up here with the Tracey Pedley disappearance.'

'Yes, but that . . . ah.'

Watmough fell silent. It must be hard, after so long responding to any mention of Tracey Pedley with the confident assertion that she was almost certainly one of Donald Pickford's victims, to admit now that the case was still open. Even when you yourself were responsible for undermining your own theory. Or at least *publicly* responsible.

Pascoe said, 'Incidentally, sir, when did you realize that it was almost impossible for Pickford to have abducted the Pedley girl?'

Watmough said, 'Not while I was still in the Force, if that's what you're thinking. What are they saying down there? That when I realized Pickford actually had made his call that afternoon I hushed it up for fear of looking silly?'

'No, sir,' said Pascoe. 'No one would believe you'd ever shirk your duty.'

Watmough looked taken aback at this assurance.

'No, of course not. I'm glad to hear it. Look, are you sure

you won't have that drink? Sorry, you're on duty, aren't you? Well, I'm not any more, so if you don't mind . . .'

He went to a bureau and took out a bottle and a glass. It was scotch, Pascoe was interested to note, not the goat-piss sherry for which he was justly infamous. And he didn't have to remove the stopper.

He poured himself a modest measure and returned to his chair.

'No,' he said, 'it wasn't till I started on my articles that I realized that Pickford wouldn't have had the time to . . . no, that sounds as if I had a sudden inspiration, like Sherlock Holmes, doesn't it? It wasn't me at all. It was Monty Boyle who got on to it. He's very impressive in his own way. Very professional.'

'Very elusive,' said Pascoe. 'I've been trying to get hold of him for a couple of days. Of course, his office would cover for him if he didn't want to see me. But when I rang this morning I got the impression they genuinely didn't know where he was . . .'

He looked at Watmough hopefully.

'Sorry. Can't help. I haven't seen or heard from him since our last so-called creative session last week.'

'No? Tell me, sir, how does it work, this partnership? Boyle updates your stuff with his own research, then knocks it all into *Challenger* shape?'

'More or less,' said Watmough without enthusiasm. 'It was fun at first. Boyle and I got on well. I'd go over my notes with him, then we'd sit and have a drink and chat about old times. He had a tape-recorder so he wouldn't miss anything. He'd obviously done a lot of background research before ever I signed up with the *Challenger*. Almost as if they knew . . . never mind . . . but he was thorough. I'll give him that. A damn sight more thorough than your precious Sergeant Wield had been.'

He glared at Pascoe accusingly.

'He carried out his instructions to the letter,' said Pascoe carefully.

'Very loyal of you, Peter. There's a lot of loyalty in Mid-Yorks CID. Perhaps a bit too much on occasion.'

173

'And what occasion would that be, sir?'

'Nothing. I speak generally. Perhaps bitterly. I'm sorry. But when Boyle told me that Pickford had kept his appointment on the Avro Estate, I felt stupid. I'd been so definite about him being responsible for the Burrthorpe girl's disappearance. Boyle said it didn't matter. The Pickford case would still be presented as my personal triumph. But here we had yet another unsolved case and it was our duty to let the public know. I still wasn't happy. I said that new evidence should be handed over to the police at once. I saw Ogilby. He said the evidence would be handed over simultaneously with its publication in the *Challenger*. That was to be this coming Sunday.'

'Was to be?'

'Things may have changed with last night's news,' said Watmough.

Pascoe said, 'These allegations that there was some kind of vigilante group in Burrthorpe after the girl disappeared, how much truth is there in them?'

'I don't know. Who's making them?' said Watmough.

Pascoe was taken aback by this superficially disingenuous answer. Was Watmough trying to force from him an admission that he knew the content of the next article? If so, he could have it!

'You are, sir,' he said. 'In the *Challenger* next Sunday.'

For a second Watmough looked blank. Then he smiled wanly and said, 'This sounds like Dalziel.' And then all trace of the smile faded and he looked very old and tired.

'You must think me a very foolish man, Inspector, not to know what's appearing under my name in a Sunday paper,' he said.

'I assume they wouldn't print anything with no grounds at all,' said Pascoe.

'Grounds? If you call idle speculation, airy rumour, retailed over a glass of brandy after a lunch with Monty Boyle, grounds, then grounds there may be. It had never occurred to me that such things plus personal anecdote and even private animosity should provide the main colouring of my memoirs.'

He stood up. It was an effort. Pascoe glanced at the clock. It was just gone eleven. The chimes had not been triggered, he noticed.

'I have got one or two other things . . .' he began.

'I'm sure. Can we make it later? I've got a few things to take care of myself. I'm not being evasive, I assure you. I will be delighted to cooperate fully in helping with your inquiries.'

The wan smile returned as he uttered the ritual phrase.

Pascoe let himself be ushered to the door. Dalziel wouldn't like it, but for once he'd have to lump it.

'Are you just helping out with South's investigation again?' asked Watmough at the door.

'Rather more than that, sir.' Pascoe explained the position.

'So Mr Dalziel is in charge? Well, well. He's by way of being a friend of yours, I believe?'

He couldn't keep the note of interrogation, or perhaps rather of incredulity out of his voice.

'Yes, sir,' said Pascoe simply, not having the two or three hours necessary for an in-depth analysis of the relationship.

'Well, a man must be allowed to make his own friends,' said Watmough. 'As long as he is careful to make his own enemies too.'

How wise, thought Pascoe. If I found that in a Christmas cracker, I'd ask for my money back!

That was a Dalziel type joke, he realized even as it popped into his mind.

And he realized then what Watmough was saying to him.

CHAPTER 13

'This your missus?' said Detective-Superintendent Dalziel.

'Yes,' said Gavin Mycroft.

'Bonny lass,' said Dalziel, putting the wedding photograph down. 'Suits white. Nice room this, Mr Mycroft. Nice things. Someone's got taste.'

'We don't all keep coal in the bath,' said Mycroft.

His dark good-looking face was watchful, almost sullenly so. He was, Dalziel guessed, about thirty. He had already been interviewed about his encounter with Colin Farr in the pit the previous day. Dalziel had a copy of his statement in his hand.

'Load of rubbish,' he said, waving it.

'What?'

'A lot of the coal we get nowadays. Now, I can remember when I were a lad, a couple of bags of Shillbottle would keep you going nicely for a week in winter, burning hot and steady all the time and going down to nowt more than a fine brown ash. No clinker, or if there were, you'd put it in a box and ask the coalie next time he came if he'd changed his trade and gone into selling hardcore for road-making! Why is it things have got so bad, Mr Mycroft?'

'I don't know. Seems all right to me.'

'You say so? But no! I mean, look at that mucky mark up your chimneybreast. You'd not have got that with the old Shillbottle we used to get before the war.'

He shook his head as he examined the discolouration left by the washing off of Colin Farr's hand prints above the fireplace.

Mycroft said, 'We had an accident.'

'An accident? No one hurt, I hope?'

'No. It were nowt. Look, what can I do for you, mister?'

'You can help me,' said Dalziel with a broad beam. 'This lad, Farr, you know him well?'

'Well enough.'

'And the dead man, Satterthwaite. You'd know him well enough too?'

'Aye.'

'But not well enough to like either of 'em? Or mebbe too well.'

'Hold on? Why d'you say that?'

'Well, one of 'em's dead and the other's suspected of killing him and you don't seem much bothered either way.'

'All right, so we weren't that close. So what?'

'Nothing. I'm glad. It makes you a good witness, unbiased. So I can look for the truth when I ask you this. When you saw Farr on his way out, did he look to you like a man who'd just bashed someone's head in with an iron bar?'

'I didn't notice any blood if that's what you mean.'

'No, I mean his expression, his manner, how did they strike you?'

Mycroft considered.

'Well,' he said, 'he were a bit quiet, that was all.'

'Quiet?'

'Aye. When I asked him what exactly was wrong with him, he didn't give me a row or owt like that, just said his guts were bad and he felt too ill to work.'

'Normally you'd have expected a bit of lip?'

'From Farr? Too true!'

'You in particular, or any deputy?'

'Oh, any deputy,' said Mycroft a little too quickly.

Dalziel scratched his slab of a cheek. Mycroft watched fascinated as if looking for the moving finger to start writing messages.

'And he said he'd been looking for Satterthwaite?' said the fat man finally.

'It's in my statement.'

'Aye, but you don't give his exact words.'

'He said, "I can't find that cunt Satterthwaite, so can you tell him I'm taking an early lowse." '

'Lowse?'

'Knock-off.'

'He didn't like Satterthwaite? Or is *cunt* a term of endearment round here?'

Mycroft said, 'I don't think they got on too well.'

'Worse than you and Farr?'

'I never said we got on badly!'

'So you didn't. Why'd he not like Satterthwaite?'

'I don't know. They just rubbed each other up the wrong way, I suppose.'

'And you didn't see Satterthwaite any time after you spoke with Farr?'

'No.'

'Would you have expected to?'

'Not necessarily. But I expected to see him in the Cage at knock-off.'

'You usually left the pit together?'

'Not specifically. But officials are entitled to ride ahead of the men.'

'So normally you're all in the first lift? I bet that's popular,' laughed Dalziel. 'But it didn't bother you that Satterthwaite wasn't there?'

'No. Something could easily have come up at the last minute.'

'I know the feeling,' said Dalziel. 'All right, Mr Mycroft, what do you personally think could have happened?'

'I've no idea,' said Mycroft.

'That's funny,' said Dalziel. 'Me neither.'

He went to the sideboard and picked up the framed wedding photograph again.

'Lovely lass, your missus,' he repeated. 'Tell you what, Mr Mycroft. I'm off next to your Welfare Club. Mebbe you could show me the way? And mebbe, just so's I don't break the law, you could even sign me in as a guest so I could try a pint if I happen to get thirsty.'

Mycroft took the photograph from him and said, 'If you like.'

Outside Dalziel took in a deep draught of the cool air and asked, 'Is it far?'

'Not too far.'

'Then let's walk it, see the sights, eh?'

Ignoring the police car parked outside Mycroft's semi, he set off down the road with the smaller man at his side. The police driver watched them till they were about fifty yards away, then started to drive slowly after them.

As they descended the hill from the new estate their progress was remarked from behind curtains or by oblique glances from passers-by. But when they levelled out into the older central part of the village, where the pebble-dashed semis gave way to brick terraces, the curiosity was blatant to the point of aggressiveness. Mycroft responded by increasing his pace and watching the pavement with a blank stare.

178

Dalziel on the contrary tossed smiles and nods at the on-lookers with the all-inclusive beneficence of a pope and appeared unperturbed by the scowls and glowers which bounced back. There were mutterings too, but nothing audible till a round young man with a red face and a beer belly fell into step slightly behind them and said, 'Found your job at last, Gav? Guide dog to the filth!'

Mycroft slowed and would have turned but Dalziel's huge arm urged him irresistibly onward.

'Makes a change from the pickets, us escorting a bobby through the streets, eh, lads?'

This conceit clearly pleased the hearers and several other men fell into step.

'I'll tell you what, Mr Policeman, why are you only talking to bloody deputies?' pursued the stout youth, encouraged by the reinforcements. 'What's up wi' the rest on us?'

Dalziel shot him a smile radiant with enough love to convert a cannibal and muttered to Mycroft, 'Who's this comedian?'

'Tommy Dickinson, big mate of Farr's. He's a nothing. All mouth.'

Something of the tone if not the actual wording of this must have reached Dickinson, who said, 'What's that you're muttering, Gav? No use *muttering* when you're a big import-ant deputy. You've got to shout right loud, so that they can hear you on pit-top, so that your own missus can hear you back in village, even if she's got her knees over her ears!'

Again Mycroft would have stopped. Again Dalziel's arm was stronger than the deputy's anger. By now, attracted by the prospect of a bit of bother, there was a crowd of approaching fifty men in close formation behind the leading trio. Their jeering remarks were still just on the right side of good-natured to a man with a deaf ear and a forgiving temperament. But Tommy Dickinson, feeling the leadership of this small insurrection was at stake, turned up the heat of his personal contribution.

'You'll get nowt but a load of lies from that bugger, Mr Policeman,' he yelled. 'He's got no cause to love Col, except mebbe second-hand cause. What've you got on Col anyway?

179

Nowt! And you can bring in your bloodhounds and your foreskin scientists and you'll still not find owt. And something else, Mr Fat Bloody Policeman: if you're going to say Col didn't get on with Satterthwaite, then you'd better lock up every bugger in this town 'cause none of 'em did, excepting a few arse-lickers like that guide dog of yours. Wuff! wuff! fucking wuff!'

They swept into the small forecourt of the Miners' Social and Welfare Club. A flight of three shallow steps led to the front door which was firmly closed. Dalziel with Mycroft at his side went up the steps while the crowd halted at their foot. Dalziel tried the door, confirmed it was locked, and hammered his clenched fist against the woodwork with sufficient force to impress most of the watchers.

'Fat bugger must be desperate for a drink,' proclaimed Dickinson. 'He'll be out of luck, I reckon. Coppers never pay for their own and Gav there's forgotten where his pocket is. So unless Pedro's feeling generous, you'll have to do without a wet note this shift, Mr Policeman, sir.'

Dalziel turned. His size and elevation permitted him to look over the crowd. He could see his car across the street. His driver had his radio mike at his mouth. Their eyes met. Slowly Dalziel shook his head. His judgement was that this gang were still here for the entertainment, but he knew it wouldn't take much to stir up all the residual distrust and dislike of the police into a riot. The sound of fast approaching sirens might be enough.

'What you shaking tha head at, mister?' demanded Dickinson. 'Are you calling me a liar like you called my marra a liar?'

'Nay,' said Dalziel. 'I don't know about your marra, lad, but as for you, aye, certainly I'm calling you a liar.'

A great silence fell, broken only by the sounds of the Club door being unbolted and unlocked whose beginnings Dalziel had caught a few moments earlier. The men were looking at Tommy Dickinson. It was his show. He'd been given a cue which in normal circumstances could only be answered by violence or at least its threat. If he took a swing at Dalziel now, the whole village would probably explode. Dickinson hesitated, not through any weighing and assessing of action and consequence, but simply because he suddenly became aware that for the first time in his working life, he was Number One, the team leader, the man everyone was looking to for a lead. He felt the onset of stage-fright. At this point Neil Wardle, who had just joined the onlookers called from the back, 'Don't be daft, Tommy. It's not worth it,' and began forcing his way forward.

Wardle's words did what cries of encouragement might have failed to do. To back away now was probably to back out of the limelight for ever. Putting his foot on the lower step, he clenched his fists and twisting his amiable features into as ferocious an expression as possible he said, 'You'd best take that back, you fat bastard.'

'Nay,' said Dalziel, all injured. 'I'll call any man a liar who says I can't get a drink anywhere in Yorkshire.'

Behind him the door opened and Pedro Pedley said, 'What the hell's going on here? Who the hell are you?'

'Detective-Superintendent Andrew Dalziel, and I want a drink.'

'Well, you can't have one,' growled Pedley. 'First we're not open, that's the Law; and second you're not a member, that's the Rules.'

'Now hang on,' said Dalziel. 'We'll soon put that right. First you are open 'cause I am the Law, and second I'm here as a guest of a member, and them's the Rules.'

'Whose guest? Yours, Gav?'

'What? Drink with a deputy?' cried Dalziel indignantly. 'What are you saying, lad? No, I'm the personal guest of my friend Mr Dickinson here. Come on, Tommy. Get me signed in before I die of thirst.'

And stooping, he swung the sixteen stone of the amazed miner up on to the top step beside him and, with a fraternal arm round his shoulder, urged him through the door.

'Here, Pedro, are you really open?' called a voice.

Pedro shrugged and said, 'Looks like it.'

'Well, fuck me. Just goes to show, nowt's completely useless, not even a cop!'

There was a roar of appreciative laughter and the men

poured over the threshold, jostling and joking.

Soon only Neil Wardle remained.

'Not coming in, Neil?' asked Pedley. 'We'll not get into bother, not with that fat bugger in there.'

'I reckon he may be more bother than this town's ever known,' said Wardle slowly. 'Pedro, how's Maggie?'

'She's gone off to stay with her mam in Barnsley. It'll probably kill the old lass. She thought the sun shone out of Harold's arsehole. She never had as much time for Maggie and reckoned she got what she deserved when she got me. I think she blamed us both for what happened when . . . you know, our Tracey. Mebbe they can comfort each other this time.'

'I didn't know it was like that,' said Wardle. 'I'm sorry. Pedro, you realize they'll probably start talking about Tracey again, the cops, and everyone.'

'That's another good reason for having Maggie out of the way,' said Pedley. 'Me, I can take it. If I snap I'll just thump some bugger. Maggie could go right over the edge if she had to go through that again.'

'It's a pig of a world, Pedro,' said Wardle.

From inside came a cry. 'If this place is open, why's there no bugger serving drink?'

'Someone should tell that lot in there,' said Pedley bitterly.

'Never fear,' said Wardle. 'Living round here, most on 'em will find out for themselves sooner or later. Let's get inside, Pedro. I think I'd like a closer look at that fat cop. He'll bear watching, that one, and I don't want Tommy talking himself any deeper in trouble.'

'You reckon he's in trouble, do you?' asked Pedley, leading the way through into the bar.

'The way that bugger picked him up like he'd been tickling a trout?' said Wardle. 'Oh yes. He's ready to be buttered and fried, is Tommy, and served up for breakfast with a sprig of parsley in his gills!'

CHAPTER 14

Wield's job that morning had been to backtrack Colin Farr. The crashed motorbike had been recovered and the sergeant used its location as his starting-point. He was riding his own machine, a lovely old BSA Rocket. In the past, without making a state secret out of it, he'd tended to keep his bike and his job in separate compartments, but recently he had started to use it not only to get to work but, when the occasion demanded, on the job. He wondered if this was some kind of symbolic gesture to reinforce his rather muted coming-out, but having long since acknowledged the fruitlessness of self-analysis, he didn't wonder much. Today, tracing the route of a man on a motorcycle, it was the obvious choice of transport.

But first he walked, taking the shortest way along the network of narrow roads from the scene of the accident to the telephone kiosk where Farr had waited for Ellie Pascoe. There was something here not right. He liked Mrs Pascoe but his judgement was that her heart ruled her head and that whenever she felt a pressure from society or self-interest to act in a certain way, her tendency would be to rush off in the opposite direction.

Wield smiled, without visible evidence. Self-analysis might be a waste of time and spirit, but chopping up other people's minds was fun.

He returned his own mind to the job in hand.

It had taken him twenty minutes to walk from the scene of the accident to the kiosk. That was the time of a fit man in daylight knowing where he was going. He noted it down with the qualification that Farr might have taken as much as twice as long. And there was no knowing how long he may have lain stunned after the crash.

In other words it was probably all a waste of time, but Wield had long since learned to leave inspired short-cuts and quantum leaps to them with the rank to cushion their shortfall.

He returned to his bike, his eyes still searching for signs of Farr's passage, but there was a marked absence of blood-stains and footprints, and it needed woodlore more skilled than his to read anything into bent grass on the verge or broken twigs in the hedgerow.

Back at his bike he studied his map, made a decision and mounted. Here his judgement proved excellent. The first pub he called at was full of traces of Farr's passage which the landlord pointed to with a kind of melancholy pride.

'He came in, asked for a pint and it went down without touching the sides. It were only then I started realizing how cut he were. He banged the glass down, said, "Another," and I said, "Is that a good idea?" and he leaned across the bar, and, you see that jar full of ten p's? Well, that were a column for the Cancer Research till his elbow caught it. I said "Out!" and fair do's, he didn't answer back, but he knocked that stool over as he turned and it caught that table and spilt someone's drink. He didn't seem to notice. It were like he weren't really in the same world as the rest of us. He just set off through the door. I heard a bike start up and I thought: Good riddance if he runs into a wall and breaks his bloody neck!'

Wield said, 'You didn't think of ringing the police?'

'What for? They'd just come in here, all buttons and gob, frighten off me regulars, sup a couple of free pints, then bugger off home with nowt done that's any benefit to me!'

Wield acknowledged defeat, noted all relevant details and pursued his errant task. He missed out on the next two pubs but at the third, the Pendragon Arms, a large roadhouse about ten miles out of Burrthorpe, he struck lucky again. Colin Farr's arrival had been too quiet for anyone to be precise about the time. The landlord's wife had been the first to notice just how much liquor he seemed bent on putting away.

'It was non-stop. Every second person I served was him, at least that's how it felt. But he were quiet enough, a good-looking lad too, he looked a bit down in the mouth, I thought. I bet he's been stood up, I said to myself. I said to him, "Cheer up. It may never happen." And he said, "It has bloody happened. But you're right about one thing. Up's the direction. I'll not go down again. There's more dead than living down there. How much would they need to pay you to work with dead men, love?" I said, "I do it for nothing, have you seen my Charlie!" And we had a laugh.'

She laughed again in memory or illustration, and Wield thrust a question into the gap.

'How long did he stay?'

'Half an hour, mebbe. Just went like that. I glimpsed him in the passage using the phone . . .'

'He made a telephone call from here?' Wield asked sharply, not waiting for a gap this time.

'That's what I'm saying. But he didn't come back in. Can't say I was sorry. I quite liked him, as a woman I mean, but as a landlady I could see he were bad news after a while. Pity. He looked such a proper lad. That's the trouble nowadays, there's no knowing who's what just by looking, is there? I mean, I'd never have spotted you for a copper, not in a month of Sundays . . .'

Wield emerged half dazed from this assault on his ear, but with a clear picture of Farr's progress that night. He timed himself to the gates of Burrthorpe Main. Farr's progress, he noted this time, would probably have been rather quicker. From the sound of him, he wasn't the type to drive sedately. Nor was Wield when on the open road, but risk-taking on these narrow winding lanes was daft.

Work had obviously resumed at the pit after the necessary hiatus of the night before. But there were also a couple of uniformed policemen wandering around in the desultory fashion of men set to look for something which three times over the same ground has persuaded them they will not find.

Leaning his bike against the high boundary fence, Wield walked through the gate. Another policeman emerged from the gatehouse and addressed him.

'Excuse me, sir. Would you mind answering a couple of questions?'

His tone was courteous and conciliatory. Perhaps this was his normal voice for addressing members of the public, but Wield guessed he'd been told off to be especially careful to create no turbulence in the uneasy atmosphere of Burrthorpe.

He showed his warrant card. The man examined it closely, clearly as doubtful as the pub landlady that anyone in riding leathers could be a policeman.

'Sorry, Sergeant,' he said finally. 'But I thought you were one of the locals and I've been told to get the name and address of everyone who comes into this place today.'

'What are those jokers doing?' asked Wield.

'They're looking for Farr's pit-black. It weren't in his locker and they reckon he must have taken it out with him and dumped it.'

'In the yard? Why not outside?'

The man shrugged. 'There's a lot of outside,' he said. 'Any road, the gateman saw him ride off and says he definitely weren't carrying anything bulky enough to be his pit clothing and boots.'

'Oh aye? Same gateman on now?'

'That's right.'

'You been here long? Did duty on the Strike?'

'Yes, Sarge.'

'Then you should know how shortsighted some of these miners can get when they're seeing their mates getting into bother.'

'Oh aye. Right gang of crooks, most on 'em,' said the policeman a touch ingratiatingly.

'No,' said Wield. 'Just loyal to their mates. Like if your Mr Wishart asked you if them zombies out there had done a morning's work, you'd likely say yes. Whereas me . . . well, they're not my mates.'

He left and went back to his bike which was parked by the fence outside. He bent down and plucked at the dandelions and docks which were growing from the stony earth under the fence. When he had got a substantial bouquet he thrust it down the front of his jerkin so that the yellow blooms showed clearly beneath his throat.

'For I'm to be Queen of the May, mother. I'm to be Queen of the May,' he murmured to himself with a flash of that self-mocking humour which all men need who are to walk near dark edges without tumbling off.

Mounting his machine, he opened the throttle, swept through the pit gate, did a circuit of the yard and went out again. Pushing the flowers out of sight beneath his jerkin, he returned to the gatehouse.

The constable looked at him uneasily.

'See me then, did you?'

'Yes, Sarge.'

'And you, sir. Did you see me?'

'Aye,' said the gateman who had appeared behind the policeman. 'I'm not bloody blind.'

'Describe me,' said Wield.

'Describe you?' said the gateman. 'Nay, mister, if I looked like you, I'd not go around asking people to describe me!'

'Stick to the clothes and the bike.'

The constable suddenly caught on and his face contracted with concentration as the gateman said. 'Don't be daft. It were just a moment since. You were just like you are now.'

'What about you, lad?'

'I'm sorry, Sarge, but I can't see any difference,' admitted the man.

Wield reached into his jerkin and pulled out the battered bouquet with a conjuror's flourish and handed it to the bemused youngster.

'These were sticking out of my jerkin,' he said. 'You see, lad, you don't even have to be loyal to be blind.'

He felt quite pleased with himself as he rode away. An hour later, having searched both sides of the hedgerows and fences bounding Farr's likely route to the first pub, he felt a little less complacent. One remote channel of his mind had been running a video in which he quietly placed Farr's pit-black on a table in the Burrthorpe incident room. But a detective's life was more disappointment than triumph and in any case he knew quite well that even if he'd found the clothes, he'd have left them *in situ* till Forensic had taken a first look.

At the station he asked for Dalziel but was told he wasn't in and taken along to see Chief Inspector Wishart. They hadn't met before and Wield noted the cold blankness of response to his uncompromisingly ugly features with which the courteous usually concealed their shock. But when Wishart examined the sergeant's notes on his morning's researches, he nodded appreciatively.

'I'd heard you were a treasure, Sergeant,' he said. 'Now I see what they meant.'

'Thanks, sir,' said Wield, who'd never been able fully to comprehend his seniors' enthusiasm for the clarity and rationality of his notes and reports. What other way was there to do them? But dumping Farr's bloodstained pit-boots on the table in front of the man, now that would really have been something!

'You've mapped out possible alternative routes to the Pendragon, I see. But you haven't been over them?'

'I thought I'd better report, sir. I did notice, though, there was a couple of lads in the pit-yard who looked as if they might fancy a walk in the country.'

'Oh? Why'd you not send them?'

'They were your men, sir. South Yorks, I mean. And even though they'd be doing most of their looking on our patch . . .'

The door opened and Pascoe came in.

'Hello, Wieldy,' he said. 'Sorry, Alex, if you're busy . . .'

'No, come in, Peter. I was just admiring the sergeant here. Not only a meticulous worker but a diplomat too. There can't be many of them in Mid-Yorks!'

'Oh dear,' said Pascoe. 'What's *he* been doing?'

Wishart glanced questioningly at Wield and Pascoe grinned and said, 'There's nothing you can tell the sergeant here about Mr Dalziel that he can't cap from personal experience.'

'Well, after suggesting to the Indian consultant treating Farr that he might hurry things along by a bit of ju-ju, he then contrived to provoke a near-riot in the middle of the village which he only managed to quell by declaring the Welfare Club bar open an hour early!'

Pascoe and Wield exchanged glances.

'Yes, Alex,' said Pascoe innocently. 'But what's he done that strikes you as being over the top?'

'I see. You're all the bloody same!' said Wishart. 'Meantime, as the only way to get in touch with your—sorry, *our* —boss is to walk into the Welfare uninvited, which I am certainly not going to do and I don't want anyone else doing, you'd better tell me what you've been up to, Peter.'

Pascoe outlined his conversation with Watmough. It didn't take long.

'That's it?' said Wishart.

'He's promised to get back to me,' said Pascoe defensively. 'I think he needed a bit of space to get himself sorted.'

'You'll need a bit of space when your boss hears that report,' forecast Wishart. 'They say there's a lot of it in Australia.'

'Sounds to me that Monty Boyle's the chap we really ought to be talking to,' said Wield. 'Any luck there?'

'None,' said Pascoe. 'He's like the Scarlet Pimpernel. First time I contacted his office I think they were just giving me the runaround. But this morning I got the impression they genuinely didn't know where he was. Even asked me to give him a message if I stumbled across him!'

'Sounds to me you two have lost track that it's yesterday's murder we're investigating,' said Wishart. 'Historical research may go down big in the groves of Academe you lot work in, but down here life is real, life is earnest. Farr should be released from hospital tomorrow. That's when we'll start making progress, I think.'

'Meanwhile he's just helping with inquiries. When's visiting? From what I heard last night, his friends and family aren't going to take quietly to leaving him unsuccoured on his bed of pain.'

'Don't I know it. The Union brief's been threatening me with the Court of Human Rights all morning. Not that that bothers me, but I don't want another Burrthorpe riot, so I've agreed he can have a visit from his mother and other applications will be treated on their merits. Meaning if we think there's a chance of our resident bobby overhearing anything interesting, we might let someone else in.'

'You're a cunning old Celt,' laughed Pascoe. 'Me, I'm just a simple soul who's starving. Time for lunch, I think.'

He and Wield headed for the door, but Wishart said, 'A word in private, Peter,' and Wield went ahead by himself.

'It's about your good lady . . .'

'No problem,' interrupted Pascoe. 'She's in the clear on the drinks charge. So all she is now is a witness who's made a statement.'

'I wish it were as simple as that, Peter,' sighed the Scot. 'Did you know she was at the hospital earlier this morning? No, I see you didn't. She didn't get to see Farr, of course, and she won't be on my permitted visiting list either. But she did dig up some tame feminist lawyer, Ms Pritchard, you may know her? We had the pleasure of meeting her in court during the Strike. A strange choice of brief for macho Colin, I'd have thought. He seemed to think so too and told her to sod off. Which she did. Ellie unfortunately didn't. According to my information she's still in Burrthorpe. In fact she's been in Farr's mother's house for most of the morning.'

'She's a free agent,' said Pascoe.

'That's what Adam said about Eve,' said Wishart caustically. 'Look, Pete, once the Press get on to this, and the Powers That Promote get round to reading the Press, you could be in real bother. OK, I know that Big Andy loves you, but not even Mid-Yorks is a hereditary monarchy . . . no, don't say anything you might regret. Just push off and get some lunch. Take your time. You look like a wet weekend in Largs.'

Pascoe left closing the door very gently behind him. Wield was waiting for him outside.

'Everything OK?' said the sergeant.

'Yes, fine.'

It was an instinctive response, defensive, distancing. He'd always hidden doubts and sometimes pain beneath a cloak of confident control. As a graduate entrant to the police, he'd wrapped the cloak even tighter as a defence against sneers from above and mockery from alongside. And now it was a response that felt as if it had been printed in his genes.

Wield say, 'I don't fancy owt round here. Why don't we find a pub out of sight of a pit and pretend we're commercial travellers?'

'All right,' said Pascoe. 'Why not? My car's round the back.'

'My bike's out front if you're not fussy who you're seen with your arms round.'

It dawned on Pascoe that Wield was offering more than a lift.

He was offering himself as a friend, a confidant.

There had been a moment not long ago when Wield himself had needed an ear to pour his doubts into, a secure, compassionate and unjudgemental confessional, and Pascoe had proved sadly inadequate. To ignore his offer now, as he had ignored his need then, would be to fix their relationship for ever. Perhaps that was what he wanted. Perhaps that was what he had always wanted, relationships which were fixed, certain, and unchanging. Perhaps that was why he had joined the Force in the first place. To feel himself supported by a hierarchy which left little doubt where you were, and to devote himself to a job whose basic function was to preserve the sum of things by law.

These thoughts came not singly but in a bubbling torrent, confused but not uncontrollable. Control would always be an option for Pascoe, until one day perhaps he controlled himself out of this life.

That thought swam up through the maelstrom, sole and terrifying. Where the hell had it come from? No, don't answer that, he thought.

'Wieldy, I'll be proud to be seen hanging on to you,' he said. 'Only I'm not going to eat any live chickens as we ride!'

CHAPTER 15

'Just get her out of here!' screamed May Farr. 'You little whore! It was a black day you ever got your claws into this family!'

Stella Mycroft, overcome with remorse at the sight of Mrs Farr's faintness, had tried to modify her claim to having heard Colin confess.

'No, he didn't actually say he'd done it, not in so many words, but he was right upset about something nasty that had happened down pit, that was clear, and I thought . . .'

'When did you ever think about owt but your own gratification?' Mrs Farr had demanded, beginning to recover. After that one thing led to another and Stella Mycroft's remorse quickly evaporated under the heat of the older woman's fury and soon she was giving as good as she got.

'It's not me who harmed your Colin,' she yelled. 'He were glad to be shut of me. He'd been harmed beyond repair years since, like poor old Billy. Mebbe if you'd been more of a proper wife and mother, Billy wouldn't have gone wandering round the woods with other people's kids and Col wouldn't be lying in that hospital now!'

That's when May Farr had started screaming abuse and looked ready to back it with physical attack till Arthur Downey put his arms round her and cried to Ellie, 'For God's sake get her out of here!'

Stella took little persuading. At the front door she said to Ellie, 'You're seeing us at our best, aren't you? You'll have some grand tales to tell when you get back home.'

'Mrs Mycroft, what was that all about? What's this got to do with Mr Farr's death? *Did* Colin confess to you or not?'

'It's well seeing you're a copper's wife,' said Stella. 'Nothing but questions. Well, they can ask till their faces are as blue as their uniforms, they'll not get anything out of me.'

Her tiny, beautiful face was set in an expression of defiance but the flawless blue eyes which locked with Ellie's for a second were haunted by despair.

'Mrs Mycroft, are you all right?' asked Ellie. 'Can I help . . . ?'

'Round here, you help your own,' said Stella. 'That's mebbe the trouble.'

She gazed out along the frowning terrace.

'I thought it'd be better up on the estate,' she said. 'But it's just the same. People thought I were upset when Colin went off to the Navy. Well, I were. Not that he'd gone, but that he'd not taken me with him. He never wanted me but for the usual. Once I realized that, it made things easier. But it still hurt.'

'I'm not sure I understand,' said Ellie.

'Why should you, love? You've got to live it to understand it. I'm off. Good luck, missus. Once you get mixed up with the Farrs, you bloody need it!'

She teetered away on her high heels, a perfect porcelain doll, but with steel beneath the glaze.

Ellie went back in, expecting to find May Farr still in need of calming down. Instead the atmosphere had changed completely. She was on the telephone talking excitedly.

'It's the Union lawyer,' explained Downey. 'I think the police are going to let her see Colin.'

'I should damn well think so,' said Ellie. She regarded the man curiously. Stella had described his devotion to May Farr as pathetic but she recalled Peter in one of his more philosophical detective moods saying that pity, disapproval, or contempt, must not be allowed to affect judgement of an emotion's kinetic power.

Peter. Where was he? What would he do when he found out where she was?

'It's a strange business, Mr Downey,' she said to distract her mind. 'What do you really make of it?'

His long face twisted into a baffled smile.

'God knows,' he said. 'People do odd things. None of us should run to lay blame. It's like down the pit. Take all the care you can and there'll still be accidents, people killed, maimed . . . if you can look after one other person, you've done all that can be asked . . . if we all did that, life would be OK, wouldn't it.'

There was no doubt who his one other was.

May Farr put down the phone. Her face was rejuvenated.

'They've said I can visit him,' she said. 'That's good, isn't it? That must mean they don't reckon there's a case against him.'

Ellie realized that they were both looking at her attentively. I've been elected police consultant! she thought resentfully. It wouldn't have been so bad if she could have confidently confirmed the woman's optimism, but the image of Dalziel's friendly smile rose in her mind.

'It means it certainly can't be a watertight case,' she said carefully. 'Mrs Farr, let me drive you up to the hospital.'

The woman who had been putting on her top coat looked assessingly at Ellie, then said in a kindly voice, 'No, love, I'm not sure that's such a good idea. There's no point, really.'

Thinking she meant there was little chance that they'd let her in to see Colin also, Ellie opened her mouth to say she didn't mind. Then she realized that the woman simply meant she had no part left in this drama.

'Arthur will take me. Shouldn't you be getting back to your little girl, Mrs Pascoe?'

'She's in the crèche,' said Ellie. 'She'll be all right. They're very good and she loves it there. Couldn't I . . . ?'

What could she do? she asked herself.

'Look,' said May Farr as if taking pity. 'You can hang on here if you like. Someone might ring. You can tell them where I am, what's going off. Would you mind? It'd be a help.'

'Yes, of course,' said Ellie, delighted to be given a role.

'Right. We'll be off. Come on, Arthur.'

'Do you want to borrow my car?' asked Ellie. 'It's just parked around the corner . . .'

'I've got my own car, missus,' said Arthur Downey possessively.

194

He followed May out of the front door. The policeman parked against the kerb opposite made a note and resumed his paperback novel.

In the quiet house Ellie prowled around between the living-room and the kitchen. This was permitted territory, she felt. Already her mind was beginning to advance Jesuitical arguments for extending her wanderings upstairs. She was entitled to use the lavatory, of course, and what harm could there be in pushing open the door of Colin's room and peeping in. You could learn a lot from a man's room, she told herself. But what did she hope to learn about Colin Farr? The answer was chilling enough to make her sit down in an armchair and lock her arms round her legs as though they might independently convey her upstairs to some dreadful revelation. For all she could, all she needed to, find out about Colin Farr was whether his incoherent ramblings about blood, bones and death down the mine had been an admission of guilt.

A bell rang shrilly, startling her. It had to ring again before she recognized it was the front door.

There were two women. One of them she recognized as the thin chain-smoking woman she'd met last time she was here. Wendy something. The other was a tall, rawboned woman with a rubbery, expressive face.

'Hello. What are you doing here?' demanded Wendy. Walker, that was it. Clearly the local CIA had put her in the picture too.

'Mrs Farr asked me to look after things here while she went up to the hospital.'

'Oh, did she?' said Wendy, pushing past with the determination of one who would not be too surprised to find bodies tied up on the carpet.

'I'm Ellie Pascoe,' she said to the other woman.

'I'm Marion Snape,' said the other curiously.

'She's the one I were telling you about,' said Wendy. 'Turns out to be a copper's wife.'

'Look,' said Ellie. 'I've been through all this with Mrs Farr.'

'Oh aye,' said Wendy, tossing her cigarette into the

fireplace and lighting another. 'And what did May have to say?'

'She left me in charge here,' retorted Ellie. 'Are you responsible for what *your* husband does, Mrs Walker?'

For some reason this hit home and for a second Ellie thought verbal violence was going to escalate into physical, then suddenly the woman grinned and said, 'All right. If May left you here, then you can't be altogether bad, can you?'

'You must forgive her, Mrs Pascoe,' said Marion Snape in a voice tinged with relief. 'She didn't get thumped enough when she were a little 'un.'

'That's me. Deprived in every way. All right, missus, seeing as we've got ourselves a line into the enemy camp, mebbe you can fill us in on what's going off.'

The question and answer session that followed left Ellie feeling drained, but the ice was broken and melted by the time her interrogators had finished with her. Then it was her turn.

She went straight to the point.

'All this seems to be about Colin's dad,' she said. 'What did happen there?'

The two women exchanged glances, then Marion said, 'If I knew, I'd not tell you, but as I don't there's no harm in telling you the different stories.'

This interesting distinction between confidence and commonalty being approved by Wendy, Marion began. She was not long allowed sole occupancy of the stage as Wendy kept chipping in with addenda and corrections of details of date, time, meteorology, dress, disposition and genealogy, and soon it became an oratorio for two voices.

What it came down to was that Billy Farr was a man not easy of access, but once reached, his affections were given unreservedly.

'He loved May—and Colin—and that little tyke of his —Jacko—and little Tracey—he idolized that child—he couldn't have hurt her, not in a month of Sundays—he'd have loved a daughter of his own—that's why he were so fond of that Stella—'

196

'But he stopped being fond of her, didn't he?' interrupted Ellie.

'Aye, well, she chucked his lad over, didn't she,' said Marion.

'Surely that was *after* Mr Farr had died,' objected Ellie.

'Were it?' The two women exchanged glances. 'Well, mebbe it were—but there's no getting away from it—no matter what anyone says, Billy Farr couldn't have harmed little Tracey—there's no getting away from it—'

Ellie had a vague feeling that they had got away from something.

'You didn't mention Arthur Downey. When you were talking about Mrs Farr's friends.'

'Downey?' said Wendy. 'He's nowt but a big kid. Thinks two turnips and a bag of spuds'll make you love him forever.'

'He's all right, Arthur,' said Marion. 'Doesn't say much, but what he does makes sense. And he treats women like they're human, which is a rare quality round here. I've sometimes thought he'd mebbe have married May if the Strike hadn't happened.'

'That's one good thing that came out of it, then,' said Wendy.

'What's the Strike got to do with it?' wondered Ellie.

'She means May got us instead,' explained Wendy. 'Widow wanted support in the old days, there was nowhere to turn except family to start with and then mebbe another fellow. You only existed round here as a wife and a mother, so what else was there to do? But the Strike changed all that.'

And now they were into the Strike and the development of the Women's Support Groups. Ellie listened enthralled. She found herself beset by a feeling almost of envy for the way in which these women had had to struggle with traditions, backgrounds, communities and families to achieve even a modest degree of self-determination.

And behind the envy lurked something else. She tried to identify it but couldn't. Then she realized she was avoiding the obvious. What went hand in hand with envy? Could it be that just as deep down these women almost certainly resented her for having had it too easy, she in her turn resented them for having had it too hard?

She wrenched them back to the Farrs.

'Could Billy have killed himself?' she asked. 'Not because he was guilty of killing the child, but because he felt guilty for leaving her alone?'

'Mebbe,' said Wendy slowly. 'Christmas is the kiddies' time. Mebbe it just got to him, is that what you mean? But I'd not have said it was likely. He wasn't a quitter. Even them who reckoned he could have been guilty didn't all think he committed suicide. There were some who said . . .'

Marion shot her a warning glance.

'Said what?' prompted Ellie.

'They were the daftest of the lot,' said Marion. 'They said that there were those in Burrthorpe who were so sure Billy Farr were guilty that they'd tried and sentenced him them-selves and executed him by chucking him down that shaft.'

Silence fell in the room, a silence compounded of horror and excitement. It was the excitement that made Ellie feel more alien than anything else. The horror was the general human reaction to such monstrosities. The excitement was the buzz of speculation and anticipation which must have run around frontier towns when the word spread that a lynching was in the offing. Rough justice, sorting out your own messes, taking care of your own . . . all the old vigilante clichés ran through her mind. Burrthorpe was a frontier town, not in the geographic, political sense, but in terms of its monogenesis, its cultural separateness, its awareness of constant threat. Its inhabitants had put down roots in a unique sense. Deep beneath the streets and houses lay the reason for their existence, the hope of their continuance. When finally the coal was exhausted or adjudged too expens-ive to be worth the hewing, Burrthorpe would literally be cut off from its roots and die.

She didn't belong here. She was an Easterner, visiting the 'Romantic' West to collect experiences for her dinner-parties back home, and the dusty, violent, uncompromising reality was proving too much for her delicate stomach.

'You OK, love?' said Marion anxiously.

'Yes. Sorry.'

'Poor lass is probably starving,' said Wendy. 'Have you seen the time?'

'Bloody hell! It'll be shut.'

'Not if we hurry. We usually go down the Club on Wednesdays and have a pie or something,' explained Wendy. 'We'll need to get our skates on. You'll come, won't you?'

Suddenly they were just women again, reachable, vulnerable, lovable, not inhabitants of another and frightening world.

'Yes, please,' she said.

She felt quite euphoric as they hurried out of the back door and along the narrow alleyway running between the fences of the rear gardens of the parallel rows of houses. They came to a cross alley where Marion guided Ellie left towards the road. Wendy however went straight on.

Ellie paused and said disappointedly, 'Isn't Wendy coming with us, then?'

'Aye,' said Marion. 'She'll not be a second.'

Ellie could see the skinny young woman over the corner of the gardens. Then she stopped momentarily out of sight, reappeared clutching something in her hand and hurled whatever it was in the direction of the nearest house.

There was a loud splintering of glass, then Wendy came running back towards them.

'What's she doing?' demanded Ellie, amazed.

'Scab,' said Marion. 'Me, I can't be bothered any more. But Wendy, every time she comes this way, she puts a brick through his window or something.'

Wendy rejoined them breathless.

'Right through the lavvy window,' she boasted. 'I hope the bugger were sitting on it. He always spent a lifetime in there studying the horses.'

'You know him, then? Well, I mean,' said Ellie.

'I should do,' said Wendy. 'He used to be my sodding husband.'

Suddenly Ellie felt an alien once more and found herself longing for the comfort of a familiar face.

When they reached the Club, far from meeting the

lunch-time exodus as Marion had feared, they found the club room bursting at the seams with bodies, smoke and conversation.

'What's going off?' Marion asked the steward after they fought their way to the bar. 'You got an extension, Pedro?'

'Sort of,' said Pedley.

'What do you mean, sort of? Either you have or you haven't?'

'Let's put it this way,' said Pedley. 'I stay open as long as *he* stays open.'

He nodded directionally. The women turned and looked. And Ellie found that her wish had been granted, in part at least. There rising through the swirling tobacco mists was a most familiar headland, but she could take no homecoming voyager's comfort from this first glimpse across a table arctic with glasses of the five-acre face of Andy Dalziel.

CHAPTER 16

Dalziel felt he had earned his money already that day and when Ellie Pascoe came into the bar, he reckoned he was into overtime.

It wasn't that he disliked her. On the contrary, he found her a bloody sight more appealing than the majority of his colleagues' spouses, most of whom were too thick to even notice when he was taking the piss! At least you could have a laugh with Ellie, trade insults, talk straight and not give offence, and give offence but not provoke hysterics.

Nor could he get too upset at the thought that she might be putting it about. It'd hurt the boy, Pascoe, and that would be a pity, but it wouldn't be—shouldn't be—the end of the world. One thing his wide experience of life had taught him was that if a woman was inclined to put it about, you couldn't stop her, not even with an Act of Parliament. Christ, you'd have to work hard with an act of God! Better then to find out sooner rather than later, while you were still young enough to enjoy your retaliation.

But there were limits. As far as such things are negotiable, a woman had a duty not to put it about in such a way as to embarrass her husband in his workplace. And for a detective-inspector's wife to be screwing around with a boy miner who was also chief suspect in a murder inquiry over stepped these limits by a long, long way. He'd hoped he'd given her a big enough hint in the hospital car park to keep her neb out of things but clearly he'd been too subtle. It was always his chief failing.

He sighed and said, 'Whose shout is it? A man could die of thirst in a place like this.'

He'd been drinking pints with whisky chasers since his arrival. Not to be outdone, Tommy Dickinson had followed suit. Ten or more pints was a normal evening's consumption for Tommy but the spirit had changed the name of the game. Several times Neil Wardle had tried to urge him to stop or at least to stick to beer. On each occasion Dalziel had added his voice to Wardle's with the inevitable result that the stout youth had indignantly rejected the advice.

There'd been others at the table too, a steady flow and ebb as curiosity or a desire to bait this constabulary bear overcame the miners' distrust and dislike. He'd fended off attacks with equanimity, traded insults with good-natured vigour, even proffered advice to those still at loggerheads with the law. And, as Neil Wardle, still on only his second pint after all this time, noted with grudging admiration, there was scarcely a one of them who got away without answering some pertinent questions. He did his best to pre-empt the grosser indiscretions by interruption or change of subject and each time felt Dalziel's undulled gaze touch upon him with amused acknowledgement before the talk was rediverted into its previous channel by a nudge which should have been blatant but was merely irresistible.

'You're a clever sod, I'll give you that,' said Wardle in a quiet interlude shortly after Ellie's arrival.

'There's some as thinks so,' said Dalziel complacently. 'But I'm glad to have your endorsement.'

'I didn't mean it as a compliment.'

'I didn't take it as one, so no harm done.'

'When are you going to let Colin out? You've got nothing on him, have you?'

'No,' said Dickinson, suddenly reviving from a cat-nap. 'There's nowt on Col, not even them foreskin scientists can pin owt on Col.'

'I hope he means forensic,' grinned Dalziel.

'Listen,' said Wardle, very intense. 'You can get Tommy drunk, but don't you patronize him, all right?'

'I'd not even dream of it,' said Dalziel. 'I've grown very fond of Tommy. He's a lovely lad.'

'Now listen,' began Wardle angrily.

'Nay, Neil, shut tha gob, it's not a Union meeting,' said Tommy Dickinson. 'And I'm not a little lad needing looked after. Andy here's all right. If we'd had more like Andy policing the pickets, we'd not have had half the bother we did, isn't that right, Andy?'

Dalziel looked at Wardle and smiled evilly.

'Oh aye, Tommy. I think you can safely say that. Not half the bother.'

A worried-looking man of about sixty approached the table and said, 'Excuse me, Superintendent, but I'm chairman of the Club Management Committee and it's long past our closing time. Our steward reckons you said something about it being OK, but I'm not sure the licence magistrates will see it that way if they get wind of it. So unless we can have something in writing . . .'

Dalziel looked at his watch.

'By God, is that the time? You should have been shut half an hour back! Hasn't time been called? That's bad, that. You'll really have to tighten up, mister, else you could lose your licence, you know that?'

His worry replaced by anger, the Chairman returned to the bar and a moment later the bell rang and Pedley's voice bellowed, 'Come on now. Get them drinks off. The holiday's over!'

Wardle said, 'So you run scared too? It's good to see you don't really make up all the laws as you go along.'

'What? Nay, lad, you don't understand. It's nowt to do with what that old geezer said. It's just that I'm finished

202

with you lot for the time being, but I've still not had a chat with Mr Pedley there, and I can't do that while he's busy serving drinks, can I?'

As the bar slowly cleared Dalziel wandered across to the table where Ellie was still sitting with her companions.

'Hello, ladies,' he said genially. 'Hope you had time to enjoy your pies.'

Wendy looked up at him and gave him a smile of stunning sweetness.

She said, 'Piss off, pig.'

Dalziel said, 'Who's your porkist friend, Ellie? Never mind. Can I have a word?'

Of course the bold reply was 'anything you've got to say to me you can say in front of my friends' but the only trouble was that Dalziel undoubtedly would, and Ellie wasn't certain that he wouldn't be saying things she'd prefer her new friends, or indeed any friends, not to hear.

So, apology and defiance most becomingly mingling in her face, she rose and moved apart with the fat man.

'I'm glad to see you, lass,' said Dalziel in a low voice. 'Have you heard owt useful?'

Expecting at the least a lecture if not a threat of physical violence, Ellie was taken by surprise by this approach.

'Useful? What do you mean?'

'Anything that'd help us get to the bottom of this business. South are determined it's down to Farr, but me, I don't like jumping to conclusions. Mind you, I can see why they think like that. No one I've spoken to has been able . . .'

'Who've you been speaking to?' demanded Ellie.

'Well, I went round to the Mycrofts' house . . .'

'You don't want to listen to anything that stupid girl has to say! Why would Colin say anything to her he didn't say to me?'

Dalziel, who had not laid eyes on Stella Mycroft yet, though he'd heard a lot about her in his rambling chat with Tommy Dickinson, nodded sagely as though understanding Ellie's odd remark.

'Just what I thought,' he said. 'Listen, how'd it be if I got you in to see young Colin?'

203

'Could you?' asked Ellie, her face lighting up with a hope which stirred something which might have been the dusty relics of shame in Dalziel's gut. Or perhaps it was just the beer.

'Why not? If he's innocent, the sooner them dozy buggers in South get on the right track the better.'

Behind her he could see Pedro Pedley urging the reluctant women to leave.

'Best get back to your friends,' he said, putting his arm round her shoulders and urging her back towards her table. 'Mr Pedley, I'd like a word. Cheerio, Ellie love. I'll see you later.'

Transferring his arm and his attention to Pedley, Dalziel moved away. Ellie watched him go. He never lost the capacity to surprise. Ready for bullying interference and a homily on marital loyalty, instead she'd got sympathy and a promise, well, almost a promise, of access to Colin. She found herself smiling at the prospect.

Wendy and Marion were on their feet. She turned to them to include them in her little aura of joy and found herself met by suspicious, hostile faces. For a second the response took her aback as much as Dalziel's had. Then she put the two together. Divide and rule.

'Oh, you devious bastard!' she said.

But when she turned again to purge her collaborative guilt, the devious bastard had already moved out of her reach into the steward's private quarters.

At first Pedley tried to give Dalziel a bad time.

'Don't think I couldn't see what you were up to. I thought you buggers were up to date now, tape-recorders, computers, proper scientific evidence, not sitting around boozing, listening to drunken gossip. You made a fool out of me, getting the Club open and shut like it were your private bar. Well, you may pull the wool over some silly buggers' eyes and you may put the fear of God into some others. But you don't fool me, mister, and you don't frighten me either. Who the hell do you think you are anyway?'

He ran out of steam and stood glaring down at the seated

204

Dalziel, who returned a gaze of hurt bewilderment.

'Me? I'm the fellow who's going to find out what really happened to your little daughter, Mr Pedley.'

Pedley's response was surprising even to a man who reckoned that only women and lunatics were totally forecastable. He laughed, without much humour, with a great deal of bitter mockery.

'What am I supposed to do, mister? Drop on t'floor and kiss your boots in gratitude? I'll tell you what I want from you. I want you to leave it alone!' He was bellowing now. 'Can you get that into your thick skull? It can't all be bone, there's so much of it you'd fall over every time you stood up!'

Dalziel rose swiftly and brought his bulk menacingly close to the steward.

'Listen, Pedro,' he said softly. 'You may be king of the bar out there, but them buggers *expect* to be ruled. They may be wild, but in the end they live by the bloody rule book, their own or some other bugger's.'

'Meaning you don't?' interrupted Pedley disbelievingly.

'Not by any book you've read,' said Dalziel.

He sat down again as rapidly as he'd risen.

'So don't try to treat me like I'm giving you trouble at closing time. If you've got summat to say, well, say it, don't shout it.'

Pedley took a deep breath, then sat down abruptly.

'It'll do no good, that's what I've got to say,' he said. 'When it happened, I thought I'd never forget. Well, I haven't. Not a day goes by . . . but sometimes an hour goes by, mebbe more. And feeling, that changes too. Once if I'd got my hands on whoever took our Tracey, there's nothing I'd not have done. Nothing. Now . . . I were glad when they said it were Pickford. Maggie clung on to some daft idea that she'd been kidnapped and would still turn up alive, but I knew from the start she were dead. From the start. So when they said it were probably Pickford and he'd killed himself, I thought: It's over. A monster, a madman . . . someone so unnatural he couldn't live with himself. And the rest of us could at least go on living with each other.

Now what are you saying? That it might not have been Pickford after all? Worse, that it may turn out to be someone I knew and liked? Or worse still, that it may turn out to be someone still alive, mebbe someone I've been serving beer to all these years and having a joke with, and asking how his family is? Is that what you want me to have to deal with now? Well, I won't, I tell you. It'd drive me round the twist and I reckon it'd likely kill my Maggie.'

He spoke with a quiet vehemence much more forceful than his earlier shouting.

Dalziel said, 'There are two ways we can manage this, Pedro. You can refuse to talk to me and then we get a hold of your missus and she can refuse to talk also. Then I pass it on to my bosses to let them sort out any question of impeding the course of justice or owt of that. Or you and me can have a nice cooperative chat and I guarantee no one, not police or Press, will go anywhere near your wife. It's up to you, lad.'

'Oh, you cunt,' said Pedro Pedley.

'Oh, I could,' said Dalziel. 'Now, about your brother-in-law, Harold Satterthwaite . . .'

CHAPTER 17

Colin Farr sat up in bed and held his mother's narrow pale hands loosely between his own.

'You've not asked me if I killed him, Mam,' he said. 'Why's that? Because you're sure I didn't? Or because you don't want to hear the answer.'

'You're sometimes so like your father,' May said sadly.

'What's that? Good or bad?'

'I don't know. He were always looking to see the inside of things too. No such thing as a straight answer, either giving it or taking it. Always looking for something hidden. And always hiding himself as he looked.'

'You're not so bad at ducking a straight question yourself,' said her son, smiling. But she wasn't deceived by his smile.

'How'd you get in anyway?' asked Colin.

'That Union lawyer, Mr Wakefield, fixed it. Said if you weren't being charged, it'd create bad feeling to keep me out.'

'Threatened them with another riot, did he? Perhaps Wakefield's not as daft as he looks.'

'I wish you'd pay heed to him, Col. You need help.'

'I'm getting it,' said Farr. 'Just lying here with lots of time to think and only one thing to think about, that's a great help. Slaving down that bastard hole all day, then getting pissed to try and forget you've got to go back down tomorrow, that doesn't leave much time for thinking. At sea now, you've got lots of time for thought . . .'

'You'll go back to sea then when this is all over?' said May hopefully.

'So I'll have more time to think? Depends, doesn't it?'

'What on?'

'On what I've got to think about,' said the young man, laughing strangely. He pulled himself up when he saw the distress on his mother's face and said with an effort at matter-of-factness, 'What's the crack, then? They can't have had as much fun as this in the village since that parson started flashing at the Reform Chapel.'

'Everyone's upset, natural,' said his mother. 'Arthur's been round since first thing . . .'

'Didn't stay the night, then?'

'No. But if he had done, it'd be my business, not yours.'

'Sorry,' said Colin. 'What's he reckon to it all, then?'

'He's not said much. But he's been a grand help fending folk off, like.'

'Oh aye? Well, if you look like a mangy hound, you might as well act like one. Sorry.'

'You should be. He's been a good friend.'

'And that's all?'

'How many times do you need told?' she asked angrily. 'And don't you think you would have been told a hundred times in that bloody club if there had been owt going on? Why's it bother you so much, anyway? Am I supposed to live like a nun just to keep you happy? You ought to practise what you preach. I've had a houseful of your fancy women this morning, most on 'em married.'

'You wha'?' said Colin, his face contorting into a look of pantomimic amazement. Despite herself, May Farr laughed.

'All right,' she said. 'Only two. That teacher, Mrs Pascoe. Did you know her husband's a bobby? A CID inspector?'

Now her son was genuinely amazed.

'What? No, I bloody didn't, but it explains . . . or mebbe it doesn't. Any road, get one thing straight, she's not my fancy woman.'

'Suit yourself. She doesn't seem a bad sort, bit wet behind the ears, though. Your other little friend who called was Stella. I suppose you're going to say you've never laid a finger on her either?'

'You know that's been over for years!'

'Oh aye? And that bother down at the Club? And you visiting that fancy house of hers in broad daylight when you should have been on shift? Social call, were it?'

Farr shook his head in disgust.

'Bloody Burrthorpe! The Russkis should send the KGB there for training. Who told you? One of your Action Women, was it? Or that other gabby tart, Downey? All right. Sorry again. Look, what did Stella want?'

'Just to see how you were, she said. Me, I'm not sure she knew what she wanted. She seemed a bit mixed up. One thing she said was that you'd phoned her last night as well as that Mrs Pascoe.'

'She said that? And what did she say I said?'

May Farr hesitated, then replied, 'That's where she seemed mixed up. I couldn't make right sense of it. I sent her packing. We've got enough trouble without having jealous husbands looking for you with pick-handles.'

'Gav?' The young man laughed. 'Gav's no bother. We understand each other, me and Gav.'

May Farr looked at him uneasily.

'I wish I knew what was going on in that head of yours.'

'Like you wished you could have known what was going on in Dad's head?' said Farr savagely.

'Oh no. Not like that.'

208

'But you said we were the same, always hiding ourselves.'

'Aye, but there were a difference. I knew your dad's limits. Even if I didn't know what he was thinking, I knew what he could and what he couldn't do!'

'And with me you don't?' He didn't seem displeased with the thought. 'So you just *knew* he couldn't have anything to do with Tracey's disappearance? That must have been grand for you. Saved you having to lie awake nights wondering why he just dumped her at the bottom of the lane and never bothered to see her properly home!'

She shook her head sadly at his vehemence.

'Of course I wondered. Of course I asked him. Of course he told me.'

'Told you? What? And if there's something to tell, why have I never been told it?' he demanded.

'Because of what you are, Colin. Because there's a wildness in you . . . and I didn't want trouble. But it doesn't matter any longer, does it?'

'What doesn't, for Christ's sake?'

So she told him. He listened without interrupting and when she had finished, he shook his head and forced a smile and said, 'Even then? By God, you've got to give it to them. They must have been real clever, else it would've been scrawled all over pit-yard wall.'

'Is that all you can say?' demanded May Farr passionately. 'This is about your dad, about what was going on in his mind, about what he could and couldn't do! But I shouldn't need to be telling you this, not you, his own son . . .'

Her voice broke under the weight of her emotion.

'Mam, Mam,' said Colin, drawing her to him. 'Don't upset yourself. You're right. I knew he couldn't have done it. I've always known it. Sometimes you lose sight of things a bit. It's like being down that bloody pit. Sometimes the dark seems to get inside you so that a lamp's no good, nowt but the sun will clear it away. You're the sun, Mam. I see things clear now!'

He kissed her forehead. She pushed him away and wiped the tears from her eyes.

'You talk daft sometimes, Colin, always did. Is this the way you charm that schoolteacher with your fancy words?'

But she smiled as she spoke to take any sting out of what she said. Now she rose and said, 'I'll be off now. I want to talk to that solicitor again. And I want to see the doctor. Is there owt you need, son?'

'Here? No. I'll be discharged tomorrow, they reckon. As far as cop-shop at least. Take care, Mam.'

'You too.'

They exchanged smiles, hers loving, his loving also but with an admixture of something else. She hesitated uneasily, then opened the door. Constable Vessey rose from the chair outside.

'Did you get a draught from the keyhole then?' she asked caustically.

He cupped his ear and said, 'What?' and grinned, but she was paying no attention to his antics. She'd spotted Gavin Mycroft standing at the end of the corridor, framed against a swirling autumn sky which the tall narrow window tried in vain to give hospital corners to.

'What's he doing here?' she demanded.

'He's come to see your boy,' said Vessey. 'It's all right. He's got permission, like you.'

'I don't care if he's got a letter from the Queen, get him out of here!'

Mycroft had advanced and caught her words. He said, 'It's all right, Mrs Farr. No trouble, I promise you. I've just come to see how he is. Col says he'd like to see me.' She looked at him doubtfully. He looked pale and strained but returned her gaze unflinchingly.

'No trouble,' he repeated.

'Hey, is that Gav Mycroft out there?'

It was Colin's voice through the half-open door.

'Aye, it's me,' said Mycroft, raising his voice.

'Well, send the bugger in. If I can't have a telly, I might as well try a bit of live entertainment.'

'Excuse me,' said Mycroft, edging past May Farr and into the room. He closed the door firmly behind him. May stood irresolutely looking at it for a while, till Vessey said slyly, 'Like to take a peek through the keyhole, missus? Be my guest.'

'Sorry. I can't get low enough for your kind of work,' she said.

The constable watched her walk away. Once she was out of sight, he resumed his seat, pulling the chair forward so that his ear came close to the jamb of the door. Not that he could hear anything more than a murmur of voices. It was all right for bloody Wishart telling him to listen, but in these days of electronic bugging, why was he expected to manage without as much as an ear-trumpet? Also it was embarrassing to be spotted by passing nurses in this farcical position.

He jerked upright now as one approached, a little Scottish girl with a satirical tongue.

'Busy again, I see,' she said. 'Too busy for a cup of tea, I dare say.'

'I could murder one,' he answered. 'And I'd make it a mass murder for a quick drag.'

'Light up here and there'll likely be a mass murder,' said the girl. 'But if you have your cuppa in Sister's cubby-hole, you'll be all right with the window open. She's not around just now.'

Vessey was tempted. Sister's room was just round the corner and there was no way out from this blank end of the corridor without passing it. With the door open, he could keep as good a watch there as here. As for listening . . . he applied his ear to the jamb once more. Only the indistinguishable murmur of voices. He looked up into the nurse's face. The child was choking back her giggles! It was too much.

'Right,' he said rising. 'I reckon I've earned a fag. Lead on!'

CHAPTER 18

When Dalziel finally left the Welfare the first thing he saw across the road was Tommy Dickinson, sitting on the lowest step of the village War Memorial, his head resting on a bronze boot. Beside him sat Wardle.

'Not waiting for me,' asked Dalziel genially.

'You must be joking,' said Wardle. 'Waiting for *him*. I'm not doing my back lifting him.'

'Very wise.' Dalziel signalled to his car. As it approached his gaze drifted down the list of names on the Memorial.

'I thought mining were a reserved occupation,' he said.

'There were always plenty who thought the Germans gave you a better chance than the bosses,' said Wardle.

'Aye, it helps to know your enemies. Let's get him in, then.'

'What? No, it's all right. Thanks, but I'll manage him.'

'Oh aye? Next copper who comes along will likely arrest him for causing an obstruction. Come on, sunshine.'

He reached down and seized Dickinson's shirt at the neck, giving him the option of rising or being strangled.

'You coming too?' he said to Wardle after Tommy had opted for life and allowed himself to be bundled into the back seat.

'I best had. He lives with his mam and she might be upset.'

'To see Tommy pissed?' said Dalziel incredulously.

'To see the company he got pissed in,' said Wardle.

'You're a puzzle to me, Mr Wardle,' said Dalziel. 'I mean, you try to be like the rest of 'em, knee-jerk reaction to the sodding pigs, that sort of thing. But that's not you really, is it?'

'You'd better not start thinking I love you buggers, mister,' said Wardle.

'No. But you love order, I'd say. I bet you ran around

during the Strike kicking people into line, making sure things were done according to the book.'

'You lot could have done with some of that.'

'I dare say. They brought a lot of cockneys up from the Stink, but, Bloody Cossacks, them lot. All they know is pillage and rape. Well, they're back in the compound now and it's sweetness and light time again.'

'You're a fucking optimist,' said Wardle.

'Not me, friend. But I'd say that *you* were, Neil, lad. Which makes your attitude . . . disappointing.'

'I'm sorry. I'll try to be nicer. Here we are. Next to the street lamp. Thanks a lot. We'll be OK now.'

'No. No. We'll see him safe inside. Hello, lass. Here's your wandering boy come home.'

He helped the semi-conscious miner past the diminutive woman who'd appeared on the front step, and laid him on a sofa in the tiny living-room.

'My advice is leave him here with a bucket by his head. Once he's spewed, kick him up to bed. Lovely place you've got here, lass. And you keep it real nice. I'll just get myself a glass of water from the kitchen then I'll be on my way.'

He went through to the kitchen. Behind him he heard the woman say, 'Who's that daft bugger?' but Wardle was too keen to come after him to reply.

He found Dalziel standing looking out on to the long narrow back garden. A stretch of lawn petered out into a rectangle of vegetables. At the juncture of grass and earth stood the grey remains of a small bonfire.

'Good for your greens, a bit of ash,' said Dalziel.

'I'd not know, I'm not a gardener,' said Wardle.

'No? People's more your line, eh? Planting them, feeding them, helping them to grow. But you ought to know, Neil, you can't make a carnation out of a carrot.'

'What the hell are you on about?'

'I'm on about doing the important things yourself. Or was there a committee meeting more important than covering up for a friend? Or was it mebbe less of a cover-up and more of a finger-pointing?'

'You slab-faced bastard!'

213

'Thank Christ for a heartfelt insult from you at last,' said Dalziel. 'Now let's go and scatter the ashes, shall we?'

As Wield's motorbike coasted down into Burrthorpe, Peter Pascoe looked at his watch and groaned.

They'd gone far afield in search of a pub out of sight of a pit-head, and drunk too much of the landlord's excellent beer, then had to spoil the taste with pints of his awful coffee. For a while the return journey with the rain-spotted wind cold on their beer-flushed cheeks, had been exhilarating. He and Wield had opened their hearts to each other in the pub, or at least as much of their hearts as men in their kind of situation, in that kind of place, in those sort of circumstances, are able to open; but by the time the winding gear of Burrthorpe Main came into sight, Pascoe was already beginning to regret the immediate past and fear the immediate future.

For a while after they re-entered Burrthorpe Police Station they felt themselves lucky. Dalziel had not yet returned. That was the good news. But Chief Inspector Wishart wanted to see them urgently.

'Where the hell have you two been?' he demanded angrily. 'Three-hour lunches might be OK in never-never land, I bet you have picnics and hay-rides up there. Down here life is getting to be so fucking real we don't even have time to be earnest.'

'Sorry, Alex,' said Pascoe. 'Trouble with the bike. Sorry. Any developments?'

'No. The mastermind of Mid-Yorks isn't back from his lunch either, so I don't suppose I can blame you two skivers too much. To tell the truth, we don't seem to be getting anywhere. I've got all the men I can spare taking statements from every bugger they can lay hands on. And them as can't do that are combing the ditches between here and the Pendragon Arms in search of Farr's pit-black. No sign so far, no weapon, nothing. It's going to be all down to hard graft this one, and that's what I want from you two. None of your pastoral fancies, just some honest to goodness police work.'

'At your service,' said Pascoe. 'Have you had another go at Farr?'

'Not yet. Thought I'd let him relax a bit. I want him somewhere where there's no bloody doctor rushing in every two minutes to say I'm being too rough. His mother's up at the hospital seeing him. And here's an interesting thing, Mycroft's turned up too.'

'What can he want? I thought they didn't get on?'

'So did I. But I told Vessey to let him in if Farr didn't object, then press his ear to the keyhole.'

'You're letting him have visitors without supervision?' said Pascoe doubtfully.

'That's right,' said Wishart defensively. 'Wakefield insisted Mrs Farr was entitled to some privacy. As for Mycroft, I know these miners. They'll give nothing away if they don't want to. Much more chance of Vessey picking something up if he keeps his ear pressed to the door.'

'Otitis, most likely,' murmured Pascoe.

'What's that?'

'Nothing.'

'No? Listen, you two had better bear in mind that down here, you're on *my* patch and we'll do things *my* way. Out there somewhere there's a nice big clue which can tie this thing up. It's Farr's pit-black. I want it found if it means raking every ditch and emptying every dustbin in South Yorkshire.'

Through the air a plastic carrier bag came sailing. It landed heavily on the table, and a fine grey dust rose from it and settled on Wishart's papers.

'No need for these gents to dirty their lily-whites, Chief Inspector,' boomed Dalziel from the doorway. 'There's Farr's pit-black or what's left of it.'

Wield looked sadly at the bag and recalled his own fantasy of doing just that. Not for him, it seemed, the extravagant gesture; professionally or personally.

'There's not a lot left except the soles of his boots,' said Dalziel advancing. 'Still, it'll give the mad scientists something to play with.'

Wishart said, 'Where'd you find it, sir?'

'Tommy Dickinson's back garden,' said Dalziel. 'He went back to the lockers and fetched it out after they found Satterthwaite's body. Covering up for his mate.'

'Some cover-up,' said Pascoe. 'Taking this stuff pointed straight at Farr. Unless . . .'

'That sounds like the labour pangs of an idea,' said Dalziel. 'Glad to see lunch-time boozing hasn't fuddled your brain, lad. But it's not on. No way would Dickinson be trying to shift interest on to his mate. He's about as devious as a backward tortoise, our Tommy. It wasn't even his idea. Neil Wardle, branch secretary and bright enough to be a CID man, he cottoned on that Farr was likely to be Number One suspect. And before you ask, he wasn't trying to point the finger either. If that had been his game he'd have lifted it himself as he came off shift. No, it was later when the word got round about the body that his mind got to working. He couldn't get back himself so he asked Tommy to go. What he really wanted Tommy to do was check to see if there were owt incriminating in Col's locker but Tommy watches a lot of Yankee crime stuff on the telly and he knows they can prove owt they like with their tests. So to be on the safe side, he took the lot home and burnt it.'

'And did you get him to say if there *were* any bloodstains on the gear?' asked Wishart.

'Got him to say nowt,' said Dalziel. 'Wardle told me all this. Tommy's flat out on his mam's sofa and liable to stay that way till tomorrow. Weak heads, these miners have. Any road, he's not going to incriminate his mate, so it's down to Forensic. Not that I can see young Farr leaving the stuff if it were covered with blood. He struck me as a clever cunt, that one. So none of this seems to leave us much further on.'

'Sir,' said Wield, thinking that even if high drama seemed out of his reach, he might as well get credit for his bit part, 'there is one thing. It seems likely Farr made another phone call last night, before the one he made to . . . Mrs Pascoe.'

'And we've not had much help from *that* quarter, have we?' said Dalziel genially. 'So, Sergeant Wield, you think it might be helpful for us to talk to this person who got Farr's first call?'

'Yes, sir.'

'Well, get to it, lad.'

'But we don't know . . .'

'Mycroft, Stella Mycroft's the name. Used to be Farr's fiancée, but got wed to that deputy Farr talked to on the way out of the pit. Gavin Mycroft. We went down to the Welfare together today, but I noticed he didn't stay long. Overcome by an irresistible urge to visit the sick, I gather. Unsupervised, I also gather. I hope that lad you've got on duty up there's got ears like Dumbo, Chief Inspector!'

The bastard's got us bugged, thought Pascoe. And just look at that five-acre face beaming smugly as he pulls his smart little rabbits out of his great sodding hat. Oh for a stone-bow to hit him in the eye!

Sergeant Swift appeared at the door. He didn't look happy. Wishart rose immediately and went out into the corridor with him. Dalziel moved round the desk and sank gratefully into Wishart's chair.

'Thought he'd never offer,' he said. 'Right. Here's what we do. You two, seeing as you're such good friends, you can stick together and get yourselves round to this fellow Mycroft's house. Pick yourself a pretty little WPC as chaperon on your way out. I want the Mycrofts and I want them simultaneously but separately. You deal with her, Wieldy. You should be a bit less susceptible to female eye-flutter than this lecherous sod. I want to know why Mycroft went visiting at the hospital today. And just in case there's any dispute, I'll head back to the Infirmary and ask that young bugger, Farr, the same questions. All right?'

'Hold it.'

It was Alex Wishart's turn to interrupt from the doorway, but Pascoe could see that he wasn't motivated by anything like Dalziel's unbearably condescending oneupmanship. If any emotion showed on the Scot's still face, it was an untypical trepidation.

'Yes, lad. What's up? Another body, is it?'

'On the contrary, sir,' said Wishart with an immediately quenched flicker of humour.

'Eh?'

'It's Farr, sir. We've just heard from the Infirmary. He's done a bunk. Taken off. Disappeared. Sir.'

PART THREE

And next, a wolf, gaunt with the famished craving
Lodged ever in her horrible lean flank,
The ancient cause of many man's enslaving;—

She was the worst . . .

CHAPTER 1

Now all was furious activity as the terrified souls trapped in Burrthorpe police station scurried hither and thither, fearful that a pause might bring them to the painful attention of Detective-Superintendent Andrew Dalziel who sat, massive and baleful and still, at the centre of all this movement.

To Wishart's protests that he'd thought all for the best, he simply replied, 'I bet your lot backed Bonnie Prince Charlie.'

Constable Vessey was advised to change his name, have plastic surgery, flee the country. He'd returned from his cuppa and drag (no more than three minutes, God help me!) to find Gavin Mycroft in his underclothes, tied by a bloodstained bandage to his chair.

'He threatened me with a knife,' said Mycroft. 'What could I do? Bugger's mad, that's my opinion.'

Mycroft was now at the Station, making a statement. Dalziel had despatched Wield to fetch in Stella Mycroft for questioning about Farr's phone call.

'And don't mention he's escaped. And don't let her see her husband when she gets here,' he bellowed after the departing sergeant.

'What about me?' said Pascoe.

'You? Aye, it's time you got sorted, lad,' said Dalziel enigmatically. 'You go off and see if Farr's headed for home. Take that Sergeant Swift. He looks the freshest of this bunch of zombies and he knows his way around. Check Farr's mates' houses too, Wardle and Dickinson. And check the Welfare. I want you to find this sod a bloody sight quicker than you've found Monty Boyle!'

At May Farr's house, Pascoe knocked at the front door while Swift and a constable went through the alleyway to the back. After a little delay, the door was opened on a chain by a man who regarded Pascoe with the watchful distrust of a guard dog and growled, 'What do you want?'

'Police,' said Pascoe. 'I'd like to see Mrs Farr.'

'Hold on.'

He vanished; there was a distant mutter of conference, then he returned and the chain was released.

'Weren't you at the Station last night?' asked Pascoe.

'That's right. Name's Arthur Downey. Friend of the family. In here.'

Pascoe was pointed into the kitchen.

Round a blue formica table three women were sitting.

One, middle-aged, handsome, but with her face pallid with strain, rose as he entered. He recognized her from the previous night as May Farr. On one side of her was a smallish woman with a thin pinched face, whose body gave off emanations of volcanic vitality and whose expression was one of mocking contempt.

But it was the woman on the other side that Pascoe focused on.

It was Ellie.

So this was what Dalziel had meant.

She said, 'Hello, Peter. You know May, do you? And this is Wendy.'

'So you're the good cop Ellie's been telling us about,' said Wendy sceptically. 'At least you look human, which is more than can be said for yon gorilla who was let loose in the Club today.'

Pascoe said, 'Mrs Farr, you won't have heard but Colin's escaped . . .'

'Escaped?' interrupted Wendy. 'What from? He weren't locked up, were he?'

'Shut up, Wendy,' said May Farr. 'What's happened, mister?'

'Colin left the hospital,' Pascoe rephrased. 'Neither we, the police, nor the medical staff, were finished with him. We'd like . . .'

'May! There's some bobbies in your back yard.' It was Downey this time, pointing out of the window.

'Christ, it's just like the Strike all over. Buggers thinking they can go where they please,' cried Wendy, rising and heading for the door. 'I'll soon sort 'em!'

'Wendy, sit down,' ordered May Farr. 'This is my house. I'll do my own sorting. What's going off, Mr Pascoe?'

'We're looking for your son. There's a warrant out now. I'm sorry those men have jumped the gun a little, but we've got to look. Inside too.'

'Look away,' said the woman indifferently. 'A man in a hospital nightgown shouldn't be hard to find.'

'He's got clothes,' said Pascoe. 'He took them from a visitor. At knife-point, it's alleged.'

'A visitor? Gav Mycroft were there as I left. Was it Gav?'

'I believe so,' said Pascoe.

'That explains the knife,' said Wendy. 'No other way Col was going to get anything out of that stuck-up bugger.'

'It doesn't altogether explain the knife,' said Pascoe.

He regarded May Farr steadily trying to assess her reaction to all this.

She seemed to be taking it calmly, but it was only the relative calm of one who has been pushed so close to the edge that she knows that even the slightest movement might send her over. Could it be she knew something? If her son had got this far, they'd find him in the next few minutes. A miner's terrace afforded little space for secret panels, priests' holes, escape tunnels. Even in persecution, the poor were disadvantaged.

Or perhaps Farr had been in touch by telephone. If so, given the smallness of the house and the situation of the phone which was in the hall almost outside the kitchen door, there was no way the others present could not be privy to the knowledge. He wanted to look at Ellie but he forced his gaze to remain on May Farr.

'Are you saying I gave him the knife?' she demanded.

'Not saying. Asking. It's important for us to know how he's armed, Mrs Farr. It could be important to Colin too.'

'So you'll know whether to use tanks or atom bombs? Why not ring Greenham and tell 'em to get Cruise on the move?'

It was Wendy again. May Farr ignored the outburst this time and said quietly, 'I gave him no knife.'

'All right, Mrs Farr. May we search the house now?'

222

'You'll find nowt.'

Taking this as acquiescence, Pascoe began to search. As anticipated, hiding places were few. As he came down the stairs, Swift appeared and said, 'No luck, sir? Me neither. There's something out in the wash-house you mebbe ought to take a look at, though.'

He followed the sergeant through the tiny kitchen into the yard. Here in an old brickbuilt wash-house Swift pointed to a plastic bag.

'It were pushed down behind the old boiler,' he said.

Pascoe picked up the bag and opened it carefully.

'Christ,' he said.

'I'm no path man, sir,' said Swift. 'But I'd say that that skull had been bashed in, wouldn't you?'

Gingerly Pascoe reached into the bag and brought out the tiny skull.

'Yes, I would,' said Pascoe. 'And even though you're no path man, Sergeant, would you have any ideas about whose bones these might be?'

'Oh yes,' said Sergeant Swift grimly. 'A bloody good idea.'

'Let's get inside and talk to Mrs Farr,' said Peter Pascoe.

CHAPTER 2

Dalziel's fingers inside his shirt scratched ineffectually at his ribcage. It was like trying to play a polystyrene-wrapped zither.

'Tell me again,' he said patiently.

'He rang. It were about six. He said he'd come off shift early again . . .'

'Again? He'd done it before?'

Stella Mycroft lit another cigarette and said, 'Aye. That's what again means down here.'

She was a pretty lass, thought Dalziel. Pretty and possibly passionate and certainly bright. He inserted the 'possibly' because during his alcoholic interrogations at the Welfare, he had elicited many wishful fantasies about Stella's love-life but nothing more positive than the firm assertion from Tommy Dickinson that Colin Farr had been 'shagging her rotten'.

But she was certainly bright, clubbing his googly questions all over the field with a violence that was often superfluous. Let's try her with a Yorker, he thought.

'When? Why? How do you know?' he rapped.

It was no problem to her.

'Not long back. He had a row wi' Harold Satterthwaite. He came round to see me,' she rapped back.

All this Dalziel knew.

'What did he want?'

'What do you think?'

'To bed you?'

'Aye,' she said, blowing a jet of smoke at him. 'Not that he were much bothered about a bed.'

'And?'

'I told him to get lost. We'd gone steady once, been engaged, but that were a long time back and now I was a respectable married woman.'

'And he went?'

'I thought he did. But he must have hung around in the hall. I went upstairs and when Gav came off shift he found someone had lit the fire and made a right sooty mess down the wall.'

'You told him who it was?'

'Of course. Why shouldn't I? I'd done nowt wrong.'

'What did he do?'

'He wanted to go after Col, what else? That's all you lot ever think of, isn't it? Screwing, drinking and fighting.'

'Oh aye? And which of these did he want to do to Mr Farr—screw him, buy him a drink, or fight him?'

'You're a real joker, aren't you?' said Stella.

'Some of my fans laugh all the way to the dock,' said Dalziel. 'Did your husband go after Farr?'

'No. I told him nowt had happened, I mean nowt to worry about, but if he went running off to play the hard man with Col, then all the nosey gossips round here would be sure there was something going on between us.'

'Which there wasn't?'

'I told you. Are you deaf or what?'

'So why did he ring you when he walked out of the pit yesterday?'

'God knows. He were in a really funny mood, rambling on about the pit and him never going down there again. I couldn't follow most of it.'

'Drunk?'

'I didn't think so. More confused. Upset, like.'

'And did he mention Mr Satterthwaite?'

'No,' said Stella definitely.

'He didn't confess to you that he'd killed him?'

'No, he didn't.'

'But didn't you tell someone earlier today that that was precisely why he had rung you? To confess?'

The woman thought a little while, then nodded and said, 'That copper's wife. She told you. Well, I suppose you've got to stick together. Yes, that's what I said to her. I just wanted to shock her, I suppose. I'd heard about her running around after Col like she owned him or something. I thought: Right, I'll shock you down to your stretch marks, you stuck-up old cow.'

Dalziel scratched his upper lip to suppress a smile. That was a description of Ellie Pascoe he would always treasure.

'And did it shock her?'

'Not as much as I thought. And that set me to thinking. I knew he'd rung her later—I could see that *that* got up her nose, him ringing me first when he were sober, her being second choice when he'd got pissed—and I reckon he must have gone on about something happening down the pit to her like he had to me.'

'You mean you think he may have confessed to Mrs Pascoe?'

'No! I didn't say that either. Do you buggers never listen? He didn't confess to me. And I'm bloody sure he didn't confess to her.'

'But?'

'But he said enough to make us both wonder just what

the hell it was had happened. And when we heard about Harold Satterthwaite . . .'

'You put two and two together?'

'That's it, mister. Are we going to be much longer? If we are, I'll need to go for a pee.'

'Be my guest,' said Dalziel.

Alex Wishart was sitting drinking a cup of coffee in the incident room.

'Finished, sir?' he asked when Dalziel came in.

'I don't know,' said the fat man uncertainly. Wishart felt alarmed. Lack of certainty here was like a shortage of fivers at the Bank of England.

'What did you make of Mycroft?' said Dalziel.

'Sticks to his story that Farr pulled a knife from under the pillow and said he'd cut his eyes out if he didn't give him his clothes. Vessey says he was sitting there calm as you like when he found him.'

'That Vessey,' said Dalziel evilly. 'I'd plant him in a slag heap if he were mine.'

'He'd probably grow,' said Wishart. 'The alternative is almost as far-fetched as the knife attack. Mycroft helped Farr voluntarily. But why should he? They hated each other's guts as far as I can make out.'

'Then why go to see Farr at all?'

'To gloat? Or maybe to try to find out for himself if Farr did the killing. Mycroft was a big mate of Satterthwaite's.'

'That could be it. Who's with him now?'

'Sergeant Wield. You've got a treasure there, Super. He must get confessions just by sitting there looking at people.'

'You reckon? From what I've seen round here he'd likely win prizes in a beauty competition,' said Dalziel shortly. 'Look, you go in and chat to that lass. She's nervous. I want to know why.'

Wishart looked at the bulky figure louring over him like the wreck of a cooling tower and sought for the words of diplomacy.

'Some people *are* made nervous by the police, sir,' he ventured.

226

'So they bloody should be,' grunted Dalziel. 'Only *her* kind, fitted carpets, duck-down duvets, no kids, and Christmas in Morocco, I'd have expected her to come on all lady-like with simple nerves. Instead she's playing it real hard. Mebbe she's just reverting; must have been basic survival kit round here, being able to fight your corner. But I think that Farr said something to her a bit more positive than she's saying now.'

'And she told her husband and he went to see Farr to check?'

'Mebbe. Except, in *that* case, Mycroft should be shouting it out of the windows that Farr killed his mate.'

Wishart finished his coffee and stood up.

'I'll give her a whirl anyway,' he said. 'Good Lord! Hello, sir. What brings you out here?'

Dalziel turned. Standing in the doorway was Neville Watmough.

'Hello, Alex,' he said, shaking the Scotsman's hand. 'It's good to see you again.'

'And you, sir. Of course you know . . .'

He looked from Watmough to Dalziel and said, 'Of course, you do. Look, I've got to go now. See you later, shall I?'

'I hope so.'

With considerable relief to everything except his curiosity, Wishart left, closing the door firmly behind him.

'Well, Andy. Here we are. Just like old times.'

'Oh aye? You look fucking terrible, Nev. Retirement not suiting you?'

Watmough smiled faintly and said, 'It suits me well enough. There are things I miss, things I don't. You for a start, Andy. No point in beating about the bush. Let's start by saying I don't like you. Never have. Not from way back when there was a lot less of you to dislike. No need to tell me it was mutual. Me, I was always aware the job had a public face. You never were. What-you-see-is-what-you-get-Andy.'

'Hiding lights under bushels either gets you a burnt bushel or puts out the light,' said Dalziel.

'Except that I always suspected you were really twice as clever as you let on. And I always knew you were a good cop in the strict sense.'

'You mean I went to church regular?'

'No. You put thieves away regular.' Watmough pulled out a chair and sat down. He really didn't look well. 'I fell among thieves a bit, Andy,' he resumed. 'I didn't realize just how much they'd stolen till Pascoe came to see me this morning. He's your public face really, isn't he?'

'Or I'm his public behind, depending how you look at it,' said Dalziel equably. 'So, Peter came to you in a flash of blinding light and you fell off your rocking-horse, right?'

'It was when he started quoting next week's article at me that I realized how far things had gone.'

'That must have been a shock,' said Dalziel complacently.

'More than you realize. The shock was not that you'd had access to it. I don't think I can any longer be shocked by any of your antics, Andy. No, the shock was that I didn't recognize it at all. I'd been a bit taken aback by the trailer that they printed to my memoirs, but Ogilby told me they had to do a big come-on to pull the readers in, it was just a form of advertising hype which even the most serious papers and publishers went in for. Then the first episode appeared. I'd done a draft, Monty Boyle had taken it to edit it for the paper, the result . . . well, I dare say you saw the result . . .'

'You mean you weren't threatening to tell the world what a useless lot Mid-Yorks CID were?' said Dalziel disbelievingly.

'Your Sergeant Wield did make a balls-up, and that had to come out as it threw a whole new complexion on the Pedley case. But I'm not interested in pillorying good officers like Wield. Admittedly it'd be nice to see you squirm, but you've got more blots than copy in your copybook and it's never seemed to bother you, so it's hardly worth the effort.'

Surprisingly, this hurt Dalziel far more than any frontal assault could do. To be savaged by Rover the Wonder Dog was comic; to be ignored was demeaning.

'What do you want, Nev?' he demanded, letting discomfiture show.

228

Watmough savoured his reaction. It had not been anticipated—he was not a subtle enough psychologist for that—
but once appreciated, the lesson would not be forgotten.

'I saw Ike Ogilby at luncheon. I told him that I had no
intention of letting any more of my alleged memoirs be
published in his paper. He was unimpressed and assured
me that Boyle had enough material from our informal
conversations and his own research to continue with the
articles for some time. He also assured me that if I read my
contract, I would see the *Challenger* was legally entitled to
proceed in this fashion. I told him that if he did, it would be
to the accompaniment of public denials in every competitor
paper that these were my memoirs, or bore any resemblance
to my memoirs. There the matter rests.'

'Well, bravo, Nev,' said Dalziel. 'So you're not as daft as
you look. But you needn't have come all this way to let me
know. Incidentally, was Monty Boyle sitting in on this
lunch? I'm more interested in that bugger's memoirs than
yours just now and he's proving harder to pin down than a
rabbi's foreskin.'

'No, he wasn't,' said Watmough. 'Interestingly, even Ike
Ogilby was inquiring if Boyle had been in touch with me
recently. He hasn't. I should like a word with him myself.
But to get back to the point; you sent Pascoe to talk to
me . . .'

'Aye. And a lot of help you were,' grunted Dalziel.

'I'm sorry. I wasn't at my best. It was all getting me
down a bit. But I did promise to give the matter my attention
later. I didn't really pay him much attention. I said I'd
heard about this murder at Burrthorpe, but I'd really just
caught a headline on the news. I thought Pascoe's visit was
just a rather unsubtle form of harassment dreamt up by you!
It wasn't till I got my mind sorted out later and listened to
the news properly that I realized I actually might be able
to help.'

'You?' said Dalziel.

'Yes. Let's be certain the media have it straight. You have
a man called Farr helping with your inquiries into the death
of a man called Satterthwaite, right?'

'In a manner of speaking,' said Dalziel.

'And this man Farr is the son of William Farr who was the last person to see Tracey Pedley alive, would I be right in thinking that?'

'That's it. This Billy Farr who you don't seem to have investigated very thoroughly because you were so bloody sure Pickford had done the job,' sneered Dalziel.

'Don't forget Sergeant Wield's contribution to that certainty,' said Watmough. 'But you're right. It would be a poor officer who didn't check out every possibility thoroughly.'

'Aye, well, it's all water under the bridge,' said Dalziel magnanimously.

'Kind of you to say so, Andy,' said Watmough, smiling faintly. Dalziel scratched his nose. This was a different Watmough. He'd always thought of the other's rank as a shield and cover. Perhaps after all it had been simply a straitjacket.

'All the same, I'm glad that I did,' resumed Watmough.

'Did what?'

'Check out Billy Farr's story.' That smile again.

'And he was in the clear? Great. Though I don't recollect seeing owt in the record which Alex Wishart showed me.'

'It wasn't in the record.' He took a small leatherbound notebook out of his pocket. 'This is what I call my commonplace book, Andy. Quite distinct and separate from my official notes, so no need to look disapproving. Just personal observations, that sort of thing.'

'Christ, how long have you been planning your memoirs, then?'

'Long enough not to let Ike Ogilby foul them up. Here it is. Now I got this in strict confidence . . .'

'Confidence? In a murder investigation? There's no such thing!' said Dalziel scornfully.

'Not if it's pertinent to the case, no,' agreed Watmough. 'But this wasn't . . .'

'Not when it eliminated a suspect?'

'I got this information on the day that Donald Pickford killed himself,' said Watmough. 'That, God help me, seemed

230

to eliminate everyone. But Farr was definitely out, whatever way you look at it.'

'Oh aye? And why've you decided to break this so-called confidence now?'

'Because now I think it may be pertinent to a murder case, Andy. Your case. I've come to do my duty and I've come to do you a favour. But most of all, Andy, I've come to hear you say thank you!'

'In that case, we'd best both have clear heads,' said Dalziel, picking up the phone, 'Hello, young man. Could you get some coffee sent up here, please? For two. No, no biscuits. But you could ask if they've got any loaves and fishes in the canteen. Aye, that's right. Mr Watmough's going to do a miracle!'

CHAPTER 3

May Farr sat with the skull in her hands and tears blinding her eyes.

'You're quite sure,' insisted Pascoe.

'Oh yes. There was the disc as well. The leather would have rotted but there was the disc with his name on. It's Jacko, poor little tyke. Billy loved that dog.'

'And Colin brought these bones home on Monday evening and you gathered he'd found them in the old workings?'

'Yes. I knew he'd been wandering around up there. I asked him not to. But I didn't know he'd got inside. It's all supposed to have been filled in and made safe since . . . since . . .'

'How did you know he'd been up there before? Did he tell you?' asked Pascoe sharply.

'Arthur saw him. He didn't deny it.'

Pascoe looked at Downey. He'd wanted to clear the room completely before talking to Mrs Farr. Wendy Walker had got belligerent and Ellie had looked defiant but they'd allowed Swift to shepherd them towards the door. Downey, however, had shaken his head and said, 'I'll stay,' in a voice tremulous with the determination of a weak man making an unshiftable stand. May Farr had resolved matters by saying, 'Yes, I'd like Arthur to stay.' The other two women had then left the kitchen. Swift stood guard on the door, but behind it Pascoe did not doubt that Wendy and Ellie were straining their ears.

Downey was finding it hard to speak. The sight of Jacko's bones seemed to have brought his old friend back to him with an intensity of emotion matching May Farr's. He sat pale-faced now, his eyes fixed on the woman opposite, or the skull in her hands.

Finally he said, 'Aye, I saw him a few times. Well, I thought nowt of it at first. The workings are mainly on the old common, right up against the edge of Gratterley Wood. That's a popular spot in summer for walking, and for courting round the White Rock—that's a sort of limestone cliff in the middle of the wood—and there's brambling in the autumn . . .'

He was getting a grip on himself again and as he realized what he'd said he shot May an apologetic look, and went on hurriedly, 'But Col was going there in all weathers and not just in the woods either, and I thought May ought to be told.'

'Did you know he was going underground, Mr Downey?' asked Pascoe.

'Aye, I did wonder. He'd disappear so unexpected, like.'

Pascoe returned his attention to the weeping woman.

'Mrs Farr, what effect did it have on Colin, finding these bones?'

Pulling herself together visibly, May Farr said, 'It upset him.'

'Yes, I'm sure. But in what way?' persisted Pascoe. 'Was it just because it brought his dad back that finding the bones upset him? Or was it because they seemed to confirm a theory . . . ?'

'You're not daft, are you, mister?' said May, drying her eyes. 'That's right. He couldn't bring himself to say it hardly, but he didn't have to. We all thought Billy most

232

likely had an accident because Jacko had got stuck somewhere and he could hear him barking. Well, any fool can see this poor devil was doing no barking.'

Her fingers ran round the edge of the great hole smashed in the top of the skull.

'And Col reckoned that if Billy could do this to Jacko, then he must have been really desperate?' prompted Pascoe.

'Yes,' said the woman wearily. 'Yes. Living in a place like this and hating it like Col does, it gets you willing to believe the worst of people, Mr Pascoe. I didn't realize how much it had affected Colin till all this blew up yesterday, him walking off shift and getting drunk, I mean. He told me he had nowt to do with Harold Satterthwaite's death, and I believe him.'

'Mrs Farr,' said Pascoe gently. 'You thought Colin believed that finding the dog proved that his father killed himself. Did you feel the same?'

'Monday night I did,' she admitted in a low, shamed voice. 'That's why I didn't catch on how far Col's thoughts had taken him. I knew Billy never harmed that little girl, but I thought mebbe it had got to him, the things people said, and him feeling guilty anyway for leaving her on her lone, and it was Christmas, and the kiddies were running around the street with their new presents, and . . .'

She looked down at the skull and said softly, 'I'm sorry, Billy, but you always did keep things bottled up, and I thought . . . any road, mister, I didn't pay as much heed to what our Colin was thinking as I should have done. But when I realized that he could actually believe his dad was a . . . was like that, I soon put him right.'

'And how did you do that, Mrs Farr?' asked Pascoe.

'I went up to the hospital and I told him what had happened when Billy took little Tracey brambling in Gratterley Wood that day.'

It had been a warm ripe Indian Summer day, a jewel in September's golden crown, a day when a man could feel it a real blessing not to have to ride the pit any more, even if the price were a stiff leg and a nagging pain in the knee joint as he tried to keep up with the impatient little girl by his side.

'The brambles'll wait,' he assured her. 'They're not going anywhere. Look, there's some over there. Why don't we start there?'

'No, no, no,' she insisted, tugging at his hand. 'The best ones are up by the White Rock. They always are. You told me that, Uncle Billy.'

'Did I? I must've been daft,' he said with a laugh that few adults ever heard. 'Well Jacko seems to agree, so we'd best go, I suppose.'

The Jack Russell, which was way ahead of them up the track, looked round to make sure they were following, then scampered on.

Fifteen minutes later the creamy limestone of the outcrop was visible. The little girl was soon absorbed in searching for blackberries. She was a very choosey picker and it was going to take her some time to fill the plastic seaside bucket she'd brought as her container.

Billy Farr strolled on. Life seemed good. It would have been marvellous to have had a little lass of their own but it wasn't to be. And as Pedro had once said, with Tracey he was getting all the pleasures of fatherhood without losing the sleep. Well, not all. There was nothing to match that sheer joy of *creation*, that was the only word for it, that he felt when he looked at Colin. But it would come again. When Col settled down and married Stella and they had kiddies of their own, a little girl perhaps. Probably would be little too if she took after her mother! Little Stella, but beautiful as a porcelain doll and strong with it, physically and mentally. They'd become really good friends since Col joined the Navy. She too was like a daughter to him. He looked back to Tracey absorbed in passing judgement on a bramble and felt a frisson of sheer pleasure. Two daughters by act of God, and the promise of grandchildren to come. It was good to be alive.

He hadn't seen Jacko for some time, he realized. Nor had he heard him. This probably meant he was on to something.

234

Never a noisy dog, he fell absolutely quiet whenever he got a scent or spotted a movement.

Now Billy Farr saw him, up a steep slope on the far side of the White Rock, where the ground rose in lynchets, each level screened by a profusion of furze and dogberry and wild eglantine. He could just see the terrier's hind quarters, rigid with attention. Something was up there. Possibly a bird or a rabbit. Farr began to ascend, aware that his approach would probably startle the prey, but not worried. A dog was a dog and hunting was his instinct, but he didn't want anything to end its life on such a glorious day.

He needn't have worried. Nothing was here which the dog might threaten. Nor was there much chance that his own approach would disturb this prey. Putting one hand firmly on Jacko's nape, he carefully parted the foliage in front of him.

Here in a scoop of ground, luxuriant with brome and hair-grass, and fragrant with willowherb, a man and a woman wrestled naked, now the golden tan of her narrow back showing on top, now the pallid breadth of his. He bore the marks of a collier, slab-muscled in the shoulder and upper torso, with his skin etched by carbon where the coal dust had soaked into small cuts and abrasions. It looked as if his weight and strength must surely tear the woman apart, but she clung to him with such tenacity, her slim legs locked round his heavy buttocks, her nails digging into his back, that there flashed into Billy Farr's mind an image from a TV wildlife programme of a tiny golden scorpion destroying a huge black beetle.

The image was his mind's attempt to escape from the physical truth he saw before him. But the mind is its own traitor and already as he slid back down the slope and hurried back down the path, seizing an amazed and distressed little Tracey as he passed, a new image, eidetic in its intensity, had printed itself permanently on his brain. He could never forget, or forgive, the sight and the sound of the girl he loved like a daughter as she gave herself willingly and with a joyous lust to Harold Satterthwaite.

*

There was a silence in the tiny room after May Farr had finished. Pascoe broke it. 'So Billy left Tracey at the back of the Club and went off by himself.'

'That's right,' said Mrs Farr. 'He'd never have done that normally, but he didn't want to see Pedro or Maggie or anyone. He just wanted to be alone for a bit. To think what to do, what to say. He were a very trusting man, my Billy. He didn't let a lot of folk get close, but when he did it was absolute trust. Stella Gibson had shattered that. And Col would need to be told. It was all too much for him. He just went off and sat in a field and smoked his pipe for a couple of hours. Then he came home and the news that Tracey had gone missing near on finished him off.'

A thousand questions arose in Pascoe's mind.

He said, 'And did he tell Colin?'

'He never saw Col again.'

'He could have written.'

'No,' she said certainly. 'It's not the kind of thing you write to someone so far away.'

'Then Colin never knew?'

May Farr said, 'When he came back for the funeral, I were ill; half dead, now I look back. It were like living in a fog. When I started coming out of it, Col and Stella had already broken up, so there seemed no point in saying anything, especially not when she got herself engaged to Gav Mycroft and married him. And there was bad blood enough between Colin and Satterthwaite without stirring up more. Mebbe I was wrong. But I never guessed that Col might get round to thinking his dad could actually be the killer!'

Her voice trembled with love and loss, and indignation too. The only words of comfort that rose in Pascoe's mind would be no comfort at all. Colin was a proven violent man, he wanted to say. It wouldn't be surprising if he began to wonder whether beneath his father's calm exterior a like darkness lay.

He forced his mind back to the job in hand. May Farr was telling the truth, yet there was still a hesitation.

He pressed on—'And what was Col's reaction when you

236

told him today?—' and knew he had reached his goal.

'What do you mean? Naturally he were relieved to know at least what happened that day.'

'But was he surprised to learn about Stella and Satterthwaite?'

'Surprised that it was happening *then*,' she said, sounding herself surprised, as if she hadn't really considered this before. 'But no, he didn't sound surprised at the idea itself. As if . . .'

'As if perhaps it was still going on and he knew all about it?'

Pascoe glanced at his watch. The afternoon was drawing on. It was time he got this information back to Dalziel.

'Thank you, Mrs Farr,' he said. 'I wish you could have told us this a lot sooner . . .'

'Sooner? Sooner than what? You've known about Billy seeing them two at it up in the wood for long enough . . .'

'No, I assure you,' said Pascoe, taken aback.

'Not you. You're an off-comer, aren't you? But this lot who were here when it happened . . .'

Pascoe looked at Sergeant Swift whose long face grew even longer in surprise.

'First I've heard of it,' he said. 'First I've heard anything about Satterthwaite and Mrs Mycroft. They must've been clever to get away with it round here!'

'But you told someone, Mrs Farr?'

'That's right. I couldn't put up with Billy being under suspicion any more. He wasn't going to open his mouth to a soul, he was so upset by everything. But in the end I went along and saw the man in charge and told him straight he were wasting time and money keeping my Billy under suspicion.'

'Who was this you told?' asked Pascoe. 'Do you recall his name?'

'Aye, it's him who's writing them things in the *Challenger*, isn't it? Watmough. That's his name. Mr Watmough.'

Now more than ever it seemed imperative to contact Dalziel. He would do it from the car, though, not from this house where there were so many ears.

He said, 'Thank you, Mrs Farr. I'll have to leave a constable here in case Colin does come home or tries to ring you. I'm sorry.'

'You're doing your job, mister,' she replied wearily. 'Now, Arthur, I reckon it's time you went off home and stopped supping my tea like it grew on bushes. And take them two out there with you. Go on now. I'll be all right. I need some time to myself.'

It was probably true. But Pascoe suspected too that in the midst of her own woes, this remarkable woman was finding time for a bit of compassionate diplomacy. He'd been wondering how to get Ellie out of the house without it seeming like a plea or a command. And he guessed Ellie had been wondering how to respond without losing face in front of the fearsome Wendy. Now May, by lumping them all together, had provided an out.

'Thank you, Mrs Farr,' he repeated. 'Try not to worry eh? Probably Colin will come in of his own accord when he sits down and considers how daft he's been.'

A wintry smile touched her frost-pale lips.

'You think so? Talk to someone who knows him, Mr Pascoe.'

He left now and stood at the front door waiting for Wendy and Ellie to make their farewells. They weren't long. Wendy seemed to have Downey in a kind of loose armlock.

On the step she said, 'See you, Ellie. Come and visit some time when you can get a pass. Come on, Arthur. What are you going to do? Curl up here and howl?'

Ignoring Pascoe, which he took for her highest courtesy to a policeman, she led the still reluctant Downey away.

'Well,' said Pascoe. 'I suppose you heard most of that?'

'Most,' admitted Ellie. 'It explained a lot.'

'Like what?'

'Like Col going on last night about bones and blood in the pit. He wasn't talking about Satterthwaite at all, he was talking about the dog!'

'Was he? Does this mean you'd like to put it in your statement now?'

She looked at him angrily, decided the grounds of her anger were unsafe, made herself relax.

He said, 'Walk you to your car?'

'All right. I'd best get home and pick up Rose.'

Pascoe glanced at his watch. Four-thirty. It felt later.

'It's been a long day,' he said. 'For both of us. Your blood test was negative, by the way.'

'What? Oh, that. It seems years ago.'

'Does it? Perhaps. Ellie, if you rush to meet trouble, you usually find it, so I'm not rushing. But shouldn't we talk?'

'Here? Now?'

He looked around. The terraced houses of Clay Street stretched away on both sides, the façades grey with indifference, their windows like blind eyes. But he guessed their indifference was delusive and their blindness like a professional beggar's.

Ellie's car, parked round the corner, was now in sight. They could sit in it and talk, but it wasn't the place, this wasn't the time. A wise man picked his own ground for a battle.

'No,' he said. 'I'll see you at home.'

'Don't tell me. You'll probably be late.'

'I wouldn't be surprised,' he said.

'I'll try to be awake,' she said.

'Just try to be at home,' he replied before he could stop himself.

She shook her head in disbelief.

'If you want to know the time, ask a policeman,' she said. 'It's always the Middle Ages. I'll see you when I do.'

She marched away towards the car and got in. He noticed she'd left it unlocked. Demonstrating her implicit trust in these knights of the dusty face, he thought savagely.

As she accelerated past him, he looked for some sign of softening, for at the very least that expression of humorous irony with which she had once laced her indignation.

But her face was set and cold and unrelenting and she drove by him without even looking in his direction.

He turned away sadly and went to update Dalziel.

And in the car Ellie said, 'You can sit up now,' and watched in the mirror to see the smiling face of Colin Farr rise into view behind her.

CHAPTER 4

'Why'd you not turn me in?' asked Colin Farr.

'God knows,' said Ellie. 'I don't.'

She'd turned off the road as soon as they were out of sight of the village, bumping the car a few yards along a deep-rutted, bracken-fringed track before switching off the engine.

She lit a much-needed cigarette. The effort of not screaming when she first glimpsed him lying in the back, the greater effort of not looking at Peter in silent appeal as she drove by him, had left her nerves in tatters. Now she did let out a smoky gasp as suddenly he slipped with practised ease through the narrow space between the passenger seat and the roof and sat beside her, saying, 'There. That's cosier, isn't it?'

Reacting against her nervousness, she demanded aggressively. 'Did you kill Satterthwaite?'

'Now why should I do a thing like that?' he mocked.

'Because he was screwing lovely little Stella,' she snapped.

'Oh aye? Nowt to do with me,' he said.

'It was something to do with you when you were still engaged!'

'Here, your ears have been flapping, haven't they? Aye, that did surprise me a bit.'

'That she could prefer another man to you?'

'That it had been going on so long. Mebbe it stopped when she got wed, then started up again when she got bored with Gav, which'd be about twenty minutes, I'd say.'

'How did you know about them? Did she tell you?'

'Oh no.' He grinned. 'We're not on such close terms as that. I put two and two together, with some help from a "friend" who left me a note on my lamp-hook. Then I paid

Stella a visit unexpected, like, and I felt she were expecting me somehow and there were only one bugger I could think of who could have warned her. Then just as I was leaving there was a phone call. No one spoke, but I could feel that bastard on the other end of the line. Just feel him. And suddenly a lot of other little things came together.'

'What did you do?'

He smiled wickedly. 'I left Stella a little going-away present.'

Behind them a lorry sped along the road. Ellie turned to look at it in alarm, Farr remained indifferent.

'Anyone sees us, they'll just imagine there's a bit of quiet humping going on,' he said.

'Not if it's the police,' she said fearfully. 'And they're probably checking cars along this road by now.'

'I'm not going any further by car,' he said. 'Up there I'm going, and it'll take more than a few flat-footed bobbies to catch me, over or under the ground.'

He was staring ahead at the tree-clothed ridge above them, incandescent in the declining sun.

'They'll have dogs, helicopters . . .'

He laughed at her.

'I'm not Lord Lucan!' he said. 'Just an ordinary pit-lad who's got in a bit of bother.'

'Did you kill him?' she asked once more.

'I suppose I did, in a manner of speaking,' he mused. 'But that's not the bit of bother I'm worried about. My dad's dead and I'd got so muddled and muddied with this bloody place that I actually got to thinking that mebbe he was a killer, aye, and a child molester too. God, I must have been near on mad! But I got to thinking lying in that hospital this morning, everything so quiet and light and clean, I got to seeing how daft I was. I didn't need Mam to come along with explanations. I knew as I should have known all along that Dad couldn't harm any living thing! He didn't much like it if Jacko caught himself a rabbit. And as for my dad hurting Jacko . . . you should have seen the poor little sod's skull . . .'

'I did.'

'What?' said Farr, jerked back to the present. 'When?

How? Oh, they searched the house, did they? Bastards.'

'That's what you were talking about when you started rambling about blood and bones last night, wasn't it? Jacko.'

'I went on about blood and bones, did I? I don't recall.' He looked at her speculatively. 'Did you tell your husband's mob, then?'

Ellie shook her head.

'Secrets? Best not to have secrets, Ellie,' he said. She felt their ages reversed, distorted, he the elderly experienced sage, she the youthful naive disciple.

'No,' she said. 'Colin, come back with me now. There's no need to run. There's nowhere to run to.'

'Who's running?' he said. 'But I'm not coming back, not just yet.'

He opened the door and got out.

'Colin,' she said. 'Why did you ring Stella when you came out of the pit yesterday?'

'Ring her *first*, you mean?' He smiled. She found him insufferable but had to persist. 'Why?'

'I owed her a warning,' he said. 'That much at least I owed her. Do me a favour, Ellie. Ring my mam and tell her I'm OK.'

'Surely,' said Ellie, disproportionately pleased at this request for help. 'But I won't ring. There's a copper there. He'll listen in. I'll go back and pretend that I forgot something. Col, is there anything I can get you while I'm there? Food, clothes, anything? I could drop it off here as I pass.'

'No,' he said. 'Too dangerous for you to try to bring owt from home and I'm not going to hang around by the roadside anyway. But you're right, a bit of grub and something to drink wouldn't come amiss. You could mebbe get someone else to fetch it for me.'

'All right. Who?'

He thought a moment, then smiled.

'Arthur,' he said. 'You'll have met him, Arthur Downey, always hanging around our house, trying to be useful. Now's his chance. He lives in the street backing ours, number thirty. Tell him to bring whatever he can up to the White Rock. But not turnips. I hate his bloody turnips!'

'The White Rock? He'll know where that is?'

'Oh aye. Even Arthur'll know where the White Rock is. Right, I'm off.'

'Colin,' she said urgently as he turned away. 'What was it you warned Stella of?'

He turned back, his face troubled.

'I met Gav on the way out of the pit. He were his usual charming self. He warned me to keep away from Stella. I didn't really know what I was saying. All I wanted was to get out. So I told him not to fear, I'd not be messing with Harold Satterthwaite's leavings. He wanted to kill me then, I think, but I just didn't have the time to fight. So I ran off shouting at him to ask Satterthwaite himself if he didn't believe me. When I got up on the bank and started thinking straight, I knew I shouldn't have told him so I rang Stella to warn her. She deserved that.'

'But Colin, that means . . .'

He leaned through the window and kissed her full on the lips. She responded with a passion that frightened her. Finally he broke away and regarded her with a smile that hardly mocked at all.

'Goodbye, Mrs Pascoe,' he said. 'You've come off lucky. Not many do as have much to do with me.'

Then he turned again and began to run up the track, as lithe and fluid and lovely as a cat. She watched him out of sight. And still she watched and seemed to see him still. Finally a cloud caught the slanting sun and dulled the golden glow in Gratterley Wood.

She started the car and backed out on to the road and turned once more to Burrthorpe.

CHAPTER 5

After Watmough had finished, Dalziel rose and went to the door.

'If I see any blind lame lepers, I'll send 'em in,' he said as he passed through it, leaving Watmough to sip his coffee uncertain if he'd been complimented or not.

Dalziel ran up the stairs, very light on his feet for such a big man. He opened a door and peered in. Alex Wishart was sitting at the far side of a desk facing Gavin Mycroft.

'Alex, a word,' said Dalziel.

The Scot got up and came towards the door. The deputy turned and said, 'Look, can I go home now? I've been here for hours and it's bloody nippy for one thing.'

He was still wearing the white overall they'd provided at the hospital.

'We'll have some of your clothes fetched in,' said Dalziel.

Wishart came into the corridor. He made to pull the door shut behind him but Dalziel's large foot got in the way. He looked in surprise at the fat man and was taken aback to see his pumpkin face wrinkle into a wink.

'She's coughed,' said Dalziel in a whisper Henry Irving would have been proud of. 'I told her we'd definitely be charging Farr and that did it. What he told her when he rang up last night was that on his way out of the pit, he'd blown the gaffe on her and Satterthwaite to Gav. Poor sod. He must have flipped it. Straight off he went and thumped Harold. Overdid it. He'll likely get off with manslaughter if he plays his cards right. Don't be too rough on him. He's had a lot to put up with.'

Another wink for the upper balcony and Dalziel went noisily down the stairs.

Now he re-entered the room where Stella Mycroft was sitting puffing angrily at a cigarette. A WPC stood by the door while opposite her sat Sergeant Wield. He stood up as Dalziel entered and flickered his eyes negatively.

As Dalziel took the vacated chair, Stella began to rave, 'How long's this going on, for God's sake? Does Gav know I'm here? Does any bugger know I'm here? I've told you all I know which is bugger-all, so why'm I being kept stuck in here with you pair of ugly sods popping in and out like rats from a compost heap?'

As she raved Dalziel reached across the table and to Wield's amazement put his huge hand over the woman's delicate hand and peered deep into her eyes. It would have been beyond the will of Boadicea to keep on shouting in such circumstances and rapidly the indignant flow sputtered to a halt.

'It's over, love,' said Dalziel softly.

She tried to pull her hand away but he held it fast.

'You wha'?' she said.

'It's over. Gav's told us everything. The lad had no choice once Col started cooperating. But not to worry. I reckon it could come down to manslaughter, accidental killing, couple of years, suspended, on probation even, what do you think, Sergeant?'

'I'm not sure of the precise circumstances, sir,' said Wield, taking his cue.

'Farr lost his temper with Gav, told him that Stella here was having an affair with Harold Satterthwaite. Now I don't know if that's true or not, and it's none of our business anyway. But Gav went to talk it over with Harold. Well, he would, wouldn't he? Things got heated, it was dark, bang! Who can say exactly what happened?'

'Col's said . . . I don't believe you!' burst out Stella.

'He felt sorry about letting the cat out of the bag,' said Dalziel. 'That's why he rang you, of course, to warn you. But it's one thing feeling sorry, it's another carrying the can. I'm sorry too, love. All I can say from old experience is that these things seem terrible at the time, but it'll pass, you'll be amazed how quick it passes.'

She looked at him distrustfully, but when she spoke her voice was subdued.

'Can I see Gav?' she said.

'Of course,' said Dalziel genially. 'Just give your statement to the young lady here, then we'll ferry you along to have a nice chat with your husband. OK?'

One last bone-cracking squeeze of her hand and he rose and left the room. Wield followed. This time Dalziel made sure the door was firmly closed.

'Has he coughed?' asked Wield.

'I'm not sure, but he will the minute he sees her statement,' said Dalziel.

'Did you really get this from Farr?' asked Wield.

'No way. That mad bugger's still missing as far as I know. No, it were a combination of things, a few hints that Pedley let drop when I talked to him earlier, and then a bit of help from my old chum, Nev Watmough, a few years late, true, but we've all got to move at our own speed. I'd been wondering why Mycroft went to see Farr in hospital and why he helped him escape. It were obviously a put-up job, weren't it?'

'Oh yes,' said Wield. 'Obviously. But why didn't Farr just speak out when he woke up this morning and realized what we were after him for?'

'Because he's bloody mad, because he wants to be on the run, because . . . I don't know, Sergeant, and I doubt if he does, either.'

'But we can call off the hunt for him?' said Wield. 'I mean, what do we want him for?'

'Impeding a police inquiry,' said Dalziel. 'All right, it's not much and it's certainly not worth the dogs and heli-copters and appeals on the telly. But I'll tell you something, Wieldy. My piles are aching again and I'll not rest comfort-able while yon mad bugger's running round free!'

He headed back up the stairs to check on Wishart's progress. A uniformed constable intercepted him.

'Sir, Mr Pascoe's been on the radio, says he needs to talk to you.'

'Has he found Farr?'

'Don't think so, sir.'

'Then what's he playing at? Whistle him up again and tell him to meet me at Mrs Farr's house in half an hour. And straighten yourself up, lad! Haven't they found a cure yet for rickets down here?'

Pascoe got Dalziel's message as he came out of the Welfare Club. Pedley had been very cooperative, which made Pascoe guess his search was a waste of time. So it had proved. Next he and Sergeant Swift went to Neil Wardle's house, but could get no reply. Tommy Dickinson lived just a couple of streets away. Swift told him, not without pride, that even for Burrthorpe, this was a rough area. When he started

246

reeling off a list of folk-heroes who'd drawn their first blood here, Pascoe cut him off brusquely. Alex Wishart's ironies were one thing, but he didn't have to take ancient sergeants implying that life in Mid-Yorks was a pastoral idyll.

The door was opened by a wirily muscular man with greying hair and watchful eyes.

'Hello, Neil,' said Swift. 'We've just come from your house.'

'I hope you left it like you found it,' said the man.

'Mr Wardle?' said Pascoe.

'Aye. You must be Pascoe. You're with yon other bugger, right? The one who could cut coal with his teeth.'

A man would need the skill of a Scarlet Pimpernel to lead a private life here, thought Pascoe.

'We're inquiring about your friend, Colin Farr?'

'I've nowt to say about Col,' said Wardle.

'Or *to* him?'

Wardle thought a moment then said, 'He's buggered off, then?'

'Very sharp,' said Pascoe. 'You wouldn't happen to know where?'

Wardle didn't even bother to reply.

'It'll do him no good,' said Pascoe, irritated. 'Running away never does.'

'You reckon? Ever been a thousand feet under and heard the timbers cracking over your head?'

Pascoe was further irritated by this easy assumption of a risk-given moral superiority. The sods really believed their own myths!

'Is Mr Dickinson in?' he asked.

Wardle stood aside and beckoned him in with mock courtesy. On an inadequate sofa, a stout young man sprawled and snored. A plastic bucket rested close to his hand.

'If you care to hang on a bit he'll likely make a statement,' said Wardle.

'What are you doing here, Mr Wardle?'

'Tommy's mam had to go out so I said I'd sit here with the lad and make sure he came to no harm.'

'How long will Mrs Dickinson be? We'd like to look round just in case Mr Farr has got in, without anyone's knowledge, of course.'

'I'd not wait till his mam comes back, then. Sergeant Swift here'll tell you she sucks coppers' blood.'

Upon this hint, Pascoe and Swift went quickly through the house.

Unless he'd wriggled under the floorboards, Farr wasn't here. They returned to the parlour.

'Just in time,' said Wardle. 'His mam's coming down the street.'

On the sofa, Dickinson stirred, opened his eyes, smiled up at Pascoe.

'Mr Dickinson,' Pascoe began. 'I'm a policeman . . .'

The stout youth turned his head away and was comprehensively sick into the bucket.

'There,' said Wardle. 'I told you he'd make a statement.'

CHAPTER 6

As he drove back to May Farr's house, Pascoe saw Arthur Downey on an old bike making his way down the High Street. It was almost dusk and there was no sign of any light on the machine. Well, that was the locals' responsibility. Pascoe guessed it would be a brave cop round here who pulled up a miner for not having lights on his bike.

As he turned into Clay Street, to his surprise he saw Ellie's Mini. Instead of wondering why she'd returned, he found himself thinking the car was parked dangerously close to the corner. I'm beginning to think like a traffic cop, he told himself.

He parked his car with exaggerated care. As he approached the front door, he could hear two voices more familiar as solos now upraised in discordant duet. He opened the door without knocking and went in.

'Hello, hello, what seems to be the trouble?' he inquired.

Ellie and Dalziel turned to face him.

'I just came round here to tell Mrs Farr her lad's off the hook and your missus flew at me like a mad ostrich!' said Dalziel, all hurt innocence.

'All I did was tell May not to trust the fat sod!'

Pascoe moved so that he could see Mrs Farr who was sitting down, partly screened by Dalziel's bulk. She was pale and clearly distraught.

'For God's sake you two, why don't you have your squabbles somewhere else?' he said angrily. He pulled up a chair and sat down in front of the woman and took her hands in his. 'It's all right, Mrs Farr,' he said.

'Is he telling the truth, this one?' she asked, looking him straight in the eyes. 'Ellie says not to trust him, he's likely just lying to find out where Colin's hiding.'

Pascoe glanced towards Dalziel, who said bluntly, 'He's off the hook.'

'He's telling the truth,' said Pascoe to Mrs Farr. 'He'd not lie about something like that, not to me anyway.'

Dalziel looked ready to dispute this assertion, then pulled on a conciliatory expression like a nylon stocking over a bandit's face.

'But Ellie's not altogether wrong,' he said. 'I do still want to find the lad. Before he comes to any harm.'

Pascoe followed his gaze to Ellie. Her cheeks were still flushed from argument and her eyes were bright. Usually he felt proud and turned on when he saw her in full Valkyrie flight, but this time he felt separated from her by Colin Farr who had occupied her mind so exclusively that she had been able to ignore May Farr's distress.

'Why did you come back, Ellie?' he asked quietly.

Still she looked defiant, then May Farr said, 'For God's sake tell him, woman. Do you not trust your own man?'

The reproof seemed to bewilder Ellie, then the tension ebbed from her body and she said, 'Oh shit. He asked me to tell May he was all right. Peter, he was hiding in my car. I dropped him off along the road that runs up to the pit. He went up into the woods on the left-hand side.'

'Gratterley Wood,' said Mrs Farr dully. 'He'll be up by the White Rock, isn't that what you said, lass?'

Ellie said, 'He asked me to get Mr Downey to bring some food up to him.'

'And have you seen this Downey fellow yet?' demanded Dalziel.

'Yes. I went to see him first, before your spies got on to me,' flashed Ellie.

'Damn.'

'It's all right. I just saw Downey cycling down the main street,' said Pascoe.

'Good. Mebbe we can catch him.'

'You don't think Colin's going to hang around once he sees you lot, do you?' demanded May Farr.

'There'll just be the two of us,' said Dalziel. 'I don't want to scare him off, just get close enough to let him know the heat's off. Sergeant Swift, you know where this White Rock is, I dare say?'

'Yes, sir.'

'Right. Let's go.' He headed for the door, closely followed by Swift.

Pascoe looked at Ellie.

'It'll be all right, won't it?' she said.

He didn't dare to ask what she was talking about but said, 'Yes.'

Outside, Dalziel said, 'We'll take your car, Peter, in case there's any rough driving.'

They got in, Swift in the back.

He said, 'Head for the main street.'

As he drove, Pascoe's mind was filled with a nagging unease.

'Why are we still chasing around after an innocent man, sir?' he asked.

'Why's an innocent man not bother to tell us he's innocent?' said Dalziel. 'That farce with Mycroft. He hates the guy. Why not just point the finger at him instead of blackmailing him into helping him escape?'

'Perhaps he felt partly responsible for Satterthwaite's death.'

'So what? He hated him too. In fact, come to think of it, there aren't a lot of people young Mr Farr likes.'

'So what's your theory, sir?'

'No theory, lad. But a man who doesn't give a toss about being chief suspect for a murder he didn't do isn't someone I want running round loose.'

They had passed down the High Street. Now at Swift's instruction, they swung left up the lane alongside the Welfare Club.

'It gets a bit rough,' said Swift, 'but if you can get round this bend we'll be out of sight of nosey eyes.'

Pascoe managed it with some slight protest from his silencer box as it grated against a stone, but it wasn't concern for his undercarriage that made him stop. Up ahead was another car blocking the way.

They got out and approached it. From the damp bloom on its paintwork and the yellow leaves clinging to the roof and bonnet, it had been there a little while, overnight at least.

'It's that reporter's,' said Swift. 'Boyle. I saw him in it the night Farr chucked him through the window.'

Dalziel swept his hand through the screening dampness on the front window and peered inside.

'Nowt,' he said. 'Except a cauliflower on the back seat.'

'The boot?' suggested Pascoe.

Dalziel came round the back, sniffed, shrugged.

'Best be sure.'

And raising his foot he drove his heel with great force against the lock.

The boot flew open. There was nothing there that didn't belong in a boot.

'I hope he's got good expenses,' said Pascoe.

'He'll need 'em if the bugger's up there, queering my pitch,' said Dalziel.

They all looked up the track to where along the looming ridge desperate fingers of light were still scrabbling for purchase. Even here, by the car, with the Welfare's chimneys still visible, industrial South Yorkshire seemed a long way away and Pascoe thought coldly that this was a wilderness long before man had made it so and these had been hills under which a lost traveller could dream and never waken.

251

'You coming or not?' demanded Dalziel, who was already ten yards ahead in close pursuit of Swift.

Reluctantly Pascoe set out after them.

A few yards further on, Swift said, 'Look, sir. That'll be Downey's bike.'

Dalziel put his hand on it.

'Seat still warm,' he said in his best Sherlockian manner. 'We can't be far behind.'

Now the track became a path. Pascoe glanced back. No sign of the cars nor even of the bike, surely they couldn't have come so far so soon? He hurried on, suddenly fearful of being left behind in this frightful dark wood in which mist was beginning to drift like the fetid exhalations of some lurking troll. What was he doing here, for God's sake? It occurred to him that he had never laid eyes on Colin Farr! What a great qualification for a searcher! If someone dropped down out of a tree in front of him at this very moment, he wouldn't know if it were Farr or some passing primate.

His acceleration had brought him up against the other two. For the simple sake of hearing a voice, he said, 'Sir, I don't even know . . .'

'Shh! We're almost there,' hissed Dalziel. He was peering ahead and upwards to where the mist seemed to have concentrated at the far end of a narrow glade. Pascoe strained his eyes and became aware that in fact the area of whiteness was not all mist but a patchy overhanging outcrop of striated limestone. Presumably this was the famous White Rock, not much to write home about, not perhaps unless you spent your days digging black rock out of the earth.

A choking cry cut through his thoughts, there was a flurry of movement at the foot of the overhang, and Dalziel lumbered forward a few steps, shouting. If it was meant to be reassuring, Pascoe couldn't blame anyone for missing the point. A writhing shadow separated, became two men, one upright, one prone. The upright figure took a couple of steps towards them. One of the last drowning fingers of light caressed his face. It was so young, so defiant, so despairing. So beautiful. Here he was at last, the marvellous boy. The phrase no longer a mockery. I was fooling myself when I said I'd never recognize him. I'd have picked him out in a riot.

The prone man was pushing at the earth like an ageing athlete trying for his fiftieth press-up.

The young man stooped and ran his hands over the ground in search of something. He seemed to take the sunlight with him and the prone man was revealed as Arthur Downey. Sergeant Swift took advantage of Farr's distraction to move forward saying, 'It's all right, son. We know it wasn't you. It's all right, believe me. You know me, don't you? It's Sergeant Swift.'

He was almost on top of the crouching man. It was going to be all right, thought Pascoe. Back down the hill, apologies all round, drinks in the club, back home for supper.

'Oh yes,' said Colin Farr. 'I know you, Sergeant Swift, You're very handy with your stick.'

And in one lithe movement he uncoiled. In his hand he grasped a rubber-covered torch. Swift ducked away but his reflexes were no match for the young man's speed; and the torch crashed against the side of his neck with a noise like a mallet on meat. The sergeant staggered sideways, collided with Downey who was still trying to push himself off the ground, and the two of them went over in a blackly comic tangle of limbs.

Pascoe found he couldn't move but Dalziel was rushing forward now yelling, 'Farr, you bastard!' For a moment the young man looked as if he might stand his ground. Then he smiled, turned, and with an easy unhurried grace which nevertheless left Dalziel lumbering like a man in a morass, he loped away into the trees.

Now Pascoe's strength returned. He rushed forward. Dalziel was stooping over Swift. 'Get after the bastard!' he shouted at Pascoe more in frustration than expectation, or so the Inspector decided as he helped Arthur Downey to sit up. The man looked at him without any recognition.

His face was bleeding and there was some bruising round the throat. A broad-bladed knife lay on the turf between his feet, but the visible damage seemed to have come from blows rather than stabs.

'It's me, Mr Downey. Inspector Pascoe. We met at Mrs Farr's. What happened here?'

'Nothing. I don't know.' He was clearly still confused. Pascoe said, 'Take it easy for a second,' and turned to Dalziel who was kneeling by Swift.

'Is he OK?' he said anxiously.

'He'll live,' said Dalziel. 'But he's going to have a stiffer neck than a fossilized giraffe!'

The sergeant tried to say something, only managed a grunt, then reached into his tunic and plucked out his personal radio.

'Good thinking, lad,' said Dalziel. 'How's your patient, Peter?'

Downey answered for himself.

'What are you lot doing here? Did that foreign woman tell you?'

Ellie. That foreign woman. Would there be a time when he could tell her this and laugh? Pascoe said, 'She had to. Colin Farr's off the hook, you see. We know he didn't kill Satterthwaite, so there's no reason for him to be running around up here.'

'*Was* off the hook,' Dalziel corrected grimly. 'All we had on him earlier was suspicion of topping a deputy which rates at slightly less than a misdemeanour round here. Now it's assaulting a police officer and that's really serious.'

He switched the radio to 'transmit'.

'What are you going to do?' asked Pascoe.

'What I should have done before. Whistle up some reinforcements. I've tried it soft, and even if I felt inclined to try it soft again, we can't. This time we don't know where he is.'

'I know where he'll be,' said Downey unexpectedly.

Once again Dalziel lowered the radio.

'You do?' he said.

'Pretty certain,' said Downey. 'It's the obvious place he'll hide.'

Suddenly Pascoe felt himself converted to Dalziel's previous viewpoint.

'Why'd he attack you, Mr Downey?' he said in an attempt at diversion.

'God knows,' said Downey. 'Why's that mad bugger ever do anything?'

'He likely backtracked you a bit to be on the safe side,' said Dalziel. 'When he spotted us back along the path, he must have thought you'd brought us with you. Can you take us to this hiding place, Mr Downey? I mean, are you fit enough?'

'Aye, I'm fit.'

'But what about the sergeant?' said Pascoe.

To his dismay Swift had a fit of nobility and croaked. 'OK. Go down by self.'

'No way,' said Dalziel to Pascoe's relief.

But it was short-lived. The fat man started bellowing into the radio till he got a startled response.

'Superintendent Dalziel,' he said. 'Send a bit of support up to the White Rock in Gratterley Wood, would you? Sergeant Swift's got himself slightly injured. Nothing serious but I don't want him walking around here by himself. Send a couple of strong lads to see him safely home. Inspector Pascoe and I are continuing our search for Mr Colin Farr. Chief Inspector Wishart has all details. Out.'

He returned the radio to Swift.

'There you are, lad. See if you can get Luxemburg while you're waiting. And take that knife down with you for Forensic to check out.'

'Sir,' said Pascoe. 'It's getting very dark. Shouldn't we perhaps ask for some lights and a tannoy?'

'What are you planning, lad? To hold a dance? You've got your torch, I've got mine. And Mr Downey here can probably see in the dark. Lead on, Macduff. The sooner we find this madman, the sooner we can all get home to our beds.'

Pascoe's reluctance was more than compensated by Downey's eagerness. He was away so quickly that Dalziel cried, 'Hold on!' and said to Pascoe. 'Move your arse, lad, or we're going to lose ourselves another miner!'

Pascoe whose night eyes were never particularly good

soon felt himself completely out of touch with their guide, but Dalziel ploughed ahead with apparent confidence. The pale gleam from the torches showed no path beneath their feet, the trees seemed to be pressing together, and the thickening mist to have a strong odour of decay. At last Downey came to a stop and let them catch up.

'All right,' said Dalziel. 'I'm getting too old for this kind of sport. Where the hell are you taking us?'

'Nowhere,' said Downey.

'Eh?'

'We're here.'

The two policemen looked round. The little there was to see was indistinguishable from what there had been to see for the last ten minutes. Trees and mist and undergrowth.

'Where?' said Dalziel.

'Here,' said Downey impatiently.

He stopped and started to pull at a clump of gorse bushes. They parted easily and he said with satisfaction, 'I knew it. He's been through here.'

'Where the fuck's *here*?' roared Dalziel.

But Pascoe staring into the even darker darkness revealed beyond the bushes was having his worst suspicions confirmed.

'It's a drift,' said Downey. 'Well, it leads into a drift. Original entry got filled in donkey's years ago. They all did eventually, but there's still ways. This ridge is riddled with workings. First mining in Burrthorpe were all done this side of the valley . . .'

'I've had the history lesson,' growled Dalziel. 'What makes you think Farr's gone in here and not in some other hole?'

'Look, this is where he'll be,' said Downey impatiently. 'I've seen him coming out of here. And I can tell someone's been through here recently. Give us one of your torches and I'll go in after him and try to talk some sense into him.'

'Hold on! Just how far does this drift go?'

'Far as you like,' said Downey. 'God knows what it links up with. But not much over a furlong on the level.'

'You mean that? Level?'

256

'More or less,' said Downey.

Pascoe did not like the way this discussion was going. He had an ingrained dislike of dark confined places which he suspected could readily develop into a full-blown hysterical phobia, given encouragement. He could have embraced Downey when the man argued, 'Look, I'm used to being underground. Besides, Colin's more likely to take notice of me alone. You two wait here till I get back.'

'He didn't seem inclined to take much notice of you at the White Rock,' said Dalziel.

Oh God. Let this be token resistance, prayed Pascoe.

But God was deaf behind the drifting mist.

'No,' said Dalziel, making up his mind. 'Can't let you go in there alone, Mr Downey. More than my job's worth. And as long as it's level, a bit of blackness won't hurt us, will it, Peter? Lead on, Mr Downey and let's see what we can find.'

He handed Downey his torch. The man shrugged but didn't argue. Stooping, he stepped forward into the dark cavern. Dalziel followed close behind.

Pascoe still hesitated on the threshold. It was stupid to let some absurd police machismo prevent him from confessing his fear.

'Come on, lad! Hurry up with that torch o' thine, will you?'

He took a deep breath, glanced up at the sky. God might be deaf but he wasn't humourless. Even as he looked the mist was drawn up as though by a sharp intake of breath prior to a good belly laugh, and the sky scintillated with a million stars.

'Oh shit,' said Pascoe. And stepped into the dark.

CHAPTER 7

It wasn't as bad as he'd feared, he assured himself. A man could walk almost upright in here and there was the occasional draught of cold air like a lifeline with the outside world. Nor was there much chance of getting lost. After the initial narrow squeeze, they'd found themselves in a tunnel which took them straight forward with no sign of any side passage in the torch's bright cone, though it did seem to be descending rather more sharply than Downey had promised.

Dalziel was just ahead. At least he assumed that hunching hulk was still Dalziel and not some time-travelled troglodyte luring him to its bone-strewn lair.

'Sir,' he whispered. 'Sir!'

'What the hell are you muttering about, lad?' said Dalziel irritatedly over his shoulder.

'You shouldn't make too much noise in places like this,' said Pascoe defensively.

'Oh aye. You an expert or something?'

No, but I've seen a lot of movies where people made too much noise, was Pascoe's proper reply.

He said, 'Shouldn't we try to make contact? I mean, we're never going to actually catch up with him, not unless this all comes to a dead end, are we?'

'You mean you want to start shouting to the lad? I thought you were worried about making too much noise just now?'

'I just think we ought to do *something*,' said Pascoe desperately. Though he couldn't be absolutely certain, he thought he sensed a slight curve developing in the tunnel. Also those comforting draughts of fresh air seemed less frequent here.

'What do you suggest?' said Dalziel.

Pascoe examined his thoughts, tried to separate proper procedure from personal terror, came to an identical conclusion in both cases, and said, 'I think one of us ought to go back and get this thing properly organized.'

Ahead, Dalziel halted, sighed deeply, turned with difficulty, the better, Pascoe guessed, to administer a rebuke.

Instead the fat man said, 'You're right . . .' and Pascoe's heart soared '. . . I'll go.' And great was the fall thereof.

But before he could find a method of contradiction short of outright refusal, Downey who'd got some way ahead during this discussion returned.

'He's not there,' he said, causing Pascoe's heart to raise its head hopefully.

'Not where?' said Dalziel, who always seemed to have trouble with Downey's locative adverbs.

'At the end of the drift,' said Downey.

'You mean he didn't come in here after all?' said Pascoe, torn between relief and indignation.

'He must have turned off,' said Downey.

'Turned off?' Pascoe echoed derisively. 'Into solid rock?'

Downey didn't reply but retreated a few paces and did just that.

'Oh God,' said Pascoe.

But Dalziel went forward and said impatiently, 'Bring that bloody torch!'

There was a side passage here. It looked as if a natural fault had been widened by a pick. A draught of air blew through it, not fresh night air, but slightly warmer and with something slightly fetid on its breath.

'Downey!' called Dalziel.

There was no reply and no sign of the miner's torch.

'Come on,' said Dalziel.

'But what about getting help?' demanded Pascoe.

'The bugger who'll need help is that half-wit Downey if he catches up with Farr and we're not there,' retorted Dalziel. 'Come on.'

There seemed to be no way the fat man was going to get through the gap but somehow he seemed to mould his bulk to fit the contours, and like a squid squeezing into a crevasse he vanished from sight.

Pascoe followed. Why not? It had been a day for new and deteriorating experiences. Now the drift seemed to him like a well-lit road. It was his fate, it seemed, to search for the tunnel at the end of the light.

His torch showed he was in a new world now; long stretches were wholly natural as if some ancient movement of the earth had prised these rocks apart. In places he had to duck beneath the atrophied roots of distant trees, sent deep-probing in search of fresh layers of earth and water which they never found. He glimpsed fossils in the walls of rock, leaves and ferns and ammonites, and his imagination turned other ridges and hollows into bones and skulls. And finally he knew that he was quite alone and this was that old nightmare come true in which he went further and further along a tunnel till it grew so narrow that he became wedged in it, unable either to retreat or advance.

Dalziel got through here, he assured himself. Dalziel got through here. Oh God! What he would give to hear a few comforting words from that deep certain voice.

'Look at the state of this fucking suit! Hurry up lad and shine that torch on it. It's bloody ruined. Look at it. Best tailor in Yorkshire made this, back when they knew how to cut cloth. It'll be three years before I can get him to do another one.'

'Why three years?' asked Pascoe, trying to control the joy in his voice at this summons back to a real world even if it were still subterranean.

'That's how long he's still got to do. I put the sod away for receiving stolen cloth, don't you remember? He blamed it on the government allowing unfair competition from the Far East. I reckon the trouble were a bit nearer east than that. Scarborough. That's where he set his fancy woman up. Expensive tastes, that one. Where's that daft bugger gone now? Downey!'

They were through the fissure and back in a tunnel which the timbered roof showed to be man-made. Up ahead a torch beam appeared and flashed urgently at them. They went forward and found Arthur Downey waitng for them.

'What now?' demanded Dalziel.

'Not so loud,' whispered Downey. 'The roof's a bit dicey here.'

Pascoe shot a triumphant glance at Dalziel, who said, 'Then let's not hang around under it. Mr Downey, if I can't communicate with young Farr by shouting, what're the odds of us getting within whispering distance of him?'

For the first time since this lunatic chase began, Downey seemed to have run out of certainties. he stared around as if surprised to be where he was. Pascoe knew the feeling, hated to know it was shared.

'Mr Downey,' he said gently, 'is there any point in going on?'

'What?' Downey looked at him as if taking this as a general philosophical inquiry and feeling inclined to answer no. Then he shook his head and said, 'A little further. He might be . . . a little further.'

He set off once more. Dalziel looked at Pascoe and shrugged his shoulders before following. Pascoe once more found himself bringing up the rear. He walked slowly, letting his torch beam run up and down the walls in an effort to memorize their features. Of course, as long as there was no choice of route there was no chance of getting lost but he still felt as if he should be dropping white pebbles, or leaving a clue of thread to guide him back. But as he had neither thread nor pebbles, he'd have to make do with memory.

Of course he could always unravel his pullover, but Ellie wouldn't like that. Her mother had knitted it for him and though Ellie herself would rather do hard labour on the Gulag than practise such a female submissive craft, she was fearsomely defensive of her mother's artefacts.

Ellie. He wished he hadn't thought of Ellie for now this thought turned naturally to Colin Farr and the relationship between them. What it was, he didn't know. That it was intense he'd had plenty of evidence. It might not be sexual but that didn't matter all that much. There are other kinds of jealousy just as corrosive.

He'd stopped walking. His mind might go wandering in search of mental escape routes but his stay-at-home eyes, directed perhaps by his roaming thoughts, had spotted something on the wall. He beamed his torch sideways. It was unmistakable. A rough arrowhead scratched on the crumbling wall behind the line of wooden props. And another. Someone else had recently been this way, beset by fears of unreturning.

He let his torch beam move onward and upward. The unknown trailblazer had been wise to carve his traffic signs on wall rather than wood. The roof must have been particularly troublesome along this stretch. Props of warped and rotting timber bowed like the ribs of an ancient wreck under sagging cross beams. If Dali had painted the aisle of some ancient cathedral it might have come out looking like this.

We're mad to be down here! thought Pascoe. Yet it had a strange fascination. A man could get used even to this. He had to breathe deep now to remind himself of just how rotten the atmosphere stank! God, it must be like this in a charnel house. Bones and blood and decaying flesh . . .

He flashed his torch ahead, fearful that he'd lost contact with the others, but there they were. They'd stopped still and he hurried to catch up with them.

He saw the reason for their hesitation. There was another side-passage. Dalziel was peering into it but Downey was shaking his head.

'No, he'll not have gone down there. It's a dead end down there. And the roof's really rotten round here, we don't want to hang around, just look at the state of it.'

Pascoe raised his torch beam. The roof indeed looked bad but little worse than it had for the past many yards. Dalziel grunted and said, 'All right, you're the boss down here,' without much conviction, but he did resume his progress down the main tunnel with Downey at his side. Pascoe was about to follow when his peripheral vision caught something he'd rather have missed. It was one of those lightly scratched arrows turning into the side passage.

He could ignore it. He could call the others back. The one thing he couldn't do was go down there by himself. Why then were his feet moving slowly, inexorably, into the passage?

The air here was thicker, the stench of decay intensified. He took another couple of steps. The torch beam oozed ahead and touched something bulky, something still beyond mineral stillness. Tiny paws scuttered away. The torch rose slowly in his hand, involuntary as a diviner's wand, tracing a crumple of dark-trousered legs; a swelling paunch; a broad chest on which lay like a tribute a narrow cassette recorder; two chins; a gaping mouth, a ragged moustache; eyes—one staring and one which something had begun to eat—a forehead laid open like a pathological model to show the brain beneath.

And Pascoe knew at last why Monty Boyle had proved so elusive over the past couple of days.

He went down on one knee by the body, motivated neither by piety nor professionalism, but merely by a weariness which had little to do with muscular fatigue. Everyone had limits and he suspected that he had come a body too far. Touch nothing, was the rule and he felt little incentive to break it, but that cassette recorder, Monty Boyle's trade mark, might tell what the Man Who Knew Too Much had known.

He stretched out his hand to take it. Then froze as the horrors which he had thought to have climaxed, resumed. The darkness beyond, which he had taken for the gallery's dead end, shifted, took shape, became distinct, advanced. And Dali's cathedral had its resident angel.

'So we meet at last,' said Pascoe inanely for the sake of hearing his voice.

But Colin Farr returned no words, though his face spoke for him as his young fair features contorted in rage and hate from guardian angel to avenging demon.

What have I done to inspire this? Pascoe wondered in terror. Then the young man launched himself forward. But the name he was screaming was not Pascoe's but 'Downey!' He was past in a single bound. Pascoe twisted round to see the deputy standing at the entry to the side passage. He must have come back to see what was holding Pascoe up.

He only had time to retreat a half step before Farr was on him driving him backwards by the force of his attack into the main tunnel.

His paralysis broken, Pascoe followed. Somehow Downey had broken loose. Pascoe seized Farr by the shoulder and cried, 'For God's sake, the roof!' But the young man hurled him away with incredible power for so slight a figure and flung himself on Downey with a brute force that drove him against the wall. Pascoe had fetched up against a prop which he distinctly felt give. On the other side he saw a couple more snap like matchsticks as Farr and Downey crashed against them. And overhead he heard the roof start to groan and creak like an old windmill straining into life. Neil Wardle's words sounded mockingly in his head. *Ever been a thousand feet under and heard the timbers cracking over your head?*

'Peter! Get out of there!'

It was Dalziel's voice behind a torch beam which seemed a half mile away. He looked at the struggling figures locked together like a pair of lovers for whom the earth is about to move. There was a noise like an explosion. Then he was running towards the voice and the light through a hail of earth and stone with chaos on his heels. The light seemed as far as yesterday and as dim as lost love, but he still thought that by running faster and striving harder, he might make it. Pebbles hit him like bird-shot, a larger rock clipped the back of his head; he stumbled, half fell, half recovered; then something much bigger and heavier crashed against the back of his legs, forcing him to the ground and pinning him there with pain and pressure till the darkness of the pit rushed in to take away pressure and pain together.

CHAPTER 8

'Hold on,' said Dalziel. 'Give us that torch. There's a foot here. By Christ, I've reached a foot. Question is, whose is it, and is it still attached? Answer is . . .'

He gently rocked the foot from side to side. Pascoe screamed.

'I reckon it's thine,' said Dalziel judiciously. 'Right, let's clear away a bit more of this rubbish and mebbe the dog can see the rabbit.'

Pascoe had long since ceased to register the passing of time in any normal mensural way but Dalziel had numbered every crawling second of the hour that had elapsed since the roof fall. He had no way of knowing precisely how long it would be before the roof immediately over their heads came down too, but that it would come he did not doubt. He had not trodden the rocky path to his present modest eminence without developing a keen scent for disaster.

At last his bloodied fingers had carefully picked the debris away from both Pascoe's legs. The left he judged was merely severely bruised and lacerated, but the right was undoubtedly broken. He touched it with infinite care. The tibia had snapped and penetrated the skin. The fibula had probably gone too but he couldn't be sure. The recommended course would be to leave him alone till a doctor could get there with morphine and a stretcher. Dalziel was not a man who'd ever found recommended courses much help, and with a roof groaning above him like a junior officer half-way through a staff college lecture, he saw no reason to be converted now.

Various sections of timber unearthed during his digging he'd set to one side. Selecting a thick splinter from a collapsed prop, he trimmed its edges with the boy scout's knife he always carried. Another piece got the same treatment. Then he pulled off his shirt and tore it into strips.

'Peter,' he said. 'Even allowing that this shirt cost me twenty quid, this could hurt you more than it hurts me.'

The pain brought Pascoe momentarily out of the timeless mists into the black present before it cut off consciousness altogether. When he came round again, he was over Dalziel's shoulder and his bound and splinted leg was being gently steadied by the fat man's huge paw to prevent it from swinging as he was carried along.

'Where are we going?' he croaked after three dry runs at it.

'Is that you, lad, or am I being followed by a frog?' said Dalziel.

'Where are we going?'

'I'm not sure but I know where we're coming from. Listen.'

Behind them in the darkness there was a grinding, cracking sound which crescendoed into a discord of rushing earth and crashing rock as another section of roof came down. Pascoe felt a blast of air against his face, then he was coughing again as the tidal bore of dust projected by the fall swept by them.

Carefully Dalziel lowered him to the ground.

'We'll rest here a while,' he spluttered. 'Till this lot clears a bit.'

'You should have left me,' said Pascoe.

'That's the kind of thing they say in movies,' reproved Dalziel. 'Your missus always said you watched too many movies.'

'Did she? At least you know where you are with a movie.'

'Paying to sit in the dark and be frightened, you mean? We're getting all that free, gratis and for bugger-all, here,' said Dalziel.

'What's my leg like?' asked Pascoe, after a timeless excursion into the misty hinterland of his mind.

'Well, you'll be hard pushed to play full back for England unless you've got an uncle on the selectors,' said Dalziel. 'But I dare say you'll be able to turn out for the Chief Inspectors' darts team, if selected.'

'Chief Inspector . . . ?'

'You're not that far gone, then? Aye. Congratulations. Not official yet, but it'll be posted next week.'

'But I thought . . .'

'. . . thought that being in my company so much had likely scuppered your chances? Nay, lad, I've got influence where it matters. I used the threat of resignation to make 'em take notice.'

Even through his pain, Pascoe was dumbfounded.

'You threatened to resign if I didn't get my promotion? But . . .'

He couldn't say it, not even in these confessional circumstances; he couldn't say: But why didn't they jump at the chance of getting rid of you?

Dalziel coughed a laugh.

'I think mebbe you've got things wrong,' he said kindly. 'I didn't tell 'em I were going to resign if you didn't get promoted. I told 'em I'd not even think of retirement until you *had* been promoted! That must have made the buggers take notice. So you can see, I've got a big investment in you, Peter. If you snuff it, they'll never learn what verbal understandings are really worth, will they? So come on, let's find our way out of here.'

'Is there a way out?' asked Pascoe faintly.

'There's still plenty of air, isn't there? I'm sure I can feel a draught on my face,' said Dalziel as once again he lifted

266

Pascoe and draped him over his shoulder. 'Any road, I don't think yon wild bugger, Farr, was daft enough to go running into a dead end, do you?'

The renewal of pain made it impossible for Pascoe to give this a considered answer. He closed his eyes and tried to will the darkness to blank him out once more, but just as success seemed close, Dalziel halted and lowered him to the ground again.

'I think you've come to the end of the road, lad,' he said.

'What?'

'No, I don't mean euthanasia, I just mean I reckon this might be the exit, only I don't think I'm going to be able to get you through there without help.'

He shone the now very faint beam of his torch ahead. The tunnel began to slope sharply up and the ground was covered with debris. A few yards on the debris was piled high to the roof and at first glance it seemed as if the way must be blocked. But high up the pile, almost at roof level, there was the dark circle of a smaller tunnel as if someone had burrowed their way through. More significantly, there was now an unmistakable draught of air blowing towards them.

'I'll not be long,' said Dalziel. 'You'll be all right?'

Pascoe nodded. He looked longingly at the torch but knew that it would be ridiculous to ask if he could keep it when Dalziel's need was so manifestly the greater. But to lie here alone in the dark . . .

'I'll be off, then,' said the fat man.

Pascoe's mind was searching feverishly for some excuse to delay Dalziel's departure.

'There was no food at the White Rock,' he gasped. 'Did you notice? And the knife . . . if Mycroft helped Farr to get out of the hospital, he'd not have needed a knife . . .'

'That's right, lad,' said Dalziel. 'That's good. Funny how it takes a leg dropping off to get some people thinking like a Chief Inspector. Pity you hadn't thought about it earlier, though. Mind you, neither did I. But I'm excused on account of being uneducated and nearly senile. Take care, lad. And don't move from here, promise?'

267

He watched the pale cone of torchlight zigzag slowly up the slope.

Then the maw of the secondary tunnel swallowed it up as Dalziel wriggled his surprisingly flexible bulk into the gap and sent the darkness pouring down on Pascoe in a mighty torrent.

He lay in that flood and tried for unconsciousness but the best he could manage was to drift outside of time. Pictures formed on the shifting surface of the dark, and when he closed his eyes they were on the inside of his eyelids too. He saw Downey, dog-like, wolf-like, drowning in darkness; he saw a young girl with long blonde hair drift by on the stream of the dark with a posy of dog-rose and bramble leaves clutched at her breast; and he saw a young man moving gracefully through the dark like an Arcadian shepherd boy splashing through the shallows of Alpheus and laughing at the silky naiads as they tried to draw him down. It seemed to Pascoe that the youth stooped over him and applied sweet damp cresses to his parching lips and that as he turned and loped gracefully away, his head was framed by a sky of Dorian blue.

Then the darkness surged upwards and the boy disappeared, and towards him, wading chin deep, came a full-faced man with a ragged moustache, talking incessantly into a cassette recorder which he held to his desperate lips. He seemed to see Pascoe and reached out to him as the dark came bubbling up, then fell forward and vanished from sight. But his outstretched hands grasped desperately at Pascoe's waist and took a firm grip on his jacket and he screamed as he felt himself also being dragged down beneath the darkness.

Then he awoke and found that the darkness and the terror at least were no dream. He shifted his position uneasily. The pain was still hot in his leg. But his mouth no longer felt so cracked and dry. The power of auto-suggestion, he told himself. There was something digging into his side.

A body in pain often finds the smaller discomfort a greater distraction and he set about removing this lump of stone he had settled upon. Except that it wasn't a lump of stone, it was something actually in his jacket pocket. He reached in, pulled it out. He couldn't see it but his fingers told him what it was.

Monty Boyle's cassette recorder.

Then he was back in the side-gallery finding Boyle's body. Now he remembered everything so clearly that he knew why he had wanted to forget.

Except that he couldn't remember pocketing the recorder.

In fact he would have sworn that in that moment of terror at Farr's appearance, he had let it fall back on the dead man's chest. But here it was.

'And I don't believe in ghosts,' he said out loud.

And shrieked as a little red eye winked at him and the cassette vibrated gently in his hand.

It was of course voice-operated, tuned and directed so that even in a crowded pub it would pick up the conversation between Boyle and the man directly in front of him without admitting enough peripheral noise to mask the words.

The Japanese were truly marvellous, thought Pascoe, not least for creating something sturdy enough to survive what he'd been through. And what Boyle had been through too, of course, poor bastard. Ike Ogilby got value for money out of his reporters. Recently Pascoe had helped get one of them jailed. Now here was another getting himself murdered. In-house scoops, impregnable exclusives. Lucky old Ike.

As his mind wandered idly, his fingers were moving to more purpose. They had found the button to run the tape back. When it stopped, he pressed the next button. And suddenly he was no longer alone. There were voices with him in the darkness and as he lay there and listened, his mind's eye gave them form and substance also.

'Christ, you scared me!'

Monty Boyle. But he didn't sound scared. He'd probably heard someone coming and gone towards him, preferring for some reason to meet him out of that horrible side-gallery.

'Did I!'

Downey. Always sneaking up on people, Downey. A bad habit.

'You surely did. What are you doing down here, Mr Downey?'

'Same as you, likely.'

'I was watching the Farr boy. I saw him go down this hole, so when he came back out again, I thought I'd take a look.'

'Me too.'

'To tell the truth, I'm pleased to see you. I've marked my way back, but I'm not used to crawling around like a mole, so it's good to have an expert along.'

'What have you found, Mr Boyle?'

'Sweet f.a. I reckon I've ruined a good suit for nothing. Come on, let's get back topside and I'll buy us both a stiff drink. I don't know about you but I'm gasping for one.'

'How far did you go, Mr Boyle?'

'Just a bit further. Not much. I thought: This is pointless. And dangerous. So I just turned round and . . .'

'You didn't go down that gallery?'

'What? That side passage, you mean? No, I didn't like the look of that. Come on . . .'

'Your marks turn in there.'

'Do they? Surely not. I mean, I may have taken a glance but . . .'

'You're a liar! You've been in there! Why are you lying to me?'

There was a pause. Classic interrogation technique, thought Pascoe with professional detachment. Test a good story with total disbelief. Make the suspect budge an inch and you had him. The best never budged. But perhaps Boyle was more used to asking questions than answering them . . . He waited. It was quite suspenseful, even though he knew the outcome.

'I'm sorry. You're right. Look, I can tell you. I did find something. A child's bones. You see what this means, Mr Downey? I didn't want to distress you, but it means your friend, Billy Farr, must have hidden the girl there after he . . . after it happened. Look, I've been thinking, maybe there's no need for this to go any further. What can the police do now? What can anyone do? Maybe it's best just left forgotten. Let's get out of here and talk about it over that drink, shall we?'

*

270

Boyle knew, thought Pascoe. Perhaps he was sharper than the rest of us and had his suspicions already. And I should have had mine too! He recalled Downey's face when they'd confronted Mrs Farr with the dog's bones. Pale and trembling. Memory of a lost friend, they'd thought. But it had been the shock of realization just how close to the truth Colin Farr must be getting. And when he got Ellie's message and guessed that Farr was proposing to hide down here, he knew that discovery was getting ever closer.

I was slow! Pascoe told himself in anguish. When I saw that Downey hadn't brought any food . . . when I saw that knife . . . if I'd stopped to think, I could have stopped all this. They could still have been alive, Downey . . . and Colin Farr . . .

'Billy'd not do that! You didn't know Billy. He was my friend, he'd not harm a fly let alone that lass . . . Never!'

'Well, if it wasn't Billy, it must have been Pickford after all. Killed her and brought her down here. That's what I'll write in my paper. You'll be able to read all about it next Sunday.'

Poor Monty. The Man Who Knows Too Much. The man with an answer for everything. Monty Boyle, confidant of cops and robbers alike, equally at home in the corridors of law and the alleys of the underworld. Except that now he'd found himself in an underworld whose geography was beyond his plotting, facing a mind whose workings were dark and twisting beyond his understanding. And now The Man Who Knows Too Much knew everything . . . or nothing.

'That's what you'll write, is it? Not the truth? You wouldn't rather write the truth?'

Downey's voice no longer strident, but teasing, wheedling. The suspect ready to cough, eager to cough, just requiring his audience to be grateful, attentive, sympathetic . . . Leave it, Boyle! Walk away from it! Show no interest. You can still survive . . . could still . . .

*

'Yes, indeed, Mr Downey. I'd very much like to write the truth. Why don't you tell it to me?'

So there it was. In the end poor old Monty Boyle had died of journalism. He gave up any chance he had of talking his way above ground because he could not resist a good story, an exclusive, a scoop . . .

'I saw them that day, Billy and Tracey. I were lying up above the White Rock, watching . . . you get a grand view up there, all sorts of things. The tricks some of these young 'uns'll get up to! Not just the young uns either, I were watching Harold Satterthwaite that day. Christ, he were really giving it to her! She were young enough to be his daughter too, and he's older than me . . . was . . . it makes you think . . . it made me think: Why'm I up here watching and he's down there . . . never mind. I saw Billy go back down the path with the girl, and a bit later Harold and Stella got dressed and went straight down through the woods towards the road. I started scrambling down the side of the White Rock and I got up a bit of speed, you know the way you do when your legs are nigh on running away with you! And I came down the last bit to the path right fast. Well, Tracey were there again. She must have come back up by herself. She were dead scared when she saw me. It's understandable, someone bursting out of the bushes like that. She just turned and started to run. And I set off running after her. All I wanted was to tell her it were all right, it was only me and I meant her no harm. But when you start chasing someone . . . have you ever chased someone, Mr Boyle?'
    'Not like that, Mr Downey. Not like that.'
    'No? Well, it's . . . exciting. But all I meant was to stop her and tell her . . . all I meant . . . Then I caught up with her and I grabbed her. I had to get hold of her, you understand, I had to touch her, to make her stop so's I could tell her . . . that's all I wanted . . . but she kept on struggling and she started yelling and I had to stop her in case folk heard and got the wrong idea . . . and I kept on thinking of Harold . . . And then she were dead, Mr Boyle. All slack and loose. Dead!'

Pascoe lay in pain and darkness and felt the other's darkness and pain. But the sharing stopped a long way short of

272

forgiving. He thought of Rosie (What time did that crèche close, for God's sake? Surely they wouldn't just dump her out on the street . . . ?) And he thought of where these first desperate steps had led this pathetic murdering bastard. Even Pickford in the end could not live with himself. But Downey was determined to live his stunted life for ever, no matter who else had to die.

He'd drifted a bit, missed a little of the tape. It didn't matter. He could fill it all in now. Super-tec, that's what he was. Super Chief Inspector tec . . .

'. . . I didn't mean to harm Billy. He were my mate. I'd have done anything for Billy. I'd not have let him get in bother for me, you can be sure of that. I'd have come forward . . . But once the coppers decided Pickford had done it, I thought it'd be all right . . . they seemed so sure . . . so sure . . . sometimes I began to wonder if mebbe Pickford hadn't really done it after all. Mebbe she were just unconscious when I left her . . . mebbe he came along and found her . . . I mean, he did it to all them other lasses, didn't he? Bastard! Any road, I went out for a walk that day, Boxing Day, it was. I could see that brother-in-law of mine wanted me out of the house and I knew what for. He'd be at it every hour that God sends if he could. I don't know how my sister puts up with him. I lie awake nights and I can hear them in the next room . . . So I went for a walk and I went up along the ridge where the old workings are, no special reason, just for a walk. Then I spotted Billy's dog, Jacko. He were worrying away at this old overgrown pile of spoil near the old shaft. I just stood and watched for a bit, never thinking anything except that Billy'd likely be along shortly and we could have a crack. I swear I never thought . . . can you believe it? This was where I'd put the girlie's body, and I'd forgotten!'

Forgotten. Who has remembered? who has . . . but the world will end when I . . . forgive . . . forgo . . . forsake . . . forlorn . . . back to the waking nightmare, the living darkness! Concentrate, concentrate. Listen to the mad bastard!

*

273

'. . . I'd come this way looking, most of the others searched in the woods and down near the road where I dumped the pail, but a few of them wanted to check the covers on the old entries, so I came up here too. I'd covered the spoil up so it didn't look touched and now I brought some stuff I had for the allotment, keeps dogs off your veg, and I sprayed it round there so that if the coppers did bring dogs in, they'd not go near. I thought that were pretty clever . . .'

'Oh yes. Very clever, Mr Downey. But now . . .'

'Oh aye. The stuff had washed off long since, I expect, though being so cold you'd have thought . . . any road, here was Jacko scratching away and suddenly it dawned on me what he were scratching after! I tried to shoo him off, but he paid no heed. Once that little bugger got a scent, he'd not leave it alone till Billy told him. I gave him a kick, a right belt, and he took a snap at my ankle. But he still went back to his scratching. I had to do something, didn't I? I picked up this rock and I brought it down hard. I just meant to stun him, that were all. But mebbe the rock were sharp or mebbe he had a thin skull. Anyway, it just seemed to go through the bone like tissue paper. I could see he were dead right away. And when I looked round, there was Billy standing watching me. He looked like . . . I don't know . . . I went to him to explain it were an accident . . . I hadn't meant . . . I held out the rock to show him how sharp it was. He knocked my hand aside. He went to Jacko and knelt down by him. He was right next to where the beast had been scratching. I had to get him away from there before he noticed anything. I put my hand on his shoulder and he turned and looked up at me and I . . . it were an accident! He was my best friend. It were an accident . . . !'

So many accidents. The child, the dog, his friend . . . Arthur Downey, the man who lived by accident . . . And here am I! Just another piece of debris on the fringe of a Downey accident, laughed Pascoe unconvincingly.

'. . . I broke open the covering, it were half rotten anyway, a real danger, someone like Billy walking up there by himself could easily have fallen through it, it's a scandal the way the council . . . Any road, I tipped Billy down so it'd look like he fell. His head weren't so bad to look at, but I knew that any fool could spot that Jacko hadn't just got hurt in a fall, so I had to get rid of him . . . and the *lass too, I couldn't leave her so close to the shaft, not when all them buggers would be tramping round there once they found Billy. So I had to . . . dig . . . and I wrapped her in my donkey jacket and I climbed down the shaft, I just dropped the dog down, but her I carried. I'd been down here when I were a kid, we were wild young buggers in them days, me and Billy, we went everywhere together . . . and I knew I could get through to the roadway. I just left them a short way in-bye. I only had a lighter to show the way and bare flame's bloody dangerous. Then I got off home, needn't have worried about sneaking in, that dirty bugger was still at it. But I were worried about them just lying there, so soon as I could I came back up with a torch and a little shovel. They'd found Billy by then and they'd started to seal off the shaft, but I know other ways of getting down here, like you found, Mr Boyle. And I brought the lass down here and I buried her in my jacket and left the dog at the entrance, like a guard sort of . . .'*

'There's no dog bones in there, Mr Downey. Just . . . no dog bones.'

Poor Monty. Still thinking he was getting a story he could write. Still wanting loose ends tied up. Of course there were no dog bones. Farr had removed them. The same night. This must be . . . when? Monday, that was it. Tuesday, Farr had come out of the pit, turning Mycroft into a ticking time-bomb en route, before getting drunk and ringing Ellie . . . Ellie . . . better to think of Monday, only two days ago, unless it was past midnight . . . could it be so late? It could be *any* time! Back to Downey, justifying himself like a word processor and feeling all the time that a malevolent fate was pushing him to an unmerited downfall . . .

' . . . It's Farr, the bastard! He's not half the man his dad were . . . I knew he'd been snooping . . . all I wanted was that he'd go off again . . . he did before, just up and left Billy . . . not that I minded . . . he was always getting in the way, Billy couldn't see what a useless bugger . . . I've tried to get shut of him . . . I've let him see his mam would be well taken care of . . . I tried to stir up trouble between him and Harold so he'd go too far and get the sack . . . I told Harold he'd been saying things . . . and I left him a note

*hinting that Harold were still stuffing Stella . . . but he'll not go
. . . and now he's found Jacko . . . and you've found . . . why's he
not go? He doesn't like it round here, he keeps telling everyone. So
why does everyone love him?'*

The voice became a scream. The climax was near. To be
unloved, this was the worm which gnawed at Downey's
heart. One man he had been able to claim as friend and
perhaps that friendship had really only flourished in his
imagination. He had built a life and personality around
being pleasant and helpful and amenable; unable to inspire
love, he had given vegetables; and when he murdered his
'friend', he had tried to create a living memorial to the
friendship by a dog-like devotion to May Farr. But no dog,
this; a wolf rather, slinking and treacherous.

And now from the tape came the sounds of poor Monty
Boyle's death. Convinced at last by that final despairing cry
that he was in deadly peril, he must have panicked and tried
to push past Downey and follow his marks to the surface.
But he was already in his grave from the moment he allowed
Downey to tell his tale. There was a noise like a dog panting,
a crunch like a cleaver splitting a cabbage, a bubbling
groan. Then Downey's voice, faint, uncertain, speaking the
inevitable epitaph.

'It were an accident . . .'

Then silence. It lasted two days in real time but only a
few seconds on the tape before the next voice alerted its
sensors.

'Oh Downey, you bastard.'

Colin Farr. Running from the police simply because be
scorned to run with them. Had he suspected Downey before
the man attacked him at the White Rock? Or had he perhaps
disliked the man too much to suspect him? But now as he
flitted easily through these dark galleries, his mind must
have been working, working, till his feet brought him here

where he had found Jacko's bones, and there was Boyle stretched out like a confession on a charge-room table . . .

'So we meet at last.'

Who was that? The voice had startled him almost more than anything else he had heard. Not Farr. Not Downey. He'd know their voices anywhere. This was a stranger. Who else had been down here? Who else had spoken in that narrow corpse-chamber to alert this hidden witness? A phantom . . .? A spirit . . .?

'And I don't believe in ghosts!'

And now Pascoe smiled.

It was himself of course. Speaking before he plucked the recorder from Boyle's waistcoat and thrust it into his pocket where it remained muffled till he took it out a few minutes ago.

He had come full circle and met himself. In folklore, the shock of that strange meeting always brought death.

He lay back now and closed his eyes. There seemed to be less pain now. Soon it would be gone altogether. And with it, hate and jealousy and striving; touch, taste and sight, and scent, and sound.

Already the passions had died and now the senses were fading too. Another hour would have probably set him completely free.

As it was, he didn't hear the noise of the men digging down to rescue him and he couldn't feel the gentle touch of their rough hands as they bound him to a stretcher.

But he never lost the taste of wet cresses from his mouth. And eventually the scent of a soft night breeze caught at his heart and stirred the slow blood in his veins.

And when he opened his eyes, he saw the stars again.

ENVOI

. . . Then he turned round,

And seemed like one of those who over the flat
And open course in the fields beside Verona
Run for the green cloth; and he seemed, at that,

Not like a loser, but the winning runner.

After the ambulance had borne Pascoe away, with Ellie grey from worry at his side, and Dalziel a-glow from whisky at his head, the men of the Mine Rescue Service descended once more into the old workings.

Monty Boyle they brought up first, to be laid with reverence beneath the headlines of his own exclusive. Then Arthur Downey they dragged from his lair back to a world which had patted his head and scratched his ears but never let him into its living-room.

Finally they bore Colin Farr's body and Tracey Pedley's bones into the clear night air, softly scented by the westerly breeze sighing through the golden-leaved, owl-haunted trees of Gratterley Wood, where the little girl had played with her forgotten and forgetting friends, and where the young man had first tasted and given love, and the world had seemed to promise both that all manner of things would be well.

Beyond the wood on the next rise, blocking out the bright slant of the northern stars, loomed the pit-head. The Wheel turned, the Cage descended, the conveyor clacked endlessly, the trucks were filled, the spoil heap grew.

An alien spirit or a simple child watching from Gratterley Wood might have thought that the process consisted of pouring men into a dark pit where by some strange sorcery they were changed into dust and coal, and so returned to the surface.

The spirit or the child might have been right.

THE END